Acclaim for Christa Parrish

STONES FOR BREAD

"A beautiful story of love and friendship, of redemption and forgiveness, *Stones for Bread* is uplifting and hopeful. It satisfies like a warm loaf of freshly made bread."

— Lynne Hinton, author of
Friendship Cake and *Pie Town*

"Christa Parrish has once again proven herself to be a powerful voice in inspirational fiction. *Stones for Bread* is delivered in Parrish's trademark lyrical style, and its content—a mix of spiritual journey, history, love story, and cookbook—is expertly woven together with Truth. An excellent choice for book clubs and individual readers alike, *Stones for Bread* does not disappoint."

— Alison Morrow, author of
Composing Amelia and *The Heart of Memory*

"No one knows how to plunge the depths of what our souls hunger for like Christa Parrish. *Stones for Bread* is a masterpiece, a story that is more than a story. You'll never look at a loaf of bread the same way again."

— Susan Meissner, author of
The Girl in the Glass

THE AIR WE BREATHE

"A fast-moving, suspenseful, enrapturing novel . . . Fans of Christian fiction with kick and psychological depth will be engaged and touched by Parrish's exciting third novel."

— *Booklist*

"*The Air We Breathe* is a compelling and emotional novel about identity, redemption, and faith. Expect it to be popular among women of all ages."

— *CBA Retailers & Resources*

"If you are a fan of Jodi Picoult or Anita Shreve, Christa Parrish will be your new favorite discovery . . . Likewise, if you have experienced loss or heartache, or just want to be assured of God's transcendent presence, you will certainly find solace here."

— Rachel McMillan on Novel
Crossing blog

"Parrish has created an exceptional look at trauma and its aftermath, as well as hope and recovery from grief at its best. Readers will love it for sure."

— *Publishers Weekly*

Watch Over Me

" . . . Christa Parrish writes a compelling story that is filled with real-life problems and raw emotions."

— 5MinutesforBooks.com

"Parrish's deft characterization pulls readers into a storyline filled with raw emotion . . . comes together seamlessly for an unforgettable conclusion."

— *Romantic Times Book Reviews*

Home Another Way

" . . . written with heart and soul. It is always refreshing to read books with imperfect characters; they seem more real."

— *Romantic Times Book Reviews*

"Parrish . . . adeptly avoids the clichéd happily-ever-after ending while still leaving the reader satisfied."

— Cindy Crosby, FaithfulReader.com

"Christa Parrish manages the rare accomplishment of telling a very good story peopled with flawed and very human characters."

— Lynn Spencer, All About
Romance (LikesBooks.com)

"With its vast array of richly imagined characters, its humor and its substance, this debut is sure to resonate with a wide and appreciative audience."

— *Publishers Weekly*

STONES *for* BREAD

STONES *for* BREAD

Christa Parrish

THOMAS NELSON
Since 1798

NASHVILLE DALLAS MEXICO CITY RIO DE JANEIRO

Published in Nashville, Tennessee, by Thomas Nelson.

Thomas Nelson titles may be purchased in bulk for educational, business, fund-raising, or sales promotional use. For information, please e-mail SpecialMarkets@ThomasNelson.com.

Scripture quotations:

Genesis 3:19 appears in chapter 1; Luke 1:46–47 appears in chapter 11; Romans 8:14–17 appears in chapter 20; excerpts from John 6:67–68 appear in chapter 22; excerpts from Matthew 7:9–11 appear in chapter 23; John 6:49–51 appears in chapter 23; all taken from THE ENGLISH STANDARD VERSION. © 2001 by Crossway Bibles, a division of Good News Publishers.

Romans 7:15 appears in chapter 3; Matthew 25:40 appears in chapter 12; Matthew 4:3 appears in chapter 22; 2 Corinthians 12:9 appears in chapter 23; all taken from the HOLY BIBLE: NEW INTERNATIONAL VERSION®. Copyright © 1973, 1978, 1984 by Biblica, Inc.™ Used by permission. All rights reserved worldwide.

Library of Congress Cataloging-in-Publication Data

Parrish, Christa.
  Stones for Bread / Christa Parrish.
    pages cm
  ISBN 978-1-4016-8901-8 (Trade Paper) — ISBN 1-4016-8901-9 (Trade Paper)
  I. Title.
  PS3616.A76835S76 2013
  813'.6—dc23   2013023669

Printed in the United States of America

13 14 15 16 17 RRD 5 4 3 2 1

For Chris
If I could choose again, I'd choose you.

Liesl's Glossary

baguette: a long, slender loaf of bread, approximately 3 to 4 inches in diameter and 24 to 36 inches in length with an almost even ratio of crust to crumb.

banneton: a proofing basket; traditionally made of coiled willow or cane, the basket holds the dough's shape during the final rise.

bâtard: an oval or torpedo-shaped bread, shorter and wider than a baguette.

biga: a pre-fermented dough, commercially leavened, used in Italian baking to make the bread's flavors more complex since sourdough is not being used. It is drier than a poolish.

boulanger: a French baker.

boule: a round loaf of bread, from the French word for *ball*.

brotform: the German term for a proofing basket, literally "bread mold."

couche: a proofing cloth; traditionally made of linen, the cloth is used to shape and/or cover the dough during its final rise.

crumb: the inner, soft part of the bread.

culture: the flour and water used to make the wild yeast (sourdough) starter before it is ready for use in baking.

degas: to deflate the dough.

dough trough: an oblong or rectangular container for holding larger amounts of dough; traditionally made of stone or wood, but now available for the commercial baker in sturdier materials, such as stainless steel.

lame: a handled razor used to score bread dough.

Maillard reaction: the chemical process by which bread browns.

miche: a large boule of French country bread, weighing more than 4 pounds, most often made with whole wheat flour.

peel: a paddle-like board with a handle, used for taking pizzas and breads in and out of the oven.

poolish: a pre-fermented dough, commercially leavened, used in French baking to make the bread's flavors more complex since sourdough is not being used. It is wetter than a biga.

proof: the dough's final rise.

rooms: the holes in the bread's crumb.

sponge: a general term for a pre-ferment; it is made with all fresh ingredients, not sourdough.

starter: the flour, water, wild yeast, and bacteria mixture used in sourdough breads.

One

I'm young, four, home from nursery school because of snow. Young enough to think my mother is most beautiful when she wears her apron; the pink and brown flowered cotton flares at the waist and ruffles around the shoulders. I wish I had an apron, but instead she ties a tea towel around my neck. The knot captures a strand of my hair, pinching my scalp. I scratch until the captive hair breaks in half. Mother pushes a chair to the counter and I stand on it, sturdy pine, rubbed shiny with age.

Our home is wood—floors, furniture, spoons, bowls, boards, frames—some painted, some naked, every piece protective around us. *Wood is warm*, my mother says, *because it once was living*. I feel nothing but coolness in the paneling, the top of the long farm table, the rolling pin, all soaked in January.

At the counter, the smooth butcher block edge meets my abdomen, still a potbellied preschooler's stomach, though my limbs are sticks. Mother adds flour and yeast to the antique dough trough. Salt. Water. Stirs with a wooden spoon.

I want to help, I say.

You will, she tells me, stirring, stirring. Finally, she smoothes olive oil on the counter and turns the viscous mound out in front of her. *Give me your hands.* I hold them out to her. She covers her own in flour, takes each one of mine between them, and rubs. Then, tightening her thumb and forefinger around a corner of dough, she chokes off an apple-sized piece and sets it before me. *Here.*

I poke it. It sucks my fingers in. *Too sticky*, I complain. She sprinkles more flour over it and says, *Watch. Like this.*

She stretches and folds and turns. The sleeves of her sweater are pushed up past her elbow. I watch the muscles in her forearms expand and contract, like lungs breathing airiness into the dough. She stretches and folds and turns. A section of hair comes free from the elastic band at the back of her head, drifting into her face. She blows at it and, using her shoulder, pushes it behind her right ear. It doesn't stay.

She stretches and folds and turns.

I grow bored of watching and play with my own dough, flattening it, leaving handprints. Peel it off the counter and hold it up; it oozes back down, holes forming. I ball it up like clay, rolling it under my palm. Wipe my hands on the back pockets of my red corduroy pants.

My mother finishes, returns her dough gently to the trough. She places my ball next to her own and covers both with a clean white tea towel.

I jump off the chair. *When do we cook it?*

Bake it. Mother wipes the counter with a damp sponge. *But not yet. It must rise.*

To the sky?

Only to the top of the bowl.

I'm disappointed. I want to see the dough swell and grow, like a hot air balloon. My mother unties the towel from my neck, dampens it beneath the faucet. *Let me see your hands.* I offer them to her, and she scrubs away the dried-on dough, so like paste, flaky and near-white between my fingers. Then she kisses my palms and says, *Go play*.

The kitchen is stuffy with our labor and the preheating oven. The neighbor children laugh outside; I can see one of them in a navy blue snowsuit, dragging a plastic toboggan up the embankment made by the snow plow. But I stay. I want to be kissed again and washed with warm water. I want my mother's hands on me, tender and strong at the same time, shaping me as she does the bread.

I watch their hands, thinking I may be the one to discover the next Lionel Poilâne, as if the knowledge of bread were some sort of gifting imbued before birth. Instead, I see only kindergarteners clumsily stretching the pizza dough, ripping great holes I try to fix for them, saying, "Don't worry, the cheese will cover it." Seven of them from the Montessori school in town, along with their young teacher, stand at the long farm table at the back of Wild Rise, white paper chef hats perched atop their heads. That's one of their favorite things about the cooking class, their names written around the band in black Magic Marker. They spread cornmeal over their pizza peels as if feeding chickens, flicking their wrists, granules bouncing everywhere.

The sauce is next. "You only need a little," I tell them as they splash spoonfuls onto the raw crusts, their shredded mozzarella cheese floating in a puddle of red. Most of the children add pepperoni in a smiley-face pattern, and then my apprentice, Gretchen, gathers the peels for baking.

"How long before it's done?" they want to know.

"About ten minutes," I say. "Until then, who can tell me something about bread? It can be something you learned today, or even something you already had tucked in your brain." I tap my index finger against my temple as I say those last four words, one word for each beat. The children laugh and waggle their hands in the air, above their heads. I begin by motioning to a petite, flame-haired girl.

"Bread can be made from beans and nuts," she says.

"I'm allergic to nuts," the girl next to her whines, her flat face pink and indignant.

"Ooh, ooh, ooh, pick me," the dark-eyed boy at the end of the table calls out. He's bigger than the other children, and his thick brows meet in the middle.

"Yes . . . Kalel," I say, reading his hat.

He clears his throat and stands. "Yeasts go into bread at the start. The more they eat, the more they—"

"Thank you, Kalel," the teacher says, but the other children have already filled in the missing word. They giggle and whisper to one another.

I give the teacher a sideways look. "He's six?"

"Seven. He started school a year later," she says, voice puckering with familiar exasperation.

I gather the remaining answers, calling each child by name. The last girl to respond—Cecelia—says, "Jesus fed lots of people with only five loaves of bread."

More nudging and tittering. Cecelia melts into her chair, reaches behind her shoulder to find the end of her long, blond braid, and sticks it in her mouth.

"Who wants to eat?" Gretchen asks, returning from the kitchen with seven plates. She remembers who belongs to which pizza and warns them to wait for their food to cool. "There's nothing worse than burning your tongue on hot cheese."

The children drink fresh-squeezed lemonade, slurping the last drops from the bottom of the cups and scooping out the ice to eat, some with their fingers, some with their straws. Kalel uses a fork. Gretchen and I slice their pizza into wedges. The two boys sit at one end of the table. Four of the girls huddle together in the center, so close their elbows keep tangling. And Cecelia at the other end, alone.

"I liked your answer," I tell her, taking the chair between her and the gaggle of girls, my body a fortification between her and the others.

Her hazel eyes shine. "Really?"

"Really, really."

"I learned that in Sunday school last time I went."

A customer comes into the bakehouse. Elise Braden, devoted librarian and Thursday regular, because she loves the Anadama sandwich loaves sold only one day each week. I make twelve and she buys three. "I don't know why you can't have them all the time, Liesl," she says as she hands me eleven dollars.

"Because I'm only one person," I say, giving her two quarters change.

Elise Braden grins. "You could hire better help."

"Hey, I heard that," Gretchen calls from the back of the shop. She's soaking up spilled lemonade from beneath Kalel's pendulous sneakers. "I'm wounded. I thought I was your favorite library patron."

"Convince Liesl to have this bread every day and you will be. And," the slightly stooped woman says, "I'll cancel your overdue fines."

"You don't need it every day," I say. "You buy plenty of it to last all week."

"Ah, yes. But it tastes much better fresh."

A few more patrons come for lunch. I wait on them, though it's usually Gretchen's job. She relates better with the students, no matter the ages, stepping into their worlds, drawing them out, connecting. Perhaps it's her college coursework in anthropology. Perhaps it's who she is, relaxed and round and fizzy. I have too many angles for people to get close.

It's one thirty when the kindergarten class finishes eating. I thank them for coming on the field trip and give them each a loaf of chocolate sourdough to take home with them. I pack the bread in paper bags. Six of them are printed with the shop's name in the center. The seventh has the words *I am the Bread of Life* stamped in front of a simple line drawing of two umber ears of wheat. I give that bag to Cecelia.

Until the most recent of human history, bread came with a price. Touted as simple wholesomeness, it is deceptive in its humility, requiring more painstaking labor than any other basic food. Fruit and vegetables are planted and harvested, and some indigenous types require only to be picked off the vine before eating. And while it's true meat animals must be raised and fed and cared for before slaughter, the option of wild game exists. Milk flows and is consumed, pasteurization a relatively newfangled innovation good for increasing shelf life but not required for drinking. But bread has no raw form. It begins as seed sown, the grasses then reaped, the grains threshed, winnowed, ground, sifted, kneaded, fermented, formed, and baked. Modern home cooks think nothing of tearing open a bag of silken flour and a package of active dry yeast, and pouring the dry ingredients into a machine with a couple measures of water and a two-hour wait for a fresh loaf. Bread's dark history is unknown to them.

And the sacrifice.

By the sweat of your face you shall eat bread, till you return to the ground, for out of it you were taken.

What can man do but toil under Eden's ruin? Those who work the fields know of the stinging sun, the dust in their nostrils, the ripping of soil to create a warm, dark cradle for each seed. And when the wheat grows tall and gold, the reaping comes, sheaves cut and tied. Early wheat is hulled, the grains imprisoned in toughened glumes requiring extra pounding to free them. Threshers beat the wheat with a flail, or oxen walk round and round over it, loosening the husks.

This chaff must be blown away during winnowing, by fan or fork, leaving behind the heavier grains.

The first millers, almost exclusively women, kneel on the ground, scrubbing one stone against another, the naked wheat between them crushed into meal. *The marrow of men.* And the woman who grinds it stretches her body long, ankles deformed by her work, her belly in the dirt like the cursed serpent who began her misery so long ago.

Wild Rise closes at three. I lock the door and flip the sign. Gretchen cashes out the register and we pack the unsold bread—fourteen loaves today—into paper sacks bearing the Bread of Life ministry logo. Those go into a large plastic trash bag. Someone from First Baptist will pick them up early tomorrow and distribute them to those in need.

We both go to the kitchen. Tee is there, simmering tomorrow's soups. She always makes them a day ahead because, according to her, the flavors need at least twenty-four hours to marry.

I hadn't wanted food served at *my* bakery. To me, bread is bread. There's a purity to it, a dense completeness that nourishes all on its own. A food that began as an accident. Perhaps a bowl of ground barley and water left too long in the afternoon sun, baked flat and chewy. A portable food, and with the domestication of grain, a convenience food, made at home, without the effort required of hunting game or gathering fruits. Bread built the first cities, established cultures, drew people into community. It was buried with Pharaohs and dug from the ashes of Mount Vesuvius, perfectly petrified loaves, gray and hard as stone. It survives.

Those credentials don't need a side dish.

But three weeks after I opened, Tee showed up with her tiny John Lennon spectacles and short cropped hair and declared in her Ukrainian accent, "You need soup."

"Pardon me?"

"I have some. You try." She opened the basket she carried and gave me a warm container. "Try. Try."

I uncovered the paper carton and blew on the steaming liquid. Then I took a sip. The subtle sting of cumin and mellowness of sweet potato coated my throat as it slid to my stomach. I closed my eyes and exhaled an involuntary sigh.

"Ah, good. You see. We serve it in a little baby *boule*." She indicated the size with her cupped hands. "Everyone will love, eh?"

So I hired her.

"What's on the menu for tomorrow?" I ask.

"Celery root soup with bacon and green apple. And bean and Swiss chard."

"Why don't you ever do something normal, like chicken noodle?" Gretchen asks.

"If you want that, buy a can," Tee says, stirring the creamy goodness in her speckled enamelware pot.

Gretchen begins preparing for the morning. I hover, watching, though by now she knows what to do. She'll make the dough for the soup boules, challah, sticky buns, and Friday's featured sandwich loaf, cinnamon raisin. I start the *poolish*—a pre-fermented dough—for my own seven-grain Rustica as she weighs the flour and fills the stand mixer. The machine wheezes, rocking a little too much, as it spins the ingredients together. It's old and will need to be replaced soon. Vintage, Gretchen calls it. My early morning bakery help, Xavier, calls it a piece of junk.

I can feel when the dough has been kneaded enough. But Gretchen, still unsure, stops the mixer and pulls out a small piece. She stretches it, holding it toward the light, and a perfect thin membrane appears. The gluten window. It's beautiful, milky, the late afternoon light caught in the elastic strands of protein.

"Looks good," I say.

"Thanks."

We work without speaking, only the sounds of the machines, the pot lid, the cooler door opening and closing. Some days one of us remembers to switch on the radio, but not today. At four Tee goes home. Gretchen's shift lasts another hour and her day is finished as well. But she stays longer, as she sometimes does, telling me about the graduate class she's taking online, about what a total bummer it is to still be living with her parents at twenty-four, and about her plans to go to the movies with friends tomorrow night. Then she says, "You've seen that *Bake-Off* show, right? The one with Jonathan Scott?"

"Yeah, a few minutes here and there." I'm distracted, reading my notes, following a checklist even after three years in business. I still fear forgetting a step, or an entire bread. Each tick of the box is a pin-prick in my billowing anxiety, releasing it so I won't explode. Baguette dough next. Flour, salt, and yeast first.

"Do you like it?"

I shrug, thermometer in a bowl of water. Perfect at 40 degrees Fahrenheit. I add it to the flour mixture. "It's fine, I guess."

"Have you ever thought about being on it?"

"No," I say with a snort. "Why would I?"

"I don't know," Gretchen says, and then runs her hand over her mouth while continuing to speak, mashing her words back against her lips.

I stop. "What?"

"I said, promise not to fire me."

"You didn't."

"I did."

"Gretchen, what in the world were you thinking?"

She throws her hands up. "I don't know. I was watching a few weeks ago and there was this lady on, baking these rather anemic bagels, all pale and puffy and misshapen, and I was like, 'Liesl could do so much better than that!' So I checked out the website, and all I had to do was fill out a form and attach a couple photos and, well . . . tell me you're not too angry."

"Don't worry. Do you know how many bakeries probably apply to be on that show? There's little to no chance they'll pick us. So you're safe." I smirk. "But if Jonathan Scott does come calling, then I'll fire you."

Gretchen laughs with me. "I'd gladly be fired for a chance to meet him. Even you can't help but notice how stinking good looking he is."

"Get out of here. I don't pay overtime."

Quiet now, alone, I add wood to the oven, a blend of oak and cherry. It will burn all night, until Xavier comes at three a.m. to extinguish it, enough heat held in the bricks to bake all morning. On the proofing table, four troughs of dough wait for me. They're for my wild yeast breads—sourdoughs—and I let no one work with them but me. The starter I use is more than eighty years old, cultured by my grandmother and brought from Germany when she came here, widowed, her nine-year-old daughter in tow. Even when I wasn't baking—running from the memory of bread, of my mother, of the warm, brown scent I associated with everything I'd lost in my life—I still kept that starter in a jar in the back of my refrigerator and fed it. Sometimes not as often as I should; once half a year passed before I unscrewed the lid and mixed fresh flour in with the pungent, yeasty slime it had become. And there was a time when I needed to leave it in foster care for an extended period. But I always came back to it, and it always resurrected, those not-quite-animal, not-quite-plant organisms waking to feed again. So I covet this part of the bread making, each loaf imprinted with a bit of my mother's soul.

I shape the dough, all of these boules. The plain Wild Rise sourdough, though nothing about it can be considered plain—it's simply unadorned to spotlight the complex flavors—is left to proof in *bannetons*, the coiled willow of the basket leaving its distinctive pattern on the crust even after baking. The dark, earthy Farmhouse *miche* is freestanding boule, nearly four pounds, formed and left on linen *couches*. I chop ripe pears and knead those into the third dough, along with cardamom and fresh ginger, to make the Spiced Anjou. Tomorrow I'll add a candied pear slice to the top, to bake into the crust—Xavier's idea. And finally the Sweet *Chèvre*, with its sharp goat cheese and fig filling.

It's nearly nine. Some dough goes into the cooler. Some I cover with plastic wrap and leave on the table. Then I go upstairs to the apartment above the bakehouse, eat an apple and shower, and set my alarm for four thirty in the morning.

Two

They bake together, my mother and grandmother, performing the dance of *brot* without hesitation, their bodies confident with a sense of space I'll never have. I watch, not because they don't want to include me, but because I'm fascinated by their movements. Even from behind, their kinship is clear. They share a shape—open hips, thick legs, narrow shoulders—Oma's body the shorter and more compact of the two, like a shadow when the sun is just beyond noon. Their hair is the same brown, shimmery with the undertones of fire, Oma's with streaks of soot gray where her youth has burned away. When I draw them up into my mind, it's always their backs I see first, and I must will them to turn around to remember their faces.

I look nothing like them.

I'm all points to their curves, nose, chin, elbows, ribs. I ask about it, and my mother tells me I favor Daddy's side. Later we sit together and flip through a photo album, the plastic pages squawking, and she touches the face of a black-and-white woman with pale hair, long cheeks, and downturned eyes. *Your father's Aunt Elinor.* She's plain and pointy and never married. I have to admit I resemble her more than not, and wonder if that's how they see me, the pointy girl destined to become an even thornier spinster.

Oma takes me on her lap and tells me of Germany, good Lutheran tales because my father is Irish and Catholic and she believes I learn nothing of the things I should. She tickles my armpits and whispers other stories from *Der Struwwelpeter.* My mother tries to intervene but she's shushed and waved away. *Du machst aus einer Mücke einen Elefanten!,* Oma tells her, gravel in her voice. You're making an elephant out of a mosquito. But my mother knows I'll have nightmares of thumb-sucking boys with sheared-off fingers and a giant Santa Claus drowning me in ink.

But then Oma tells me of bread, of the six hundred kinds made throughout her homeland, white and gray and black in color. Loaves heavy with pumpkin seeds. Pumpernickel. Rye. All with long, dense names like *Sonnenblumenkernbrot* and *Roggenmischbrot.* Each word is music to her. She has never eaten tinned bread bagged in plastic with a little twist tie, a pride she wears all over. *It matters,* she tells me. *Wes Brot ich ess, des Lied ich sing.*

Whose bread I eat, his song I sing.

I come into the bakeshop at five in the morning, a film of coffee and toothpaste on my tongue. Xavier, as steady as time, loads bread into the oven with a long-handled peel. The first loaves of the day. The rest proof on the tables, one final rise, one last chance for the Saccharomycetales to feast before entering the fiery furnace. They aren't the first domesticated creatures to be sacrificed for the stomachs of their masters, but perhaps the only ones to have their immortality stolen from them. As individuals, yeasts eventually die, but the colony can live forever, mother cells budding daughter cells into eternity.

Xavier wears swimming trunks and a sleeveless tank shirt, the heat from the oven washing over his skin. Perspiration shines on his bald head and catches in the hair of his long, fibrous arms. I recall the photos I've seen of Parisian *boulangers*, clad only in thin, white cotton shorts, baker's lames in their teeth.

"'Morning, Zave," I say.

He nods. "I sliced and sugared the pears for you."

"I would have done it."

"I know," he says, and then motions to the tables. "Beautiful work."

I would love him, I think, if he were forty years younger, or I forty older. He once hugged a still-warm miche to his chest, pressed his cheek to it when he thought no one would see him, and right then I read our kindredness on his face. I understand now why some believe in reincarnation, two people learning one another over and over into infinity, retaining pieces in the persistence of memory so they will recognize something of the other when they meet again. Xavier peers through me like glass.

My first instinct when seeing the domes of yellow-white dough is, always, to put my hands on it. The taut skin of unbaked bread, the puffiness pressed up just beneath the surface. It's a woman's stomach, swollen with maturity, beautiful in its generosity. As a child I would poke my finger into it, deeper and deeper until the dough no longer sprung back but created a divot in the otherwise perfect mound. "Look, Mama, a belly button."

"They're scars," she'd tell me. "Everyone begins life with a scar."

She knew.

And now Xavier scores the dough and it opens in gaping, bloodless wounds. The crust will bake differently in those places—rougher, thinner, blistery. More scars.

This is my body, broken for you.

When Wild Rise first opened, I did all the bread making myself. I brought Gretchen on when it became clear I couldn't keep up with the demand and thought she would make the things I didn't like to do—the enriched breads, the sandwich loaves, cinnamon buns, breadsticks. For five months I woke at two a.m., shuffling downstairs with the grit of sleep in my eyes. I fell into bed by eight, though by the time the lunch crowd left I dreamt of curling beneath the blankets. But the quality of the bread suffered. I had to hire someone, and after several weeks of help-wanted advertisements in the local classified section of the *Green Mountain Sentinel,* and several applicants I wouldn't trust to pour a bowl of cornflakes, let alone work in my bakehouse, I found Xavier. Or he found me. He'd owned a bakery in New Hampshire, started in the seventies and built to three locations, his bread in supermarkets across the state. He retired here, to Vermont, and gave the business to his children, but the lure of dough can't be buried with golf games and winters in Tampa. "I'm seventy-one," he told me when I mentioned the ungodly hours. "I don't sleep anyway."

Three years later, I still couldn't guess his age if I did not know it.

We pull loaves from the oven, Xavier shoveling them onto the peel, me catching them in the baskets and setting them on the racks. The air snaps with cooling crust, a symphony of dried twigs crunching beneath my feet, of cracking knuckles, of Rice Krispies. I'm home within that sound.

I keep notations, like my mother. She had notebook after notebook of trials and errors, all written in her perfect penmanship on quad-ruled pages, a square for each letter to nest in. My journal is a thick black hardcover with unlined pages. Like her, I'm a technician, a statistician, copiously documenting slight variations in texture, color, taste. I'm a chemist. A quarter cup of rye flour added to the white wheat gives a sweeter flavor. A half teaspoon more salt and 78 percent hydration of the dough result in those coveted large, irregular rooms in the crumb. Mastering formulas, not recipes, in the quest for the perfect loaf. Xavier tells me not to bother. He doesn't believe in perfection. "Forget the ingredients. Forget the environment. *You* are different each day. You can't replicate yourself. Your hands are stronger, or weaker. Your mind thinks different thoughts while kneading. Life is all over you, changing you. All that goes into the making comes out in the bread. It won't be the same from one batch to the next. Not ever."

"It'll be close, though."

"Close only counts in horseshoes and hand grenades."

He's the artist. He makes me brave enough to try. With his encouragement, I've focused on the creativity of bread, writing my own recipes, exploring nontraditional flavors and shapes. Not all of them turn out well, but he tastes my failures with me, with layers of warm butter.

Xavier fills the oven again. I scrawl a few notations in the corner of my journal while his back is turned, twist a pencil into my hair, and after adding cinnamon and star anise to the bowl, plunge my hands into the wet flour mixture. Pans clatter, and I see him stirring brown sugar on the stove. The sauce for the sticky buns. "I would have taken care of that," I say.

"I know," he says. "But your hands are a mess."

"Tee's gonna throw a fit when she finds out you used her pots."

"Only if someone tells her."

I laugh. "I don't have to. She'll know anyway. She has some sort of psychic chef sense."

"We'll see about that. I'll turn the handle to point exactly where she left it."

"Wager on it?"

"Oh, I'm not a betting man," he says, and winks because we both know I'm right and he'll lose.

Yes, kindred.

Liesl's Orange Chai Boule

Makes one loaf

LIESL'S NOTES:

This bread uses commercial yeast, but it's an excellent introduction to cold fermentation, a way to extract more flavor from the bread by slowing the fermentation process. It's delicious toasted with cream cheese for a little bit of sweetness.

INGREDIENTS:

360g (3 cups) unbleached bread flour, organic if possible
6g (1 teaspoon) finely ground sea salt
5g (1 teaspoon) instant yeast
120g (1/2 cup) fresh-squeezed orange juice
140g (1/2 cup) plus 2 tablespoons cold water
10g (1 teaspoon) orange zest
1/2 teaspoon ground star anise
1/2 teaspoon ground fennel seed
1/2 teaspoon ground cinnamon
1/4 teaspoon ground allspice
1/8 teaspoon ground cardamom
85g (1/4 cup) honey

EQUIPMENT:

mixing bowl
wooden spoon
stand mixer with dough hook (optional)
olive oil or nonstick cooking spray
glass or ceramic bowl
cornmeal
pizza peel or parchment paper

plastic wrap
broiler pan
pizza stone or baking tiles
serrated knife or razor
baking thermometer (optional)

Do Ahead

Combine all of the ingredients in a mixing bowl. Use a large wooden spoon and stir for 1 minute, until well blended; the dough should form a coarse, shaggy ball.

If using an electric stand mixer, switch to the dough hook and mix on medium-low speed for 2 minutes. The dough should stick to the bottom of the bowl but not to the sides. Or knead by hand for about 2 minutes, adjusting with flour or water as needed. The dough should be smooth and soft but not sticky.

Use olive oil to lightly coat the inside of a clean bowl. Transfer the dough to this bowl, cover with plastic wrap, and refrigerate overnight or up to 4 days.

On Baking Day

Remove the dough from the refrigerator about 2 or 3 hours before you plan to bake. Gently transfer it to a lightly floured work surface, taking care to degas it as little as possible. To form a boule, hold the dough in your hands and sprinkle with more flour so it doesn't stick to your hands. Stretch the surface of the dough around to the bottom on all four sides, rotating it as you go. When it's correctly shaped, the ball will be smooth and cohesive. This should take less than a minute to accomplish. Generously sprinkle cornmeal on a pizza peel or sheet of parchment paper. Lightly coat the plastic wrap with olive oil or non-stick cooking spray, loosely cover the dough, and proof at room temperature for about 2 hours, until increased to one and a half times its original size.

About 45 minutes before baking, preheat the oven to 550 degrees Fahrenheit or as high as it will go. On the lower shelf, put the empty broiler pan. Position the pizza stone on the shelf above.

Just prior to baking, score the dough 1/2 inch deep with a serrated knife or razor. Transfer the dough to the oven, pour 1 cup of hot water into the steam pan, then lower the oven temperature to 450 degrees Fahrenheit.

Bake for 25 to 35 minutes, until the crust is a rich golden brown, the loaf sounds hollow when thumped, and the internal temperature registers about 200 degrees Fahrenheit in the center, using a baking thermometer. For a crisper crust, turn off the oven and leave the bread in for another 5 minutes before removing.

Cool the bread for at least 45 minutes before slicing or serving.

I open the back door for the third time in fifteen minutes. My delivery-man hasn't come and I need the fresh flour to begin tomorrow's dough. Flour is temperamental—the fatty acids in the wheat germ reacting with the air the moment it is ground—and it eventually becomes rancid. This cycle takes up to nine months, but freshness matters to me. I won't use anything older than two weeks from mill to loaf.

Good bread, like wine, has depth. Subtle layers of flavor emerge by the use of different flours, by the length of the rise, the smallest ratio change of basic ingredients. I always make everyone taste. "Notice the nuttiness of this one," I say, chewing slowly.

"Mm, yeah, nutty," Gretchen says, laughing. "Totally nutty."

I savor the differences, even if no one else can.

"If I didn't know you better, I'd think you had a boyfriend."

Gretchen. She reties her apron and leans against the counter. Scratches a bit of dried dough off the edge with her purple thumbnail.

"Brent's late."

"He'll be here. He always is."

"He should have been here an hour ago."

"Liesl, chill. And have some caffeine." Gretchen hands me a Coke. "I'll call the Coop, okay?"

The Coop—that's what the locals call the natural food co-op. I nod. The pain in my head reverberates as Tee clatters around the kitchen, still muttering in Ukrainian. Contrary to his promise to reposition the pot exactly as Tee left it, Zave turned it upside down and marched his fingerprints around the otherwise shiny stainless steel. "You have to instigate?" I said.

"She has to lighten up. It's not good for her health, to be so serious."

"You better watch out. It might not be good for yours when she gets done with you."

The two hours she and Xavier worked together this morning were nothing short of torture. She threw sour glances at him and banged things. And after he pinched some freshly grated mozzarella from the plate she left at her workstation, she marched across the room and rapped his knuckles with a wooden spoon. He grinned and swiped some more.

After Zave leaves, she says she will buy a padlock for her cookware if *that man* doesn't stop touching it.

"But I use them too, Tee."

"You are the boss," she says. "He is a pig."

The woman holds grudges.

I hear the front door open and Gretchen swings back through the kitchen. "Someone for you."

"Hello?" I call, coming into the bakery. A man stands near the counter, a sack on his broad shoulder, the side of his head white with residue from a tiny slit in the paper. More flour flakes onto the cash register. I brush it off.

"Are you Liesl?"

"Yes?"

"Delivery. From the Coop."

"I gathered that. Where's Brent?"

"Who?"

"Brent. He usually brings my flour."

"I can't say. It's just me today."

The man belongs in Vermont, with his curly copper hair and equally unruly beard. He conjures images of lumberjacks, without the plaid shirt, or perhaps a long-retired linebacker, body still thick but softening with age. His work boots scuff my wide-plank pine floor.

My headache grows.

"You need to go around back and unload there," I tell him. "I'll meet you at the door."

"No problem."

"Gretchen," I shout, stumbling back into the kitchen. "Where's that Advil you offered me earlier?"

"Right here," she says, rattling the bottle.

"I need some."

She uses her talented thumbnail again, this time to pop the lid off the painkiller. Her polish, I see now, is glittery. She shakes a couple pills into my hand; they're the same color as the delivery guy's hair.

"He tracked flour and dirt all over the café," I mumble.

"I'll take care of it."

A horn honks. The man drives a small box truck, dirty white with the hint of a logo peeking through the paint someone used to cover it over. Backs to the door and parks, engine idling. I shout at him to turn the truck off. I don't want the fumes in my kitchen.

He calls out the window, "What?" and I make gestures with my words now, turning my wrist as if I clutched a key and then running my hand across my throat. He shuts off the engine and swings the driver's side door open. "I couldn't hear you. What did you say?"

"I said I didn't want your carbon emissions in my bread."

"Oh. Sorry." He looks genuinely chagrined.

"It's fine. Let's just get the flour."

But the guy is a chatty one, introducing himself as Seamus and saying he's only been living in Billingston for a month. This is his first day delivering for the co-op, though he's had other jobs with other businesses. "Liesl, that's not a name you hear too often."

"I guess not." I direct him to put the bags on the table. I've yet to clean the old flour from the bins; it will be bagged and donated with today's leftover bread.

"Only time I've ever heard it was in *The Sound of Music*. Are you German?"

"It's Austrian."

"You're Austrian?"

"No. *The Sound of Music* takes place in Austria."

"Oh. Sure. Well, my daughter couldn't remember your name. She called you the bread lady."

Confused, I shake my head. The slight movement vibrates the head pain around my skull and down into my face. "Your daughter?"

"Oh, she was here yesterday with her class. Cecelia."

I wriggle my jaw from side to side. My ear pops. "She was very sweet."

"She said you were really nice to her. And your bread wasn't too bad either."

"Not bad?"

"I had some this morning for breakfast. Peanut butter and fried egg sandwich. I have to admit, I've never had chocolate bread before. I thought it would be sugary, but it wasn't."

"You ate peanut butter and eggs on my bread?"

"Yeah. We usually do Friehoffer's, but it wasn't bad."

"Liesl," Gretchen warns. *It's only bread*, her look says.

Only bread. And *not* only bread, all at the same time. "If thou tastest a crust of bread, thou tastest all the stars and all the heavens," Robert Browning wrote. That's how I feel. Others, I need to remember, gunk it up with pulverized peanuts and unfertilized chickens.

Gretchen turns to Seamus. "Thanks so much for bringing this over."

"Yeah, no problem. That's my job." He peers at me, scratches his thick beard. "Are you okay?"

"Yes. Just a headache. I didn't eat enough today."

"Okay, well. You should do that. Eat more, I mean. It's important."

I give an exaggerated nod. Exhale. "You're absolutely right. Thank you. We'll see you next Friday."

He squints at me, cheeks twitching. "Good, okay then. Have a nice week." His truck pulls away from the back door and out the driveway. Through the window at the front of the building I see him disappear down the street. I groan instead of saying what I'd like to say, which would not only be rude but breaking more than one commandment.

Tee drops a pot lid, grunts something unintelligible, and rummages through the refrigerator. "All cheese is gone. That man ate it. I know he did to spite me. I spit on him."

Gretchen looks at me, hides a smile against her shoulder. "I can run to the Coop."

"No, let me. I need some air," I say. "And I want to find out when Brent's coming back."

Three

We vacation each year, somewhere small and coastal and boring. This year it's Maine, a ten-hour drive and a rented cottage on a bluff overlooking the sea. Little for me to do but toss rocks into the ocean and poke yellow-green seaweed with dead sticks. I wish we can visit somewhere exciting, like Disney World or the Grand Canyon. Or even Lake George, where the neighbors go every year, coming home with T-shirts and taffy and sunburns, and already-broken prizes from the boardwalk arcade.

The water is too cold to swim. I wear my suit anyway, sand creeping into it while I make castles; eventually I run home to bathe and change because it's like wriggling on sandpaper.

I wash and find my parents on the deck, sitting close, chairs touching, arms touching, maybe silent for hours, maybe silent only now that I've come. They soak one another in. I feel like an outsider, trapped in the intensity radiating from them, until my father makes room for me on his lap. He props his legs on the splintery gray railing. I rest my feet on his, curling my toes over his own, his nails scratching my skin. He kisses my hair. Mother offers me a sip of her wine, liquid jelly in a squat glass. *Nur einen kleinen Schluck!* She rarely speaks German in the home if Oma isn't visiting, and never to me. I feel giddy and older than eight, and try not to pucker after I gulp down a sharp mouthful of purple. The coughing comes anyway, and my parents laugh. *Sie glaubt, sie ist ein Fisch!*

Invariably, they tell me—again—how they met. More for them than for me.

I wish I can say it's in some tiny Parisian café or a neighborhood bakery in Brooklyn with the most perfect Jewish rye. But they meet in an appliance store. My father works there, twenty years old and earning money for city college. He and the other young salesmen wager to see who can get customers to walk out with items they never intended to buy. My father's item this day is an electric fondue pot. The customer is my mother.

Ice to Eskimos, boys. Ice to Eskimos, he says.

She comes in for vacuum cleaner bags and leaves with only that. He loses two dollars to the guys but manages to get her phone number, which he feels is more than a fair trade.

They marry three months later.

I don't understand them. Even as a child I see how different they are. Perhaps their unrequited passions glue them together, the daily failure to live lives other than ordinary. My mother puts aside her passion for baking to work as an elementary school secretary because we need the money. She buys cheap blenders and toasters from garage sales for my father to deconstruct in the basement. She always has dough crusted in her engagement ring. My father, a lunch meat deliveryman, works thirteen-hour days bringing black forest ham and logs of salami to grocery stores. A proprietor of three failed businesses. He's a tinkerer, a connoisseur of spare parts. He builds metal whirlygig sculptures in the garden, much to the complaint of the families on our street.

They live on crusts of what may have been.

I'm hungry, I say.

Let's go out. It's vacation, my father says. None of us like seafood so we find a near-empty Italian place, and when the hostess asks, *Booth or table?* my mother nudges me to answer and I pick the booth. My parents sit across from one another and I'm next to my mother, against the window, my bare legs sticking to the red vinyl. The air conditioner blows above my head, and I try to rub the gooseflesh from my arms. We order, and the waitress brings our salads and drinks—I have ginger ale, a rare treat—and a basket of bread.

We all snatch a slice. The crust is thin and flaky, the crumb a blinding white pillow. My mother nibbles a corner and places the remainder on her saucer. My father finishes the first piece and takes a second, peels the foil off a little plastic pot of margarine. *Have you tasted this?* he says. *It's just like yours.*

My mother's face doesn't change.

The waitress brings our food, and in the shuffle of dishes I break the corner off my bread and sneak it into my mouth, a puff of warm, moist cotton ball. Tasteless, like the time I licked my fingers after sticking them into a torn bag of bleached all-purpose flour at the grocery store.

Beneath the table, I reach out and rest my hand on my mother's thigh. She doesn't respond and I think I've made a mistake. My fingers tremble. I begin to pull my hand away, wiggle my tongue around my closed mouth to work up enough saliva to excuse myself to the restroom, but as soon as my lips part my mother blankets my hand with her own.

My father never notices we don't finish our bread.

On the last Sunday of every month, Wild Rise offers sanctuary.

I'd been open nearly two years when the pastor of the community church on the outskirts of town called, one of three churches collecting my leftover bread. He asked if I'd be interested in hosting the fellowship meal, and his question captured my undernourished spirit, famished for connection in ways the rest of me hadn't realized. Or ignored. *Yes*, it said, but my flesh wanted no part of it. Sunday was my only day off, and I told him so.

"We'll make it easy for you," Ryan said. "We'll open, close, clean, and provide the food. You don't even need to be there. We'd just like to use your space."

"Who said no already?"

"I haven't asked anyone else."

"Fine, but you can't use the kitchen."

"Not even the sinks?"

I sighed. "Only the sinks."

Ryan calls these Sundays *Sanctus dies Solis*—sacred Sunday. Bread is passed and broken. Simple foods are served. There's a blessing and a five-minute message, but mostly people talk to one another, sharing life in groups of three and four around the tables. And in a year it has grown from a dozen members of his own congregation to sixty people each week. Some come from area churches, some make the trip from an hour away or more. Some are tourists leisurely strolling the sidewalks of Billingston who walk into Wild Rise expecting to order lunch and instead find the hospitality of strangers. Some are people of the community—curious, seeking, occasionally antagonistic—all handled with grace, their questions welcome. And some come only for the free meal.

I'm there too.

I tell myself it's because it's the bakehouse, and no one but Xavier and I are allowed in there alone. Half-truths are easy, but they're always only half. Eventually the other side bobs to the surface and demands attention.

The room fills quickly. I nod to Ryan as he shakes hands and welcomes each person who comes through the door. He smiles and waves me over, but I hover near the counter, watching plates fill with fruit salad and triangles of turkey and ham sandwiches, today's offerings. In the center of each table a loaf of my bread—extra from yesterday—has been placed.

I lean into the kitchen door; it opens for me, accepting me into the solitude of the back room. More self-imposed isolation. I've been doing it since I was twelve; after twenty-one years it's my body's natural response, those neural pathways firmly established, and I tell myself I can't expect to act differently.

I've only been navigating this faith thing slightly longer than I've been running Wild Rise, and I'm much, much better at bread. But these Sundays make me hungry for more.

Monday through Saturday I have no time to be empty. From the moment I wake in the still-dark early hours to the moment I fall asleep each night, my hands stay busy, my mind churns with business and baking, and if a wisp of loneliness somehow manages to invade my day, I brush it away with a wave, like smoke. Like flour dust. The first three Sundays of the month are not much more difficult. I usually set my alarm with every intention of making it to church. Sometimes I do, but mostly I toss restlessly between sleep and excuses until noon. I get up, eat, run errands, and catch a sermon or two on the radio while I prep the next day's dough. It's not enough. I know it's not enough. But I can't seem to do differently. And during *Sanctus dies Solis*, that still-undernourished part of me cries out, unable to be ignored. I promise myself I'll get to services or open my Bible. The conviction never lasts past Monday morning, though, once the hustle becomes bustle and I can feed that emptiness with tasks galore.

For what I want to do I do not do, but what I hate I do.

Thirsty, I drink a glass of cool water in long, loud gulps, counting how many it takes to finish. Six swallows, or seven, if I count the residual moisture my throat instinctively pulls from my mouth at the end. Then I nab one of Tee's tomatoes and eat it like an apple. I'll have to replace it before tomorrow, and even then, she'll somehow know it's not the same one she bought, even if I bury it under the nineteen other ones in the bag. Seeds drip over my fingers; as I rinse them, I hear Ryan's voice. I stand by the door, shoulder propping it open enough for me to understand his words. He speaks on community, on the inherent need humans have because we are created in the image of the Godhead to be in close fellowship with one another. Without it, we shrivel. Without it, we deny who He made us to be. "And even if you think you don't need it," he says, "you do. Sorry, folks. No one can go it alone and experience the fullness He has for them."

I wriggle quietly through the door as the message ends. Several weekday customers gesture, so I weave through the tables and make small talk with them and others. "Liesl. Liesl," a small voice calls, and I look around until I see a bobbing blond girl at the back, waving her arm in the air.

Cecelia.

She sits next to her father, that sloppy lug of a truck driver. What was his name? Something odd and Irish, I think. Ryan stands behind them; he motions to me too.

"Liesl, I take it you've already met Seamus Tate and his daughter, Cecelia?"

"I have, yes."

"The Tates moved here not too long ago and have been attending Green Mountain Community for the past month," Ryan says. He notices a young family making their way to the front door. "Excuse me, would you?"

Seamus takes a quiet bite from the corner of his sandwich. Cecelia plucks a purple grape from the fruit salad and begins tearing the skin from it. "Do you like green grapes or purple ones better, Liesl?"

"Green, I think. Are you peeling that?"

"I don't like the skin. And once it's off, it feels like an eyeball."

"Oh. Have you felt many eyeballs?"

"No, but once in preschool there was a Halloween party and we had to stick our hands into boxes but we couldn't see what we were touching. One box was s'posed to be eyeballs, but they were just grapes without the skin on. I peeked."

"Oh."

Cecelia stood up on the chair then, tall enough to whisper loudly at the side of my face, "Daddy doesn't like Halloween and we don't go trick-or-treating, but he let me go to the party anyway."

"Honey, sit. And stop talking Liesl's ear off," Seamus says. He looks at her, not me.

"Sorry." She jumps to the floor. "What are you doing today? Do you have to bake more bread?"

"Not today," I tell the girl. "But later I'll prepare some dough."

"How much later?"

I shrug. "Probably close to your bedtime."

"Oh, good," she says, clapping twice. "Then you can come with us."

Seamus glances up now. A crumb clings to his beard. Not my bread. The packaged kind used by whoever made the sandwiches. "Cecelia, don't bother Liesl. I'm sure she's plenty busy today."

"Oh, please, please, let her go. Please, Liesl."

"Um, go where?"

"To the farm. For the fiber tour."

"The what?"

"It's this thing where people involved in the artisan fiber industry open their farms and businesses to the public to learn more about it," Seamus says. "I'm sure it wouldn't interest you. I'm sorry for Cecelia's exuberance."

"She'd like it, Daddy. We get to pet sheep and see alpacas and sometimes there's cotton candy too. If she wants to go, can she? Please, please, please?"

He narrowed his eyes at the girl in that way parents do when their children force them into an awkward corner and they can't escape without either looking like a fool or breaking their little ones' hearts. As soon as the expression comes, however, it softens. He itches his beard and the crumb falls away. "Of course she can. If she wants to, she can."

Cecelia turns her face to me. It shines with hopefulness, and that part of me that I don't want to exist, the one that needs people, the one that comes awake on these Sundays, drinks in her light. And it says to me, *More*.

"Sure," I say. "Why not?"

Yeast. The word comes to us through Old English, from the Indo-European root *yes*—meaning boil, foam, bubble. It does all those things, and more. And would it not be the Egyptians, who construct the largest, most sophisticated buildings in the land, to also harness the tiniest microbe?

Of course, they know nothing of yeast. To them, it is magic.

They are called the *bread eaters*. "Dough they knead with their feet, but clay with their hands," Herodotus wrote with derision. The Egyptians do not care. They understand their bread is from the gods, for king and peasant alike. They invent ovens to bake this new, breath-filled dough because it cannot be cooked like the flat breads they know first. They construct clay vessels to hold it. They watch it rise in the heat. They add butter and eggs and honey and coriander, and save soured dough from one batch to add to the next. They eat.

They live.

It becomes a symbol of morality; a beggar is never to be denied bread. It becomes the cornerstone of their society, their currency. The poor are paid three loaves a day, the temple priests nine hundred fine wheat breads a year. Pharaohs have an abundance for this life and the next.

But the ancient bakers are not only magicians. They are artists, creating shapes limited only by imagination. Spirals and cones and shells. Fish and birds and pyramids. Does each shape have significance, each flavor its own power? Perhaps. Or perhaps even the ancients created only to create, celebrating beauty for beauty's sake.

And what is lovelier than warm bread?

Seamus insists on taking his truck, so I struggle into the front seat after Cecelia. She wriggles into the center, sticks her hand deep into the cushion to fish out the belt. "Here's one. And here's two," she says, metal fasteners clanging. She clicks the seat belt into place and pulls the end.

"Not tight enough," Seamus says. He gives the strap another tug.

"I can't breathe."

"Any looser and you'll slip out."

She squirms and tugs at her waist. "Daddy."

"Okay, okay," he says, "just a little." He unlatches the belt, pretends to lengthen it, and buckles her in again. "Better?"

She fills her belly with a deep gulp of air. Exhales. Nods. "Much."

Seamus meets my eye, the thinnest smile at one corner of his mouth. He starts the truck; it wheezes like an old man, emphysema in the exhaust. Cecelia drapes her legs on my side of the gearshift; they don't stop moving, her sandaled feet constantly scraping up against my leg. Dirt smudges my pants. I try not to reach down and rub it away.

They're my favorite pair.

The truck rattles around us. Conversing is an effort, the words vibrating into pieces difficult to hear. Seamus and I try to exchange a few polite sentences, but after a few minutes we fall into a concentrated silence—him staring out the windshield, me counting trees on the side of the road. Cecelia talks enough for all of us, about anything and everything. Kindergarten. Her rabbit she gave away when they moved from Massachusetts. All the things she wants to do this summer. And then, her mother.

"She left us." Her legs jiggle faster.

Seamus tightens his grip on the shifter, skin thinning over his knuckles until I worry the bones will burst through.

"I'm sorry," I say.

"Daddy says she doesn't know how to love us 'cause she never learned it." The girl's cheeks tremble. "I didn't know loving was something you hafta get taught."

"My mother died when I was young," I tell her. "It still hurts not to have her around."

"Did she love you and your dad?"

"Very much."

Cecelia chews the end of her ponytail. She pokes the buttons on the cassette player without turning the radio on. Fiddles with the tuning knob and opens the vents, blowing her bangs back with stale, barely cool air. "Have you been married before? I know you're not now."

"Oh really?" I give her a little pinch in the side. She giggles. "How, may I ask, do you know that?"

"Because you don't have a ring on. Daddy says you always hafta look for the ring."

"Okay," Seamus says, his fleshy ears glowing pink. "We don't have to tell Liesl all our secrets at once."

We turn, and turn, and turn again, each time my elbow banging against the metal door, on farm roads now where the pavement has been all but driven away. The truck bounces us through ruts and potholes, churning loose stone up beneath it.

Cecelia continues her chattering, now about the small garden she planted all by herself, stressing those words. *All. By. My. Self.* She has snap peas and two bean bushes, a couple of cucumber vines, and one tomato plant. Leaning close to me, she holds her hand up to her mouth and whispers, "I didn't grow the tomato from a seed. Daddy bought it for me from the market. Does that still count?"

"Absolutely."

"Okay, everybody," Seamus says, coming to a stop on the shoulder, a steep embankment on my side of the truck. "You might want to get out over here."

"I'm good," I say, pushing open the door. It swings wide, handle out of reach, so I cling to the seat belt and lower myself into the tangle of grass below. Cecelia scrambles out backward on her father's side and he catches her. With them out of sight, I take a moment to brush at the scuff mark on my pants. It doesn't come off.

Outside the cab of the truck, silence grows over Cecelia, thick as ivy on the walls of a manor house, and she melts into her father's thick body, behind it the stone wall surrounding the home. The sparkling, talkative girl from the previous hour is gone, replaced with this nearly invisible one.

We wander around the farm for a little while. Cecelia feeds the goats, cranking quarters into the red machines and catching handfuls of pellets for the billies to nibble from her fingers. Then we move on to the sheep, who seem bored with all the attention they're receiving, the petting and baby talk animals inevitably bring. They chew and stare in calm, ordered lines against the fence. "Aren't you a pretty girl? Yes, you are. So pretty," coos the woman next to me.

"Gross," a boy with her says. He's about twelve. "They smell like sh—"

"Gregory." The mother grabs the skin of his upper arm and twists. "Watch your mouth."

The boy pulls away. "Ow, geez, Mom. Don't be so psycho."

Quietly, Cecelia lifts her hand from the ewe's back and creeps it up toward her face. Wrinkles her nose. Her father pumps liquid sanitizer into her palm. She rubs and then flaps her hands in the air.

"What next, pumpkin?" Seamus asks. "Thirsty?"

"Not yet."

We pass a gray-haired woman at a spinning wheel. Its compact style and blond wood look nothing like the wheel next to it, one of those tall, thin antique ones. The woman pumps both feet against the pedals and smiles at Cecelia. "Want to try?"

She shakes her head.

"How about you?"

"Me? I don't think so," I say.

"Yes, Liesl, you try," Cecelia says.

It did look soothing, the subtle swaying motion of the woman's head, the rhythmic up-and-down of her naked feet against cool wood. I think of the home I grew up in, the sheen of pine and oak and maple all around us because my mother loved it so much.

"Okay. Sure."

I sit. The woman points at the wheel and throws out terms—maiden, flyer, staple length, double treadle—then gives me the wad of gray wool. It's coarser than I expect, slightly greasy. My hands rebel at the unfamiliar texture, fingers curling too tightly into it. I push my chest forward, arching my back, settling my tailbone into the stool. "Now," she says, "you want to stretch and feed the roving onto the bobbin in one smooth motion." She turns the wheel manually; my feet move with the treadle, and I try to draft the wool but I only understand dough. My hands are too clumsy for spinning. The yarn is so fat in some places it won't fit through the eye, so thin in other places it simply falls away like cotton candy. "You need to breathe," the woman instructs. "And be gentle. Don't strangle the fiber."

Cecelia is giggling behind her hair, which she's wrapped over her mouth. "You're making faces, Liesl. Like this." She shakes her pony-tail away and crosses her eyes, brows and nose scrunching together. Even Seamus tries not to laugh.

I hold on to the roving too long and it spirals around itself until it snaps.

"That's it. I give up."

"It takes practice," the woman says, "sometimes."

"I think Daddy should try," Cecelia says.

"That's a great idea," I say. "Let's see how you do, Mr. Delivery Man."

My words hurt him. His shoulder twitches and he slides his eyes away from mine. But he nods and says, "Sure," and waits for me to stand. Then he takes my place, his booted feet as large as the treadles. The woman stutters a few words of warning, clearly worried this bull of a man will crush her precious wheel.

Gently, he begins spinning. One perfectly drafted ply of yarn twists from his giant hands, as if he is Arachne's son, human or spider it doesn't matter, it comes away from him lovelier than even the demonstrator herself can make.

"You've done this before," the woman says.

"A few times." Seamus unseats himself, pulling the legs of the stool out from the ground, having sunk under his weight.

Cecelia, so pleased her father has surprised his audience, wraps her arms around his waist and hugs her face into his stomach. He presses her head deeper into him.

"Did you know he could do that?" I ask her.

Her eyes crinkle in impish delight. "Uh-huh."

"Okay, missy, I see how you are."

She simply laughs, her shyness freed a little in the shared victory with her father. "Can I feed the goats again?" Seamus fishes a handful of quarters from his pocket and she takes them, palms cupped together, before walking down the dirt path toward the animal enclosure.

I look at him. "Well."

"Sorry," he says, and he smiles so I know he's beyond his annoyance. "But you were asking for it, kind of."

"I suppose I was."

He motions toward Cecelia, who keeps glancing back at us. "We should head down there. She's getting better, but she's still worried she'll lose me."

We walk, and Seamus waves at the girl. She waves back and plunks another coin into the machine. Even from here, I can see more feed falls to the weeds below than into her hand. I find an elastic hair band in one of the cargo pockets of my pants and gather my hair into it; it feels dry, tangled from the farm dust and the wind.

"So, you're not going to tell me?" I say finally.

"You mean the spinning? It's no big deal. My parents were hippies in the seventies and eighties. We lived on a commune with a bunch of other back-to-self-sufficiency types and one of the men taught me."

"Were hippies? I take it they're not anymore."

Seamus buzzes his lips in amusement. "Heck no. My folks divorced right after I graduated high school. Dad left my mother for some actress-slash-model-slash-waitress and went to LA. I hear from him once a year at Christmas. I stayed in New England, bumped around for college and work. Mom moved just outside Nashville and opened a dog grooming parlor. She lives in a condo and votes Republican now. Whoever would've thunk it."

"People change."

"That they do."

Sometimes right in front of your eyes.

We meet Cecelia and she says, "Someone gave me a bag to use," holding up a small Ziploc she's filled with pellets. "Take some too, Liesl."

I do, offering the mound to the goat on its back legs right there next to me. I feel its tongue, rough and slick. But my eyes are on Seamus, kneeling behind his daughter, their heads so close they're touching as he holds his hand beneath hers to catch any wayward feed. She pulls her arm back as soon as she's nuzzled, wiping the saliva on her shorts. He kisses her cheek, and she wipes it away before patting his unruly beard. Their silent ritual. Seamus raises his equally wild brows and then tilts his chin into her neck, rubbing it back and forth as she laughs with her entire six-year-old body. And the goat at the fence continues to lick between my fingers, cleaning away every crumb of the old Seamus, the inconsiderate, sloppy, truck-driving oaf who tracked dirt through my bakehouse, leaving only the Seamus who spins wool better than Athena herself and who loves his little girl with abandon.

Four

I'm older, ten, old enough to sense sadness the way only a woman can, though it takes me longer than one who has been through all the things yet to come to me—cramps and discharge, nine months of swelling, birth, forever good-byes, the casual, careless words of a lover slicing all the way through to tendon. My intuition isn't sharp yet. That sensitivity comes with years, sprouting like the first tiny hairs under a young girl's arms, the ones she only notices when some boy teases her about it while she dangles from a tree branch, and immediately she knows she's passed into some new realm.

The kingdom of Womanhood.

It's in the air when I walk in, but before I notice it, I see the bread. It covers the counters, the top of the refrigerator, the table. My mother stands in the center of the floor, facing me. I open my mouth to make a joke, something clever about exploding loaves, but the smell of mourning overpowers the crustiness in the air and I stop. *What's wrong?*

Your grandmother is dead.

I've never heard my mother speak in this tone. It's utterly flat, like paper, and so blank I almost miss it as the words float past me. The corner of the hard *d* hooks my ear, though, and the rest of the sentence stops with it as my brain does the deciphering, winding each letter in.

I snap.

I grab one loaf after another from the counter and smash them against the floor, grind them beneath my feet. *No,* I scream, and the words are not flat or blank. They blaze with a pain I have never experienced before.

My mother takes me against her. I still hold a boule, and as she squeezes me I dig my fingers into the soft bread and imagine it's my own face I'm tearing apart. *No, no, no,* I repeat until the bread disintegrates between us and my voice runs out. Mother finally unwraps me and wipes my face with her apron. I drop the remaining loaf, my body swaying with weakness as my emotions drain away.

She leaves the room, only for a moment, and I hear the closet in the hallway open, shut. She returns with the broom and dustpan. I reach for her, but my hand closes around the broom handle and I accept that instead, lean into it, and it holds my body upright.

It's grief, my mother says. *All of it.*

Placing the dustpan on the floor, she comes behind me and begins moving the broom, rocking me and sweeping broken bread all at the same time. I lean back against her. She hums and we sweep, and she tells me, *It will come again, Liesl. Grief always does. And in the face of it, you'll need to decide if you'll step over the pieces and leave them to be trampled, or if you'll gather them up for salvage.*

I don't know what salvage means, but understand the crumbs cannot stay on the floor. We finish cleaning, the mess emptied into a bentwood basket given to my mother by Oma; it carried some of their belongings from Germany to their new home here in America. Mother hands it to me and I open the lid of the trash pail, but she stops me. *Take it outside for the animals.*

I do, sowing the pieces like seeds beneath the Rose of Sharon where the hummingbirds come for nectar. Before I finish, a chipmunk scampers over from its hiding place in the drain spout, pads its cheeks full of bread with disconcertingly human-like hands, and runs away toward the greenhouse, carrying my grief with it.

Cecelia blows bubbles into her chocolate milk through a straw, the sticky sacs of air mounding at the top of her glass and then popping, one by one, splattering tiny droplets onto the table. It annoys me, the *glub-glub-glub* sound, but she takes such delight in her frothy accomplishments I can't bring myself to stop her. I have Gretchen swing through with a damp rag and wipe the mess every few minutes.

Tee gives her the milk so dark it looks like the Mississippi flooded into the cup. I can't imagine Tee using any sort of bottled Hershey's or Nesquik, and I'm right. She makes her own syrup, whisking Dutch-process cocoa and home-brewed vanilla extract with sugar and salt and water. And her secret ingredient, which she pulls from her pocket in a little fabric pouch and sprinkles over the boiling pot, scowling at me when I peek at her a few seconds too long. That's the other reason I won't tell Cecelia to stop slurping and splashing, because Tee doesn't leave for another twenty minutes. She's taken what my father would call "a shine" to the girl, and heaven help anyone who crosses Tee and the things she loves. I see how she protects her skillet and the apples for tomorrow's soup. This is her *zayka*, her little bunny.

Gretchen and I bag the leftover bread; I leave two loaves of white sandwich aside for Seamus to take with him when he picks up Cecelia, which could be in ten minutes or two hours. I don't mind. I'm here and the girl is no trouble. And I suppose it was my idea.

Two Fridays ago Seamus arrived with my flour delivery, late as usual but yet to make the same mistake as he did the first time, dragging a mess through the bakehouse. He brought in the bags and handed me a clipboard to sign, his manner much more brisk and unfriendly than usual. Then Cecelia's face appeared between our elbows.

"I told you to wait in the truck," Seamus said.

"I know, but I wanted to see Liesl." She shifted from one leg to another. "And I hafta, you know."

"Can she use your restroom?"

"Sure, of course," I said. "Gretchen can take you."

"I know where it is," Cecelia said, glancing around the kitchen. She wrinkled her nose. "Once I get out of here."

"Come on, honey. Through this door," Gretchen said, leading with a hand gently pressed on her shoulder blade.

"Thanks," Seamus said. "And sorry. She had someone watching her after school, but I just can't manage that anymore. Not with all the money I just put into this stinkin' clunker." He jabbed his thumb at the truck.

"So she rides around with you?"

"I try to finish up by five so she won't have to sit too long. But, yeah. I pick her up at two thirty and, well, that's that."

Seamus looked smaller. His size hadn't changed, but the layer of pride we all have beneath our skin, the one reminding us how well we care for our own, that had lost some of its girth. I'd seen it in my own father, as one business venture after another failed. In my mother, as dishes piled up and cocoons of dust huddled in corners and her *dark moments* overcame her. No one should have to shrink this way. "I guess you could bring her here."

"What?"

"After school. She can stay here."

"You're serious?"

"Gretchen leaves at five, and I'm always in the kitchen until at least seven. She can do her homework or whatever."

"She's in kindergarten."

"Then she can do whatever she does while she's driving around in the truck with you."

Seamus laughed. "Talk, mostly."

"I believe it."

"Liesl, thank you." And then he crowed. Literally lifted his fists into the air and *cock-a-doodle-doo*ed like a fat, fortyish Peter Pan. When he brought his arms down, he closed them around me, the briefest squeeze, but long enough for me to breathe in Mennen and the workday soured on his shirt. He went, holding his daughter's hand, some of his plumpness returned.

Cecelia integrates herself into the rhythm of the bakehouse. She colors and drinks her milk and eats the grilled cheese and tomato sandwiches Tee prepares for her, thick wedges of bread coated with mayonnaise and fried brown. She charms the few late customers who come in to grab a loaf for supper. And even Gretchen, who declares several times a week she will never have children, allows the girl to follow her, filling napkin holders and saltshakers and scrubbing handprints off the front window.

The phone rings. My hands are in dough. I call, "Gretchen, could you get that?"

"She not here," Tee says. "I send her to Coop for the chives you forgot yesterday."

I sigh. "Well, could you—"

"I not secretary." She turns her back to me, flips the sautéing vegetables in her pan.

"Tee," I say, but she begins humming.

"The phone's ringing," Cecelia calls, spinning through the kitchen door. She holds the cordless receiver.

"Just a sec."

I begin peeling dough from my fingers. Cecelia pushes a button. "Hello. Thank you for calling Wild Rise. This is Cecelia. How may I help you?" She grins, having repeated Gretchen's script perfectly. "Yes. Just one moment, please."

She covers the mouthpiece with her hand. "It's for you. Somebody from something-something. She talks really fast."

"That's okay. Just come stick it here." She holds it next to my head until I can clamp it between my ear and shoulder. "Hello?"

"Is this Liesl McNamara?"

"Yes."

"My name is Patrice Olsen and I'm a producer for *Bake-Off with Jonathan Scott.* Are you aware that one of your employees, a Gretchen Manske, submitted your bakery for consideration to be on our show?'"

"She mentioned something like that," I mumble. *This is not happening.*

"It's my pleasure to inform you that you've been selected. Congratulations." She doesn't sound pleased.

My neck cramps. I rush to the sink, wash my hands, and look for a towel. I snap my fingers at Cecelia and point to the one across the room. She rushes to grab it and Tee sighs loudly. She's forever ordering me to wear an apron, but I've never been comfortable in one; they were my mother's realm. I swipe my palms over the rear of my jeans and reach up for the phone, but it slips through my still-damp fingers. Cecelia and I both crouch to find it, the towel forgotten, and I fish it out from beneath a metal rolling cart.

"Sorry. I dropped the phone."

"That happens all the time. The excitement and all. Let me verify your e-mail address and I will send you all the necessary rules and regulations, contracts, release forms, and other paperwork. You may want an attorney to approve them for you. We at *Bake-Off* and the Good Food Channel are not liable for any misunderstanding you—"

"What if I don't want to be on the show?"

Silence. Then, "Pardon me?"

"I'm not sure I want to do this."

Patrice clears her throat. Again. I hear her sip some liquid and swallow. "Of course, that's your choice, Ms. McNamara. I do want to mention, though, Mr. Scott was very complimentary of you and"—papers shuffle—"Wild Rise. And I haven't yet told you about one of the rather large changes to the upcoming season, which you would be featured on, should you agree."

"Which is?"

"The ten-thousand-dollar prize. If you win. If you don't, it's donated to a charity of Mr. Scott's choice." She pauses. "I don't suppose you could find a use for that kind of money."

I swallow. "I'll look at the information."

"That's all I ask."

I doubt that.

Patrice solicits the answers to a few more questions and promises I'll find all I need to know in my e-mail box by the close of business today.

"Sorry I took so long," Gretchen says, two canvas produce bags draped over her shoulder. "There was an accident on Baxter. What's going on?"

I toss the phone at her, still working to comprehend the five-minute call. "You're fired."

Wild Yeast Starter

Liesl's notes:

Warmth is vitally important for proper yeast development; it may be difficult to grow a starter during colder months.

The formula below utilizes observation and some approximation along with its precise measurements. Because wild yeast are living organisms and the other variables—temperature, time, flour, water—also change even from day to day, culturing a starter is far from an exact science. There is often much trial and even more error. Don't be surprised if a first or second attempt fails. The success, however, is well worth the effort.

INGREDIENTS:

water (in all instances, the temperature should be
   approximately 85 degrees Fahrenheit or feel neutral to the
   touch)
rye flour
white all-purpose or bread flour

EQUIPMENT:

kitchen scale (optional but recommended)
1-quart (or larger) glass jar or bowl with lid (or plastic wrap to
   cover)
spatula or dough scraper
instant-read thermometer (optional but recommended)
wooden spoon
transparent tape
permanent marker

DAY ONE, MORNING

Add 100 grams water (1 cup), 50 grams rye flour (3/8 cup), and
50 grams white flour (3/8 cup) to a clean, dry jar. Mix thoroughly
and then scrape the sides of the jar or bowl with the spatula or
dough scraper to make the culture level easier to see. Use a piece
of transparent tape and marker to indicate the culture's level.

   Cover and leave the culture in a warm area for 24 hours,
ideally around 80 degrees Fahrenheit. If using a screw-on or
snap-on lid, do not tighten; allow it to rest loosely on the jar to
allow gases to escape.

DAY TWO, MORNING

Inspect the jar to see if the culture has risen or if there are bubbles.
(If neither is present, allow the culture to rest for another 12
hours.) Discard 75 grams of the culture (approximately 1/3 cup).

Add 75 grams water (1/3 cup), 25 grams rye flour (5 teaspoons), and 50 grams white flour (1/3 cup). Again mix well, scrape the sides of the jar, and record the level with tape and marker.

DAY TWO, EVENING
(AS CLOSE TO 12 HOURS LATER AS POSSIBLE)
Repeat steps from Day Two, Morning.

DAY THREE, MORNING
Repeat steps from Day Two, Morning. The culture may appear unresponsive, but continue anyway.

DAY THREE, EVENING—AND EVERY 12 HOURS THEREAFTER
Repeat steps from Day Two, Morning. The culture should become livelier with each feeding. When the culture doubles in volume over a 12-hour period and is quite bubbly, begin feeding with a mixture of 75 grams culture (1/3 cup), 75 grams water (1/3 cup), and 75 grams white flour (1/3 cup plus 5 teaspoons); this can take 7 to 10 days. (When the culture doubles itself in 8 hours or less, it is ready to use as a starter; however, do not refrigerate until after at least one full week of feedings.)

STORING THE STARTER
Since a starter is comprised of living organisms, it needs to be fed regularly or it dies. A starter left at room temperature needs to be fed a minimum of once a day at a ratio of at least 1:2:2, meaning one part starter, two parts water, and two parts white flour. This ratio is *by weight*. (Without a scale, approximate one part water to two parts flour *by volume*.) Many professional bakers recommend keeping a starter at room temperature for at least 30 days.

Home bakers, however, who are not making bread every day or who have busy lives and can't spend a month remembering to feed a jar of starter every 12 to 24 hours may want to store it in the refrigerator after it matures (again, after about 7 days). Keep the starter in a glass jar or bowl; the container should be no more than half full. While many starters have been revived after long periods of dormancy in the refrigerator, it is best to routinely feed it to prevent diminished performance or accidental death. Once a week is a good guideline. Choose a day of the week—perhaps every Monday?—and remove the jar from the refrigerator. Take 75 grams (1/3 cup) of the starter and place it in a clean, dry jar or bowl. Again begin feeding this starter at a 1:2:2 ratio, so add 150 grams water (2/3 cup) and 150 grams white flour (11/8 cups). Discard the remaining starter, freeze it, or use in baking. Continue to feed the new jar of starter every 12 hours until it doubles in size—usually two feedings is sufficient. Refrigerate and feed again next week.

Seamus comes to pick up Cecelia and wants to know about all the commotion.

"Liesl's gonna be on TV," his daughter says, her sparse eyebrows lifted as high as she can make them go, nearly to the center of her forehead. "For real."

"Maybe," I say. "Probably not."

"I think not," Tee says from the stove. "She is rooster."

"Chicken," Gretchen says.

Tee frowns at the correction. "If you are clever as you think, you do not give her photo to television cooking show."

"But she made it."

"A cooking show?" Seamus asks.

"The one we watch, Daddy. The one where the guy goes to different places and tries to beat them."

"They're all like that."

"*Bake-Off*," Gretchen says.

"You have to do it, Liesl," Cecelia begs. "Please, please, please? Maybe I can be on TV too."

The room spins with all the voices and people and the different odors on their breaths. Chocolate milk. Orange Tic Tacs. Something fishy, like tuna salad or perhaps liverwurst. Onions. I can't find a speck of clean, silent air.

"Okay, everyone out."

They stop and stare at me.

"I mean it."

No one speaks. Tee turns off the stove and packs away the food she's prepared for tomorrow's lunch. Seamus zips Cecelia's bag, not stopping to put the crayons back in the box but simply sweeping them into the main pouch with everything else. Gretchen takes a stainless steel bowl from the rack hanging above the dough prep table. "I'll start the breadsticks, then."

"Even you, Gretchen. Go."

"You're seriously firing me?"

"No. I'll see you at nine tomorrow." I rub my hand along my jawline, over a painful nodule close to my ear. A stress pimple already. It hadn't been there an hour ago. "I just need some alone time now."

I lock the door behind everyone and open my notebook, listing all the things Gretchen usually takes care of so I won't forget anything, lest Ginny Moren come looking for her sticky buns in the morning and find none. "Sticky buns? Might as well stick them to my buns!" she says every time she buys her two, shaking the bag near her already ample backside. I flip through to find a few more simple, time-worn recipes and prepare the dough for them too, cheating with the stand mixer when I usually knead by spoon and hand. I'm tired. And for the first time in a long time, I don't want to be making bread.

I finish, finally, and go upstairs. Turn on the computer. An e-mail from Patrice Olsen waits for me. I ignore it, but navigate over to the Good Food Channel and find a past episode of *Bake-Off* to watch online. I've seen pieces of it previously but force myself to sit through an entire show now. I don't hate it, almost appreciate the respect shown for those participating and their abilities, unlike other cooking competitions. I click over to Jonathan Scott's bio.

He apprenticed in a Parisian *boulangerie*.

I suddenly want France so badly it fills my mouth in a rush of saliva. My mother had been there once as a child but remembered nothing of the trip, except for slipping on the uneven cobbles in the rain and scraping her knee. Grandmother, there too, recalled much more. And while fully believing all things German superior, especially the bread, she had a baker's admiration for the *pain des Françaises*. She told her daughter, and later me, about loaves in every shade of earth, with flavors just as deep and armors of crust around them. My mother saved for years to return, putting away what she earned selling her bread and any little extra she could scrape together buying store brands and going without new panty hose. Not long before my grandmother died, all those pennies added up to more than enough for a round-trip plane ticket to Paris.

And all those pennies ended up given to my father.

He needed the money to get out from under yet another failed business venture. For years resentment grew within me over this transaction between husband and wife, something I wasn't supposed to know about but learned by overhearing my mother speaking on the telephone to a friend. She sounded defeated, and I hated my father and his ineptitude for robbing her of a dream when she had so little of them left. Once, while I was in high school, I told him so in a venomous rant, spilling all those things I'd kept inside since finding my mother dead in the garage when I was twelve. Would she still be alive if he hadn't stolen that money from her? "You left her with nothing," I said.

My gentle father, who began wilting the day he lost his beloved and would never again straighten, said, "Do you think I could make her do anything? If I had that kind of power, she would be with us now."

I didn't believe him then, and I saved so I could go in her stead. In the beginning it was to honor her, and then it grew larger than that. The bread called. I quit my job. I planned a three-month tour of France and Germany, mapping out both famous and little-known bakeries throughout the countries. I would travel by bicycle and train and bus. I would sleep in hostels. And I would feast and learn and come home changed.

And then I, too, had a choice to make.

Less than a week before my flight from JFK to Charles de Gaulle, I was given the opportunity to open Wild Rise. The rent was reasonable, there was an apartment above the store I could live in, and the former pizzeria was already outfitted with a wood-fire oven— something I would never be able to afford on my own. The start-up cost? Enough of my travel fund to worry me. I'd need some sort of income within three months of opening.

Yes, choices.

I took it. I knew the chance would not come again. I trusted God in it, both the business opportunity and the reconciliation of my relationship with my father. Sometimes understanding is long coming.

But I still want Paris. I will, I decide, sell out for it.

Selecting Patrice Olsen's e-mail, I click Reply and let her know I am honored to accept the invitation to be on *Bake-Off*.

| Five |

They take a trip without me, to the ocean again even though it's
November. My father brings me down into the basement, amidst his
springs and scrap and wire, and asks me to understand. *Because she's
sad about Oma*, he says. *Not because we don't love you or want you
along.* He gives me five dollars and tells me I can use it for ice cream
in school or for a Fanta at the corner grocery. *Just remember to brush
your teeth afterward.*

The grief sticks to my mother, coating her, like dirt on the mouthful of Bubble Yum I cough to the ground while swinging in the play
yard at recess. When I find it, only bits of pink gum show through
the grit and grass, and no amount of rinsing in the water fountain can
clean it. Only bits of my mother show through the sadness. I can't
imagine the ocean any more effective than the fountain at school.

So I stay home for two weeks with Great-Aunt Mary. She cooks
brown meat for every supper—liver and dry London broil and
crumbled hamburger pie—and tries to help me with my homework
the one time I ask if she knows the secret to adding fractions. She

doesn't, but tries valiantly to understand the model problems in my textbook before writing a note to Mr. Sanchez explaining my *home situation* and asking him to please give me extra tutoring. Otherwise, she watches her game shows and eats pudding desserts and tells me to go to bed at eight thirty.

My mother seems plumper and happier when they come home. I expect gifts from the seashore, a jar filled with sand and shells and dehydrated starfish, or a box of saltwater taffy. My father hands me a bag of hotel toiletries, shampoo and soap and lotion and a plastic shower cap. Mother hugs me against her neck until I can't breathe; her body trembles next to my own. *You know I love you*, she whispers.

Oh yes.

Promise me you won't forget.

My eyes flick to my father. He smiles tightly, takes my mother's arm. *Why don't you lie down, Claudia? It was a long drive. I'll be up in a moment.*

She lifts the small case at her feet and carries it up the stairs with her; something rattles inside with each step. My father smoothes my hair, one of his bony, long hands positioned on each side of my part, sliding them down to my ears once, twice, and then giving a little tug on the ends. *Don't worry. The doctor gave her some new medicine. To make her feel better. It will be all right now.*

Doctor? I thought you were at the beach.

He opens his mouth in response, but my mother's voice creeps down to us. *Alistair?*

Coming.

He twitches, as if he wants to come to me once more, but the floorboards creak above our heads and he's upstairs in seconds. My parents' bedroom door closes.

I stand on the edge of the living room rug, a braided wool island in the center of my mother's most loved pine plank floors, and listen. Only the trees talk to me, thin fingers tapping the panes on the east side of the house. I dump the toiletries onto the couch, peel my jeans off, and sit, legs straight out. Thigh to toe, I squeeze one long line of lotion down each leg. Then another, though I get only over my second knee before the bottle empties, spitting a blob on the nappy fabric of the sofa. *Mayonnaise.* My hands are knives. I spread the cool cream over my skin. Slick. White. I'm a ghost; maybe no one will see me.

I smack my legs, the sting snappier because of the lotion. I hit myself again and again, harder each time, the moisturizer thinning and opening to show speckled red below.

And then I slap my face.

I'm stunned. My cheek radiates heat, buzzing like a neon sign. Bright, dim, bright. Dim. Fading. I try to hit myself again but cannot seem to make my hand apply the same amount of force as the first time, my body protecting itself.

A door opening upstairs. I pull on my pants and wipe my fingers on the top of the couch cushion, flipping it over to hide the stain.

Xavier knows about the television show when I find him the next morning, already pulling baguettes from the oven. I reach for a basket to help, banging my hip on the corner of the counter. "Ow."

"Slow down, dear one," he says, swinging the peel with grace through the air and sliding the hot loaves into the basket on his own. They stand perfectly at attention, thin pointed sentinels of wheat. "Save some of that enthusiasm for Mr. Scott."

"Ha-ha."

I rub my hip and, turning from Xavier, lift the corner of my shirt and peer down my jeans. A bruise greets me, puffed up and purplish-blue, a color I've only seen artificially induced in a grape snow cone. Lovely. I snatch the lame from Xavier's apron and give each unblemished round of dough four cuts across the top. I'm in no mood for dainty.

Xavier notices. "Remind me to stay out of your way."

"I'm going to do the show."

He wrinkles his forehead. "Glad I'm not a betting man."

"There's prize money. Ten thousand dollars."

"Paris," he says.

He sees through me like glass.

Xavier has been to France a dozen times. He's charmed me with stories of bread, but more so of people. Of *Jérôme*, the Gaelic-music-promoter-turned-boulanger because he wanted to save a beloved building from demolition. He has one of the first LeFort ovens in his basement and only uses pre-1800 bread recipes. Or Marthe, who owns a small inn close to the northern border of France, who accepted Xavier's gift of bread as if it were from the Magi.

"Tell me I'm a sell-out."

"I'll do no such thing. But I do have a favor to ask."

"What's up?"

"I'd like to take on an apprentice."

"Zave, I can't pay anyone else."

"I know. You don't have to worry about that." He hesitates. "My grandson is living with me."

"Since when?"

"Since yesterday. He showed up on my front porch. It was either my place or the street, I imagine. Things haven't been good with Jude for a while. He's always struggled in school, failed his junior year. Says he's not going back. No interest in anything. His parents told him to get a job or get out, so he hitchhiked over to good old Vermont. I spoke to his father last night. Bill, my middle boy. I guess there are . . . many things Jude's dealing with now."

I wait for Xavier to elaborate but he stays silent. I suck my lips together and a puckering sound escapes. "Can he bake?"

"Not a lick," he says. "But, Liesl, he has the hands. I just know it."

❦

Bread plays favorites.

From the earliest times, it acts as a social marker, sifting the poor from the wealthy, the cereal from the chaff.

The exceptional from the mediocre.

Wheat becomes more acceptable than rye; farmers talk of losing their *rye teeth* as their economic status improves. Barley is for the most destitute, the coarse grain grinding down molars until the nerves are exposed. Breads with the added richness of eggs and milk and butter become the luxuries of princes. Only paupers eat dark bread adulterated with peas and left to sour, or purchase horse-bread instead of man-bread, often baked with the floor sweepings, because it costs a third less than the cheapest whole-meal loaves. When brown bread makes it to the tables of the prosperous, it is as trenchers—plates— stacked high with fish and meat and vegetables and soaked with gravy. The trenchers are then thrown outside, where the dogs and beggars fight over them. Crusts are chipped off the rolls of the rich, both to make it easier to chew and to aid in digestion. Peasants must work all the more to eat, even in the act of eating itself, jaws exhausted from biting through thick crusts and heavy crumb. There is no lightness for them. No whiteness at all.

And it is the whiteness every man wants. Pure, white flour. Only white bread blooms when baked, opening to the heat like a rose. Only a king should be allowed such beauty, because he has been blessed by his God. So wouldn't he be surprised—no, filled with horror—to find white bread the food of all men today, and even more so the food of the common people. It is the least expensive on the shelf at the supermarket, ninety-nine cents a loaf for the storebrand. It is smeared with sweetened fruit and devoured by schoolchildren, used for tea sandwiches by the affluent, donated to soup kitchens for the needy, and shunned by the artisan. Yes, the irony of all ironies; the hearty, dark bread once considered fit only for thieves and livestock is now some of the most prized of all.

He picks up Cecelia earlier today, not quite four yet, his one arm sunburned because he hangs it out the window as he drives. It's summer now, so he wears work boots with his socks pulled up nearly to his knees, shorts, a gray t-shirt with a logo on the chest so faded I wonder if it's actually there. I won't stare to find out. It's the first day I've seen Seamus's limbs uncovered, his forearms surprisingly narrow, his calves bulgy, pumped full of Popeye's spinach.

"Business good today?" He asks this almost every afternoon.

"A little slow."

"Just wait 'til that show rolls out." Something akin to disappointment discolors his words.

"We'll see."

We stand watching his daughter, the bottoms of her pigtails matted with saliva from chewing them, spray water onto a chair and wipe it. "Every little spot," Gretchen tells her, and Cecelia scrubs quicker and harder to finish before her, and they race to the next table and start again.

Seamus rakes his top teeth through the hair on his chin. "Her last day of school is tomorrow."

"She told me." I take a deep breath. "I can't have her here all day. I'm sorry."

"Oh no. 'Course not," he says. "I found her a place, at the Y. Gave us a scholarship, or whatever they call it so you don't feel like a charity case. It's just . . . look at her. You don't know her outside of here, except when we were on the farm. The shy girl you saw there, that's more what she's like everywhere else, with everyone else. The Cecelia she is when she's here . . . it's the most like the one she was before Judy left. This is her magic place."

I know what he means. I am more *me* here than anywhere. So much so that when I'm outside the bakehouse I sometimes need to remind myself I'm something other than ether, that I can bump into passersby and be heard when I make comments aloud. Maybe I am *only* me here.

I poured out my soul when decorating Wild Rise. The aqua-green wainscoting, treated to look worn and topped with peg molding head-high. Then the plaster walls, Van Gogh gold rising high to the metal pipes and ducts, original tin ceiling, all a deep eggplant color. Wooden floors, absolutely. Mismatched chairs, painted the same purple as the ceiling. My father came to the grand opening and couldn't suppress his astonishment at my choice in colors. "It's so bright," he said. "Not you at all." I muttered something about vibrancy being good for the stomach and tried not to be too hurt because, really, what else would he think. We had always been that *quiet* family. We didn't shout— usually. No one gesticulated while talking or hung our emotions on the clothesline for all the neighbors to see. We never seemed overly excitable or sought out rugged adventures, or even had much fanfare at the holidays beyond a wreath on the door and a few paper hats. We wore dull clothes in dull colors, moths not butterflies. Those looking in on the McNamara family must have thought us as wan as over-watered chicken broth, without meat or noodle.

So where did these colors come from? So deep I didn't know I had them inside me until I left my beiges and yellows and twenty-seven shades of white sample chips in a pile at the Home Depot paint counter, carrying out my cans of color instead. But on my surface I still wear only brown and gray and denim and fatigue green.

I don't want to be noticed.

Seamus gathers Cecelia, and they stand together at the counter to pick their loaf, a liturgy for them when he's here before we pack away the extra. Most days they choose sandwich bread or a loaf of Italian if they plan on spaghetti for dinner. But today Wild Rise offers Cecelia's favorite—chocolate sourdough. She won't leave without it. Seamus knows this very well, but rituals must be played out, despite know-ing the endings. "I'm not sure, Ceese. It all looks good. Too many choices." She giggles, and he points to the Sweet Chèvre. "How about something new?"

"What's chev-ree?" she asks.

"Goat cheese." He doesn't correct her pronunciation.

"Yucky. No way."

"Well, then maybe the one there, with garlic and sun-dried tomatoes."

"The chocolate, Daddy. It's right there. And there's only one left."

There's always one left. I keep it aside, just for her, each time I make it.

Seamus *hmm*s loudly, pretends to deeply contemplate her words while stroking his beard. "I don't know. I heard a little girl in Montpelier turned all sweet and melty because she ate too much chocolate bread."

Cecelia giggles. "You did not."

"True, true."

"Please, please, please?"

"Aren't you sick of it?"

She shakes her head, pigtails slapping her face.

"Alrighty then. I suppose we can all be a little sweeter. One choc-olate bread. Thank you much, Miss Liesl."

I bag the loaf and give it to Cecelia. "And you?"

"Oh no. We're good," Seamus says, taking a step back from the counter. "We can't take any more from you."

"I told you, it was a slow day. There's too much left, and it will just be donated. So pick."

He chooses a cinnamon raisin. I add a whole wheat sandwich loaf. He protests, hand fumbling to the back of his pants for his wallet, but I tell them to go. Seamus thanks me again, pinching both breads between his elbow and ribs. With his other hand, he cups the back of Cecelia's neck, guiding her through the tables and out the door. They stand on the curb, and I hear his blurry words reminding her to look both ways. He turns her head left, right, left, right, fast enough she begins to laugh. Then they stampede across the street to his truck, and he boosts her into the driver's side before climbing in after her.

I want to call my father.

In the kitchen, Tee and Gretchen argue. Tee brandishes a ladle, stabbing it toward Gretchen with each angry word. "What on earth?" I ask.

"I have no clue," Gretchen says.

Tee bites her lip. "She insult my food."

"I didn't. No one ordered her silly ankle soup today—"

"*Solyanka.*"

"—whatever it is. No one wanted it because they have no clue what's in it. Or they didn't want to look like fools trying to pronounce it. I just told her to call it something different, like summer sausage stew or something."

"It is Ukrainian solyanka." Tee shouts this and flings her spoon into the pans on the counter. Her nose reddens, her glasses steaming with tears. "Only that. Only."

And she goes, without cleaning the stove, without putting away the food. Gretchen looks at me and shrugs. "I didn't mean anything by it, Liesl. I was trying to help."

"It's fine. She . . . she's Tee."

"I can call her tonight. Apologize."

"Leave it alone. She'll be back in the morning, her normal prickly self."

We work for some time, falling into our rhythm, kneading and mixing and shaping and staying out of one another's way. Gretchen offers to wash Tee's pots before she leaves, but I send her home and do it myself, spending extra time making the stainless steel shine and storing the leftover soup in the cooler for tomorrow.

Then, upstairs, before changing my clothes or eating, I dial my father.

I don't expect him to answer. Most of the time he doesn't, ignoring the ringing and letting the machine handle it, sometimes listening to his messages, occasionally returning them. More than once I've had to contact old Mrs. Grimm, the neighbor, asking her to knock on my father's door and tell him to call me. She doesn't mind; she finds him charming and likes an excuse to make conversation. And I have to not mind, because when it comes to telephones, I do the exact same thing.

But tonight he picks up.

"Dad, it's me."

"Liesl, darling heart, how are you?"

He still has a bit of brogue left in him, passed on from immigrant parents, though he was born in Brooklyn. There have been times he's worked to snip it out of his speech, and mostly he thickens it to sound like a Lucky Charms commercial. "It's good for business," he would tell me during the few times I made deliveries with him, "the accent." The middle-aged women thought it delightful, the men felt as though they were talking with their buddy from the corner pub. My father came home exhausted from playing the game.

"I'm good. Busy with the bakery. What are you up to?"

"Oh, this and that." He retired a few years ago from the deli meat truck but works part-time at the local Ace Hardware, instructing the lost on how to fix their perpetually running toilets and faulty light sockets. "They made me head usher at church. Speaking of which, remember Selah Bates, the one you used to play with in high school?"

"It was elementary school."

"That long ago? Any which way, she got married last weekend. Real nice boy. A podiatrist, I think. Which gets me to wondering when you'll—"

"Dad."

We are close, he and I. Not as tightly knit as we were when I was a child, but better than those teenaged years when I railed against his earnest and imperfect attempts at loving me, despite my hostility and the blame I placed on him for my mother's death. We can get no closer, though, because she is always there, a placeholder for the past.

"I have some news," I say. "I'm going to be on TV." I tell him about *Bake-Off* and ask him to come to the taping, on July seventeenth. *Five weeks away.*

"I wouldn't miss it for anything," he says.

I want him there. But when he comes, she'll be with him, her ghost inflated between us.

Cecelia's Dark Chocolate Pain au Levain

Makes one loaf

LIESL'S NOTES:

If you haven't been able to culture your own wild yeast starter yet, there are many places selling it commercially online, or you may want to check with a local bakery.

INGREDIENTS:

400 grams (3 cups) unbleached white whole wheat flour, organic if possible

65 grams (1/2 cup cocoa) powder

200 grams (1 cup sourdough) starter commercial or homemade (see page 45)

100 grams (1/2 cup) sugar

250–300 grams (1 1/4 to 1/2 cups) water

6 grams (1 teaspoons) salt

50 grams (1/4 cup) chocolate, 70% cocoa, chopped very fine

60 grams (1/3 cup) dried cherries (optional)

EQUIPMENT:

2 mixing bowls

wooden spoon

stand mixer with dough hook (optional)

olive oil or nonstick cooking spray

plastic wrap

parchment paper

broiler pan

pizza stone or baking tiles

serrated knife or razor

Do Ahead

Combine ingredients, except chopped chocolate, in a large mixing bowl. Use a large wooden spoon and stir for 1 minute, until well blended; the dough should form a coarse, shaggy ball.

Add chopped chocolate (and dried cherries, if using them). If using an electric stand mixer, switch to the dough hook and mix on medium-low speed for 2 minutes. The dough should stick to the bottom of the bowl but not to the sides. Or knead by hand for about 2 minutes, adjusting with flour or water as needed. The dough should be smooth and soft but not sticky.

Use olive oil to lightly coat the inside of a clean bowl. Transfer the dough to this bowl, cover with plastic wrap, and let stand 8 to 10 hours at room temperature (overnight works best).

On Baking Day

Gently transfer the dough to a lightly floured work surface, taking care to degas it as little as possible. To form a boule, hold the dough in your hands and sprinkle with more flour so it doesn't stick to your hands. Stretch the surface of the dough around to the bottom on all four sides, rotating it as you go. When it's correctly shaped, the ball will be smooth and cohesive. This should take less than a minute to accomplish. Rest dough on a sheet of parchment paper and proof at room temperature for about 3 hours, until double its original size.

About 45 minutes before baking, preheat the oven to 550 degrees Fahrenheit or as high as it will go. On the lower shelf, put the empty broiler pan. Position the pizza stone on the shelf above.

Just prior to baking, score the dough 1/2 inch deep with a serrated knife or razor. Transfer the dough to the oven, pour 1 cup of hot water into the steam pan, then lower the oven temperature to 450 degrees Fahrenheit.

Bake for 25 to 35 minutes, until the loaf sounds hollow when thumped and the internal temperature is about 200 degrees Fahrenheit in the center. For a crisper crust, turn off the oven and leave the bread in for another 5 minutes before removing.

Tee doesn't show up for work the next day. I call the number on her employment forms and a woman answers. Her landlord. She tells me Tee is out of town for a family emergency, something about her sister's unexpected death yesterday morning.

I reheat the solyanka, and in yellow chalk Gretchen writes *Hearty Sausage Dill* under *Soups* on the menu board. It sells out before the lunch crowd finishes.

Six

Madness is a sugar cube dissolving in warm water. The sharp edges melt away first, then the white brick shrinks until nothing is left but a few crystals and fog. Eventually the water clears too, and looking at two glasses—one sweetened, one not—no difference is detectable. But the sugar is there, invisible, permeating everything, even though the sturdy, solid cube is long gone.

I never see a sugar cube dissolve like this, not then. Not yet. All mine disappear into murky cups of tea, doubly hidden by a blanket of cream. I think if I had, I would recognize it better—my mother rounding off, melting away, clouding over.

By the clearing, it's too late.

It takes a year for her to disintegrate. The sticky sadness only tightens around her, even with the pills, when she takes them. More than once, late at night when he thinks I'm asleep, I watch through the old-fashioned keyhole my father trying to wrestle the lithium into her mouth, one wiry arm restraining her, the other curling around her head to push the capsule through her lips. She doesn't want it, insists she's fine without it, says it makes her too tired and too slow and too fat. But she's tired and slow without it. I come home from school and she's asleep on the couch, all the shades pulled low. Or she's in the bathroom, in the dark. Or the bedroom closet.

My father stops reassuring me.

There's no one left to hold us together. My father, too worried and absentminded. He forgets to pay the bills—her job—and more than once I pick up the phone only to find it disconnected. He buys odd food at the grocery, jars of beets and frozen corn dogs and peanut butter. He doesn't remember things like Q-tips or conditioner, and my hair snarls so badly I cut it off with my craft scissors, to my chin first, then my ears because I can't get it even. I try to cook us supper using the ingredients in the pantry and fridge, cutting up chunks of salami and mixing it with the beets, serving it over still-crunchy elbow macaroni. Sandwiches are easier, but anytime my father buys a loaf of packaged bread, we find it in the garbage can the next morning, unwrapped, each slice mauled to crumbs. Even when he hides it in the Crock-Pot at the top of the linen closet.

So we have no more bread in our home. Until one day I walk through the door and the entire kitchen is bread. Not like when Oma died. This is chaos. Deformed boules tumbling into the sink. Burnt loaves are stacked four and five high, shaky ziggurats beckoning the untidy gods of imprecision. My mother kneads with frenzy, sprinkling this and pinching that, rolling great blobs of dough through her hands. *Help me, Liesl. There's so much to do.*

For what?

The party.

What party?

Why, the one I want to have. She laughs, loose and jangly and unconcerned. I'm frightened, because my mother's entire world spins with concern. Everything is well cared for, everyone holds value to her. She is loving-kindness.

This is madness.

Maybe we should call Dad, I say.

She slams the dough onto the counter. *Spielverderber. Both of you*, she hisses. Then she sweeps the car keys into her hand. *You're a teen-ager now. You can stay home alone.*

She leaves me. I'm not yet twelve, my birthday seven weeks away.

Jude is Xavier in miniature. Narrow in the shoulders, tattered shorts cinched bag-like on his hips, thin-limbed and graceful. His features are finer but positioned the same, his mannerisms nearly identical. Jude has hair, though, a shocking mess of bright blue, and a silver ring at each corner of his bottom lip. And glasses, thick black plastic frames. He wears Adidas flip-flops and a white sleeveless undershirt every day.

I expect a sullen, resentful teenager. What seventeen-year-old wants out of bed at three in the morning? But he works hard, and Zave is right—those hands. He has the fingers of a sculptor, twisting bread in ways I only see in glossy, oversized books on artisan baking. The designs he cuts into the crusts—birds and vines and abstract swirls—make my stick-figure-drawing self bubble with envy.

"Where did you learn to do that?" I ask him. "It's just . . . wow."

Jude shrugs. "Tenth-grade ceramics studio, I guess."

"Zave, can't we get some sort of, I don't know, coating or sealer or something to put on these and preserve them? I've seen other bak-eries do it."

"Don't bother," Jude says. "There'll be more tomorrow."

"Well, maybe you should go up against Jonathan Scott."

He shakes his head. "It's all just window dressing." And he goes out the back door, down the street to the shiny blue public bench—nearly the same color as his hair—and smokes two cigarettes. I watch him puff and blow, stubbing out the butts on the sidewalk, sometimes tossing them in the trash, other times flicking them into the gutter.

I think about tobacco residue slipping from the oil on his fingertips into the dough, but say nothing and charge nearly five dollars more for his designer loaves. They sell out before noon.

Patrice Olsen has made certain every possible publicity outlet in a hundred-mile radius knows about Wild Rise and *Bake-Off.* All four local television news affiliates run stories, poking their cameras in patrons' faces and taking some footage of Gretchen and me preparing dough. They promise to return for the contest, now less than two weeks away. The one daily and two weekly papers feature articles, as do the two big city newspapers. All the coverage increases business. We make thirty more loaves a day, closing most afternoons with no more than five left over. When Tee complains she needs more help too, Xavier volunteers Jude. She leaves him notes about what to prep each morning before she arrives; he chops carrots and marinates chicken and dices onions into tiny slivers while wiping the tears away. Tee dotes on him much the way she does with Cecelia, making him thick Panini sandwiches for lunch dripping with provolone and bacon. "You need to get fatter," she says, bringing him desserts too, made at home the night before, *perekladanets* and *fruktovykh ta horikhovykh shtrudel.* Or sometimes plain old chocolate chip cookies, big as saucers. Xavier delights in breaking off small pieces of the sweets and popping them in his mouth while she watches. She thumps him with every sort of utensil, across the knuckles or on the top of the head. "Only for the boy. None for the pigs."

Tee returned to work three days after the death of her sister without apology or explanation, though her landlady must have told her I phoned. She worked silently and efficiently, eyes downturned, taping to the cooler a list of ingredients she needed for the next day. We all let her be, even Xavier, until he decided she'd been sullen long enough. He took her favorite spatula, greased it with raspberry jam, and planted it, handle down, in a loaf of bread. "So it waves to her when she come in," he said.

"Zave—"

"Trust me, my dear girl. She needs this."

When she saw the spatula, she shimmied it from the loaf and scoured it clean, saying nothing. *She's crushed*, I thought. *Under the weight of loss.* Twenty minutes later Xavier couldn't find his lame. He searched under towels, in aprons, in the cooler, even checking the bread baskets and the oven. The beginnings of a smirk whet Tee's lips. We all noticed. "Tatiana, darling, you wouldn't happen to have seen my razor, have you?" Xavier asked.

"I believe, yes," she said. "But my memory runs away from me. I think I forget."

He scored the dough with a serrated knife instead of giving her the satisfaction of borrowing mine. The next day he brought a half dozen, hiding them various places, even duct taping one beneath the worktable. He found the missing one several days later, submerged in the jar of raspberry jam.

Tee was back.

I, however, want to disappear.

No one talks to me about the show. They tried to ask a question now and then, but each time were met with a caustic, short answer or an "I'm not talking about it." Patrice Olsen sends e-mails almost every day. I read half of them, maybe, and respond to less. Others remain unopened, glaring at me in their bold print. I forward them to Xavier. Some he takes care of on his own. The ones requiring my attention he boots back to me. I don't look at them.

Finally, Xavier shows up at Wild Rise as I'm finishing for the evening.

"We need to talk," he says. "That Olsen woman and her crew will be here in four days."

"What? The show isn't supposed to shoot until next Saturday."

"If you had read your mail, you would have learned the crew comes early for preproduction work."

"I can't do this, Zave."

"Too late for that, my friend."

I press my fingertips against my closed eyes until it hurts and then blow a slow, flat stream of air from my nose, willing my body to deflate, to go limp and empty and slide off the wooden stool, slipping under the table where Xavier, if he's kind, can roll me up and store me in some closet until the show passes. I avoid, like my father, plugging my ears and closing my eyes, singing, "Nana-nana-nana, I can't hear you," when facing something with which I don't want to deal. Returning a confrontational phone call. Balancing the business checkbook when I haven't looked at it in months. And lately, Seamus. Eventually, though, I force myself to face things, usually the day of the deadline or sometime within the grace period. Today is eventually for *Bake-Off.*

Another deep breath. A thumbprint of warmth blooms in the cavern beneath my breastbone, a penny on the sidewalk in the sun. The Comforter. The sensation fills my chest and dribbles down my limbs, and a perfect peace comes over me for a moment. The guilt comes seconds later. I think of how few times I've been to church this year, about the dusty spiritual disciplines book on top of the toilet tank, my sporadic bursts of two-second prayer only when I need something. I don't deserve comfort. And yet he gives it to me anyway, warmer and deeper, clearing out my shame until I can raise my head and say, "Okay, what do I need to know?"

"You'll bake for two challenges—"

"Two? What do you mean, two?"

"Yes, two. The first is a basic baguette—"

"Baguette?"

"—your choice of recipe. The second is a secret ingredient challenge—"

"Are you joking? What ingredient?"

"You won't find out until the day of the competition. Hence, secret. And if you don't stop repeating what I say in questions, I'm going to let you read all your messages and handle this on your own."

"Sorry."

"The competition will last seven hours, beginning at nine in the morning. You'll have to close that day, obviously. You can have the dough prepared ahead of time and allow for the final rises on Saturday."

"We're baking here?"

Xavier nodded. "But they're doing the tasting and judging in Centennial Park, since they're expecting a crowd."

"And please shock me. Who's judging? The mayor? Betty the crazy cat lady down the street?"

"Seriously, Liesl. At least try to enjoy this a little. And give them some credit. They're getting one of the bakers from King Arthur's to come. And that chef who lives not far from here. Marianna Dutton? She has a couple shows on Good Food."

"And about a hundred cookbooks, lines of cookware, gadgets, and her own magazine."

"So, you're impressed?"

I bite my lip. "I suppose."

"Good," he says.

The Hebrews come into the bread eaters' land with no bread of their own. It's famine, and Jacob's sons travel to Egypt in hopes of finding something to save their families. They find not only grain but forgiveness. Joseph is there, whom God takes from them so he can later deliver them. They find a new home. And they, too, find the miracle of yeast.

Surely the descendants of Abraham bake their grains, mixing flour and oil and kneading it to dough. But this is *uggah*—a flat cake baked on hot stones or in the ashes, the same given to the Lord by Abraham when he visits and pronounces Isaac's birth. Nomads have no time for fermentation, for waiting for dough to ripen. They have enough to carry from place to place. And they have no ovens, probably have never conceived of such a thing. Again, too heavy to move.

So what must it have been like for them to see these risen loaves come from strange Egyptian baking containers? It becomes part of them, the first thing they cry out for in the wilderness, not any bread but that of those who enslaved them. The Hebrews have freedom. Instead, they want food, their bellies filled with the earthly comfort they know. And God, the heavenly Comforter, sends bread of a different kind.

What is it?

They call it *manna*. And it's given *to* the wandering children of Israel, but not only *for* them. For us. For all who brush away the veil and will one day lay eyes on the true manna, a child they do not yet know will be born in *Beth-lehem*, the house of bread.

Seamus and Cecelia come for Saturday brunch, she in a yellow sundress with one strap stubbornly falling from her shoulder, he with his summer beard, not much more than stubble on his cheeks and a pom-pom of bristles hugging his chin. They've been regulars since May, since school ended. She orders the same thing each time, a cinnamon roll and hot cocoa, no matter how warm it is outside. He gets an off-menu sandwich; Tee gladly serves up anything he imagines, and I shake my head at his bizarre requests. This week it's scrambled eggs, sautéed green bell peppers, and grape jelly on toasted rye.

My poor bread.

We all miss Cecelia's presence at Wild Rise. She spends only one afternoon with us now during the week, and sometimes not that. The other day she said to Gretchen, "Daddy doesn't like to in-pose on Liesl," and then clamped both hands over her mouth as if a great secret accidentally snuck out. Gretchen promised she wouldn't tell, but

I overheard and knew I'd caused Seamus's unease by my curt attitude toward him the past month. I haven't been ignoring him, but close enough to it not to matter what my real intentions are.

Tee slides Seamus's plate onto the counter beside her. "You take to him."

"Gretchen will," I say.

"I send her to the store."

"You can't just send my only waitress out on errands. And without asking?"

"She back before all the people come for the lunchtime."

"That's not the point."

"The boy is helping," Tee says. She drops the plate into my hands. "Go now. Shoo."

The boy is Jude. He stands at Cecelia's chair, watching as she unrolls her cinnamon bun into one long strip, breaking off the final center swirl to save for her last mouthful. She's told me, every time, she thinks it's the best part, squishiest and drenched in buttery sugar. I give a tiny smile and wave, and give Seamus the plate. "Thanks," he says, eyes seeking to connect with mine. I look at the floor.

"Liesl, Liesl," Cecelia bubbles, "Jude said Daddy and I can come to the taping. He said only super-special people can come, and we're on the list."

"Oh? Am I on this list?"

"Don't be silly. You *have* to be there."

"Maybe," I say.

Jude adjusts his glasses. "I thought Pops told you. This place is too small to fit everyone who wants to come. You had to submit names."

"I didn't."

"We know. Pops took care of it for you."

I start to itch in my anxiety places, beneath my kneecaps, the back of my neck at the hairline, my navel. I cross one leg over the other and rub, trying to scrape away the irritation with my jeans.

It doesn't work, so I bend and scratch in earnest. Cecelia giggles, a tongue of cinnamon roll hanging from her mouth. "Martin does that when he has fleas."

"Martin?"

"Miss Betsy's dog."

"Our neighbor," Seamus adds.

"No fleas," I say. "I'm allergic to being on television shows."

Even Seamus smiles at this, a very small, seemingly wistful smile that straightens his lips rather than curls them. He hasn't touched his food since I brought it. I tuck Cecelia's dress strap back on her shoulder and give the top of her warm head a kiss. "Well, it's back to the kitchen for me."

"Wait, Liesl, can you come to church on Sunday? You can sit with me and Daddy and Jude."

I sigh. She asks every week. "Oh, sweetie, I'd love to, but I just can't tomorrow. I'm really, really busy."

"You always say that." Her eyebrows dive toward the bridge of her nose. "Daddy says we can't ever be too busy for church."

"That's us, Cecelia," Seamus says. "Liesl has much more work than we do."

"Another time," I tell her.

"Promise?"

I hesitate, feeling her father's gaze on me. I don't have to turn to read it. *Don't say it if you don't mean it. She's had enough of that.* "Yes."

Cecelia bounces from her chair and squeezes me. "When, when, when?"

"Cecelia," Seamus says.

"Soon. Just give me a few weeks to recover from this whole circus, okay?"

"What circus?"

"The TV show," Seamus tells her. "Sit, okay? I'll tell you when you can ask."

The girl motions as if she's zipping her mouth closed, then turning a key and tossing it over her shoulder. Then she nods with conviction. "Not until Daddy says. Got it."

I hug her again and wander to the other tables, talking to patrons and offering to refill glasses of iced tea. Everyone wants to ask about *Bake-Off.* I answer diplomatically, my knees and neck throbbing for a good scratch. Jude spends a few more minutes with Seamus and Cecelia, then clears the dirty dishes left around. Gretchen reappears, hurrying by with an apology, and right away takes the order of a couple who sat down only moments ago. I lock myself in the bathroom and rake my nails over my legs until pinpricks of blood appear. Then I hold wads of toilet paper on the tiny wounds until they scab.

Seven

It lasts three weeks, what I call my mother's possession. Possessed by what or whom, I can't say. But something has evicted her spirit from her body and taken over. I wonder if my real mother is tethered in the house somewhere, waiting to sneak back in. I comb the air, feeling for some thread of her. There's none.

My father calls it *mania*. At least he does when he's on the phone with the doctor, closed in the front room we call the library, speaking with hushed but urgent words. I try to listen at the door, but he sees the shadow of my feet beneath it and says, *I'll call you back*. I scurry up to my bed and hide in the blankets.

My mother is a tornado, blowing through projects and money. She cuts her hair short as a boy's and colors it platinum. She peels the flowered paper off the bathroom walls and begins painting them tangerine, but bores of the job halfway through, leaving us with a patchwork mess. She rearranges the furniture. And she bakes. All with seemingly endless energy.

Between the secret calls and his long hours at work, my father tries to clear the wreckage my mother scatters all around us. He gathers up the shopping bags full of clothes and shoes and jewelry she purchases on her lone JC Penney credit card, returning them to the store. He rescues party invitations from the mailbox before the postman comes, the yellow envelopes smudged, stamps upside down, handwritten addresses marching wildly in all directions. He hides the checkbook under the spare tire of his truck. He washes bar smoke from her blouses.

I get my first key to the house after finding myself locked out twice because my mother is gone when the school bus drops me off. The first time I sit on the stoop, waiting, the neighbors eventually inviting me in as dusk falls and the shadows grow long. I eat a Hungry-Man roast turkey dinner on a TV tray while Mr. and Mrs. Grimm watch *Wheel of Fortune*, and when my father finally pulls into the driveway, I run home without a thank-you. The next time it happens, I hide in the backyard, eventually managing to shimmy open a basement window with a screwdriver from the shed; I climb down onto the water heater and, once upstairs, make a peanut butter sandwich and start my homework at the kitchen table. After that, my father gives me a key on a tooth-shaped fob advertising our dentist's name and address. *For the back door*, he says. *Don't lose it.*

And then it stops. The shopping, the redecorating, the baking. Instead of moving on to some new, frenetic activity, my mother is still in bed at noon. A day passes, another. My father tells me she's resting and to leave her be. I peek in on her. The shades are pulled low and she's curled on the very edge of the mattress, eyes open. I roll in behind her, smell the oil on her scalp and dried saliva on the pillow. My arm loops over her body. *Tell me something*, I say, *about bread.*

If she hears me, she gives no indication. Her respiration slows and grows loud with sleep. I try to match my breaths with hers, like stepping in footprints left behind by another. But the prints are too big, the breaths too widely spaced, and I feel light-headed. So I fall into my own pattern and it's hypnotic. I start to doze.

Never punch down.

My mother's voice floats through to me, and I say, *What?*

You never punch down dough. No matter what the recipe says. Never punch it down.

Several days later my mother is dressed and washed, her unnaturally blond hair hidden in a silk scarf. She makes her special tea for us, brewing the loose leaves in warm milk instead of water, sweetening it with honey. We sit and eat zucchini muffins and she asks me how school is going, her hands fidgety, her words nervous. She's almost my mother again. Close enough, I think, to believe things will be back to normal soon.

Patrice Olsen is nothing I expect. I think metropolitan mama, in tailored trousers and pointed white blouse, hair slick and severe and pulled away from her face. I think triangle-toed shoes and slender hips and seamless boysenberry lip color. And not much older than I am, if at all. Thirty-five at the most.

She is none of those things, and when she comes to the counter, I ask if I can help her, like any other chubby, middle-aged customer in denim and comfort clogs. "Patrice Olsen," she says. "You're Liesl McNamara, correct?"

"That's me." I shake the plump, dry hand she offers, and while I've never held a live snake, I imagine it feels like her skin, rough and taut and sort of shimmery. I can't help but wipe my own palm on the leg of my jeans.

"Good. Do you have an office? There's quite a bit to go over."

"I don't, actually."

"Well," she says. She adds no more to the sentence.

"My apartment is upstairs. We could talk there. Or we can just sit at one of the tables. Maybe that one, in the corner?" I motion to the back of the café.

"The kitchen. Is that an option?"

"I suppose. If you don't mind—"

"I don't."

"Okay then." She follows me into the back. I introduce her to Tee and Gretchen.

Patrice tucks her frizzled gray hair behind her ears. I offer her a stool and she struggles to perch her short, round body on it. "And your manager? Xavier Potter? I have been corresponding with him."

"He's gone for the day." Manager? I don't correct her.

"I see." She lifts her oversized quilted bag onto the counter, removes a yellow legal pad, and gives me a binder with the *Bake-Off* logo custom-printed on the front. "Page three, please. Let's review the schedule, which I sent you. This afternoon you'll meet with hair and makeup. And wardrobe. Tomorrow will be a day of filming interviews and voice-over segments and speaking with customers. The color." She crosses off several words from her pad. "You do have those photos together?"

"Uh, yeah." I have no idea what she's talking about, but she doesn't seem like the kind of person I should admit it to, so I make a mental note to call Xavier as soon as possible.

"Fine." Another check mark. "On Friday you'll be closed, of course. The restaurant will be prepared for the show. Things will need to be rearranged, lighting brought in, some props. We may need to record more fill footage. And then Saturday, it's hair and makeup by six a.m., contest begins at nine, and judging at five p.m. This is all familiar to you." She stares at me, her green eyes unblinking, and I realize she meant that final statement as a question.

I nod. "Oh yes. Absolutely."

Patrice caps her pen and sets it on the pad, folds her hands over it. "Ms. McNamara. I have been doing this a long time. There are two types of people who come on these shows—those who seek them out, who believe their half hour of fame will bring happiness and unicorns and make all their dreams come true, and those who find themselves in the middle of it all without ever intending to be there. We both know where you fall."

"Ms. Olsen—"

"Patrice. Please. To the first group, I tell them, 'Enjoy it. But realize it's not going to change your life.' They never believe me."

"And the second?"

"I tell them, 'Enjoy it. And realize it's not going to change your life.' They rarely believe me either."

I look at her. Her face is soft with unexpected kindness. "I understand."

She opens her pen and flips to the next page of paper.

Even in times of want, men seek out bread, as if any substance milled and kneaded and shaped and baked provides the sustenance of a wheaten loaf. Perhaps they know this isn't truth, but convince themselves of it because bread brings them comfort. Each slice has the potential to become the body of the risen Christ, the church tells them—with the proper priestly blessing, of course—so they fashion their gleanings to something almost bread, hoping for a miracle of their own.

Animals are slaughtered first, not only for food, but for their feed. The grains eaten by cows and chickens can be used to nourish a family in the form of pottage, a mash of boiled cereals and water, unseasoned probably, because all the sugar, honey, and maple is finished—if they could ever afford it at all. And then the flour disappears, the housewife telling her family this is the last loaf, and she cuts it thin so it will last several days, toasting the stale pieces over the fire to revive them.

And then it's gone too.

What is to be done now? The French make acorn bread, shelling and grinding the bitter little hatted pods into meal, sometimes mixing it with other meals or flours, if there are any to be had. Those eating it do so in disgrace, since acorns have long been used as food for swine. The Germans harvest wild oats and shore grasses with heads mimicking those of wheat, and even reeds and rushes. Any vegetable seed one could find is dried and crushed. In Sweden, pine bark and needles sometimes comprised upward of three-fourths of the loaf. And if water is scarce, animal blood may be used to mix and bind it all.

Anything resembling grain is consumed. Straw is plucked from the thatched roofs of village homes. The hungriest eat grass like cattle, on their hands and knees, unable to wait for it to dry; they often die of dehydration due to continued diarrhea. Men even mix what little flour they can afford with dirt, cooking it into flat cakes, consuming the very medium from which both they, and the wheat they desperately desire, have been conceived.

Patrice slides her fingers over a touch-screen phone nearly the size of her pad, pecking here and there with beak-like precision. "Technology," she sighs. "I'm forced to keep up with it, but give me pulp and pen any day." A vibrating beep mocks her. "Hair and makeup await outside."

"Will this take long?" I ask.

She glances at me. "Yes."

"Give me a minute, then."

Wild Rise closes in ninety minutes but it buzzes with an unusual intensity, customers drawn in by the monstrous Good Food Channel bus outside the building. Gretchen assures me she can handle the crowd. "They're not ordering much anyway. No food, really. And the bread is practically gone—they're only here to gawk." She assures me she'll come find me if I'm needed.

They wait on the sidewalk, two people more like I expected Patrice to look, a post-thin man and woman, both wearing tight black jeans and t-shirts. His is flamingo pink and too small, with the words *blue bells* scribbled all over it, maybe by his own hand. Hers is oversized and hangs off one shoulder, fat aqua and gray stripes circling her torso. Patrice introduces them as León and Janska. I shake hands. "These nails will never do," the woman says.

I tuck my fingers in my back pockets.

"I trust you'll remedy that, Janska," Patrice says. "Ms. McNamara, it's been a pleasure. I'll see you tomorrow morning. Early."

She disappears into the bus. León sweeps his palm over my hair. "My, my. When was the last time you had a trim?"

"I don't remember." And it's true, though I estimate it has been at least a year.

León doesn't need my memory. His days are measured in split ends and half inches. "I *have* seen worse," he says. "Don't worry you that. We can use the bus, but Miss Patty-Cakes thought you'd feel more comfy in your own abode. So let's take this party up one story, if that's good with you."

"Uh, okay. Sure."

I never lock the downstairs door, the one beside the entrance to Wild Rise, and we climb the narrow wood steps to the landing, where I take the key from an otherwise empty clay planter hanging on the wall. "We ain't in the Village anymore, Toto," León says. He and Janska laugh.

Inside, I offer them drinks and both ask for coffee. While I start the pot brewing, they agree hair before makeup or wardrobe, and León opens his suitcase, a vintage hard shell with loud, popping latches, atop the kitchen table. He shakes open a sheet of plastic and covers the floor, setting one of my chairs in the center. "Your throne awaits."

I arrange two coffee mugs—my favorite ones, matching hand-thrown pottery with sharp angles and mottled gray glaze; I don't want them to think I'm completely unsophisticated—on the counter with the milk and sugar. And then I sit. León wraps more plastic around my neck and paws through my hair more intently, like one baboon grooming another. "We're gonna fix you right up, girl."

"What are you going to do?"

"Color first. This blond does you no good at all. Too much ash, not enough sparkle."

"Sparkle?" My voice breaks.

"Not real sparkle," Janska tells me. She pours two mugs of black coffee. "He won't glitter you."

"Oh, good."

"Chickadee, you need some major chillage. I got you read. We'll brighten you up and add itty-bitty highlights. Nothing you wouldn't want your mama to see." León peers into my sink. "Mind if I wash your hair here?"

I shake my head. He closes his suitcase and has me sit on it, folds a towel over the edge of the counter, and gently leans my head back. Warm water sprays over my hair, tickling my scalp at the base of my neck, sending reverberations through the muscles of my back. He massages my head, fingers kneading deep, and I think of dough. Rinse, condition, rinse. He squeezes the wetness from my ends and wraps me in a turban. I stand, wobbly, my body soft beneath his fingers.

"Is this what you mean by chillage?" I ask.

He grins. "You just let León take care of you."

As he paints my hair and twists the foil around it, I listen to them talk of television shows and trendy nightspots and people they both know but I'll never meet. I realize how confined my days are, to the two floors of this building and the stairway between them. To the Coop once a week and Target, four miles away, when I need a shower curtain or a new notebook. But León and Janska also live on their own narrow island of reality, limiting their daily tasks to what fits them best.

While waiting for the color to set, Janska manicures my nails, clipping away teepees of dead skin at the cuticles and filing ragged keratin edges. Her own are painted aqua to match her top and set with tiny rhinestones, long and shiny, Egyptian scarabs perched on the end of each finger. "Um, what were you thinking for me?" I ask.

Laughing, she says, "Just a coat of clear polish. If that's okay."

I nod.

Patrice Olsen does understand people. I would not have been able to handle all this in the network bus surrounded by unfamiliar words, smells, noise. In my own space it's bearable. When I look at my hands and don't recognize them, there's something else I know. The chipped Formica table I bought at the Salvation Army and love because the top is the perfect shade of *Oma Opal*, just like my grandmother had in her small cottage. The braided wool rug, a spiral rainbow hiding the drab commercial carpeting already installed here when I rented it. The loveseat, with its two wrinkled canvas cushions. The slightly yellowed light. I can breathe here.

Janska finishes my manicure and asks to see my closet. "I'm wardrobe too. Did you have any thoughts about what you wanted to wear Saturday?"

I shrug, gesture to the clothes I have on now, linen-look drawstring shorts and a sleeveless blouse. "I don't know. Something like this?"

"Do you have anything more . . . fun?"

"No."

"Let's take a look anyway."

She opens the bedroom closet and stares at the few things I own. "What about this?" she asks, removing a gauzy tunic-style shirt with a bold, violet geometric design tumbling over it. "The tag is still on."

"I bought it on clearance a couple years ago, but every time I put it on I just feel too . . . I don't know. Too purple, maybe?"

"It's perfect for the camera. With these." She takes a pair of dark capri jeans, cuffed beneath the knee, off the hanger. They are hand-me-downs from Gretchen. "Great. That was simple."

León beckons me back to the kitchen, to the waiting chair at the sink, where he removes the foil from my hair, rinses it, and buffs it until damp. Then I'm coated with a plastic cape and he cuts a part in the middle of my head and combs my hair straight against my cheeks. *Seaweed*, I think, reminded of my time at the ocean as a child.

"What do you think of bangs?" León asks, twisting chunks of hair into alligator-mouthed clips.

"I haven't had them since I was ten."

"They're making a comeback. On you, anyway. You have too much forehead without them."

My cheeks burn. "Oh."

"I'll keep enough length for you to be able to pull it up out of your face still."

"How much are you taking off?"

"To the shoulders. A smidge more."

"That's how long it is already."

"Oh my. Janska, we pegged her right. She doesn't look in the mirror."

He begins to snip. I close my eyes and listen. I rarely use the mirror for more than making sure my hair isn't too lumpy when I tie it into a ponytail. I brush it through in the shower to save time. The lighting in the bathroom is so poor, I can't see much anyway. Sometimes I lean close to tweeze a stubborn prickle of hair from my chin, or to pinch away the blackheads from my nose when they become large and dark and tempting. Otherwise, I'm grab-and-go. And if I leave my hair down, as I do occasionally on winter Sundays when my neck is too cold and I don't want to wear a scarf around the apartment, I still fasten back the front and sides in a single tiger-striped Goody barrette at the horizon of my skull, that place where the top begins curving into the back, the same way I've done since junior high.

León shoots a puff of mousse into his palm and rakes it through my freshly sheared hair. Then the blow dryer; he brushes and tousles and finally finishes. "Peek-a-boo now or after Janska has her way with you?"

"Now," I say, at the same time Janska says, "After."

She opens her bag, black with trays of shadow and gloss, and rummages until she finds tweezers. I know she'll attack my eyebrows, but the pop of each filament releasing from my skin is oddly comforting. Then she shakes my cosmetics pouch. "It was on the bathroom counter."

"I wear makeup. Sometimes."

She unzips the cracked plastic bag, given to me as a teen by someone at the church my father attended for a while, a white elephant gift at a ladies' Christmas tea. Shakes the contents onto the table. "You're better off without it," she says, and sweeps it all into the trash can.

"Wait—"

"Your mascaras are expired and none of those are even remotely good colors for you. I'll replace."

Janska winds paintbrushes in her hair, knowing the position of each particular size and plucking them out as needed. She explains to me each step, though I won't remember, lightly dusting my skin with mineral powder, highlighting my eyes at the corners and the brows, adding color to the top lids and liner to the bottom. "Focus on your eyes. They're small but amazingly vivid. Making them seem larger is easy." My lashes are thickened. My lips are glazed. She tells me to smile big and finishes with a few strokes of blush. "There. Go peek in the mirror."

I do. And I look beautiful.

I shake my head, my hair airy and layered around my face. I'm not used to it against my skin, but I resist the urge to tuck it behind my ears. The makeup reminds me of those five-minute miracle routines boasted in every issue of *Cosmopolitan* or *Woman's Day*, the ones I tried but always failed to make look anything like the glossy, airbrushed photo. I don't want to be so pleased. I've always considered myself above such nonsense, the idea that denim or hair or lipstick can—or should—make someone feel better about herself.

I can't help it.

"So, what do you think?" Janska asks when I return to the living room. Both she and León are packed and ready to move on.

"It's nice. Thank you."

"Nice?" León clutches his chest. "I am wounded. But never fear. León always survives. It's what all artists must do. Now," he says, holding up his cell phone, "Miss Patty-Cakes is gonna want some evidence of your transformation."

"You don't call her that to her face, do you?"

"Seriously, girl? You think I have a death wish? Patrice Olsen may look like she's off to the PTA bake sale, but she's one sly cupcake, that one. Smile pretty for the birdies."

My mouth twists and I blink with the flash. León sighs and snaps one more photo. "Good enough."

I thank them again and show them the door, then resist the urge to run back to the bathroom and stare in the mirror again. I'm thirsty, but don't want to smudge my lips. After five dry minutes, I go downstairs to the kitchen. Everyone stops and stares.

"Liesl," Gretchen says. "Holy cr—"

"You look lovely." Xavier.

"What are you doing here?" I ask. It's twenty minutes until six.

"I called him and Jude 'cause I didn't know when you'd be done," Gretchen says. She still looks stunned.

"Oh, thanks. I can take over from here."

"We're nearly finished," Xavier says. "Let us do it. You, I believe, have plenty of other things needing your attention at the moment."

I nod. "Okay."

My plan is to skim through the binder Patrice gave me and perhaps sort the e-mails previously sent. But once in the apartment again, I'm too airy to read. Or sit. Can split ends weigh a person down so much? Foolishness, I know. Suddenly I want to be outside. I want— heaven forbid—to be seen. I check my face again and add a little more lip color; Janska gorged my plastic pouch with samples. Then, with only the leanest pause, I slip into my only dress, a little black knee-length thing I bought for a wedding when I lived in the city. Baby-doll style with a rounded neckline, the kind that can be dressed up with rhinestones and shiny shoes. Or dressed down, like I do now, with a single silver bangle and turquoise flip-flops.

I leave the building, turning away from the window of Wild Rise, and go quickly down another street, in the opposite direction either Xavier or Gretchen travels home. I walk toward the park, where families feed the ducks after supper and eat ice-cream cones and young couples twist around themselves on blankets under the trees. I walk, and feel eyes on me. My shoulders straighten; usually I hunch into myself, disappearing into my bland, midsized clothing. I make eye contact, smiling at the young mothers wrangling their toddlers, nodding and responding, "Yes, it is," to the hunched, wrinkled couple walking arm in arm, the husband saying, "Beautiful night, isn't it?" as I pass. I engage the community around me, something I reserve almost completely for within the four walls of the bakery. I feel, for a few minutes, a part of something outside me. As if I can belong somewhere, can root myself without having my hands trapped in dough to keep me from drifting away.

I am more beautiful than all my pieces allow—ankles and elbows powdered with dry skin, bony shins, knees turned in, bread-puckered thighs neatly hidden beneath my dress, no breasts to speak of, lips stretching to invisible when I smile. And stirring within is that distinctly feminine tickle, an awakening, an acceptance of how I'm made.

I want Seamus to see me this way.

Some evenings he goes to this park with Cecelia. I sit on a stone bench by the fountain so I don't look lost and scan the area for them. Of course they are not here. I stay a few more minutes, hoping with a kind of hope more like prayer they will appear. I don't pray it, though. For all my religious shortcomings, I do take faith more seriously than lamp rubbing for God-the-Magic-Genie to come grant my three foolish wishes.

They don't show up.

I can drive there, to their home, invite them out to a movie, or a milk shake at Friendly's, or simply tell them I missed them.

Him. I miss him.

I won't go. All the hair dye in León's enchanted suitcase can't hide my true color, that of a woman who chooses bread over all else, who refuses to allow people too close. I walk home, the dress and mascara and admiring glances losing most of their luster, and instead of preparing for *Bake-Off*, I eat the supper of the spinster—Lean Cuisine pasta primavera and an entire bag of chocolate-coated, peanut butter–filled pretzels—and scrub my face with a washcloth until it burns.

Eight

There's a difference between the air of a house that's occupied and an empty one. I've always been able to tell, waking up on Sunday mornings and knowing, as soon as awareness washes over me, whether my parents are downstairs or in the backyard. Or gone, as is the case recently with my mother's strange behavior. *Mania.*

My father says her new pills are working.

It's because of the vibrations. We inhale and exhale, sending ripples out around us. Our bodies radiate heat, another silent wave jostles the air. Perhaps even the sparks jumping from one neuron to the next leak from our skin, electrifying the atmosphere. However it happens, the world around us quakes with the living. Stillness comes only in the empty spaces. Or death.

I'm home from school, and as soon as I'm inside I know I'm alone. The door is unlocked. "Mom?" I call, not expecting an answer. A tingle of apprehension smolders in my pelvis.

The garage is closed. I saw that as I stepped off the bus. We have a one-car garage and no electric door opener. My mother's Buick stays in there; Dad parks his work truck in the driveway. When she goes out, the door gets left up until she returns.

I know I'm alone, but I check each room anyway, beginning upstairs. Unoccupied, all of them. In the kitchen, dough rises in the trough on the counter, a blue checkered tea towel blanketing it. And then I see it. The shade is drawn on the door leading out to the garage. It's never down. Sometimes my mother closes the yellow half curtains, but the shade always remains tightly rolled behind the valance. The fear grows. I don't want to, but my arm moves of its own volition, tugging the thin rod at the bottom of the shade. It retracts, shooting up with a slapping sound.

My eyes are closed.

And then they're not.

The Buick sits in the garage; it's not running—not now, at least. The hose from our vacuum has been taped to the exhaust pipe, pulled tight over the hood, and threaded through the driver's side window, which is open only enough to trap the hose in the glass. A towel hangs from the window too, pink with seashells printed on it, from our guest bathroom. Another is on the ground, crumpled next to the front tire. My mother's body slumps against the steering wheel.

I float to the sofa—I must have because I have no recollection of my legs moving—and sit on the center cushion. The ghost of a thought comes to me, that I should call my father or an ambulance, but it's gone so quickly I wonder if it was even there at all. And then nothing is there but the sensation of everything inside my head— the *me* I was when I jumped off the bottom step of the school bus, over the puddle, before opening the front door of my house—melting from between the wrinkles of my brain and dripping, dripping, dripping down, pulled by gravity. Down the back sides of my cheekbones, my throat, my chest cavity, coating my stomach like Pepto-Bismol in the commercials, into my pelvis. It doesn't move to my thighs, though; they are straight out, and the laws governing the universe won't allow these memories to go anywhere but down. But all the old *me* must escape somehow, and it does, through the baby fat of my puberty-swelled backside, through my pores, soaking into the couch cushion beneath me.

I am completely emptied, ready to be refilled by a life without my mother.

We've settled into a routine, the three of us. Or maybe more so, Jude has settled into ours. He knows I always move to my right when I'm bringing the dough to the cooler, no matter where I begin in the kitchen. He knows Xavier begins whistling two minutes before the bread is due out of the oven; Jude watches the clock, waiting for sixty more seconds to tick off, and then stands with peel in hand before his grandfather reaches for the door. The bread dance. My mother had it perfectly choreographed with Oma; I never learned the steps. I used to think I would have, if I'd been given more time with her. At eight, nine, ten, I still knocked over measuring cups of water and tripped over the edge of the rag rug in front of the sink, falling against my mother as she weighed the flour. But even now, as I still sometimes bump into Xavier and I see how seamlessly Jude glides around us, I wonder if it's a giftedness I don't have.

It's more than grace of movement, though. He has a sense of bread I cannot fathom. I'm not certain Xavier expected so much either. He reads flour, senses its properties, knows which grains to use to achieve his desired results in texture and flavor and body. I offered him several books on baking science and artisan recipes, and he shook his head, saying, "Thanks, but I don't read so well. And I can't figure those dumb formulas to save my life." His experimentation isn't random and driven by emotion, like his grandfather's. He simply *knows*.

I admit a little envy.

Not even my mother could do what he does. She toiled, and there was a pride in all the hours she devoted to cultivating and improving and *becoming*. My grandmother, perhaps, baked on instinct. Children only understand so much and memories metamorphose as they're replayed over and over, but I think I saw Oma sprinkle this and pour that, and somewhere in the recesses of my mind I dust off snatches of conversation, times my mother told me how my grandmother could make bread from sand. Talent like that must skip a generation or two.

Once the first batches of bread are taken from the oven, I ask Jude to open and work the counter. Already a small line has formed outside. "You sure?" he asks. "They're coming to see you."

"They're coming to be on TV."

"Okay then." He strips off his white, sweaty tank and buttons on an oversized tent of a Hawaiian shirt.

"In my kitchen? Really?" I say.

He shrugs and smiles in this four-year-old way. "Sorry."

"Tropical doesn't seem your style, if you don't mind me saying."

"It's borrowed," he says, and then, "Pops, heads," while throwing the balled-up shirt at Xavier.

The older man catches it and checks the tag. "So is this."

"I don't have anything clean."

"Washer's in the basement."

"Yeah, I know. But your dresser's just a few steps from my bed."

Xavier throws the shirt back at Jude as he scuttles out into the café. "Teenagers."

"How's he doing?" I ask, picking up the shirt between two fingers. "This is gross."

"Give me." He crams it back into Jude's canvas bag, washes his hands. "I don't know. About the boy, I mean. He's quiet. We talk, but not about what made him leave. I'm not certain it was a particular event, but everything leading up to it heaped onto him and he finally suffocated."

"You were right, though. About his hands."

"If his father—" He stops. "Yes, but not nearly as right as I thought I was."

And there's stillness as Xavier wedges between his son and grandson, loyalties tangled like the metal Slinky I played with as a child, invariably knotted beyond mending after a few ill-fated tumbles down the stairs.

When the silence goes on long enough to make me think he's burrowed too far into his own thoughts to come back without an interruption, I say, "Oh, I forgot. Patrice Olsen said something yesterday about photos?"

Xavier blinks. "Of your mother. And grandmother, if you have any."

My arms go cold. "What on earth for?"

"Backstory," he says, circling his shoulders until one pops. He lifts the corner of a damp towel, checking the dough, his work carrying him away from the sadness still graying his eyes.

"What did you tell her?"

"Nothing. She's read your website. You mention baking with your mother. That Olsen woman likes the intergenerational aspect."

"What about the quitting my day job aspect? Fleeing the big, bad city for the mountains of New England."

"Won't resonate the same way with viewers, I'm afraid."

"How would you know?"

"It's what I was told when I suggested the same."

"You tried to get me out of it."

"That I did."

I shake my head, flicking my hair from my face. I washed and dried it this morning and rubbed in a blob of gel from a tube I found in the linen closet, in the basket where I toss all those things I buy for a certain occasion and use only once—wart removal pads, Nair, gauze bandages, melatonin capsules, Tums. The new style makes me dress differently too. It's fine to slump around in shapeless clothes with my hair tied back in a rubber band, but nice hair requires accessories, so I wear beaded earrings and a coordinating necklace. The earrings distract me; I keep brushing them away, thinking some insect is crawling up my jaw. "I guess I'll go look for them now."

"Is that quiet resignation I hear in your voice?"

"Maturity, I think," I say. "Your Liesl's done gone and grown up."

He laughs. "Not too much, now. Sulking does a bit of good every here and again."

"All right, if Patrice Olsen comes looking for me, tell her I'm being a good girl and I'll get in touch with her sometime this afternoon."

"She'll find you, don't you worry about that."

I push open the kitchen door just as Jude swings through in the other direction, knocking me backward. "A little help out here? It's psycho."

"Zave, call Gretchen and ask her to come early. And that friend of hers who fills in sometimes. Erika?"

"Will do. And I'll get some extra loaves in."

The bakery has been open an hour and already the bread is half gone. Jude and I work the counter, the line of customers snaking toward the screen door. A few of the women pull compacts from their handbags and touch up their lips. Those who aren't regulars ask about the *other* baked goods—muffins and scones and bagels—they can eat with their coffee while waiting for the cameras to catch sight of them. I tell them we don't do those things here, my voice scuffed with irritation. Jude smiles and explains things much more personably than I, slicing and toasting thick pillows of cinnamon-coated raisin and offering that to people, topped with a pool of melted cultured butter, fresh from the farm down the way. The day tourists find this quaint; the green eaters, sustainable and local; and the rest happy to have something sweet now that the sticky buns are gone. Everyone is smiling, and I wonder if Jude can also turn water into some sort of fermented beverage.

Patrice Olsen weaves through the crowd with a cameraman, asking questions and filming the chaos. The local newspapers are back as well; Jude looks at me in a way that says, *Be nice*, and it's his grandfather's face fifty years and forty pounds ago, and I try my best to answer all the reporters' questions without growling. One of the papers also photographs Jude in front of the sunflower-shaped art bread he's made this morning. I haven't seen it until now and am as amazed as those *oohing* and *aahing* around me. The bread is made in two parts: the center a simple boule covered in ground sunflower and sesame seeds, the outer a disk of curved petals. Jude tells the journalist he baked this outer part around a stoneware bowl so the seeded inner loaf could be cradled within it. He's made three of them. I price them at twelve dollars, and could have easily sold two dozen more.

It's ten before Gretchen arrives—her normal time—because, as she rushes to explain, her cell phone is dead and lost, and she spent the night away from home. And Erika can't be tracked down. So I work until the lunch crowd fades and we've run out of bread to sell. Then I leave Jude and Gretchen on their own and run upstairs to find the photos, and to escape the tornado around me.

It changes hands, at some point. The labor of milling grain, of baking it. Before it's woman's work, low to the ground and accomplished only with stone and sweat. After it becomes trade, an occupation, a man's livelihood and a way to feed his children. Still with stone. Still with sweat.

And lower still.

The miller is an evil man, the peasants whisper. What do they know of the soke forcing them to bring their wheat for grinding to the stranger who lives outside the gates of the city? Or that these laws compel the miller to spy into village homes to make sure no one is grinding their own grain at home? *It's one thing to use four-legged beasts to do his work*, the townsfolk say. But now the miller dares control the gods of water and wind, harnessing their power to turn the mill-stones. And as the rocks move against one another, they speak with the voices of demons, low, loud rumblings echoing through the belly of the earth. What do the peasants know, but that their freshly milled flour is returned to them mixed with sand? They accuse the miller of adding it to make it weigh more, make them pay more. Sometimes he doesn't, as the grinding process produces the grit, the medieval conditions. Sometimes he does; after paying the lord of the manor his share, the miller has barely enough flour for his own family.

They're in my bedroom closet, on the topmost shelf, in a manila envelope. My father must have given them to me, though I never asked for confirmation, and he never brought them up. I found the envelope in a box of measuring spoons and pot holders and other odds and ends I packed up from our own kitchen when I went away to college. There is no reason to the collection; it appears he grabbed and stuffed random handfuls into the package. He probably did because, for all my mother's talents, keeping memories wasn't one of them. Film canisters lingered on the counter for weeks or months before some-one dropped them off at CVS to be developed. We'd look through the pictures together, laughing and pointing and smudging them, and then they'd make their journey to the attic, first perched on the bottom of the stairs waiting for someone to grab them on the way up, then on my mother's dresser, then to a box in the dusty crawl space above the house, forgotten unless I needed one for a school project or special occasion. I marveled at my friends' homes where photos decorated every wall, school pictures and family sessions from Olan Mills, and collage frames displaying candid shots, the remaining snapshots arranged in albums at the bottom of the bookcases and pawed through every Christmas or birthday.

I stand on a chair and take the envelope down, spread the contents over my bed. The photos with stray fingers accidentally in the frame, the blurry ones, the ones of tree branches and feet and cars parked along the side of the road, those I pile aside. And then I find it, the one I knew was here, a Polaroid of my mother. She wears a yellow apron with gathered sleeves, half turned toward the camera, toward my father, giving him a look that might find them in bed later. Her hands are deep in the dough trough, the sunlight from the window above the sink painting her brown hair gold. A streak of flour mars her cheek, so perfectly positioned that if this were a magazine advertisement, the whiteness would have been patted on with a makeup puff.

She is alive.

I sort through a few more. There's one of my mother and me baking Christmas cookies, both of us licking dark icing from the beaters. One of Oma, pulling a loaf of German rye from her oven, hair swirled in a loose knot like grandmothers in storybooks, bread held in her terry-cloth mitts. And then one of me the same day, sitting at her table, eating a slice of the warm rye with butter and jam. I think I'm about five, in short pigtails that curl and ribbons. I loved ribbons then, wanted them in my hair all the time. I wear navy corduroy overalls and a white turtleneck, sturdy liver-colored shoes on my feet. The soles were so hard I limped until they finally broke in. But I loved the laces and called them my candy cane shoes because the two-tone cords reminded me of my favorite candy.

There are three black-and-white photos. One is my mother as an infant, posed and professional. Another is my mother somewhat older, maybe three, holding the hand of a man only captured from the waist down. *Opa.* I've seen so few pictures of him I can't recall what he looks like. And then this one, of my grandmother in her wool peacoat and panty hose drooping at her ankles, one arm around my young mother's shoulders, the other holding a paper sack of groceries, three baguettes pointing from the top. I add this one to the others I have for Patrice Olsen. That's five. That's enough.

As I sweep the remaining pictures together, two more flip to the surface as if placed there intentionally by some invisible hand. My mother and me at the beach. Our Maine vacation. We're laughing because the wind keeps blowing our hair across our eyes, into our open mouths, and my father is telling us we look better this way. Then taken moments later, another shot of all three of us, his arm over my mother's shoulders, gently holding her hair in place. And mine too; he's collected it in his fist, and I'm nestled against both of them, face upturned. My father whispers something into my mother's ear and her eyes are scrunched in laughter. "Say cheese," the stranger holding our camera instructs. *"Der Käse,"* we all say, and giggle as the man gives the camera back to my father and jogs down the sand with his dog.

Why didn't you stay? I squeeze the photo, smudging it. *Why couldn't you have stayed with us?*

I sense then I'm not alone. I turn, and it's Seamus in the doorway. "I . . . I'm sorry. I didn't mean to scare you." He peers down at me. "You're crying."

I sniffle, touch my face. Tears stick in my eyelashes, dangle at my jawbone. "I didn't know."

"Are you okay?"

"Yeah, maybe. I guess." I wipe my chin again. "What are you doing here?"

"They told me downstairs you were up here."

"Is Cecelia with you?"

"No." He tightens his thumb and forefinger around his clump of beard and tries to shrink his massive frame into something smaller and less present. "I haven't picked her up yet. I was going to, but I thought, it's early, and, well, I've been thinking about you, I mean about everything going on here, and I thought maybe I could help with something or . . . something."

"The producer asked for pictures," I tell him, and hold one out to him. "My mother. She killed herself when I was twelve. She was bipolar."

"I'm sorry."

And I step into him then, because he's there, because I need something solid and he's nothing if not that. I lean my head against his chest and he hesitates only a flicker before tightening his arms around me, both firm and mindful. Even my father—who hugged me as much as I needed or wanted—couldn't provide that. He wasn't solid, not after my mother died. Her death ate away at his sturdy parts, his bony parts, his armor, leaving him spongy despite his best efforts to be strong for me.

I'm so comfortable here. *Too comfortable.* And I sway backward with the smallest hint of pressure against his arms. As soon as he feels it, he releases me and moves away.

"I have to meet with the producer now," I say.

"Right, then." He swings his arms, fist slapping his open palm. "I think I'll go pick up Cecelia."

"See you Saturday, I guess?"

"We're on the list, I've been reminded by a very excited little girl. Many, many, *many* times."

I walk him to the door and watch him as he descends the stairs in front of me, a sasquatch in this narrow corridor, hair at the nape of his neck matted with July's heat. I wait for him to turn out of the doorway, then I run back through the apartment grabbing the *Bake-Off* binder and the photographs and go downstairs myself. Seamus is there at the bottom, sitting in the passenger seat of his truck with the door open. As soon as he sees me, he jumps out, slams the door. "I'm not stalking you, really," he says. "I just forgot to tell you that your hair looks really beautiful." And he walks around to the other side of the truck, dodging a few passing cars, and drives away.

Inside Wild Rise, Patrice Olsen sits at a table, waiting for me.

Gretchen gives me an arched eyebrow look as I join the producer and then continues to sweep the floor. I slip the photos across to her. Silently she looks at them. Nods. "These will be fine."

Her words sting me with their compassion, and I know Xavier has told her everything.

Nine

Sometime later my father arrives home. It's dark. No lights have been switched on. I hear the crinkle of paper bags, his elbow fumbling against the wall, and then a burst of incandescence from the overhead bulb.

Liesl? he says.

I find enough voice to answer, *The garage.*

Only sounds now. My father's parcels and keys crashing to the floor. His heavy footfalls behind me, to the kitchen. A moan. *No, no, no.* The door from kitchen to garage swinging open, banging into the wall. *Claudia. No. Oh, God, Claudia.* His voice on the phone, calling the emergency number, explaining, pleading. Another call, angry, to the doctor.

Red flashes outside the living room picture window, muted by sheer umber drapes. More pounding and scampering and heavy feet. Voices, so many of them. If my eyes are open they trace the mortar lines between the fireplace bricks. Mostly I keep them closed.

Finally, someone speaks to me. It's not my father. I still cannot recall who, only that it is a man, his voice soft and low and indecipherable to my traumatized ears. He puts a hand on my arm, his pale blue shirtsleeve folded to his elbow, his watch white-faced with a fat black band. With gentle pressure he lifts me from the couch, the back of my pants damp from sitting so long, from my soul sweating out, and the coolness of the air against me is startling. I'm led upstairs, to my bedroom. The arm peels down the quilt and blanket from my bed but not the top sheet. I'm helped into it, covered. The hand touches my hair. *Rest now.*

In the days following I look at arms. I don't find his again.

We wait for Jonathan Scott to make his entrance.

I see the cameras outside, following him down the sidewalk. He's talking, and then suddenly laughs, along with the cameraman, and he makes his way back down the street to try the take again.

Yesterday Wild Rise was transformed for filming. All the tables were removed. Lights strategically placed. Two work spaces—one for the celebrity chef, one for me—were placed toward the back of the room. I've claimed my station already with my baguette dough; it proofs in my mother's dough trough, my couches folded beside it.

Patrice Olsen motions to us and holds a mini megaphone to her lips. "Ready? Here he comes."

The crowd follows her earlier instructions. When Jonathan Scott opens the door, they cheer.

He smiles and waves and shakes hands. "Are we ready for a bake-off?"

"Yes!" everyone shouts.

Clapping, he says, "Awesome," and rubs his palms together as if plotting my demise. His two assistants move to his prep table and unpack his prepared dough. He joins them, giving the audience the standard, brief introduction to the show and its rules. He then says,

"We're baking two types of bread today. The first is the traditional French baguette. No other shape or type of bread is more recognized in the world. Everyone who sees these long, slim loaves knows what they are, or at least where they're from. *Baguette* can be translated into English as 'stick' or 'wand' and has only four ingredients, usually—water, flour, yeast, and salt."

I form my baguettes and bunch the couches around them. Jonathan does the same, facing the camera, giving instruction to the future home audience. The second camera records my hands. Patrice Olsen instructs me to say something, and I fumble around for a smudge of something interesting or significant. My mother always told me something new as we baked together, or whenever I asked, "Tell me something about bread." I said those words that day in the bed with her, when she'd come down from her mania into the miry clay of despair. My fingers pick the edge of the linen cloth cradling my loaves.

"You should never wash your couche," I say finally. I think of my mother, holding hers over the sink and gently fluttering away the excess flour dust. "The yeast and dough residue is what helps give baguettes their signature crust. You want your linen to be seasoned with it. Just brush them off."

"Great advice, Liesl," Jonathan says, and then removes a wicker picnic basket from beneath his table. "Now it's time to reveal the secret ingredient to be included in our second type of bread. This can be made of any type of dough, but must prominently feature whatever is in this basket."

The crowd hushes and he opens the lid, removes two containers, and holds them in the air so all can see. "Chèvre," he declares. "Goat cheese."

Jude looks at me. "What a joke. I thought you would get something good, like sour gummy worms or turkey feet or something."

Jonathan speaks to the camera as he works a new lump of dough, explaining how he's using the same base formula as his baguettes, but adding the sweet twist of maple syrup and apples.

"Ciabatta," I tell Jude.

"Seriously?"

"I need you to caramelize some onions for me."

He snorts. "I can't cook."

"Where's Tee?" I scan the room. "Or Zave."

"Pops is checking on the oven. Tee's so short, she's probably stuck behind someone out there."

"Tee can't be here until this afternoon," Xavier says, coming from the kitchen. He dries his hands on a towel, carefully slipping his wedding band to his knuckle so he can wipe beneath it. Annie has been dead five years. "I'm still married to her," he told me once when he caught me looking at the ring. "Don't matter that she's not here. I know."

"I need someone to caramelize some onions." I motion to Jude. "Apparently boy wonder here only works in bread."

"He can use a can opener, but heating the contents is a challenge. And forget frozen pizza. I've had to scrape more than one blackened crust from the oven rack."

"Electric oven?" I ask.

"Unfortunately," Xavier says.

"I suppose we can forgive him, then."

"Whoa," Jude says. "Not cool, people."

I ask him to pull the buttermilk sourdough; I'd taken several of my wet starters, fed them vigorously yesterday, and created three different dough variations early this morning, giving them time to rise. "The green bowl."

"Yeah, okay," he grumbles.

"And I'll take care of the onions," Xavier says. "Why do you need them?"

"Ciabatta," Jude says.

"Dough." I point to the door. He goes and I show Xavier the container of goat cheese. "I need something splashy. I thought a caramelized onion and Chèvre ciabatta."

"Using the buttermilk starter as a base?"

"I consistently get the biggest rooms with it."

"You need a third ingredient, I think. Apricots?"

I nod toward the other table. "Scott's going sweet already. I'll stay savory for contrast. Sun-dried tomato?"

"Meh. Expected."

"What are you folks conspiring over here?" Jonathan Scott asks. He comes between us, tosses an arm over both our shoulders, and grins for the camera. There's an easiness about him, all loose and simpering and almost *greasy*. Perhaps it's because he's too handsome, and this close to him I see it's not all makeup and lights. Genetics has been kind.

I, on the other hand, cannot figure out the whole television thing. Face this way, keep smiling, eyes toward the camera. I'm certain my face contorts with all manner of odd and unattractive expressions, and I search instead for people in the crowd I know. My father, talking with Seamus. Cecelia and Gretchen. A few loyal customers. I ignore the reporters and the rest who seem only vaguely familiar.

It wasn't as difficult yesterday when Patrice Olsen sat me in a chair and asked me questions, the footage to be spliced in with the competition to help viewers connect with me—about past jobs, my training, my mother and grandmother, why I opened the bakery. I talked for almost an hour. But the candid aspect is, at best, disconcerting. No wonder Xavier offered to do the kitchen grunt work. Patrice told me this morning not to worry; the show has a fantastic editing team.

"Fess up, you two. What's your plan?"

"A wild yeast ciabatta," I say.

He raises an eyebrow. "Competition. I like that."

Jude returns with the large ceramic bowl and a glass bottle of milk. Xavier disappears to prepare my onions. I take flour, olive oil, and salt from the shelf beneath the tabletop. Jonathan motions to the cameraman. "Tell me what you're doing," Jonathan says. He points to the bowl. "What's this?"

"A buttermilk starter-based dough I made this morning. It's already been through its first rise."

"Buttermilk?"

I nod. "It's one of the starters I like to keep around all the time."

"How many do you have?"

"Right now, about eight. My five favorites, and then three I'm experimenting with. Oh, and two more cultures I'm developing."

He whistles. "Impressive."

"Not really," I say, smoothing part of the table with olive oil.

"And what are you doing now?"

I'm almost annoyed. I don't need him hovering, asking questions to which he must already know the answers, and I'm about to tell him so when Patrice Olsen swoops over. "It's for those watching, here and when the show airs. Be natural, like you're teaching one of your baking classes. And smile."

Smile. Right. "Well," I say, "ciabatta dough is a very wet dough. I don't want it to stick to the table, but I also don't want to add any more flour because all the hydration is necessary for good results. So I use olive oil instead."

I turn the dough out onto the oiled surface; it oozes flat. "If you've ever had really good, well-made ciabatta, you've seen the large, irregular holes when you've sliced it. Bakers call those holes *rooms*, and the inside part of the bread the *crumb*.

"One of the most fascinating things about bread, though, is that conventions change. What's considered good and desirable and well-crafted changes. Texture, color, crust, flavor—every aspect of bread, really—is like fashion, in a sense. Certain things are in style at different periods of time. Now it's large, irregular rooms. During other times in history, soft, compact crumb was considered premier. It's bell-bottoms versus skinny jeans."

Jonathan Scott watches me with an odd, quiet look of—I don't know—relief, perhaps? As if he's decided I'm not the bumbling dud I appear at first glance. I try to continue before he can prod me with another idiotic question, but he asks, "What's the hydration on this?"

"About eighty percent. Maybe a tad more," I tell him, then remember to look directly into the camera. "The wet dough contributes to these large holes. But you can see how soft and shapeless it is. We want to firm it up without working it too much, so another important part of preparing this bread is a specific stretch-and-fold technique. Jude?"

He gently tugs one side of the dough, forming two corners. I do the same with the other, and we lift and pull together. The mound becomes an almost-rectangle. Jude folds his end into the center and I then blanket my half over it. We turn the dough ninety degrees and stretch again. Another fold. Another turn. We continue the ritual several more times. "You want to be very careful while doing this because you also don't want to deflate the rise already done by the yeast. It helps to have two people. And now, we let the dough rest for a couple hours."

The baguettes are almost ready to bake, but otherwise there won't be much to see for a while. Patrice Olsen explained this to the crowd when they came this morning; now she dismisses them with instructions to return at one this afternoon.

My makeshift Wild Rise family surrounds me. I introduce them all to Jonathan Scott; he engages each of them, speaking a kind word, drawing them in. He tells my father how talented I am, thanks Gretchen for submitting my name to the show, touches Cecelia's twin French braids and says they're beautiful, like her. Charisma, I suppose. Or showmanship. I can't imagine anyone could possibly enjoy being so kind to strangers day in and day out, signing autographs, always aware each person encountered is a potential viewer who has the power to choose a pot with Jonathan Scott's face on it rather than any of the dozens of other television chefs who stamp their name on cookware.

Seamus hesitates when Jonathan offers his hand, and when he does take it, he only pumps it once before taking one step closer to me.

My father tells me he's going upstairs for a nap; he hugs me and vanishes. I desperately want to join him, chugging along on three hours of sleep, up so early to finish preparing dough, then makeup and hair with Janska and León, one more preproduction meeting with Patrice Olsen, and forty minutes of nerves while waiting for filming to begin. Gretchen wants to know if I need help with anything, which I don't. She lingers anyway, her T-shirt more fitted than usual, her skirt shorter, her sandal heels higher, exchanging a few more pleasantries with the good-looking celebrity. If she smiled any bigger, her cheeks would split. Cecelia melts around my legs and waist. "Can we stay with you for a little while, Liesl? Daddy's gonna take me to McDonald's for lunch. You can come, but it's still too soon yet. So there's no place to go."

"We can go home," Seamus says.

"McDonald's?" Jonathan Scott's eyes widen in mock horror, and he crouches to Cecelia's height. "Oh no. I couldn't let you eat that food. I hear it makes kids lose their front teeth."

Cecelia giggles, her two missing bottom incisors clearly showing. "It does not. My teeth fell out 'cause I'm seven."

"I thought you were at least eight."

"The doctor says I'm tall since my daddy's tall."

"That makes sense. You're one smart kid."

"I know. I get all Es in school. They mean excellent."

"All excellents? That calls for a celebration. How about I cook lunch for you, your dad, Liesl, and anyone else here who wants to stay."

Cecelia puckers her mouth until her lips hide her nostrils. "I don't know. I really, really like cheeseburgers. And McDonald's has a PlayPlace."

"Well," Jonathan says, sighing, "it's up to you. But I've been told I'm a pretty good cook."

"Thank you anyway, but I think we're going to head out for a while," Seamus says, and Cecelia is relieved she doesn't have to choose between her charming new friend and the twisty slide with a side order of fries.

Seamus glances in my direction. No, it's more than a glance. His eyes stay fixed on me; I feel them even as I look elsewhere around the room. A strange, almost protective energy radiates from him, strong enough for me to hear. *Ask us to stay. Want us to stay.* He won't push his way through; he will come only if invited, the awkward giant in this delicate land of TV stars and artisan baking.

I'm not certain I want him here.

"I'll see you both around two, then," I say. "Have fun."

"We will," Cecelia chirps.

Whatever passed between us the other day, in my bedroom with the photograph of my mother, evaporates. Seamus withdraws his attentions, and I am left to wonder if I read him wrong.

Wild Rise Petite Baguette

LIESL'S NOTES:

This wild yeast baguette variation takes approximately two days from start to finish, if the wet starter is active and ready to use. If the starter has been refrigerated and needs to be refreshed, be sure to add that time—usually two or three feeds, about 24 to 36 hours—to the total preparation time.

INGREDIENTS:

400 grams (2 cups) wild yeast starter (page 45, or use your own starter or a commercial starter)

900 grams (7 cups) unbleached white flour, divided (organic, if possible)

35 grams (¹/4 cup) whole wheat flour (organic, if possible)
450 grams (2 cups) water
18 grams (1 tablespoon) finely ground sea salt

EQUIPMENT:
mixing bowls
spatula or dough scraper
plastic wrap or clean kitchen towels
stand mixer with dough hook (optional)
wooden spoon
olive oil
couche, baguette form, or cotton tea towels
baking or pizza stone
peel
spray bottle of water

DO AHEAD
PREPARING THE FIRM STARTER

In a mixing bowl, combine the active wild yeast starter with 120 grams (1 cup) of white flour and whole wheat flour. Stir well (a tablespoon of water may be added, if necessary), scrape down the sides of the bowl, and cover with plastic wrap. Let the firm starter rest at room temperature for 8 to 10 hours, until it doubles in volume and appears to have bubbles throughout. The consistency of the starter will be more like dough (rather than the batter-like wet starter).

ON BAKING DAY
PREPARING THE BAGUETTE DOUGH

In a large bowl or stand mixer, combine the firm starter and the water, stirring until the firm starter is partially dissolved and the mixture is slightly frothy. Add 120 grams (1 cup) of flour and stir with a spoon until well combined. Add the salt and just enough of the remaining flour to make a stiff ball that can no longer be stirred. Turn out onto a well-floured surface and knead until the dough is firm and smooth, about 15 minutes. Or use a stand mixer with dough hook on low to medium speed for 10 to 12 minutes. The dough is ready when a pinch of dough pulled from the ball springs back quickly.

Shape the dough into a ball and place in a lightly oiled bowl, turning once to coat. Cover with a clean, damp towel or plastic wrap and let ferment for two hours. It will increase about 1/4 in volume.

Divide and Shape

After 2 hours, turn out the dough to a lightly floured surface. Knead briefly and then cut into 6 equal pieces. Shape each piece into a small, tight ball and cover with a damp towel or plastic wrap for 30 minutes. After the half hour has passed, shape each ball into a baguette. To do this, flatten the ball of dough with the heel of the hand and stretch a little, until it resembles an oval. Fold the top edge of the dough one-third of the way down and seal with the side of the hand. Then fold the bottom edge one-third of the way up and seal—like folding a business letter so it fits in an envelope. Use the side of your hand to crease the dough down the center and fold in half. Again, seal the edge, creating a taut, smooth log shape. Sprinkle the work surface with a small amount of additional flour and gently press and roll your dough into the long baguette form, starting with hands in the center of the log and moving outward, until the loaf is as long as your bread pan or couche—usually 12 to 15 inches (be sure the baguettes will fit on the baking stone). Transfer the baguette, seam side up, to a well-floured couche or baguette form. If using the couche, bunch the cloth around the dough so it will help hold the dough's shape. Cover with plastic wrap or a damp cloth and let proof for 2 hours, until the baguettes double in size; a slight indentation will remain when the dough is lightly pressed.

BAKE

Preheat the oven to 450 degrees Fahrenheit. Position the oven rack with baking stone in the center of the oven. Very carefully roll the baguettes from the couche to a lightly floured peel or parchment paper; the loaves will be seam side down now. Score the dough, making 1/4- to 1/2-inch cuts along the length of the loaf. Slide the loaves onto the baking stone. Spray the inner walls of the oven with cold water from the spray bottle until steam has filled the oven. Close the door, wait 3 minutes, and repeat. Bake for 20 to 25 minutes, until the loaves are golden brown and the crust is firm. Check doneness by tapping the bottom of the loaf; if it sounds hollow, it is finished baking. If not, bake for 5 more minutes. Cool baguettes on a wire rack.

Because baguettes have a nearly even crust-to-crumb ratio, they stale very quickly. If the loaves will not be eaten within 24 to 36 hours, freezing them is a good way to preserve their freshness. Wrap cooled loaves in plastic wrap and then aluminum foil, and store in the freezer until needed. To reheat, place thawed baguettes in a 350-degree-Fahrenheit oven for 15 minutes.

The baguettes are ready to bake.

With the tenderness of battlefield nurses carrying the stretcher of a dying soldier, Xavier and Jude move my loaves into the kitchen. Jonathan Scott and his assistants follow with his own dough. The oven is ready. Xavier transfers my baguettes to a cornmeal-covered peel, and I slash each one before he slides them onto the hot bricks to bake. He hands the peel to Jonathan. "Your turn."

"Thanks," the chef says, and expertly adds his loaves next to mine.

And we watch, silent, the heat from the oven uncomfortable and yet welcome. The crust browns, a Maillard reaction between sugar and amino acids, and for me the magic of bread only increases as it becomes less mysterious and more understood, the complex scientific reasons for color and flavor so . . . so . . .

"Beautiful," Jonathan says.

He speaks of the baguettes, now ready to be taken from the oven, not the thoughts rattling around my head. But either way the word fits. Xavier removes all the loaves, slipping mine into the basket Jude holds and the others into a basket for Jonathan. "There you are."

"We better not get these mixed up," Jonathan says, and his assistant takes his baguettes to his work space in the other room.

Jude tucks mine onto the counter. "Not possible."

"Loyalty. I like it," Jonathan says. "Now, do I get to see your famous starters?"

"There's not much to see. A bunch of gallon-sized buckets," I tell him, but drift toward the cooler. He follows, as does Gretchen, a bit too close. "And they're certainly not famous."

He whistles, sharp and low. "Which is which?"

Each lid is labeled, but like a parent of multiples, I know them by sight. My regulars first. A hand-ground Desem starter tied in linen, the buttermilk starter, a white flour barm, a pure rye, and then my mother's—my grandmother's, my great-grandmother's—culture. Two of them. I keep one in a bucket to feed and use. The other is tucked in the topmost, backmost corner of the cooler, in the small stoneware crock in which Oma carried it from Germany. I feed and divide that one too, but rarely bake with it—and never bread I sell.

And then the ones I'm playing with now, a spelt-based starter, a wheat and barley mix, and one with both flour and potato.

"Do you use the same build method for all of them?" Jonathan asks.

"No. I know conventional wisdom is to find something that works and stick with it, but, honestly, I get a little bored."

He nods to two other cultures on the counter, still developing. "And you don't use a proofing box?"

I shake my head.

"Living on the edge," he says with a laugh.

"Maybe just a little old-fashioned," I tell him.

"Did your mother experiment as well?"

"No."

The direct, flat answer catches him off guard, and he withdraws, not visibly, but sensing he's crossed some line I've sketched around myself. The question doesn't necessarily bother me, but I don't want it today because it only brings distance between her and me. I want to be like her when it comes to bread, and in most ways we're identical. I don't consider whether the similarities are there because we are the same in substance, because she taught me and that's what I know first, or because I won't deviate from her ways for fear of forgetting.

I am different, though, when it comes to sourdough. My mother loved to bake with wild yeast; more than half her loaves used Oma's starter. But she never considered making her own culture, or that any other was needed besides the one in the crock in her refrigerator. I made my first starter at fifteen and fell in love with the *unpredictability* of it. The yeast is wild, the process is wild. It changes minute by minute. It's observable; even years later I can't help but peek at the jar on my counter every hour or two, watching bubbles expand and measuring the slurry of flour and water as it creeps up the sides. All the things I can't seem to do with dough—the improvisation, the eyeballing of ingredients, the freedom to defy convention—I love doing within the microcosm of a Mason jar. I refuse to take notes even, despite once beginning a neat, black-covered notebook for it.

"Sorry," I say.

Jonathan touches my arm. There's no spark, nothing inherently inappropriate or forward about the action. It doesn't seem even warm, not done in a friendly sort of way—and how could it? We're not friends, or colleagues, merely two strangers brought together by the odd, reality television–driven world in which we live, knowing one another only in facts listed on websites and contest entry forms. The motion of him reaching out to me is automatic, driven by the bread within. He's like Xavier, Jude. The dough has seeped through the skin of his palms, burrowed deep, and grown. The passion we share recognizes itself before we see it there ourselves.

Gretchen, tired of being outside it all, begins to chatter. Jonathan's attention is diverted, and I hurry to the bathroom to wash my face, forgetting all about my makeup. The waterproof mascara stays put; the rest of it smears onto the rough paper towel. I take time to sit with no one around, the bulb in the ceiling humming down on me, my face gaunt in the feeble light. I read the wrapping on the toilet tissue rolls and the soap bottle label until enough time has passed. I find the kitchen as I left it, Gretchen yapping and Jonathan nodding, Xavier and Jude watching from the corner with amusement.

"So," Jonathan says. "Who am I cooking for?"

"I'd love lunch," Gretchen says.

"Too bad we need you to run some errands," Xavier tells her.

"What?"

He hands her a list. "You are getting paid for today."

"All right," she grumbles, stuffing the paper in her back pocket without folding it. "I'll be back—"

"—at two," Xavier says.

She squints at him, then turns and sweetly offers her hand to Jonathan. "It's been lovely to meet you."

"You too, Gretchen. We'll talk more this afternoon, I'm sure."

"I'd like that."

When she goes, Jonathan turns to the men. "Lunch for you?"

"No, we're on our way out as well," Xavier says. "Also have a few things to do before the judging."

Now it's my turn to narrow my eyes at him. He pats me on the shoulder as he passes, as does Jude, who whispers, "Behave."

"Don't tell me you're going to ditch me too," Jonathan says.

I want to. My head pounds with exhaustion and talk and everything else bombarding me the past week. I see he's offering to prepare a meal out of kindness and no other motive. He cooks because it's who he is, and he can't help but share that enthusiasm with others.

I understand.

"No, I'll eat."

"Don't make me twist your arm."

"I'm just tired."

"Long day?"

"Long day. Long week. Long everything."

He nods, swipes his finger over his smartphone, and pecks at the screen. "I hear you."

Minutes later one of his assistants knocks on the back door, plastic grocery bag in hand, black case in another. Jonathan takes them both and thanks her. He must know I need a break because he doesn't try to engage me in what he's doing. Or perhaps he needs the respite too, and he finds his peace in chopping and sautéing and making foods better than they can be on their own. He moves instinctively around the stove, never asking where something is, opening drawers and removing utensils. He brings his own knives, unzips the case. I'm soothed by watching him. He halves fresh Brussels sprouts and tosses them in a pan of butter and garlic, squeezes the juice of a lemon over them. He thinly slices two sweet potatoes, setting them to boil. When they're soft, he mashes and seasons them. Another pan heating on the gas burner, this one for rounds of filet mignon, seared and drizzled with a red wine reduction.

He plates the food and presents it to me, with a fork from Tee's drawer and a steak knife from his kit. "Madam, lunch is served."

"It's lovely."

"I know." His words are without pride or arrogance. He can say it to me because I understand. It's no crime to be skilled and know it.

We eat with only the sound of flatware against ceramic dishes, until finally Jonathan says, "This kitchen is really well laid out. Everything is where you'd expect it to be."

"That's Tee. My cook. She's quite . . . fastidious. When you meet her this afternoon, she'll probably give you an earful for using her beloved pots."

"Looking forward to it."

Another lull. Now I say, "Are your baguettes yeasted?"

"Guilty." He covers his eyes with his hand in mock shame. "I'm no sourdough expert. Actually, in all honesty, I've never gotten the hang of it. This is the dough I use in my restaurant, a variation on *pain a l'ancienne*."

"I can't wait to try it."

"I thought you'd never ask."

He disappears briefly into the café and returns with one of the long, slender loaves baked less than two hours ago. But before sitting, he grabs one of my baguettes too, shaking it like a sword as he comes back to the table. "Fair's fair."

"As long as it's not breaking any rules."

"I make the rules."

Taking a wooden cutting board from where it hangs on the pot rack above us, he lines both loaves on it and holds his serrated knife over them. "Some days I hate cutting into it," he tells me. "Destroying the perfection of it all."

Jonathan's baguette is much more rustic than mine, knobby and arthritic, the bony fingers of the ancients the name suggests. He slices. The crust is thicker, the crumb yellowish with erratically sized holes. I take a bite. Delicious. He doesn't expect comment, though, instead slicing through my more traditional-looking loaf. The rooms are more uniform, each about the size of the tip of my pinky—I stick my finger in them, sometimes, measuring—the texture slightly heavier. He takes a bite now, moves the bread around his mouth slowly. Then he wipes it over his place, soaking up wine and beef juice and garlicky residue from the sprouts. "You think I'm a charlatan for that."

"Of course not," I say, a grin finding my mouth.

"You won't tell anyone."

"Never." He pours more of the reduction on his plate and takes another piece of my baguette, and I laugh. "I like butter on mine. And salt."

"Now we both have our secrets." He reaches back for the stick on the counter, soft from the kitchen's heat. I spread it thinly, sprinkle a pinch of sea salt over the bread, and help myself to another slice.

Ten

My best friend, Jennie Rausenberg, lets me borrow her navy pleated skirt for the funeral, the one she wore for her band concert last spring, and I match it with a dull-colored sweater and black flats. I take a pair of nylons from my mother's dresser, still full of her things, and wriggle into them. She hadn't let me wear them yet, though I desperately wanted to. My legs look plastic, too dark and slightly orangish. I run my hands up and down them, so silky I can't stop rubbing. A sharp corner of fingernail catches, and I watch the fabric separate, the split climbing like a ladder from shin to thigh. I take off the torn pair and hide it in the bathroom trash pail inside my cousin's wet disposable diaper, trim my nails, and put on another pair, this one brand new in egg-shaped packaging.

We're leaving, my aunt—my father's sister—calls up the stairs.

The service is at a funeral home. We don't have a church, and my father doesn't bother calling around to find one; he's unsure of the Lutheran position on suicide and doesn't want to find out. He knows where the Catholic church of his birth stands, and that's more than enough for him to bear.

The viewing is short because there's nothing to see but an urn of ashes and a few photos. No one speaks but the hired chaplain, who pronounces my mother's name the American way. *Clawdia.* I think of the sand crabs in Maine, how my father took me out at night and we'd shine flashlights up the beach and watch them scamper back into the shadows, one white pincher larger than the other. *Claw, claw, Clawdia.* It sounds so harsh and nailed to the earth, unlike the German way of saying it. *Cloudia.* Ethereal. Floating. Destined for the clouds, not burned to soot and trapped in some glorified tin can.

They come back to our home, my father's relatives and my mother's friends, coworkers and meat buyers and neighbors. They eat and laugh, and I don't understand why they come at all. It's not comforting to have them here. Only loud and messy. I hide in my bedroom with Jennie, listening to my nearly worn New Kids on the Block cassette. My Aunt Anwyn finally finds me and drags me downstairs. *Guests are leaving. Say good-bye.* I collect hugs from people I barely know, their breath warm with Swedish meatballs and condolences. Finally, with everyone gone, my aunt upstairs putting my cousin down for a nap and her husband off to the grocery store for more baby wipes, my father and I stand in an empty living room between the long folding table of food and the sofa, where he found me four days ago.

Someone has placed my mother's dough trough in the center of the table and filled it with store-bought rolls. There are only four left, and a half of one—torn, not cut—and crumbs. I think my father will stand here forever, that he's turned to granite in his sadness, and I'll have to tilt and roll him into the corner and dust him once a month. And stand he does, without moving, long enough for my feet to hurt in my toe-pinching dress shoes. Uncle Russ should be home soon; his entrance will give me an opportunity to escape. It seems wrong to say something, to break through the stillness with my voice, or with motion. This is his requiem.

And then he roars, clutching my mother's beloved antique trough in his clawed hands—*claw, claw, Clawdia, the sand crab*—and smashes it onto the planked floor. It splits in two with a bellow of its own.

We stand there again, no longer still, my body trembling with fear, his heaving in rage and exertion, both of us with our eyes on the bowl. *Alistair, what happ*—Aunt Anwyn stops at the bottom of the steps, freezing at the sight of the carnage. She knows too. My mother's treasure, passed to her from grandmother, from great-grandmother, from the motherland, broken.

My trembling becomes quaking, tears spilling now, fear metamorphosing to anger. My fingers curl into my palms and I wish I hadn't cut my nails this morning. I want to claw the skin from his face.

Claw, claw, Clawdia.

And then, her voice. *It's grief. Step over it, or pick up the pieces.*

I gather the two halves in my arms. It's her body, and I offer them to my father, saying, *Daddy, it's grief.*

He holds me as he weeps in a way I have never seen before or since, and I ignore that my neck is crimped and my hair is caught between my shoulder and his, and it hurts. His tears wash away my own, and in the morning I find my mother's trough in front of the fireplace, the halves clamped together, the glue almost dry, the break nearly imperceptible.

While Jonathan Scott cleans the kitchen, I tend to the ciabatta. I do offer to wash for him, or to at least wipe the counters and load the dishwasher, but he refuses my help. "Scrubbing keeps me humble," he says.

Jonathan's secret ingredient bread continues to proof. No more manipulation is needed. My ciabatta, however, must be divided into four loaves, stretched, and folded. I slice the dough and let it rest a moment while I mash the goat cheese with the caramelized onions. I still have to decide on a third ingredient and, heading back into the kitchen, rummage through the cooler and pantry to see what Tee has on hand. Sun-dried tomatoes. Xavier called it expected, and he's right, but I need something and can't think of a better alternative. Where is Tee when I need her? She teases flavors in ways one would never consider, stretching ingredient combinations into the deliciously bizarre. Like Gretchen, Tee is being paid to be here. The only other time she's missed work is when her sister died.

I dice the tomatoes, my knife skills looking even more mediocre now that I've seen Jonathan's, and stir them into the onion. He sees me and says, "Wait. The camera."

I sigh. "Really?"

"We have to film something for TV."

He sends a text and the cameraman, who has been in the Good Food Channel bus outside the bakery, stumbles in, hair matted flat to one side of his head, cheek etched with indentations of sleep. The guy films as I stretch the dough and, before folding, spoon the goat cheese mixture over it. Now another hour to proof.

"Napping on the job?" I raise my eyebrows after the camera leaves again.

"Bread is much more exciting on television. In real life? Not so much. That's why we typically only do one or two bread episodes per season, because of the logistics. But I think it's necessary."

"Because you love it."

"I appreciate it deeply," Jonathan says. "I don't love it, not like you, or others I've met. For me, it's cooking. You know how it is when you find that thing you were born to do. Your soul sings. We are two of the lucky ones. Most people never do."

"How did you, then? If you don't mind me asking."

He realizes he's leaning against my glass display counter, his handprints smeared on top. Bending over, he blows on them, holds the bottom of his sleeve, and buffs them away. Then he settles back against the counter again, this time on his elbow only. "I was six. In kindergarten. There was this play kitchen, and I would use it with all the girls. But I'd cook with Legos. Each color was a different ingredient, depending on what I was making. And I wrote down my recipes. Seven red Lego tomatoes. Three white Lego onions. Whatever it was. One day my teacher—Miss Lois, we called her—decided to make one of the recipes in the proportions I specified. I don't know why, but she did. And it worked. So she tried another, and another. She told my parents I should be enrolled in cooking classes. My parents, a lawyer and a CEO, lived on takeout or premade grocery store meals or whatever my nanny heated up before they came home from work. They didn't take the teacher's advice, but I still found a way to experiment. The nannies—none of them cared as long as I cleaned up after myself.

"By the time I graduated high school, things were . . . strained . . . between my father and me. He was the attorney. He saw cooking as a waste of my potential. We fought and I left. I had some money saved and I went to France. I didn't have a plan, other than to eat great food and try to learn to make it. I didn't want to go to some stuffy culinary school or hit the famous restaurants with the famous chefs. I believed— and still do—some of the best food is prepared by the untrained, the naturally talented, the undiscovered in little holes-in-the-wall tucked away where only locals know about them. So I traveled and found these places. Many of the owners let me intern with them in return for scrubbing pots or doing prep work or even running to the market. I slept in barns and back rooms or in a hostel now and then. I ate one meal a day wherever I was working, if I was working, and when I wasn't I'd find produce drops at the open market or pick from the trash behind the cafés. I was skinny and sunburned with blistered toes and surviving on adventure, which was more than enough for a nineteen-year-old idealist. I lived two years like that, and then landed a real chef's position in Lyon for another eighteen months; one of those little dive owners opened his dream restaurant there and remembered me, found me, and offered me a job. I went back to the States at twenty-three and started my first restaurant. Never looked back."

"And the boulangerie?"

"You read my bio," he says, and tells me of a time in Paris, exploring the narrow streets of the less desirable *arrondisements*, one evening stumbling upon a tiny bakery in a crumbling building. It offered only five or six types of bread but all the locals bought there, carrying their newsprint-wrapped baguettes in their armpits and hurrying home after work. The business was owned by an old man called Henri, nearly eighty then, bitter and aloof, never married and with no children. After three visits, he refused to speak to Jonathan or listen to the American's very bad French. He'd wave his hand across his nose and tell the boy to *casse toi* before getting through the door. Jonathan would come every day and stand with his francs pressed against the glass. If the old man placed a loaf of bread beside the ancient cast-iron register, it meant Jonathan could come in and purchase it—as long as he didn't say a word.

Alexandre Dumas, *père*, wrote of the bakers:

> In Paris today millions of pounds of bread are sold daily, made during the previous night by those strange, half-naked beings one glimpses through cellar windows, whose wild-seeming cries floating out of those depths always makes a painful impression. In the morning, one sees these pale men, still white with flour, carrying a loaf under one arm, going off to rest and gather new strength to renew their hard and useful labor when night comes again. I have always highly esteemed the brave and humble workers who labor all night to produce those soft but crusty loaves that look more like cake than bread . . .

And this was how Jonathan saw Henri. His wood oven was in the basement—constructed in the mid-1800s—like most of old Paris, just the way Dumas described, with low ceiling and stone walls, full of crumbs and ash and the smell of sewer. Henri fashioned his dough on the first floor in a small room off the retail area and hobbled to the oven with a dozen unbaked loaves at a time, navigating his way down the narrow, uneven staircase by memory because he couldn't see over the bread board. Years of neglect caked the windows of the storefront too, and the floors. Cobwebs grew over the walls, gray blankets of dust. It didn't seem to faze the customers, but one day Jonathan brought a French friend to tell Henri he'd clean the bakery until it was spotless, if Henri would let him watch the bread being made. Henri was suspicious but agreed—as long as Jonathan promised not to say a word. He told the friend that Jonathan *"parlait français comme une vache espagnole"*—spoke French like a Spanish cow.

So he observed. Henri began at five in the morning, opened at seven. By two in the afternoon he'd shut the lights and go upstairs, where he lived, to take a nap and then reopen around six for people to buy bread for supper. And Jonathan scrubbed. First the windows, then the racks, the walls. He crawled on his hands and knees and used a toothbrush and toothpaste on the grout, foaming away years and years of grime from around thousands of those tiny white and black octagonal tiles. When he finished, he brought his friend back to thank the old man, and Henri said he could come back the next day and watch some more, if he wanted.

Jonathan did, staying on for six more months. The old man finally allowed him to work the dough, berating him for ill-formed loaves and often shouting, *"Tu as une tête en pain de sucre,"* and rapping him with a broom handle every now and again. Eventually, though, Henri told his story. His parents owned the bakery before him, and he'd worked there every day since he was eleven, except for when he tried to be a soldier during World War II. Eventually he was taken as a prisoner of war and sent to a factory in southwest Berlin to build tanks and armored vehicles for the German war effort. Conditions were harsh and hours of work long, but he could write letters. Some made their way home to his family.

Soon a man came to him, a German officer who said he wanted to help; he had met Henri's mother in Paris, ate bread from his family's bakery, a baguette so delicious he asked the woman if there was anything he could do for her. She told him her only son was forced to labor at Daimler-Benz, and could the officer help at all? The German came with a note from Henri's mother. *Do as he says. He has shared our bread and is sent of God.* Henri agreed to let the German help him, and he was transferred to a camp for French officers where no work was done. The German told him, "Make the bread of your father, and you will be safe here." Henri spent the rest of the war baking bread once a day, reading, smoking, and playing cards with the other soldiers. He went home when the fighting ended to bake in his family's oven, never again to leave.

"He's gone," Jonathan says. "My translator friend let me know when he died, oh, probably eight years ago now. He said the old man left something for me, and I received a package several months later, a tattered French bread book with a note in the front cover: *À celui avec une tête en pain de sucre.*'"

"'To the one with the egg-shaped head.' Or literally, the head out of the sugar loaf," I say. "Four years of high school French."

"You probably speak it better than I do, still," he says with a laugh. "I never did get the hang of it. But that's my boulangerie story. And that's why I appreciate bread. I mean, quite honestly, before Paris I didn't think much about it. It was something you tossed on the table with dinner or made a sandwich with, and there wasn't much difference between a good loaf and a bad loaf. Even most of the bread people here consider good—I'm talking the so-called artisan stuff in the grocery store or that fancy chain-bakery bread—wouldn't be considered fit for consumption in France. While traveling, I began seeing it differently, the skill that goes into it, the craftsmanship. The time.

Oh, do you need patience for good bread. But after Henri, and his story, it became more than food. It was something that had the power to give a man back his life."

"Is that why you came up with the *Bake-Off* idea, then?"

Jonathan's eyes darken and he's disappointed, it seems. I've tied his story together with the show, one cheap parlor trick leading the way to another. "I didn't. The network did. But I was the hot, up-and-coming TV chef at the time, so it was given to me." He laughs again, this time without a trace of amusement. "That's the biz, as they say."

And the baker starved them. He is looked upon with no less suspicion than the miller. He charges for bread what they cannot afford, the peasants say. He has no bread to sell when they are hungry. What do they know of Assize of Bread, which fixes the price of a loaf based on the cost of grain and puts more money into the pocket of the lord and less into that of the baker? The peasants watch for his thumb on the scale, even though he gives them thirteen loaves instead of twelve so they will trust his honesty. Heaven help the baker who cheats; he is paraded naked and chained around town and pelted with his own bread.

If the miller suffers loneliness, the baker suffers with his body. His chest oozes with pustules from flour-clogged pores. His knees swell, his spine compresses, his height decreases each year. Burns cover his hands. Only he is allowed to work in the night as well as in the day, and he tries to keep his eyes always open, knowing another baker who burned to death when he tumbled into the oven in his sleep. The baker must have a pact with the devil, the peasants think. He is always in the fire.

It is bread that keeps them alive. *Give us this day our daily bread*, they pray, and they praise the Almighty for it. The miller and baker they despise, those who, on earth, are most responsible for their food.

∽

Armed with our loaves of bread—the baguettes, Jonathan's maple cheese boule, and my ciabatta—we make our way to the park down the street where a crowd has gathered and judges await. We walk, Jonathan beside my father, chatting about nothing in particular, as far as I can tell, but it's difficult to make out any of their conversation because Cecelia is chirping like a mockingbird at my side, clinging to my arm, nearly yanking it from my shoulder as she bounces along. Seamus is somewhere behind the two of us.

Three hundred people cheer for us as we walk through the wrought iron gates. Jonathan zips on his television personality; hands are shaken, babies bounced, photos snapped, cheeks kissed. Patrice Olsen removes a travel-sized package of baby wipes from her floral bag and gives one to Jonathan, who manages to clean lipstick from his face in such a discreet way I wonder if the burgundy and pink and coral smudges have been there at all.

Patrice uses her megaphone to quiet the crowd. Jonathan makes a few comments about the show, my abilities, the hospitality of Vermont folk, and then directs everyone to the far tent, where the bread has been sliced for sampling. I wander, watching the cameras film men and women gnawing their bread and then answering, "Which do you like better and why?" A few children throw pieces to the ducks waddling around the pond. I close my eyes and breathe deeply, a breeze ruffling my hair, wrapping around my bare ankles. I wish, only for a most insignificant of seconds, I am one of those people who believes spirits flit around us all the time, existing on some other plane in the trees and wind and drops of rain. Then I can lie in the grass and with each blade tickling my neck think, *That is my mother.* That's not truth, though, and I am still here without her, so I find my father and loop my arm through his. He smiles at me and says, "Ah, Liesl. I'm sorry, my dear one. I tried both the long breads and I can't tell the difference. Forgive me?"

"There's nothing to forgive." I say, remembering the Italian place in Maine, the dead white bread, the margarine pots. I've been waiting all day for him to mention my mother, but he doesn't, and I'm afraid to bring her up. I don't know if he's trying to avoid it for his sake, or my own.

Cecelia has replaced me with Jude, and she's tossing crab apples to the ducks with him. The birds ignore the fruit until Jude shows her to break them open. Then they gobble the sticky bits and follow Cecelia, wanting more. She collects handfuls from beneath the tree, stomps on them, and flings them into the flock. Across the park, Xavier talks on his phone, his back to me. I go to him, touch his shoulder. He says, "Call you back," and folds the phone into his pocket.

"Everything okay?" I ask.

"Ducky," he says. "Don't say anything about your bread. They're children. The temptation is too great."

"I know, I know."

"You went with the tomatoes."

"I couldn't come up with anything better. You and Jude sure got out of there fast enough."

"Sorry."

"No, you're not. And Tee. Of all days to desert me. She better be bleeding or dying in an alley somewhere, I kid you not."

Xavier smoothes his hand across his bald head. "She is."

I stop. "She is what?"

"Dying."

"What? Wait. Tee is dying? What are you talking about?"

"Chemo. She's home sick from her first treatment. She thought she'd be able to sleep it off and come by this afternoon, but it didn't work out that way."

"Tee has cancer?"

Xavier nods.

"What kind?"

"I don't remember. Does it matter?"

I'm still confused, one sentence after the next a tranquilizing dart, each making me dizzier, more numb. "Why didn't she tell me? And how come you know?"

"She wasn't planning on letting anyone in on the news, as far as I can tell. The only reason I know is because she needed to get to a doctor's appointment the other day and was too sick to drive herself. Tee is, well . . . she doesn't want fanfare or sympathy, or God forbid, pity. She doesn't want anyone treating her different. And she certainly didn't want to lose her job."

"I'd never do that."

"I know. But she made me promise not to tell you. You have to act as if that's the case or I'll never hear the end of it."

"She'll know anyway," I say.

"Ain't that the truth," Xavier says.

A blast of the megaphone and Patrice Olsen announces judging is about to begin. She crosses the grass in determined strides, the fist-sized copper pendant around her neck bouncing with each step. "Ms. McNamara, you disappeared. I don't appreciate that."

"I've been right here."

"You were supposed to stay with Mr. Scott. Come now."

I follow her, turning back to Xavier to see him mouthing, *Woof, woof,* and giving a little pant. That's how I feel, like her dog on a leash, one who peed on the expensive Persian carpet and is now about to have my nose rubbed in it. We go to a second tent, where the judges sit. I'm introduced to Master Baker Ronald Gantz from King Arthur's Flour Company, Peter Kris-Wentworth, owner and chef at one of the ritzy Vermont B&Bs not far from here, and Good Food Channel star Marianna Dutton. I shake hands. Jonathan jokes with them. The camera films it all. Then Jonathan and I are directed to stand aside while lettered plates are given to the judges. He's plate A, I'm B. Patrice herds my father, Gretchen and Jude and Xavier, and then Seamus and

Cecelia toward me. "Look concerned and hopeful and excited," she tells them, then screeches orders through the megaphone for the crowd to quiet.

The judges taste Jonathan's bread first. "Pain a l'ancienne, I believe," Gantz says. "A little spongier than we like to see at King Arthur's."

Those around the judges murmur, and Jonathan stages an indignant expression for the camera focused on us. The other judges comment on the crispy crust, scribble notes on their ballots, and move on to the goat-cheese-maple-walnut-apple bread, which all agree is delicious and not too sweet.

Plate B now. I don't have to pretend to be hopeful or concerned or excited; I'm all those things already, and more. I cannot believe how thick my heart beats, how I can feel it bulging at every joint in my body. Cecelia stands in front of me; I drape my arms over her shoulders, clasping my hands across her collarbone simply to have something to hold. She, in turn, crosses her fingers and sticks them behind her back. And then a warm, firm sensation against the small of my back. It's Seamus. I shift my eyes toward him and contort my lips into a tortured smile. He smiles back, shifting in a little closer, but when my father's arm clamps down on my shoulder, Seamus removes his hand and leans away.

"I'm proud of you," my father says against my ear.

I nod, an itchy lump swelling behind my tongue. That's not what I want him to say.

My father's mouth quivers. *He's praying.* I've never understood the rules of prayer. Some people, I know, petition God for every single thing, from parking spaces at the mall to raising the dead. Others save their prayers for the important things—a job loss, a sick child, a failing marriage—just in case there's a limit to the number of yeses one is allowed in a lifetime. I tend to fall into the second category, but I'm not certain what's truly prayer-worthy and what's an impostor, and a reality cooking competition seems too far down the list to chance being wrong.

Still, I can't help it.

Please, please.

The judges nibble my baguette; they like the slight tanginess of the crumb, the shiny crust. The crunch. Then they taste the secret ingredient bread. "The flavors are balanced," Gantz says, "but I wish the combination was more original." They scribble on their ballots again.

I scowl. Jonathan creeps closer and whispers, "That look is going to make it on the show."

Finally, Marianna Dutton stands. "This was a very difficult decision, but my fellow judges and I have made our choice. The winner of this episode of *Bake-Off* is . . ."

I close my eyes. "Look, look, Liesl," Cecelia says.

In her hand, the judge holds card B.

Eleven

I'm thirteen, an old thirteen, coming home with a report card of Cs mostly, a B in art and a D in social studies, and plenty of *Liesl is not performing to her potential* comments to go along with the grades. I don't care and neither will my father. Neither of us is living up to our potential now. Neither of us cares much about living at all.

We manage. We exist in a home without the spoken word, except for television and the occasional request from him, or the occasional question from me. Mostly we pass one another as we wander around the cold, wood rooms we once believed were warm. My mother was the warmth, our sun, but she left us and we can no longer find the thermostat without her, even though we walk by it every day, in the hallway, on our way out the door.

I make dinner, tonight a frozen skillet meal, just pour, heat, and serve. This one has the chicken included. My father used to buy the ones where the meat was purchased and prepared separately, but I sliced my finger open cutting up strips of steak for one of them. I waited for him to come home, staring at *Jeopardy!* while squeezing a dishrag around my pinky. He saw the blood and shouted at me for not calling him sooner. I had to get eleven stiches. I was relieved to be excused from gym class for two weeks.

My father won't be home to eat with me. He works as late as possible, and on the days he doesn't work—the weekends, like tomorrow—he lives in the basement with his toasters and gears, and I bring him plates of food if I have the inclination to take a load of laundry down to the washing machine. I don't sort the clothes, and our underwear is dingy gray-blue because I toss them in with our jeans.

After my cheesy rotini primavera, I spoon the remaining pasta onto a plate, cover it with wax paper, and stick it in the microwave. Then I rinse the pan and jam it into the overly full dishwasher. It needs to be run but we're out of detergent. I add it to the list on the freezer door and hang my report card next to it, with a clay magnet shaped like a loaf of braided bread.

Everything is *her* in this house.

I think that's why he does it, because we're suffocating in the fullness of her. He will never—can never—get rid of her tables or bowls or chairs. But the sofa is safe, he must believe. My mother never liked it, great mint green cushions with embroidered peach tulips, given to us by the people across the street when they moved and in better condition than the old couch my parents bought when they married. I emerge from my bedroom well past noon Saturday and see the new sofa, a plush brown leather sectional with built-in recliners on each end. I scream.

My father is there. I don't know where he came from. *What's wrong?*

The sofa.

I bought another.

How could you?

He doesn't know that all I used to be bled into that middle cushion the day she died, that I have a plan to recover myself, to soak me back in. I can't do it yet, though, can't bring myself to sit on a center cushion on any couch, let alone our own. Now it's impossible because my essence has been hauled away to some secondhand store or garbage dumpster. My body clenches. *You don't love her,* I say.

He slaps me across the cheek.

We both recoil. It's the first time I've been struck by either parent. I stare at him, the poltergeist of his hand throbbing in my skin. His anger melts, jowls and lips sagging. I turn and run upstairs.

Liesl, he calls.

I slam the bathroom door behind me. None of the other rooms upstairs lock, old doors in an old house with brass keyholes and skeleton keys long gone missing. The bathroom has a hook and eye for privacy. I expect a knock, or another shout of my name, but neither comes. My cheek burns. It feels good, a tangible, physical pain understudying for my broken heart. I don't want it to stop.

I'm not able to hit myself in the face, but I remember the lotion, my legs, and I shimmy my jeans over my hips and down to the floor, sit on the closed toilet, and slam my fists into my thighs. It's not enough; the heaviness in my chest remains. Next to me, on the vanity, is my hairbrush. I grab it and smack my legs until they flame, prickled with broken vessels, until they go numb and I turn the brush, pointed handle end down, and stab, stab, stab. The blue welts grow, and I stop because I'm crying. It hurts too much.

I lie on the floor, on a moldy-smelling towel I left sitting wet in the machine too long but didn't rewash. Cover myself with another one, this one still damp from my father's morning shower, and clamp an arm over my eyes. My legs throb and I focus on them, content. It's the only thing I feel.

I keep drifting up from sleep, so buoyant it cannot keep me captive. I don't wake completely, but enough to be aware of a car alarm, a stray feather from my pillow, my sheets twisted around my feet. It's disorienting, and finally I give up and open my eyes. Six thirty.

Something stirs in my brain, wanting attention. For weeks after my mother died, I would swing my legs over the side of the bed each morning with dread in my belly, knowing I had a reason to be sad but not quite conscious enough to fully realize why. The cold wood against my feet, the sunlight in my face, and suddenly I'd remember. She was gone.

It's the same now, but instead of sadness there's joy. I rub my face, feeling how puffed it is with the previous night. I yawn. And it's there.

I won.

What is this—this happiness? I cannot remember feeling such delight, ever. Perhaps as a child, before the rust and moth chewed it away, leaving gaping holes where reality began seeping in. And maybe something very close to it when I opened the bakery, a few hours of excitement and anticipation of the journey, but quashed not long after by all the work needing to be done. That's how my life has been, always walking, completing tasks, moving on to the next, a constant focus on the *to do*. Drive, some call it, praise it, even. And it will come again, this evening, when the dough must be prepared for tomorrow and the weekly invoices paid and the flour ordered. But for this morning, I choose to enjoy it.

I may sleep, shower, and occasionally flop on the couch here in the apartment, but I dwell in the Wild Rise kitchen. The apostle John writes the Word became flesh and dwells among us. Tabernacles. He makes his home with us, lives in the tent with us. It's where he breathes, with us. *It's Sunday*. I shake my head. I promised Cecelia, but not today.

I dress and twist my hair into an elastic band. Downstairs, I unlock Wild Rise and hear a thud. Then another. The noise is continuous, rhythmic. The light shines beneath the kitchen door. I tiptoe close and open it enough to peek in. Jude. He stands at the table, his back to me, sinewy arms lifting a ball of dough over his head, slamming it to the table. A silent moment as the muscles in his back flex. He's folding and turning, I know. The dough comes up again. Then down. A French knead.

"Jude?"

He turns, startled. "I woke you."

"No, I couldn't sleep." Pink moisture rims his nose and eyes. "Are you okay?"

"I shouldn't be here, but I needed a place, you know?"

"I didn't think you could drive."

"I thumbed it." He drops the dough into a willow banneton. "A twenty-minute pounding is enough."

"More than enough."

I think he'll leave now, but he continues to stand, gripping the edge of the table, leaning over it slightly, his eyes closed. Then he stretches his arms forward, his hands flat and open, slowly spreading the flour residue over the wood, drawing patterns as a child will. A tear falls into it and almost immediately disappears as his hands continue to move. "I don't get it," he says finally. "What is it about this stuff? All of it. The flour, the dough, the loaves. It's like there are magnets in it, and in me. I have to touch it."

I know. When my hands are in dough, something deep and primordial can hear the voice of God, calling me forth from the earth. *It is very good.* Grain from the ground, made dust. Man from the dust. The kneading reconnects both, bringing me back to Eden in a way I've never encountered at any church service.

"It's like it's—"

"Spiritual," I say.

He's forgotten I am there. But the word penetrates, and he looks at me. "Yeah."

"What's wrong, Jude?"

He nods to his left, to the counter, where a rumpled newspaper hides his canvas bag. The front page has a story about me and Wild Rise and *Bake-Off*. The reporter also wrote a sidebar about Jude and his art bread.

"Yesterday's *Gazette*?"

"My dad, he doesn't care about the bread. None of them do. Pops gave the bakeries to them, you know? My dad, Uncle Ray, and Aunt Jilly. She makes cupcakes now, mostly. My dad and uncle bought out her part of the business, she changed the name of the place and wears a poodle skirt and covers everything in pink frosting. Dad and Uncle Ray partnered up and everything is made in a factory now. Conveyor belts and all that. I think that kills Pops more than anything. He don't say it, but it's obvious.

"Charlie—my brother—already works there with Dad. He's vice president of something and something else. My other brother Pete graduates next year with his MBA and has some other vice-president-whatever-else waiting with his name on it. You know what good ol' dad told me? There'll always be a job for me on the line, if I want it. Yeah, the assembly line. That's all I'm good for." He brushes flour from the table; it curls around the room, like smoke, and settles on our feet, both of us in running shoes.

"I don't—"

"I'm dyslexic," he says. "I can hardly read, and forget it if it's above a second-grade level. So I sucked in school. My brothers were both valedictorians. Dad only gives a care about success. His boys, his business. Whatever. I've always been an embarrassment to his perfect family. His perfect little screw-up."

"I'm sorry," I say. "But, Jude, what you can do with bread, it's amazing. Even more so knowing it hasn't come from books or research. It's all you."

"Yeah? Well, Dad's amazed too. He saw the article. Some customer around here sent him a link to it online. He called me last night, wants me to come home. Said he had no idea. Said he wants to find a place for me in the family business. He stressed the word *family*. He talked about responsibility. Said he'd get me whatever tutors or help or whatever I needed to get through high school and graduate. He told me he was proud of me. Proud. Of me. Do you know how long I've waited to hear those words?

"And I hung up on him. Because it's all crap. He only wants me now that I can do something for him. Not before. Never before."

He cries like the child he is, loud, bubbling sobs, and I think, *I can be solid for him*. Like Seamus had been for me a few days ago. So I go and tighten my arms around his thin body, and he wets my neck with mucous and spit and tear film, and when he's finished, I toss him a towel and wipe my own skin dry. Then I pile the table with flour and bowls and measuring spoons and yeast and jars of sourdough starter and salt. "Go ahead," I say, and we create together.

What is so mystical about bread that superstitions follow from the moment man conceived it to this very day? The wheat, from the ground. The yeast, from the air. The dough, alive, breathing, growing, giving itself up for the people. The gods find it acceptable, the priests use it in their rituals, the magicians want to harness its power. And yet what goes into bread is common, vulgar even, available to anyone who will pick and grind and create fire to bake.

Sacred *and* profane.

What people go through to appease the earth and, in turn, urge the forces of nature to cooperate in the cycle of bread. They carry these rituals with them well into the Middle Ages. Eggs are placed before the plow at the first groundbreaking of the season. If the egg breaks, the soil has accepted the offering. Postpartum women, people with coughs and other respiratory disease, and the dead may not— must not—come near a field. Spirits live in the grain; it quivers and sways with their presence. But the too-quiet, too-still stalks are also feared. This is the *noontide ghost*, the air hot and golden and unmoving above the tips of wheat.

In some cultures, the last harvested sheaf is dressed in clothes and mocked by women prancing around it. In others, it's honored, left unthreshed and spread over the fallow field in reverence. And during the blustery, violent winter nights, farmers praying to be saved from the storm empty sacks of flour onto the wind.

Jude and I work mostly without speaking. Occasionally he asks a question about the wetness of the dough or the amount of starter, or the difference between a poolish and a *biga*. We don't bake because the wood fire oven isn't started, and while we could use the regular gas one, neither of us considers this a viable option. Finally, at nine thirty, Jude lifts his head up and says, "You think I can bum a ride to church?"

I can't tell him no. "Ah, okay. Sure. What time?"

"Starts in an hour." He wipes his hands on the back of his shorts. "Wanna come?"

It's there again, the prodding. The Spirit. Oh, how I hate it, because it reminds me of all I should be doing and all I don't want to do, and how I allow my flesh to win time and time again. But I want it to come over me too, telling me that I've not been forsaken, that he is still gently, gently pursuing and hasn't given up on me after all.

"Okay," I say.

My soul magnifies the Lord, and my spirit rejoices in God my Savior.

"Coolness."

"I'll go get ready, then."

"Mind if I stay here?"

"No, go ahead. Don't worry about cleaning up either. I'll be making the same mess tonight."

He plucks a wire from his pocket, sticks the bud ends in his ears, and gives a wave over his shoulder.

Upstairs, I shower and wear my black dress and sandals and the silver bangle again. I style my hair the way León showed me, put on makeup, and meet Jude in the kitchen. He strips off his T-shirt and changes to another he has in his bag, then looks at me. "Uh, give me a minute to shake out my shorts?"

"In my kitchen? Again?"

He grins. "I'll do it in back."

"Oh no. I can't have you half-naked outside my bakery. Especially after yesterday. Someone will call the local news."

"Or the police."

"Wonderful."

"Then . . . ?"

"Fine. In here. There's flour everywhere already."

I wait in the dining area and he follows not thirty seconds later. We both leave white footprints on the floor on our way out to the car. I slide the air-conditioning lever to high and ask, "Which church?"

"Green Mountain Community, out on River. You know it?"

"I go there sometimes."

"Yeah? It's cool. I like it. I've never really gone to church all that much before. Just Christmas and Easter."

I glance sideways. "So how did you end up attending here?"

He shrugs. "That little Cecelia pestered me until I agreed. She's a trip and a half."

We're silent, beyond small talk, our relationship of half strangers, of boss and employee, subtly altered. The church is busy; I park as close as possible, still six rows from the front door, and follow Jude into the lobby. He ignores the coffee, so I do too, but after a restless night and early morning, I wish for anything with caffeine. We spot Seamus at the same time, Cecelia dressed in her shyness and standing close, twisting the hem of his polo-style shirt. She sees Jude first and then me, and her lips stretch wide, hot cocoa mustache growing with her smile. "Liesl!"

Seamus turns his head in our direction. He holds out his palm to Jude, who shakes it, hand devoured in Seamus's massive grasp. And then he offers it to me. I take it, tips of his fingers only, and squeeze. He squeezes back.

"You came," Cecelia says.

"Jude is quite persuasive," I tell her.

"What's that mean?"

"It means," Jude says, "I bugged her until she said yes. A little trick I learned from someone standing right in front of me."

"I do that," Cecelia says. She wraps both her hands around her father's wrist, bouncing on his arm. "I'm good at it, Daddy says. But he can't give in all the time. That makes kids spoiled."

"Who says you're spoiled?" Jude asks. He touches the tip of her nose.

"No one. Yet. Not even Daddy, and he gives in a lot." She looks at Seamus and adds quickly, "But not all the time."

We sit somewhere in the middle of the sanctuary, Cecelia on one side of me and Jude on the other. I'm distracted by the little girl's wiggling, her coloring on the bulletin, the whispers of those around us. Seamus, who keeps peeking in my direction. My mind wanders through the entire sermon. When we leave, people congratulate me on the show. I wonder if they think I'm here because I won, as if I've bargained with God about it.

"Lunch?" Seamus asks.

"I'm game," Jude says.

"McDonald's, McDonald's, McDonald's," Cecelia says.

Seamus shakes his head. "You had that yesterday. We should let Liesl pick."

"Oh, I don't know. I'm up for whatever."

"McDonald's."

"No," Seamus tells her again.

We end up at Suki's Diner because it's close and fast, Jude riding with Seamus and Cecelia with me for the two-minute trip. Cecelia immediately finds the crane machine; Jude fishes a wad of change and bills from his front pocket and gives her a dollar. The money slot spits it back out, so he smoothes it over the corner of the glass and lets her try again. This time the green paper disappears and lights begin blinking.

The sign at the hostess stand tells us to find our own table. Seamus and I sit while they play, and I say, "I've never been here before."

"I think Ceese and I have hit most of the food places in Billingston. We go out to lunch most Sundays. The afternoon just gets too long when you're home by eleven thirty and have nothing else to do all day."

I think I've eaten at two restaurants since I moved here three years ago, and one was the McDonald's drive-through. The other was a tiny bistro not far from Wild Rise where my father and I ate the first time he visited me here, the weekend the bakery opened.

"My father left last night." I watch Jude and Cecelia as I say this, the teenager now controlling the machine's stick, the little girl pointing and giving instruction and cheering him on, despite the claw returning empty once again.

I can't avoid Seamus in my periphery; he closes the menu and rests his elbow on it. Waits. *Why do I tell him things?* Because he's been there when I was bleeding—with my mother's photo, the show, now—and his hands are large enough to cover the wounds.

I had wanted my father to share the *Bake-Off* experience with me, to use it as some sort of trampoline to bounce us into the heavens and give us a glimpse of my mother as she used to be, as we so desperately wanted her to be. And perhaps we could have stayed there awhile. Instead, he drove in the morning of the taping, took a long afternoon nap, and jumped in his car to leave for home before the sun went down. I know. Being there with me, with the bread, pokes at all his still-tender places. We've both of us exhausted ourselves trying to pack those places deep and swaddled and away from anything given to irritating them. It doesn't work. We know that because we've been ducking and sidestepping for the past twenty years. Time passes, days or weeks, and we breathe deep the illusion that things are better until we're bumped too sharply by the past, and the oozing begins again.

It's harder for my father; he has less to fill time and more to remember.

The waitress brings us water and napkin-spun utensils. Seamus orders a milk for Cecelia and a coffee for himself. "And a Coke."

"Pepsi okay?"

"Sure. And do you have Mountain Dew?"

"Mm-hm."

"Okay, a Mountain Dew as well, for him." Seamus points to the empty place mat beside me.

I ask for lemonade, until she tells me it's Lipton from the drink machine. "Unsweetened iced tea, then, with lemon," I tell her.

"I can give you a cup of ice and a tea bag and hot water. We only keep the sweet stuff cold."

"Fine," I say, though it isn't to either of us. She puffs out her lower lip and crams her notepad into her apron pocket. I think snobbish thoughts about the kind of place unable to brew and chill a pitcher of unsweetened tea. Seamus motions to Cecelia, who bounds to the table with a mangy stuffed four-legged animal of some type. "Jude won it and gave it to me," she says, scooting over her father's lap to the inside of the booth, where she flips the panels of the tabletop jukebox. "They still have it."

"What's that?" I ask, also sliding in to make room for Jude.

"My song. Well, the song I'm named after." She points, and I squint at the list. "See it? By Simon and Gardenfunkle."

"Garfunkel," Seamus corrects her. He's embarrassed, cheeks almost purple. "And you're not really named for the song. Your mother and I just happened to like Cecelia."

"I never get to hear the whole thing," she says. "If it comes on the radio, Daddy always turns down the middle part."

"My name is a song too," Jude says. "It might be there. If you find it, I'll let you play it."

"Menu first," Seamus says.

"I just want chicken fingers and fries," Cecelia tells him, face to the jukebox's clear plastic front, reading each selection softly to herself.

The waitress bring our drinks and takes orders. Minutes later Cecelia shouts, "Got it. It's here. 'Hee Jude' by the . . . Beatles?"

"'Hey Jude,'" Seamus says. "And yes, it's the Beatles."

"Yuck. They have the same name as bugs?"

"Yup," Jude says, flicking her a quarter. It passes through her hands, spins on the table, and then rolls off the edge. Cecelia crawls beneath us and returns, flushed but triumphant, coin pressed over her eye.

"Had to hold my breath down there," she says, dropping the quarter into the slot. "What number again?"

I peer over. "E two eight."

She pushes each button with steady determination. The music fills the diner. "How long do these *na-na-nas* go on?" she asks finally.

"Too long," Jude says.

The food comes and we eat and talk and laugh. Cecelia deep-sea dives beneath the table again, searching for money, prying up each of our feet in her exploration. She returns with another quarter pulled from who knows where and plunks it into the jukebox. "Hey Jude" begins again. Jude hides his face in his hands. Seamus, when the *na-na-nas* begin, uses his spoon as a microphone and sings along. "Yeah, you can stop now," Jude tells him, but Cecelia joins in. Finally, the teenager adds his own *Jude-jude-ju-jude-jude-jude* above them. I try to be stern and tell them to quiet down, everyone is staring, but I'm ignored until I wad up my napkin and toss it at Seamus. He catches it in his mouth.

"I used that to wipe my nose," I tell him.

He spits it out as the waitress appears and asks if we want any dessert, or just the check. She stresses *just the check* and nods with each word, as if we're supposed to understand we've overstayed our welcome.

Jude wants chocolate cake, though, so we all order something from the bakery. The waitress grunts and collects our dirty plates.

This is what Pastor Ryan means when he preaches on community, all of us with pieces missing, all of us starfish, but instead of regenerating our amputated parts we've replaced them with one another.

"Okay, everyone. Now listen. We need to behave," I say.

We sit with our hands in our laps, biting our lips so they won't split and reveal smiles, until Seamus taps the end of the straw from its paper and blows the wrapper across the table.

Twelve

It's Christmas, our first without her, and neither my father nor I know what to do with the day. Seventy-two hours before the twenty-fifth we still have no tree. My mother's decorations sleep in tissue paper and cardboard boxes in the dark of the attic. The ratty, fur-clad Belsnickels. The long ivory stockings with red woven toes. The glass balls and Hallmark ornaments, and all the handprint reindeer I made. I pull the trapdoor chain dangling in the hallway outside the bathroom door, unfold the ladder, and stare into the rush of stale, uninsulated air from the unlit room above me. I climb the first rung, the second. The ladder settles into place, groaning beneath my weight. I've never minded going up; coming down frightens me. It's too steep facing forward, but I've slipped before trying to find my footing when going backward, banging my chin and pinching my fingers in the ladder's springs as I flailed to find something to grab before I fell.

I step down and pack the door back into the ceiling.

On Christmas Eve, my father comes home from work with a two-foot potted spruce and a plastic bag from the grocery store, handles knotted. He sets the tree on the bricks in front of the fireplace and kisses my head. *Aunt Anwyn is coming tomorrow. And the rest of them.*

Okay, I say.

Okay.

He goes to the bedroom. I stare at the tree, dotted with starlight candies and wrapped in a plastic gumdrop garland. The mints are real, wired on; I tug one from the back, twist off the cellophane, and suck it onto my tongue. Christmas fills my mouth, and along with the sweet, peppery flavor, I'm flooded with holidays past, the memories coming until I almost drown in them, and I spit the candy between the flimsy branches of the tree. I shove the empty wrapper in there too.

Christstollen.

I can shake away thoughts of favorite gifts and trips to Oma's house and building snowmen with Santa hats every Christmas Eve, as long as enough snow covered the ground. But my mother's stollen won't fall off as easily. She made it for my father; he ate the first piece with cream cheese at breakfast while I had bacon and chocolate chip pancakes and my mother drank her special amaretto tea.

The recipe is there, tucked in her recipe box, the index card translucent in places from butter stains. I hold it in my hand, considering, reading the ingredients and pawing through the cupboards and pantry. We have raisins and a bag of dried cranberries from last year's Christmas baking. There's a wrinkled orange in the fruit bin, a couple plastic packets of lemon juice that came with one of my father's fish and chips take-out orders. No marzipan, almonds, candied fruit, or mace. I'll be up all night. It's too much effort. But the card won't seem to leave my hand. So I start, soaking the fruit and preparing the sponge. I lay on the hard wood, the side of my head pressed against the brick in front of the fireplace, trying to look through the underside of the potted tree, just as I did as a child, beneath the real tree my mother chose each year. Our trees were never the full, bushy kind.

My mother liked the spindlier ones best, with short, spiky needles and plenty of space between the branches.

I doze, the beep of the microwave timer enough to rouse me for each phase of the stollen. It's past four in the morning when I remove it from the oven. I wash the bowls and spoons and pan, taking the bread and aluminum foil to my bedroom.

Aunt Anwyn knocks on my door late in the afternoon. Neither my father nor I have been downstairs, at least not since I've been awake; I've heard him in his own room, listening to television. She moves down the hall to summon him and I dress, wind the bread in foil, and search around for something else to tie around the package. I cut off the hem of a faded red t-shirt, one I wear only to bed, and use the strip as a ribbon, tying it into a limp bow.

Liesl, my aunt says as she passes my door again. I follow downstairs and put the stollen behind the spruce's pot. My father has his own unhappily wrapped gift beside the tree. The young cousins yank the ends of Christmas crackers, confetti exploding throughout the room, and give each of us a paper hat. I glance at my father. He puts his on, so I do too. My aunt tells us she's warmed leftovers on the stove and brought desserts for the rest of them, since they left their own home without having Yule log cake. My uncle sits in the corner, drinking Guinness from a can and watching a basketball game. The over-sugared cousins screech about the toys Santa brought them and throw presents at us. We open the penguin socks and woolly ice scraper mitt and angel mugs filled with toffees and travel manicure sets. My father gives me his gift—it's my favorite Christmas treat, a chocolate orange, the *Whack and Unwrap* kind. He's folded forty dollars into the front of the box.

I give him mine. His fingers tighten into it. He knows the weight, the shape, the way it indents under the pressure of his hands. Without opening it, he sets it beside him and covers it with the ice scraper and socks. He looks at me and nods ever so slightly. I try to smile back. He stands, touches the top of my head, and says, *Let's get something to eat.*

When Tee arrives for work Monday morning, I shout at her.

"Where were you? One of the biggest days here, and you don't even have the courtesy to call?"

"I am sick yesterday. It is not a crime. And I tell that man there to tell you."

"Well, I'm not paying you for not showing up."

"Your choosing." Tee shrugs, hauls her soup pot onto the stove; it's twice her girth and more than a third as tall as she is. She's always been small but seems frangible now, the knobs at her wrists, the way her collarbone juts from her T-shirt. Her head shrunken beneath a thick mushroom of hair. Has she been this way since we met, or is it recent, brought on by illness and concern? I can't remember, won't remember even if I sit for hours and concentrate. I don't notice these things, so caught up in my world of *fougasse* and lactobacilli and protein content. I choose bread over people.

Tee holds a long-handled wooden spatula in one hand, a stainless ladle in the other. I ignore them both and embrace her. She stands rigid against me, and then I feel her arms move, her fists in my back, the ladle cold against my neck. I release her and sniffle, wiping a tear trail from my cheek.

"Yeah, well, just remember, you don't have to work here," I say.

She dumps congealed beef stock into the pot, turns on the burner. Stirs. "You are boss."

"Well played," Xavier whispers as I pass. "She won't suspect a thing."

I relieve Jude of front counter duties and greet customers. The bakehouse doesn't swell with people like last week, but it is busier than usual. Several regulars who had been at the taping congratulate me. I smile politely, giving them the answer Patrice Olsen made me rehearse. "I really can't say anything until the show airs." They wink and grin and say they understand and buy a loaf of bread for dinner tonight. Others ask for the breads I made Saturday and are disappointed when I explain they were recipes I used for the show and aren't necessarily in my regular rotation. I convince them other variants are just as good, and they grudgingly agree to try a yeasted baguette or the garlic basil focaccia I made this morning.

Again, the bread sells too quickly.

I don't make many single-build recipes, where the dough is mixed, proofed, and baked in a matter of hours. Those are fine for home bakers who haven't the time or inclination for longer processes, but it does nothing to tease out the flavors of the flour, the natural yeast, the bacteria. Most of my formulas require at least two days, the dough cold fermented overnight or some kind of pre-ferment—whether a yeasted poolish or biga, or a wild sourdough starter—prepared and added to the other ingredients. Because of this, I can't boast the variety of a Baskin-Robbins–type bakery; I make eight to twelve different kinds of bread for the day, and when it's on the higher end, it's because of the different shapes or additives—seeds and spices and flavorings—not different dough. I'm not able to whip up some quick loaves to have ready to sell for the afternoon.

I poke my head into the kitchen and motion to Jude. "Watch the counter for me again?"

He nods. "They all want your winning ciabatta. I'm gonna have to beat them off with a stick."

"Tell them maybe tomorrow."

"They won't hear the maybe part, and then you'll have an angry horde."

"Then say I've taken my winnings and moved to the Cayman Islands."

Jude snorts. "I'll come up with something."

We switch places, and in the quiet of the kitchen, I sag. Every part of me. I look at Xavier, who pours a bucket of flour into the stand mixer. "I thought I'd get a start for tomorrow."

"Tell me things will go back to normal."

"You're looking at normal."

"This is all novelty," I say, motioning to the unseen patrons on the other side of the wall.

"No. Last week, with the big bus and the cameras, that was novelty. This is discovery. It's not going away."

I slouch backward, hard, head banging the cooler door. "We can't keep up, Zave."

"You need to hire more help. Someone for the counter and to wait tables. Another baker. Maybe even someone else for the kitchen."

Tee drops the lid on her pot. She grabs the knife beside her cutting board, shakes it at us, her eyes invisible slits behind her Lennon lenses. "You think I am hard to hear? You think I don't know what you say?" She taps the knife to her temple. "There is no more cook here. I am cook." Slicing the knife through the air, she turns and chops the waiting carrots with heavy strokes.

I raise my eyebrows at Xavier, who shakes his head and bats Tee's angry words away with the back of his hand, like swatting flies at a picnic. "A waitress and baker, then."

"Where am I going to find someone I can trust with my bread?"

"You found me. There are others out there, Liesl, who would be just fine. Start looking now, because once the show airs, things will only get busier."

"All I wanted to do was bake."

"If you wanted that, you could have done it in your kitchen. No, you wanted to bake good bread for others to eat. Well, they're eating it. Sometimes success looks different than we expect. Yours looks better. Be grateful."

"You're telling me to grow up."

Xavier smiles. "Something like that."

Claudia's Christstollen

Makes one large or two smaller loaves

INGREDIENTS

FOR THE FRUIT:

230 grams (1 generous cup) mixed candied fruit or 165 grams
  (1 generous cup) mixed dried fruit of your choice

165 grams (1 generous cup) raisins

120 grams (1/2 cup) dark rum or orange juice

FOR THE SPONGE:

10 grams (1 tablespoon) active dry yeast

60 grams (1/4 cup) warm water (about 110 degrees Fahrenheit)

170 grams (2/3 cup) milk

8 grams (1 teaspoon) honey

120 grams (1 cup) unbleached all-purpose flour, organic if
  possible

FOR THE DOUGH:

113 grams (1/3 cup) honey

2 large eggs, beaten

113 grams (1/2 cup) unsalted butter, softened

10 grams (1 tablespoon) finely grated lemon zest

6 grams (1 teaspoon) salt

1/2 teaspoon ground cinnamon

1/8 teaspoon ground allspice

1/8 teaspoon ground mace

60 grams (1/2 cup) slivered almonds

360 to 480 grams (3 to 4 cups) unbleached all-purpose flour

Oil, for coating bowl

FOR THE FILLING:

3 ounces marzipan or almond paste

FOR THE TOPPING:

60 grams ($^1/2$ cup) powdered sugar

DO AHEAD

Combine the mixed fruit, raisins, and rum or orange juice. Cover and set aside overnight, or for at least 4 hours.

ON BAKING DAY

Prepare the sponge in a large bowl by first combining the yeast and water. Heat the milk and add it to the yeast mixture along with the honey and 1 cup flour. Cover the sponge with plastic wrap and let rise until light and full of bubbles, about 30 minutes to an hour.

Add the fruit mixture, honey, egg, butter, zest, salt, spices, almonds, and 2 cups of the flour to the sponge. If kneading by hand, stir with a wooden spoon until combined, about 2 minutes. Gradually add the remaining flour $^1/4$ cup at a time until the dough begins to pull away from the side of the bowl. Turn the dough out onto a floured work surface. Knead, adding flour a little at a time, until the dough is smooth and elastic, about 8 to 10 minutes. If using a stand mixer, use a paddle attachment and beat the mixture on medium-low speed for 2 minutes. Gradually add the remaining flour $^1/4$ cup at a time until the dough begins to pull away from the side of the bowl. Switch to the dough hook. Continue to add flour 1 tablespoon at a time until the dough just begins to clean the bowl, approximately 4 to 5 minutes on medium-low speed.

Shape the dough into a ball and place it in a large, lightly oiled bowl, turning to coat the dough. Cover with a tightly woven towel or plastic wrap and let rise until doubled, about 1 to 2 hours.

Gently turn the dough out onto a lightly oiled work surface. For one large loaf, roll the dough into a 9-by-13-inch oval. For two loaves, divide the dough in half and roll each half into a 7 x 9-inch oval. Brush the melted butter over the top of the loaves. Between two pieces of waxed paper or plastic wrap, roll the marzipan the length of the dough. Place the marzipan on half of the oval and fold the dough over it lengthwise.

Carefully lift the bread onto a parchment-lined or well-greased baking sheet. Press lightly to seal the seams. Cover with a clean towel or plastic wrap and let rise for 1 hour.

Preheat oven to 375 degrees Fahrenheit. Bake for 25 minutes or until the internal temperature of the bread reaches 190 degrees Fahrenheit. Immediately remove from the baking sheet and place on a rack to cool. Sprinkle with powdered sugar before serving.

Variation: Omit the marzipan filling. Instead, combine 2 tablespoons melted unsalted butter, 2 teaspoons ground cinnamon, and 3 tablespoons granulated sugar and sprinkle over half the ovals before folding lengthwise. Or leave out the filling altogether. Allow to rise and bake as instructed above.

Three days later I interview Rebekah, a still, milky girl nearly as tall as Seamus. Her mother waits outside for her in a fifteen-passenger van. She's the second oldest of eleven, she tells me. This will be her first real job, outside of babysitting and helping work the family's organic farm.

"I can run a register. We have one at the farm stand."

I nod. "Where's your farm?"

"On the other side of the creek. Windsor Creek, you know?"

"That's a bit of a drive to get here."

"Thirty-five minutes. But we're in the middle of nowhere so it's at least that to anything." She uncrosses her legs beneath her almost ankle-length skirt, which she wears with a matching bandana around her hair, T-shirt, and plastic flip-flops. Her gangly feet are flat with calloused heels, her toes scrubbed clean, nails cut too short. "This is a nice place. I've never been here before. Most of our trips are in the opposite direction because, you know, Hanson has a Walmart with a grocery."

"Why are you interested in working here?"

"Well, our church gets your bread. The leftover ones you give us to give away to people? When I read the help-wanted in the paper, I was kind of hoping I could somehow be involved with that."

We sit in Wild Rise, at the table in front of the window, the bakery having closed an hour ago, the sun at the exact angle to dance on the dust particles in the air. I offer her coffee and water and Tee's special summer punch and nearly anything in the bakery. She declines all of it with a graciousness not usually seen in teenagers. Her voice is animated, but the rest of her moves so little. She's not at all the type I expected to have work here, but I have a feeling she'll fit. "Well, right now I'm looking for a waitress and counter help. Hours are six forty-five a.m. to about three fifteen in the afternoon. You get a half hour for lunch in there. I'd like you to work either Tuesday through Saturday or Monday through Friday, but if there's another day that works better for you to have off, I can accommodate, except Wednesday, because my other waitress has that off now. Otherwise, you can start tomorrow and learn as you go along."

"You mean I got the job?"

"If you want it."

"Oh my goodness, yes. Thank you, Miss McNamara. I can't believe it."

"It's Liesl," I tell her, giving her two forms to fill out and return in the morning. "As for the bread ministry, you'll be the one packing the extra loaves for pickup, but other than that, there isn't much else to it. At least for now. I'm open to ideas, if you have any."

"Really? Oh, I wasn't thinking anything in particular, but I'll pray about it." She stops, rakes her teeth over her bottom lip. She does this often; the skin beneath her mouth is chapped, her lip puffed and bruised on one side. "Is that okay to say?"

"It's fine."

Rebekah stands. She's lean and sturdy but her bones are large, the kind that too easily hold on to pregnancy weight and extra helpings of mashed potatoes and sleepless nights and worry. She won't be thin much longer. "It's the bags, you know."

I don't. "What bags?"

"The ones you put the bread in, the pretty ones that say *Bread of Life Ministries* on them. Our church gets food from different places and most of it is just thrown together in some boxes. Some of it's not even edible, you know, like all covered in mold or bruised up, or really, really old. I knew when I saw your bags that you cared."

I lock the door behind her, wave as she gets into the van and it pulls away from the curb.

It began in high school, when our Key Club collected food for a local pantry. We went out Halloween night, and instead of gathering candy we asked for canned goods and brought a van-load back to the school cafeteria. We stacked the food on a table, organizing it as best as our hormone-saturated brains could manage—pasta and sauces here, other noodles next, soups, canned meats, rice, vegetables, the pickles and strange items on the end. I took a jar of blue-cheese–stuffed Greek olives from one of the bags, the dust on the lid so thick it was sticky. I couldn't blow it off, finding instead a box of Kleenex and scrubbing the top before adding it to the tower of beets and gherkins and mince-meat filling.

It bothered me for days, and I grappled with my feelings, the idea that someone would use a food donation to rid the pantry of disliked or never-used food. I mentioned it to Jennie, who said, "Maybe they just thought someone else would want them. There are people out there who really like green olives. Or maybe that was all they had to give."

I knew it was true. Some old man on a fixed income who adores olives but couldn't afford them would feast on them in his senior apartment, picking them straight out of the jar with his fingers and squeezing the cheese onto his tongue before squishing the olive in his mouth. He'd drink the packing oil and watch *The Amazing Race*, and go to bed full and happy.

Perhaps the person who donated the olives thought this, or for her, the donation was her widow's mite. I imagined she thought nothing, though. Simply saw the jar hiding at the back of their pantry, some Secret Santa gift from the office holiday party two, oh wait, three years ago, and dropped the olives into the bag with the extra package of bread stuffing from Thanksgiving, the four-for-a-dollar can of creamed corn, and a box of Rice-A-Roni that has yet to be eaten because she accidentally grabbed the wrong flavor.

Do everything as if unto the Lord. Offer up everything as if for the Lord, including jars of olives to the food pantry. Or leftover loaves of bread. Years later, that's finally how I make sense of it, where it settles out for me. If Jesus knocks on my door today, will I rummage through my home and give him the food I don't like, the outgrown jacket with stains and a broken zipper, the dirty Crock-Pot in the basement, the one with the chipped lid and the mice nesting inside I've yet to find time to toss into the Salvation Army's dumpster?

Whatever you did for one of the least of these brothers and sisters of mine, you did for me.

So I pack the bread in bags, like I will for any paying customer. I don't send burnt loaves or stale loaves, or any kitchen experiment I don't believe is quality enough to sell. I will not give to the least of these anything I will not offer to my Lord, should he walk into Wild Rise one afternoon and ask for a little something to eat.

| Thirteen |

I'm in bed and my father shakes me, his hand warm and gritty on my bare shoulder. I wear a lace-strapped camisole to bed, satiny and sheer and something I never would dare put on if I thought he'd come into my room to rouse me. Or for any reason at all. He hasn't been in here in months.

I bought the camisole two weeks ago, when Jennie's mother took her and Amanda Craft and me to the mall. She let us wander around freely while she shopped for new shoes, and we took advantage of the freedom by eating Taco Bell in the food court and squeezing into the photo machine and buying clearance lingerie at T.J. Maxx. Jennie and I bought it, at least. Amanda hid hers in the leg of a pair of jeans she took into the dressing room and then slipped the cami on beneath her shirt before returning the jeans and the little yellow plastic "1" tag to the attendant. She truth-or-dared us to do the same, but Jennie and I paid for ours. Mine had a red sticker on the tag, marked down to seven dollars. It's midnight blue, or at least I'd call it that—I remember midnight blue being my favorite color in the Crayola box, the child of aqua and navy, worn down well below the tips of all the others—with silver filaments woven through it. The lace at the bottom hem was torn away in two places, easily mended if I wanted to take the time or thread to do it. I didn't, expecting no one to see me in it except me, in the bedroom mirror, turning this way and that, and lamenting how little my almost-an-A breasts filled out the gathered cups.

Before we met her mother to go home, Jennie and I folded the camisoles into bundles the size of an egg and zipped them into the innermost pockets of our winter coats.

Now, aware of my father's clean-shaven scent hovering above, I tug the blanket to my neck and hold it tight around me. *What?*

I'm going to mass. Come with me.

I won't roll over, fearing the blanket will somehow come loose. *Saint Andrew's or Annunciation?* Lutheran or Catholic?

No. Ken invited me with him.

Ken Burl. A coworker of my father's whom he's complained about more than once, because he doesn't drink or cuss and is too nice to everyone. *He's some sort of Baptist.*

I know.

Forget it.

He goes, shutting the door, trapping his Old Spice in the room with me. The smell, one I only ever associate with my father, and the sensation of the camisole's silky polyester against my skin—childhood and adulthood, public and private, safety and budding sensuality—they collide so violently I'm almost ill. I reach down to the floor where my laundry is strewn—dirty, clean, doesn't matter—and in one motion the cami is off and the T-shirt is on, and I'm burrowed under the blankets so far I'm breathing the hot, stale air of sheets that haven't been changed in months.

I finally get up hours later, spurred from bed by an over-full bladder and some clattering in the kitchen. I tie a bathrobe over my flannel pants and T-shirt and wander downstairs to find my father frying smelts in a pan on the stove.

He's whistling.

What's going on?

I'm making lunch.

Why?

I thought it would be nice for us to eat together. We haven't had smelts in forever. I know you like them.

I like Mom's.

He continues to transfer the crispy fish onto a paper towel–lined plate, one after the other, heads still on, bodies curling like breaded fossils. *I followed the cookbook.* He turns off the burner, moves the iron skillet to the back of the stovetop, and, without looking at me, says, *Maybe it's time we tried to let go of some things.*

She's not a thing.

Liesl—

This is because you went to that church? I yank open the refrigerator, bottles rattling on the door shelves, reach into the crisper for an apple, and take a huge, noisy bite. *You can keep your Jesus freak crap. I'll keep her.* I throw a loaf of bread and jar of peanut butter on the counter, make a show of digging around the flatware drawer for a knife. Unscrew the lid and plop a mound of Jif in the center of a slice of honey wheat.

My father turns away from me, dish of smelts in hand, shakes the fish into the trash pail, and then, as an afterthought, drops the plate in as well. Without speaking, he descends the basement stairs. I do the same with my food, gathering the peanut butter jar and hastily half-made sandwich and apple and all the bread into my arms, and push them down into the garbage, smothering the fish. Then I go in the opposite direction, upstairs, to lock myself in the bathroom with my hairbrush.

❧

They want to learn wild yeast, these women, though I suspect of the nine of them, maybe one will still have a viable starter in her refrigerator by year's end. Caring for yeast is like nurturing a beloved family pet, a puppy needing to be fed, watered, housebroken, one that whimpers all night and is lonely even though its owner wraps a ticking clock in a blanket in its kennel, hoping it will be comforted by a sound reminiscent of its mother's heart. It never works, and I tell them so. They laugh, not believing me, though several of them have tried to culture sourdough and failed. They think it's bad flour, or chlorine in their tap water, or the fact they stirred the mixture with a metal spoon. They're here to learn *the trick*. How much work can flour and water and a billion microorganisms truly be? Most of life is unforgiving, and there are no shortcuts when it comes to wild yeast.

"There are plenty of bread myths," I say. "A metal spoon will not react with the culture. You can use all the metal spoons you want, even in the dough. I just happen to prefer wooden ones because my mother and grandmother used them."

The women take notes. I compartmentalize them; after three years of teaching these classes, I can read their reasons for being here. Two are here because they believe commercial yeast destroys the gut and causes a multitude of health problems. Three are friends, housewives, mothers, looking for a life-enriching class while the kids are in school. Two are skilled home bakers who haven't yet conquered sourdough; one will be self-satisfied with the success in her own kitchen, the other wants to sell her bread at medieval Renaissance fairs. Of the remaining students, one is addicted to learning, to trying new things, to the excitement of accomplishment. By next month her starter will be forgotten, the expensive bannetons and proofing box stored in the closet, waiting to be sold at her summer garage sale, and she'll have moved on to cake decorating or stained glass. The last woman doesn't know why she's here, except she saw an advertisement in the newspaper and felt called. She's never made a loaf of yeasted bread in her life. People like her are wild cards, the seeds in the parable of the sower. She may come to love baking and, even more so, excel at it, or her culture may die on the counter as she forgets it, concerned more with her sick father and credit card debt and her son's behavior problems at Boy Scouts. She may decide even a once-a-week feeding is too much effort, or at class end, she may think, *Why on earth did I figure I'd enjoy this?*

Isn't it that way in all things, though? The birds, the thorns, the lack of soil—all reasons to give up, to fade out of life and find the easiest way to deal with all those disappointing things people, as children, never expect will come to them.

"Another myth is that sourdough is always sour. Yes, some breads made with wild yeast have that sharp taste people associate with San Francisco–style loaves, but many do not. I, honestly, don't like a strong sour taste in my bread. I sell one true sourdough, and let me tell you, it will make you pucker. But my other wild yeast breads range from very mild to just the slightest tang."

"What makes the yeast get more sour?" one woman asks. "Isn't it how long you leave the dough out to ferment?"

"That's one reason," I tell her, "but it's not the yeast that sours the dough, it's the bacteria."

All but two of the women—the two, I imagine, who have tried making a starter before—look utterly disgusted. Bacteria is bad, they think. All their bathrooms have lovely pump bottles of berry-scented bacteria-killing soap, and they wash all those nasty little critters down the drain more times a day than they can count.

I explain the symbiosis between the yeast and lactobacilli. "The wild yeast live on the grain as it grows in the field, and when the wheat is harvested they're still there, invading our kitchens whether we purchase the berries from the bulk bins at a natural food store to grind at home or pick up a paper brick of the all-purpose stuff at Hannaford. So does the bacteria. The yeast eat the simple sugars in the flour, producing gasses that make the dough rise. The bacteria, on the other hand, give off lactic acid, which is what gives the bread its sour flavor. Actually, the lactobacilli is what keeps the culture healthy.

Only the yeast strains good for bread can survive in the mixture's acidity, and it destroys stray, unhealthy bacteria and other yeasts. The lactobacilli also eat dead yeasts.

"The way to keep a starter from becoming too sour, however your own palate defines it, is to feed it more often. The bacteria eat more slowly than the yeast. The yeast die off faster without food, but the bacteria can just keep on consuming the dead yeast and their waste, making more lactic acid and thus a more sour starter. Regular feedings keep the system in balance, so the yeast don't run out of simple sugars and the bacteria never overwhelm the starter. I find it's best, once the starter is well established, to feed every twelve to twenty-four hours. That's if you're keeping it at room temperature, of course, which is best to do if you're baking daily or almost that much. Refrigeration slows the whole process down, but even then, you should feed your starter at least once a week."

"I thought you had to capture wild yeast from the air," the Renaissance fair woman says, disappointed.

"I'm afraid that's probably another myth," I tell her, and her frown deepens. "There are yeast in the air, but not necessarily the ones needed for sourdough. It's like the idea of adding grapes to a culture; that white film on the skin is yeast, but it's grape yeast—excellent for wine but completely ineffective for bread. Eventually that strain will be killed off in the culture because it can't survive in that particular environment. However," I add in the hopes of cheering her, though I doubt I will—her romantic notions have been burned away by too much knowledge, "it may be true that the more you bake with sourdough, the more wild yeast will be floating around your kitchen. Some of those very well may become part of your bread."

She persists. "But is it true that the flavor and even the strain of bread yeast will change when you move from, say, California to Vermont?"

"Well, yes, that is the case. I think most likely that's still due to the flour, since grains are regionally produced. If you have a starter from Vermont and continue to buy your flour from Vermont and have it shipped to you in California to do your baking, your starter probably won't change all that much."

"Other famous bakers still think yeast is collected from the environment around us. I always leave my bowl outside, covered in cheesecloth, of course, and let mother nature blow them into my starter."

"I suppose it's possible." I don't mention she hasn't managed to culture a stable starter, or studies in which sterilized flour will not establish colonies of yeast. I leave it alone. I was one of those hopeful wild yeast hunters—a lifetime ago, it seems. It's the Santa Claus of bread baking, something people want to believe even though they're too old to sit on his lap, even when faced with the realization the *From Santa* tags are written in their mothers' handwriting, and they've accidentally discovered their Christmas lists tucked in the secret pockets of their fathers' briefcases.

I share several more old wives' tales, and the final one, that sourdough made in a home with women would taste different from one made around men only—due to, it was believed, the natural yeast of the female body—draws more chuckles and pulls the XX-chromosome group together in a sort of gendered solidarity. *Of course some stupid man would come up with an idea like that.* I don't use the example if the class isn't all female.

Together we make the beginnings of a sourdough culture—two parts water, one part rye flour, one part wheat flour—stirring it together in a glass Ball jar. I also give each woman half a cup of one of my established starters, encouraging them to report back to me their successes and failures, to take a picture of their first loaves and come post them on the baker's bulletin board hanging just over there on the wall, and then I send them out the door before the lunch crowd begins. Then I sneak into the kitchen before any of the customers can lure me into a conversation and find Tee complaining about Jude's knife skills. He cuts celery for her, not thin or even enough, and she covers his hands with hers and directs him, counting each downward slice in Ukrainian. "See it is good like this? You do now."

"I'm trying," Jude says.

"And he's supposed to be working with Zave," I say. "I told you if you needed more help, I'd hire someone."

"I no need help," Tee says. "I have the boy."

"Hello? Did you hear me? I'm paying Jude to help with the bread, not the soup." Yes, he has a salary now, though he's embarrassed by it. I'd pay him double if I could afford it.

"Is not for soup. We make quiche."

"Tee, come on. Your job is safe. I'm only trying to make life easier for you."

My words puncture her and she droops without all her brashness to keep her puffed up. "When it is easy you forget how it is to fight." And then she smacks her spoon on the counter, inches from Jude's arm. "Enough with vegetable. See eggs in that bowl? Crack and beat. And no shells. None."

I step outside, onto the concrete loading platform, the area cool and shaded. Not quite September yet, but the scent of it is beginning, the one reminding me of digging in the backyard for earthworms until my fingers bend painfully backward in the packed, slightly damp ground and the tips of my nails turn blue with dirt. An uncovering smell, one of endings, soon to overwhelm the air as all the leaves offer their fallen bodies to this yearly rite of passage.

The screen door squeaks and bounces behind me, and Xavier appears in the corner of my vision.

"That woman," I say.

"You should be used to it by now."

"You'd think."

"The new girl is working out well."

"Rebekah, yeah. She's a godsend."

"Any inquiries for the baker's position?"

"A few," I say. I'd received five résumés. All seem qualified and eager, but I'm in no mood to schedule interviews yet. "But I'm wondering if maybe we're not doing fine without the extra hands."

"Just trying to make things a little easier for you," Xavier says, voice gilded in irony.

I don't need him to point out my similarities with Tee, or remind me of my inability to relinquish control of things I've decided are more important than breathing—my personal principles of bread, the bakery and the way I feel it should run; all things of temporal value and yet I cling to them as I should only hold on to the One who is eternal. Idols. And more exhausting each day as the business expands, explodes, and I go without sleep and food and sunlight in my lungs. I can't lay them down, though. They are glued to my palms, and I shake and shake and shake but they don't come off.

I stare down the street. Two boys, somewhere in their teens but I can't tell from this distance, smoke on the public bench, skateboards standing on end and clamped between their knees. "I haven't seen Jude smoking lately."

"He's quitting, I think," Xavier says. "Sometimes I see the ash glowing red from my window at night. But I don't smell it on him anymore, or see him with them any other time. Just in the dark."

The door swings open again. Rebekah. She holds the cordless phone. "Excuse me, Liesl? I'm sorry to bother you, but you have a call. Patrice Olsen from the Good Food Channel?"

"Thanks," I say, taking the receiver. "Hello, Ms. Olsen."

"Ms. McNamara, lovely to speak to you. I sent an e-mail, but I understand you don't always receive them, so I wanted to call as well and tell you the air date has been chosen for your *Bake-Off* episode."

"Okay, when?"

"Three weeks from this Thursday. The season premiere."

↶↷

It doesn't begin as oppression, or not the kind of oppression it later becomes. After Rome falls, after the barbarians and wanderers of the north cease their warring and settle behind the plow, there come the manors. We call them *lord* and *lady* now, but these words rise from Old English ancestors: *hlaford*, the guard of the loaves, and *hlæf-dige*, the kneader of the dough. A sense of provision, of protection. Something all at once good and necessary. But it's of no surprise this degrades into abuse—of power, of people, of food. The universe is overcome by entropy, and this of the moral kind, where eventually all that is conceived as excellent and noble and true—governments and philosophies and religions and men—begins to break apart into corrupt particles of dust.

One might call it sin.

Why, then, does the serf stay in the field, providing bread for the lord when he hardly has enough for his own children? Eventually uprisings come, but not for hundreds of years because the monks and priests have done their jobs too well. *Are all men not bondservants of Christ?* they say to the peasant. They have become people, not possessions. And at once, the lowly position is given a measure of holiness, of status.

Of worth.

Those who work with grain—who sow and reap and thresh and grind—they remind themselves they are the worthiest of all as they are pieces in the passion of the bread, making it possible for God incarnate to come to them in the Eucharist, every day, just as he told his first disciples, *This is my body.*

Autumn sweeps into Vermont with unseasonably cool nights and mornings. Afternoons are as warm as usual, plenty of people strolling in summer clothes, still buying ice-cream cones and attending the farmer's market, though snap peas and tomatoes have given way to stalks of celery and apples and squash. I wear a sweatshirt over my

T-shirt and bring a pair of socks downstairs with me in the morning, peeling off the extra layer once I get into the warm kitchen. But by evening, once the fire has died in the oven and there's a breeze sneaking in through the back screen door, my long sleeves are back on and I loosen the elastic on my hiking sandals to accommodate my socks. Fortunately, the bakehouse is closed and no customers see this statement of fashion, but even if they did, no one would think twice. Tweed socks with sandals are a very Vermont thing to do.

With children back in school, Cecelia comes again each afternoon, the bus dropping her in front of the bakehouse around half past three, on the other side of the street, and she waits there until the driver gives an exaggerated okay with his fingers and then points for her to cross. Seamus has her in public first grade this year. She runs from one sidewalk to the other and bursts through the door, which I keep unlocked for her. She remembers to turn the deadbolt and announces, "I'm here," to the room, whether empty or not. Usually Tee, Gretchen, and I are in the kitchen, and she bursts in like New Year's Day, the ends of her hair still chewed, her tummy growing a bit rounder as she readies for a growth spurt. Tee makes her a snack and Gretchen tells her it's time to make their list, and Cecelia writes each chore as Gretchen dictates, words like *shaker* and *ceramic* creatively spelled. All our routines from the spring resurrected, and I can almost pretend nothing has changed. Until the dough preparation begins. Until Seamus shows up. Until I stumble up to my apartment at night, my loneliness exposed.

We make two hundred loaves a day, and while thirty or forty of them remain unsold each afternoon at closing, Xavier tells me to trust him. Once the show airs, we'll be glad we followed his advice and became accustomed to the quantity. And all of it, he promises, will sell. He knows business, and so we work to learn how to double the bread we bake, not adding variety so much as producing more of the old favorites. It's easier now with Rebekah here; Gretchen can begin helping me with the dough earlier in the day. And Seamus comes in the evenings, rolling up his sleeves and kneading together flour and water with his giant hands. He arrives by five, right about the time Gretchen leaves, continues where she left off, and stays until seven or eight. Sometimes he brings dinner. Cecelia does her homework and plays with scraps of dough, like clay, making balls and snakes and bracelets, or watches cartoons on her father's phone. When I ask if perhaps Cecelia would be better off at home, he says, "She'd be doing the same thing there as here. And you'd be all by yourself."

Working with Seamus is different. With Xavier and Jude and Gretchen, we avoid one another, each of us in our own bubble of space, no one too close to the other. Seamus can't help but invade the borders around me, his body taking up so much volume of its own. But he also creeps close on purpose. Our hips bump. His arm against my back. My hair in my face as I'm wrist-deep in dough, and he adjusts the barrettes for me, clipping my bangs out of my eyes and saying, "I think you need a haircut."

"I haven't decided if I'm growing it out or not." And then without considering, I add, "What do you think?"

"I don't know. You look nice however your hair is." He reaches for the thermometer in the measuring cup beside him, his usually dexterous fingers suddenly ten limp tentacles, and the water washes over the table, dripping off the side and threatening Cecelia's addition worksheet. She squeals and lifts her paper high in the air. I dam the spill with kitchen towels and Seamus wipes the floor. "Sorry."

"It's just water."

"The help shouldn't make more work for you."

My face twists, one side scrunching until I can see only from the opposite eye, and I shake my head. "You're not the help."

I've sprung the trapdoor. Seamus turns my way in all his transparency, and I read his expression. *What am I, then?*

I am not Seamus, who tacks his emotions to the outside of his skin and whose words charge from his mouth on horseback. No one sees through me, except Xavier, and he does so not because I choose to give him access but because he knows himself. I will have to offer myself to Seamus, if I want something *more* with him. Part of me can't believe I'd contemplate it, even for a moment. What do I have in common with an oversized yarn-spinning, bread-mauling, divorced deliveryman attached to a seven-year-old? The rest of me doesn't know if I remember how to be close to another person. I practice mimicry, a Viceroy butterfly masquerading as a Monarch, a Superb Lyrebird echoing the calls of everything from chickadees to chain saws. I practice stories of my past, telling this sad memory or that scary one, and people feel I'm confiding in them because the words touch their deepest wounds, not because the tales hold any emotional resonance for me. My intimacies, the ones that have become my Sisyphus stones, are kept only for me. I don't tell and no one notices; my first of two long-term romantic relationships, the college one, ended with the nice young man shocked when I said I didn't love him and we had nothing in common. "We've spent two years talking about everything," he said.

Yes, mimicry.

This is why I run from God. I am not ignorant of his requirement of me to empty myself to him. I'm not lazy. Even though, cognitively, I know he is omnipotent, I don't want to surrender my most vulnerable places. And I don't want him poking around in there on his own.

Cecelia, fortunately, decides to break the increasingly awkward silence. "Daddy's gonna let me stay up late for your party. And if I'm too tired in the morning, he says maybe I can stay home from school the next day."

"What party?"

"The one for the cooking show."

I shrug toward Seamus, who says, "A surprise, Cecelia. Remember?"

The girl clamps both hands over her mouth.

"What surprise?" I ask, more insistent.

"The *Gazette* and the network set it up. They've invited everyone who was at the taping to come back for the show's premier. The newspaper is setting up a big-screen TV here. They're running some sort of story to announce you winning."

"Was someone planning to let me in on the big surprise?"

"Xavier. I guess he hasn't gotten around to it yet."

"I guess not." I swipe a hill of excess flour from the counter into my hand, shake it off into the sink. Then I dampen a cloth and scrub at the mess. "I think I'm done for the night. It's late. You both should probably be getting home too."

"Are you mad?" Cecelia asks. She picks at the corner of her homework page. I must be wearing quite the black expression.

I try to add lightness to my voice. "Mad? Nope, not mad. It's just getting late and you look like you need to get to bed."

She stifles a yawn. "I only did that 'cause you mentioned bed. Sleepy words make people yawn. It's a fact."

"Really?"

"Uh-huh. Daddy says."

"Daddy also says you get grumpy as a bear when you don't get enough rest," Seamus tells her. He zips her colored pencils into her case and smoothes her math worksheet into a glossy kitten folder. "Liesl's right. Go ahead and use the bathroom so we can get you home."

"I don't hafta go."

"You will once you've been in the truck for three minutes."

"I can't help it. All the bumps make that happen."

"Go on, grumpy bear."

He lifts her from the stool. She scrunches her face—her mean expression—and growls a generic sort of growl that could be any number of wild beasts, clawing the air and shuffling to the restroom. Once the door closes, Seamus says, "So, are you mad?"

"No." I sigh. "I'm just tired of feeling like everything is out of my control. Which it isn't, as Zave would remind me. I've had choices. Or I've made the choice not to make choices. All of it got me here."

"Here isn't so bad."

"I know. Really, I do. I'm not all that good at being thankful."

"I understand."

"Do you?"

"Yeah," he says. I wait for him to elaborate but he doesn't, instead carrying several buckets of dough to the cooler. I'll need another soon, with the increased volume, but for now I've added several recipes to the menu where the shaped dough proofs at room temperature overnight, freeing up space. I move those containers to the end of the table, spread cornmeal, and begin forming boules and *bâtards*, dipping my hands in a bowl of water to prevent the dough from adhering to my skin.

"So, I'm wondering what you're doing this coming Saturday."

"Working."

"I mean, after that. Once the store closes."

I shrug. "Same as always, I guess. Eat. Sleep. Wait with anticipation for the new season of *Bake-Off with Jonathan Scott* to begin."

"Funny."

"I'm all laughs these days."

Quiet, and then an annoying scraping sound. I look up. Seamus rakes dried dough from the table with his fingernails. "Just leave it," I tell him. "I'll get it with a spatula later."

"What? Oh, yeah. Right. Okay." He draws air in, exhales; his shaky breath rustles the escaped strands of hair around my face. "Want to go to a movie?"

"What are you seeing?"

"Anything you want. You can pick."

My sweatshirt sleeves, which I had pulled all the way past my elbows before I began working with the dough, slide down my forearms, pooling at my wrists. I try to slip them back up with my nose, then by rubbing the cloth on my thighs, but they insist on staying put. "Could you push my sleeves back up?" I hold my arms up, like a sterilized surgeon waiting for gloves, hands milky with flour and water.

Seamus gently returns the cuffs to their place above my elbows. The wrinkles in his knuckles are also filled with dried dough. "Thanks. I have no idea what's out. What does Cecelia want to see?"

"She has a sleepover that night."

"Oh," I say, surprised, and then, "Oh," again, this syllable lower and longer and more informed.

"You don't have to," he says, words and tips of his ears red with my misunderstanding.

"No, I will." My response, nearly as quick as his, catches us both off guard. He stares at me, and in the seconds he's frozen, I turn my decision around and around, peering at it from every angle my mind can conceive. *I'm doing this because I feel put on the spot, because he's been here the past two weeks preparing bread and I owe him, because I want to shield him from his embarrassment, because I don't know how to decline.*

No. I agree because I want to. It is my choice.

"Are you sure?" he finally asks, and he thinks I'll change my mind.

I nod. "I haven't gone out in ages. It sounds like fun."

The frenetic energy always surging through him builds—I feel it in the room—and his smile grows so large the rest of his head nearly disappears into a crescent moon of teeth and beard. "I'd crow if Cecelia wasn't just through there," he says, and then the little girl is there, complaining there is no toilet paper in the bathroom and she waited and waited for Seamus to come find her to see what was taking so long, and when he didn't, she tiptoed to the towel dispenser and used the rough brown paper from there, but she didn't flush it because she knew, from experience, it can clog the pipes.

"And now I am grumpy," she says, yawning again.

"Like a big, hungry, sleepy bear," Seamus roars, first lifting his hands in the air, curling his fingers into claws, and then swiping them down around Cecelia, lifting her into his embrace and nuzzling her until her pout turns to giggles.

"Let me wash up and I'll see you out," I say, but he shakes his head and tells me not to bother, manages to pack Cecelia's book bag with one arm while holding her in his other, and they both say good night.

I finish preparation for tomorrow and set the buckets and bowls and utensils to soak so they'll be easier to wash in the morning. It isn't until the lights are off and the doors locked I realize I've been infected with Seamus's smile. There's also something else, something frail and small, the wings of a moth, a spider's web, something I don't want to examine too closely for fear it will disintegrate upon too much handling. Something a little bit bubbly inside, foaming up to fill long-time-empty spaces.

In the stairwell to my apartment, the mail is on the floor, pushed through the slot this afternoon. I gather it all. On top of the pile is a folded section of newspaper. The movie section, with the words U PICK scrawled in orange colored pencil.

Fourteen

Oma's stoneware crock of sourdough nestles between a jar of bread and butter pickles and a plastic bottle of mustard in the door of the refrigerator. My mother's own jar has been bumped to the back of the top shelf, behind the milk and an ancient cardboard bucket of chicken and unidentifiable leftovers in Saran Wrap–covered bowls, too close to the cooling unit, ice crystals sparkling on the surface. I ignore them for a month after her death, then six weeks. Then eight. But ignoring doesn't mean I forget about them; I only pretend I don't see them, the visual equivalent of jamming my pointer fingers in my ears and repeating *na-ni-na-ni-nana* over and over. Soon I have anxiety over opening the door at all. I eat only from the pantry and the cabinets, dry food, canned food, and then I won't go into the kitchen at all. I buy extra Fritos and bottles of Yoo-Hoo at school lunchtime and devour them in my bedroom at night.

There's life in those jars, sluggish and sleepy in a sort of cold-induced suspended animation. It only takes twenty minutes or so once a week to care for them, but it's twenty minutes of holding my hand directly in the flame of death—my mother's, grandmother's—and once I caught fire I'd want to be there with them too.

In my haze of sadness, though, I still feel the pulse of the starters throughout the house, throughout me, beating with my own heart, pleading to be spared. They've come half a century and an entire ocean too far to be dumped in the trash.

I take them to Jennie Rausenberg's house, to her mother, and ask her to love them for me. She understands and agrees.

Time passes. More weeks. More months. My father swathes himself in religion. I cover my thighs in bruises. We're losing each other. And *her*. She is all around us in her things, in the dust, and yet she's hemorrhaging from us because we don't know how to hold her in our memories without them growing into a tangle and strangling us, and we don't know how to tuck her aside without misplacing her forever.

I try to reclaim a fragment of her, in the sourdough starter. I am not ready to work with hers—it's too close. Too fragile. I will, instead, culture my own. I borrow a book from the library, read about capturing wild yeasts from the air. On the first sunny, dry day, I mix one cup of water and one cup of flour in a Mason jar, stirring until it's sludge. I find a window screen in the basement—it's spring but our storms are still in—and cut a square of black mesh from it, not caring my father will have to repair the hole. I wash the piece of screening in soap and water, dry it with a clean paper towel, and use a rubber band to fasten it over the mouth of the jar. Then I go into the backyard.

It's overgrown, the grass highest around the trees, beside the fence. The clothesline has fallen down at one end, the rusted metal pulley rotted from the dying birch at the far end of our property, the rope embedded in the mud, then rising from the ground and up to the house, screwed into the back porch. My mother stood there, hanging all our white clothes and linens because the sun works stronger than any chlorine bleach, and there's a cannonball in my chest—I swallow over and over but it stays lodged there, heavy because I know the clothesline won't be fixed and sheets will never flap on it again.

I'm out here for a purpose, though. I hold the jar out and spin, catching air inside it. I run through the weeds, hoping the disruption will kick up yeast. Then, out of breath, I sit on the ground with the jar between my knees, April soaking through my jeans, and wait for something to happen, too small for me to see.

My father doesn't come. He says he will see it at home, and I'm relieved. Xavier and Jude also aren't here, since their shift begins at three in the morning, though I suspect at least Xavier will watch. He doesn't sleep much anyway.

The *Gazette* provides popcorn and movie candy and cans of soda. Gretchen and Rebekah set the chairs in rows, pushing the tables to the back of the room. The crowd is more subdued than on taping day; people chat and pop open Pepsi, and when Gretchen flicks the lights, they scramble into their chairs. Five minutes until showtime.

"Where are you sitting?" Cecelia asks. She wears her pajamas and plush dog slippers.

"Up front, of course," Gretchen tells her.

"No, that's too close," I say, but I'm steered there anyway, to the first row, where I manage to avoid the center seat and take the one on the very end, closest to the kitchen door.

Cecelia sits next to me, jiggling back in the chair, shaking several kernels of popped corn loose from her bag. She tries to brush them under her chair with her feet, but they don't touch the ground. "I forgot a pillow."

"This is too exciting for pillows," Gretchen says, and plops down beside the girl.

I look for Seamus. He's still near the food table, talking with Pastor Ryan and a few other men. He sees me searching for him and nods, slips a soda into each massive cargo pant pocket, and weaves his way toward me. I thank him for the Sprite and he smiles, giving me two boxes of Sour Patch Kids as well, presenting them as a magician holds out his magic cards. "I know you like them."

Now I smile; he remembers what I ordered at the movies the other night. "Thanks." Is this what happens after one date? I get the sense I've somehow been claimed, and I think I might like it.

"All right, everyone," the *Gazette* reporter says, clapping his hands. "It's about that time."

The television bursts on, already tuned in to the Good Food Channel. A commercial for another show ends and then the unmistakable *Bake-Off with Jonathan Scott* theme plays, a James Bond-esque tune, as the screen fills with short clips of previous shows between flashes of Jonathan's too-handsome face. Seamus drags a chair from the row behind us and settles next to me. "So I can whisper to you and no one will hear me," he says.

"Shh," Gretchen says.

He likes to talk through movies, I learned last Saturday. And talk. And talk. Fortunately, the movie I chose—some period drama with high critical praise and no action—had very few people in it. Us, and a trio of women who claimed the seats in the middle of the theater and must have had dinner including ample adult beverages beforehand; their chatting and ill-timed laughter drowned out most of the picture's dialogue and anything Seamus had to say.

"This is *Bake-Off*," the TV Jonathan says. "We're traveling to the tiny city of Billingston, Vermont, to see if Wild Rise, a small artisan bread shop, has what it takes to impart big flavor and take me on in the battle of baguettes."

Music. Footage of Billingston. Everyone cheers as Gretchen comes on the screen, waiting tables, and customers talk into the camera about me, about the bakehouse, about the bread—everything is "delicious" and "fantastic," all the praise effusive. I wonder how much is sincere and how much is influenced by the blinking red light of modern video.

"Those sticky buns," the television Ginny Moren says. "Oh my. That's why my backside looks the way it does!"

The crowd laughs and turns toward the real Ginny, four rows behind me, who covers her wide, pink face in embarrassment. "Never speak truth with the cameras rolling," she says.

And then I'm there on the screen.

"The secrets of baking have, until relatively recently, always passed from mother to daughter. I was young, eight perhaps, when my own mother tied her apron around my waist and told me it was time for me to show her how much of what she taught me I remembered. It was time for me to make my first loaf without help or instruction. No recipes. Just my senses. And I did."

The photographs I gave Patrice Olsen float across our field of vision with my voice. "It was a squat loaf of wheat bread. A little too dense. A little too brown. But we ate it at supper that night, my father, mother, and I, with butter and salt, rewarmed in the oven. And my mother said to me, 'You're now a keeper of bread.' It was my rite of passage."

"Wow," Seamus sighs. He touches my hand, and for a moment I think he'll thread his fingers with mine, but he pulls back, reaching into his box of Raisinets. The candies rattle around before he manages to grab some and shove them in his mouth. That's one more thing I learned about him at the movies, he eats loudly and drinks loudly, and loudly clomps from dark theaters when making his way to the rest-room. I suppose I knew this already, but it's so much more amplified in a huge, dark room requiring—or strongly suggesting, at least—as much silence as possible.

"Shh," Gretchen says again. Cecelia cuddles against her ribs, beneath her arm, fighting to keep her eyes open.

"Hanging in there?" I ask.

The little girl nods. "How much longer?"

"About half an hour."

"I can make it, if I keep my feet going." Her legs swing like pendulums, and she bumps Gretchen's own leg over and over again.

"How about some more popcorn?" Seamus asks.

Cecelia nods and Gretchen shushes him again.

"It's a commercial," he says.

"Shh anyway."

Seamus scavenges for more treats, returning with Swedish Fish for Cecelia and another box of the sour, child-shaped gummies for me, despite the fact I haven't opened the previous two. He also gives his daughter a Sierra Mist, which he opens with a crack and fizz just as the show begins again. Gretchen glares at him.

"I know, I know," he tells her, handing the can to Cecelia. "Sorry, Ceese, all the popcorn is gone."

Cecelia slurps her drink and tears open the box of candy. "This is good."

On the television, Jonathan Scott lectures on baguettes, I demonstrate the stretch-and-fold method with my ciabatta dough, and fresh loaves are filmed coming out of the oven. And then on to the park, where people sample the bread and make their opinions known. Cecelia makes an appearance; smacking on my baguette crust, she announces, "Liesl's is the best bread ever. 'Specially her chocolate kind."

"That's me," the real Cecelia says, pointing, invigorated by her ten seconds of fame and all the sugar she's consumed.

The room cheers for her, and Seamus says, "You're famous."

"Don't you ever stop talking?" Gretchen wants to know.

"When he's sleeping," Cecelia says. "But then he snores, so it's kinda the same."

"You have me confused with someone else in this room," Seamus says. "Someone eating Swedish Fish and wearing purple pajamas."

"I don't snore."

"Like a vacuum cleaner." And he imitates a noisy, rattling sawing sound.

A chorus of "Shhs" descends on Seamus from around the room.

Another commercial, and then the judges are introduced, the bread is tasted, the images on the screen bouncing from comments about taste to our faces, Jonathan's and mine, reacting to the words of the judges. He was right, my scowl is broadcasted for the world to see. But other than that one look, the editing is kind to me. I seem well-spoken and knowledgeable and at ease in front of the camera. No odd facial contortions, thank you very much.

And then the winner is announced. It's still me.

The room comes to life with applause.

On the screen, Jonathan congratulates me. He says his closing lines and the entire park shouts, "Three, two, one, *Bake-Off*," as instructed by Patrice Olsen minutes prior to the final take. Actually, there had been three takes. The credits roll. Someone flicks on the lights, and we groan and rub at our eyes. The reporter turns off the TV, thanks everyone for coming, and reminds us of the article in tomorrow's paper, when he can finally, officially, announce my victory.

Viewers mill around. Those whose images were kept off the cutting room floor grin big, cheeks warm and shiny with pride, talking about how they should have said this, or their hair was too flat, or they had a bit of lint on their shirt. A few people ask Cecelia for her autograph, which makes her giggle and blush, but she does it, printing her name on a napkin, an empty popcorn bag, the back of a wrinkled receipt from Elise Braden's purse. Finally, Rebekah and Gretchen herd everyone out the front door and lock it. They help Seamus and me reset the tables and chairs as Cecelia spins through the room, propelled by candy and soda and her new status as television star. "She won't sleep," I tell Seamus.

"We're both playing hooky tomorrow," he says. "You should too."

I snort. "We are going to be overrun tomorrow."

"An even better reason not to be here."

"You'll have to take a rain check."

"Saturday night, then?"

The room stills, slows as Gretchen and Rebekah suddenly turn their heads toward us and wipe the tables with snail-paced strokes. I hesitate to answer, because of the audience, because this is private. And because I'm ashamed. Bitter honesty fills my mouth, a pre-nausea rush of spit and scandal. It's one thing to be seen by strangers twenty miles away in a near-empty theater, or in the bakehouse, busy making dough and chaperoned by a hawk-eyed seven-year-old. It's another to be *involved*.

Is this the kind of man with whom I want people to associate me? *Lord, forgive me.*

"I'm not sure," I tell him.

"Oh, okay," he says. He licks his teeth. "We can still come, you know, to help in the afternoon. With the prep. Like we have been. That's if you need us."

"Yes. Absolutely yes. I'd still really appreciate that."

"Well then, okay. We'll see you then."

Seamus zips Cecelia into her windbreaker and I pull the hood over her hair, giving the drawstrings a tug. "You think you're sweet after eating my chocolate bread? How about everything you had tonight? Make sure you brush your teeth super-duper well. TV stars can't have rotted smiles."

"That's from McDonald's. Mr. Scott said."

"I promise you, Swedish Fish will do the same." And then I bend down to her and kiss her forehead. Seamus watches with an expression of loss I recognize too well.

They go, as does Rebekah, whose father gives a soft knock on the front window before returning to the van. I take the dustpan from Gretchen and hold it as she sweeps into it corn kernels and flattened M&M's and dirt from Seamus's boots. "You're an idiot, you know that?" she says to me.

I shake the contents of the dustpan into the trash. "I'm starting to figure it out."

⌒

They are all convinced of the power of the host, this sacred bread, the Lord's own body. So convinced, it seems, that even the unblessed wafers, the "middle stage between the flour and the Sacrament," need to be guarded by the priests, the coin-sized breads he makes on a waffle iron (so no leaven will desecrate it) locked away from the people. Still, they disappear. The peasants want them for their animals. Was not the holy child warmed by oxen and sheep at his birth? Then these lowly creatures deserve a blessing from him as well. The wafers are mixed with hay and fed to the calves. Or taken to line the bottom of beehives, to make the honey sweeter.

The poor and devoted people are not the only ones who seek such magic. This is a religion of miracles. Bread becomes man becomes God. The blind see, the lame walk, men rise from the dead. The future is foretold. Magicians and witches—yes, they are very real in those dark, medieval times—want to harness the dominion of the host and use it for their benefit. Ancient cultures find sorcery in the bread, but it is celebrated. Those practicing divination and spell casting with the body of Christ in the church are put to death.

There are stories, though, of the wafer defending itself. It clings to the walls of the tabernacle so firmly the robber cannot steal it, and instead his fingers snap, bones grinding together as he runs away howling. Other times the moon-white disks escape from the thief's bag, scampering back to their church before anyone discovers they've been missing.

⌒

Three weeks pass since *Bake-Off* aired, and while business has lessened somewhat since those first few days, we're still overwhelmed.

Xavier suggests calling a meeting, so I do. He comes back to the bake-house after it closes—Jude home, asleep—and we sit, with Gretchen and Rebekah and Tee, to discuss some sort of workable plan.

I have no idea where to begin.

Gretchen, ever organized with her lists, reads off her first idea. She thinks the menu should be expanded.

"There is nothing wrong with my food," Tee snaps. She wears a scarf over her thinning hair, knotted at the back of her neck, long, bright tails of silk hanging to her waist.

"Your food is delicious. We all know it. But we need more of it."

"This is a bakehouse," I say, "not a restaurant."

"Yes, but different people are coming now. People from out of town. They come hungry. If you don't have something for them here, they'll go somewhere else to eat. It's money lost."

I shake my head. "It's too much for one person."

"We hire someone else, then."

I wait for the explosion, but Tee says simply, "Yes."

"What?" I say.

"You get me little helper cook. I teach them. They make what I say. All is happy-happy."

"Are you sure?"

Tee shrugs. "It is good."

Like a schoolgirl, Rebekah holds her hand up. "I could help Tee?"

"You mean, instead of waitressing?" I ask.

Rebekah nods. "I love to cook. I help my mother all the time, and I make supper for all of us at least twice a week. And we cook season-ally, like you do, because of the farm. I imagine I know more ways to use acorn squash than most."

I look at Tee. She jerks her head, once, a gavel descending. "I take the tall girl helper cook."

Gretchen makes a note. "All right, then. I'll get an ad in the papers for someone else to do the counter and tables. Unless you want to take care of it, Liesl."

"No. Please, just do it. What's next?"

"A baker," Xavier says.

"Zave."

"We need someone else, my dear. That's all there is to it."

"We do," Rebekah says. "We're selling out almost every day. There's nothing left to give away."

"We only donate because it's there," Gretchen says. "If it's all sold, that's even better."

"No. There needs to be bread for the ministry every day," I say. "Rebekah, pull and bag twenty loaves each morning when you come in. Mix it up, maybe two of each kind, or three of some, if there are more than others. Just use your discretion. If we have more at the end of the afternoon, we'll add it in."

"That's, like, five hundred dollars a week," Gretchen says.

"It's also what I want to do."

Tee slaps the tabletop. "She boss."

"Yeah, no kidding."

"What's next?"

Gretchen looks at her list again. "We need a—"

"—baker," Xavier interrupts. I roll my eyes and groan, but he continues, "Listen to me, Liesl. It's long overdue. You're running yourself into the ground trying to take up the slack. What time do you get out of here at night? Nine? Ten, now? And then you're back in the morning at five? You need to let some of it go.

"I know you have at least a dozen résumés, because I've read that many e-mails asking if the position is filled. Quite honestly, I don't want to deal with it. You need an office manager as well, since you avoid your messages like the plague."

"I can't afford to hire all these people."

"You hire the baker. Then Gretchen doesn't have to do dough

anymore. She can take care of mail, inquiries that come through the website, whatever phone calls you don't want to return, all of it, in the afternoons after the lunch rush and once the bakehouse closes."

I exchange looks with both of them. "You've already figured it all out."

Gretchen laughs. "Someone had to."

"Of course," Xavier says, winking at the waitress, "Gretchen will have increased responsibility now."

"Fine, you'll get a raise too." I pluck the skin of my eyelids, making a wet, suction sound. "The first of your new duties is to schedule baker interviews. No more than two in an afternoon, though. Okay?"

"Aye, aye, Captain." Gretchen salutes.

"Lovely. Anything else?"

"How much more can you handle before your brain implodes?"

"Not much. Go easy on me."

"Well, we should talk about mail order."

I think I've dissociated for a fraction of a second. Everything fuzzes over and goes grayscale, bad reception from pupil to optic nerve. I blink, as if clearing my vision will affect my ears. "You didn't just say what I think you did."

"People are asking."

"What people?"

Gretchen hops up in a chair and a blue folder appears; she's been sitting on it. She waves several sheets of paper at me and then flips through them. "Alabama, Florida, Montreal, New York—"

"If they're from New York they can just drive here."

"—Nevada, Ohio, need I go on?"

"I can't ship bread. The whole reason to buy it here is to get it fresh."

"You could have limited items for shipping. Like stollen at the holidays. You always say it tastes better a few days after it's baked. Or maybe just charge people for overnight delivery. If they want the bread, they'll pay it."

"Poilâne does mail order," Xavier adds.

I give him a look that says, *Don't even go there.* "I can't think about this now. Gretchen, find out what other bakeries do and we'll talk about it in a few days. Otherwise, unless someone is about to tell me there's a huge meteor about to crash into the earth and destroy all life as we know it, I think we're done here."

Everyone scatters—Tee to finish her soup, Gretchen to monitor the inbox, Rebekah around the corner to the public library. "My mom's picking me up there," she says, but I wonder if she doesn't want to be around here longer than necessary with me in such an irritable mood. She's traded T-shirts for sweaters and her flip-flops for leggings and clogs beneath her skirt, but there's a chill in the air so I ask, "Xavier's leaving now. Do you want him to give you a ride over? It's a bit cool."

"I milk cows at four in the morning in December," she says with a laugh and a wave as she pulls open the door. "This is nothing."

Xavier, however, hasn't budged from his chair. "You are leaving now, right?" I say.

"Liesl, sit."

"What's going on?"

More softly. "Sit."

I do. "Oh-kaaaay." When he says nothing, I shrug my entire body and face forward, urging some sort of communication from him. "Well?"

"Mail-order requests aren't the only inquiries you're getting."

"What else do people want? My firstborn?"

"Your business."

"I'm sorry. What?"

"You've had three offers to buy your business. Or at least to discuss the possibility of some sort of merger." He coughs. "One was from my very own flesh and blood."

"You mean your son? Jude's father? What's his name, Bill?"

"That's the one."

"I don't get it. Why?"

"It's business, my dear. You're a phenomenon right now."

"I'm small potatoes."

"Ah, yes. But therein lies the rub. You don't have to be. With the right marketing, the right capital, Wild Rise can go national easily."

"I have absolutely no desire for that. My goodness, Zave, that's like my worst nightmare."

"Bill doesn't know that. Neither do these other two companies. All they know is they want to be the ones to snatch you up and reap the rewards before you figure out how to do it for yourself, or someone else clues you into the fact."

"They know you're working for me. All of them."

"I'm sure they do."

I take in as much air as my lungs will hold, don't let it out until the world begins to tremble and darken around me. I lean my head back as far as it will go and my vertebrae crackle and I stare into the eggplant pipes above me. "Patrice Olsen said my life wouldn't change." My bent throat distorts my voice.

"She's not God."

I've never heard Xavier utter anything remotely religious, not that some generic phrase indicated a kind of faith. But it gives me pause, and I lift my head back onto my shoulders. It's not how he looks, spine-rod straight as always, burnished skin from his daily three-mile runs, one blue eye frosted with a developing cataract. He's healthier than I am, probably. But he radiates mortality today, as if he's been considering the inevitable, whether three years into the future, or thirty.

If I had a bit of Cecelia's missionary zeal, I might say something. Coming from a child, unwelcome personal insinuations—*What? You don't go to church? You need to!*—are forgivable and somewhat endearing. From the mouth of a grown woman with her own questionable commitment to all things Jesus, it's on the spectrum between laughable and offensive. Xavier will respond with a polite *Thanks, but no thanks*, forget I mentioned it, and our relationship will be undisturbed. I'll know I said something, though, the conversation more an indictment of me than him. I am the other son in the parable, the one who tells his father, "I will go," but doesn't.

Xavier peers into me now. "What?"

"Nothing. Just tired."

"I meant what I said before, Liesl. Enough is enough. You don't need to come in so early. Jude and I can take care of the first morning bakes. Sleep in. Go home at a decent hour and relax. And let that young man of yours dote on you more. It keeps us feeling useful." He winks.

I open my mouth to protest, but it's Xavier, and worthless, so I mumble, "He's not my young man."

"Oh, my dear. He's been yours since the first day he saw you, I'm certain of that. Him and the girl, both, if you'll have them." He reaches across the table and takes my hands in his. "There's nothing worse than waking up one day and realizing you're old and alone, and bound to stay that way."

I want to tell him he's not old, and neither of us is alone, but it's semantics, arguing for argument's sake, because I know exactly what he means. So I nod. He gives my fingers a squeeze and a shake, and then stands. "I think that's all the lecturing I have in me today."

"Wait," I say. "What about Bill? And the others?"

"Decline their offers. Politely, of course. It won't be the end of it, though. You'll get more."

I wrinkle my nose, puff my lips, and blow air through them until they buzz. "It's easy to say no to something you don't want. Anyway, I have an office manager to do that for me now."

Xavier's smile flickers on and off in an instant. "If I were only more like you twenty, thirty, forty years ago. I wasn't satisfied with small and perfect. I wish to God I had been. Then maybe I would be still baking, with my sons, in one small shop. Like this one. Instead of cringing each time I see some mass-produced Potter's loaf on the shelf in the Qwik-Mart. It was purely ego. I enjoyed too much the power I had to make something grow."

"I have just as much ego as you, Zave."

"You have passion. That's a whole different beast." He slips a tan corduroy newsboy hat on his bald head. "I suppose I should be thankful, though, if that's one of only two regrets I have in life."

"What's the other?"

"That I didn't tell my Annie I loved her every single hour of every single day."

"Stick to Your Buns" Sticky Buns

Makes 8 buns

LIESL'S NOTES:

This sticky bun recipe uses brioche dough, a highly enriched French bread that is more like cake. The phrase "Let them eat cake"—often attributed to Marie Antoinette but one she most likely never uttered—is a translation of the French "Qu'ils mangent de la brioche," that is, not cake as we think of it, but a rich bread full of butter, milk, and egg.

This recipe requires the dough be chilled in the refrigerator overnight.

If sticky buns aren't a favorite, try the variation for cinnamon rolls at the end of the recipe.

INGREDIENTS
FOR THE SPONGE:

5 grams (1 teaspoon) sugar

6 grams (1/4 cup) warm milk, whole if possible

8 grams (2 1/2 teaspoons) instant yeast

60 grams (1/2 cup) all-purpose flour, sifted

For the Dough:

1.5 grams (1/4 teaspoon) salt

40 grams (3 tablespoons) sugar

15 grams (1 tablespoon) warm (room temperature is fine), milk, whole if possible

3 large eggs

180 grams (1 1/2 cups) all-purpose flour, organic, if possible

170 grams (1 1/2 sticks or 3/4 cup unsalted butter, room temperature and cut into 1/2-inch slices

For the Glaze:

226 grams (2 sticks or 1 cup) unsalted butter

440 grams (2 cups) firmly packed light brown sugar

110 grams (1/3 cup) honey

120 grams (1/2 cup) water

1.5 grams (1/4 teaspoon) finely ground sea salt

100 grams (1 cup) pecan halves (optional)

For the Filling:

55 grams (1/4 cup) light brown sugar

50 grams (1/4 cup) granulated sugar

57 grams (1/4 cup) unsalted butter, melted

6 grams (1 1/2 teaspoons) ground cinnamon

60 grams (1/2 cup) pecan halves, toasted (optional)

Equipment:

small bowls

plastic wrap

stand mixer with dough hook and whisk attachment

large glass bowl

saucepan

whisk

bench scraper or chef's knife
9 x 13-inch baking dish

Do Ahead

To make the sponge, stir together sugar and milk in a small bowl. Sprinkle yeast over mixture and let stand until foamy, about 10 minutes. Stir flour into yeast mixture, forming a soft dough, and cut a deep X across top. Let the sponge rise, covered with plastic wrap, at room temperature for 1 hour.

To make the dough, combine salt, sugar, and hot milk in a small bowl and stir until salt and sugar are dissolved. Fit mixer with whisk attachment, then beat 2 eggs at medium-low speed until fluffy. Add sugar mixture and combine well. Add in order, beating after each addition: 60 grams (1/2 cup) flour, remaining egg, 60 grams (1/2 cup) flour, 1/4 of the butter, and remaining 60 grams (1/2 cup) flour. Beat mixture for 1 minute.

Add the sponge to the dough. Using a dough hook, mix at medium-high speed for 6 minutes, or until dough is smooth and elastic. Add remaining butter and mix for 1 more minute, or until the butter is incorporated.

Transfer dough to a greased bowl. Lightly dust the dough with flour to prevent a crust from forming. Cover bowl with plastic wrap and let the dough rise at room temperature until more than doubled in bulk, approximately 2 to 3 hours. Gently degas the dough, re-cover the bowl with plastic wrap, and chill for at least 12 hours.

On Baking Day

Preheat oven to 350 degrees Fahrenheit. If using pecans, spread them on a baking sheet. Bake, stirring once or twice, for 7 to 10 minutes and allow to cool.

In a medium saucepan, melt the butter over medium heat.

Whisk in the brown sugar and cook, stirring to combine. Remove from heat and whisk in the honey, water, and salt. Let cool for about 30 minutes, or until the mixture reaches room temperature.

Remove dough from the refrigerator. On a floured work surface, roll out the brioche into a rectangle about 12 x 16 inches and 1/4 inch thick.

In a small bowl, stir together the brown sugar, granulated sugar, cinnamon, and 1/3 of the pecans. Sprinkle the sugar mixture and 60 grams (1/2 cup) of the pecans (if using), evenly over the entire surface of the dough. Starting at one of the short sides of the rectangle, tightly roll the dough like a jelly roll. Trim off 1/4 inch from each end of the roll.

Use a bench scraper or a chef's knife to cut the roll into eight equal pieces, each about 11/2 inches wide. (At this point, the unbaked buns can be tightly wrapped in plastic wrap and frozen for up to 1 week. When ready to bake, thaw them, still wrapped, in the refrigerator overnight or at room temperature for 2 to 3 hours, then proceed as directed.)

Pour the glaze into a 9 x 13-inch baking dish, covering the bottom evenly. Sprinkle the remaining pecans evenly over the surface. Arrange the buns, evenly spaced, in the baking dish. Cover with plastic wrap and put in a warm spot to proof until the buns are touching and almost tripled in size, approximately 2 hours.

Preheat the oven to 350 degrees Fahrenheit. Bake until golden brown, about 35 to 45 minutes. Let cool in the baking dish for 20 to 30 minutes. One at a time, invert the buns onto a serving platter, spooning any extra sauce and pecans from the bottom of the dish over the top.

Cinnamon roll variation: Omit the pecans from the filling and do not make the sticky bun glaze. Instead, bake the rolls without any glaze. To make icing, use an electric mixer to beat together 56 grams (1/4 cup) cream cheese and 90 grams (7 tablespoons) butter until creamy. Add $1/2$ teaspoon pure vanilla extract 30 grams (2 tablespoons) heavy cream (milk or half-and-half may be substituted), and 1.5 grams ($1/4$ teaspoon) salt. Gradually beat in 180 grams ($11/2$ cups) powdered sugar until smooth and fluffy. Spread over the cinnamon rolls before serving, while still warm.

Fifteen

My wild yeasts need a warm place to grow, a womb, somewhere safe and hidden away where I don't have to explain them. I won't put the jar in my room; I don't know what things live in there. It's not been cleaned since my mother's death, the sheets unchanged, the dust thickening, downy like the hair appearing above my lip. I try to remove it with a lotion from the drugstore, one smelling of lavender and toilet bowl cleaner, and it burns until I wash it away, well short of the required five minutes. My skin is left raw; I can't talk or smile or brush my teeth. I suck mouthwash through a straw, swish and spit. I eat applesauce and cream soups, which require no chewing. Eventually the irritation heals, the deepest burns scabbing so it looks like I have a scaly, dark mustache instead of the nearly unnoticeable blond one from before. My mother would have broken one of the spidery tips from her aloe plant and coated the scab so it wouldn't scar. I use triple antibacterial ointment, the aloe plant shriveled from neglect.

In our old house of twists and quirks I find a place for my jar.

The vanity in our downstairs bathroom is over a heating duct, and the previous owner who built it from a clumsy mismatch of oak and pine added a decorative screen to one of the cabinet doors to allow the hot air to escape. But the drawers are unvented, and the lowest, smallest one—the size of a bread box—remains unused. I tuck a thermometer in there before I leave for school and read it when I arrive home. An ideal 82 degrees.

I line the drawer with a nest of kitchen towels and close my jar into its incubator. I feed twice a day, removing all but one-half cup of the culture, adding in equal parts fresh water and flour. Nothing happens for four days, other than the tiniest pockets of air along the glass, only four or five I see if I squint, which may or may not indicate life. By day five there are honest bubbles, and the mixture rises a little. By day nine the culture doubles in size.

It's ready.

I don't make bread with it. I'm not certain I ever will. And I don't store it in the refrigerator, not yet, because the book I read tells me I should continue the daily feeds for thirty days to establish the colony and the flavor. And because I want to be responsible for something, I keep this starter alive. Like a newborn, it's dependent upon me.

I'm its mother.

Then I find the empty drawer.

On day twenty-two, a Saturday, I pull the wooden knob and nothing's in there. The wood is shiny and smells of lemon. I run into the kitchen and notice the lid of the garbage pail askew. Inside are the towels, clotted with the yeast and flour mixture, and the jar.

You've seen it. My father. He's come up behind me. *I found it spilling out the bottom of the drawer. Was it an experiment for science class?*

I quietly hate him then, not because he threw the starter away, but because he doesn't know what it is. He lived with my mother for more than twenty years; I think of them as desperately in love, constantly connected through ears and eyes and heart. Now I wonder, did he never watch her bake her bread? He was so consumed with his springs and wrenches he was blind to what she loved most.

Yes. For science, I say, and I go back to bed.

Hiring a new waitress is easy. Ellie is twenty-two, an art major recently graduated from college, a Hobbit of a girl, round through the middle with a shock of green-streaked hair. She mixes patterns with her vintage clothes and wears wide, silver hoop earrings onto which she threads all manner of found objects—feathers and playing cards, candy bar wrappers and empty dental floss containers. "I don't sell many of my paintings," she says. "People don't get me." The customers like her, though; she's full of smiles and kind words for everyone.

The baker decision is more difficult. I analyze résumés and interview fourteen prospects. Like Goldilocks, I find fault with them for being too hard or too soft. Too pompous or too wan. Too eager. Not eager enough. I sit in church between Cecelia and Jude one Sunday and listen to the pastor read the beginning of Acts, where the apostles cast lots to replace Judas. The sermon has nothing to do with these couple of sentences, but they don't leave me, so I go home and write each baker candidate's name on a scrap of paper and toss them all into a paper lunch bag. Close my eyes and choose.

Kelvin Morse.

During our interview I call him Calvin. He corrects me, saying he's named for the Kelvin Scale, giving me some explanation about thermodynamics, absolute zero, and triple point—the single combination of pressure and temperature where liquid water, solid ice, and water vapor can coexist in a stable equilibrium. "That's zero point zero one degrees Celsius or two hundred seventy-three point sixteen Kelvin."

"Oh," I say.

"My folks didn't know that when they named me. They just liked the sound of it. Turned out to be some sort of prophecy, though. I'm a total science nerd."

"And you went to R.P.I.?"

"Chemical engineering."

"But you're not doing that now."

"No," he says. "The small firm I helped start went under about eight months ago. Still haven't found another job. I saw the ad in the paper and thought I could do this until something else came around. Just being straight with you. In college I worked nights in a family-owned bakery. They made mostly Italian bread, soft rolls, that kind of stuff. Nothing artisan like you. But I understand the chemistry behind it, figure baker's ratios and the like. I can handle what you're asking with this position."

So I hire him. Xavier thinks I'm insane, questioning why I didn't choose someone who would be around long-term. I can't tell him I pulled a name from a hat. I shrug instead and imitate Tee with a terrible Ukrainian accent. "I boss. I do what I do."

Kelvin proves to be capable with dough and uninterested in creativity. He follows my formulas to the last decimal. I'm pleased with his work. However, his hiring makes it unnecessary for Seamus to come and help me in the evenings. He still picks up Cecelia during the week, after he's finished the day's delivery route, but stays minutes instead of hours. We do go to lunch, the three of us and often Jude, after church—I now attend almost regularly—and Seamus and I have been out twice more, alone. I suppose I should think of those outings as dates, but I can't seem to manage it. Our relationship hovers somewhere between *friendship* and *more*. My protective instincts won't allow me to consider what that *more* might be.

All I know is I miss him when he's not around.

Cecelia and Seamus both have a day off, Columbus Day, and I invite them to the bakehouse for . . . well, for no reason in particular at all. They show up midafternoon while my hands are varnished with molasses and rye because I have it in my mind to tweak my mother's pumpernickel formulas. While I respect dark breads, I'm not a particular fan of eating them. I know I should offer the classic at least weekly, though, so I first find and then photocopy the pages in my mother's journals where she'd kept notes about her adventures in pumpernickel bread. She has three versions—one using the crumbs of stale rye bread, one with a hint of cocoa powder, and one featuring a commercial yeast booster—all of them with ingredients I want for my own version, and also with this and that I plan to eliminate.

"Eww, what is that?" Cecelia asks.

"Pumpernickel dough," I tell her.

"Does it have nickels in it?"

"Nope. It has caraway seeds and onions and coffee." I look at Seamus. "Actually, it sounds a lot like something you'd eat for breakfast."

"Ha, ha," he says, but I know he likes that I've taken the time to tease him. A role reversal. I'm the boy who ties a little girl's braids together when he has a crush on her. He's the girl telling all her friends the reason some guy *just has* to be interested, because he poked her in the ribs when she was taking her books from her locker and gave her an extra chocolate milk carton at lunch.

"It sounds so yucky," Cecelia said. "Who would come up with something like that?"

"Well, the Germans."

Suddenly, the screen door bangs shut and another voice speaks. "And have you told your young friend what the name literally means?" It's one I recognize and can't place, until I look up and see Jonathan Scott standing in my kitchen. Still, I can't speak. Apparently, neither can the others. Tee and Rebekah stop their chopping, and Seamus's winter beard—almost full, curling from cheekbones to mid-neck—doesn't hide the greenish cast that's come over him.

"Those Germans have quite the sense of humor," Jonathan continues. "*Nickel* is the word for sprite."

"What's that?" Cecelia asks.

"It's like a fairy, but one who makes great mischief."

"Oh."

"And *Pumpern* means . . . well, I'm afraid I'll have to whisper it in your ear."

And he bends down to Cecelia. His mouth moves, and she begins giggling, little snorts punctuating her laughter. "Really?"

"Yes, really," I manage, knowing full well what he's told her. Pumpern is the gas the bread tends to create in the intestines. I shake my head, wipe my hands on a towel. "What are you doing here?"

"Well, let me tell you," he says, and it's his television voice, the smooth, perfectly styled Jonathan Scott ready for crowd and camera. "I woke this morning and thought, It's a gorgeous autumn day. I think I'll get out of the city and drive somewhere I can see the leaves turning and buy some real maple sugar candy. Wouldn't Vermont be the perfect place to do so? And while I was driving, I remembered seeing an episode of some cooking show on the Good Food Channel about a little bakery in Billingston that has the best bread in the area, so I figured I'd stop in and see what all the fuss was about."

"I saw that show too," Cecelia says, oblivious to his joking. "I was even on it."

Jonathan snaps his fingers and points at her, flicking the end of her nose. "And you were amazing. Now, if only—"

"Tee," Gretchen calls, pushing through the kitchen door, staring down at the order pad in her hand. "There's a woman out there who wants to know if your soup has—" She sees Jonathan. "What are you doing here?"

"I'm not quite sure anymore," he tells her, "since everyone seems to be shocked and dismayed at my appearance."

"Maybe shocked, that's for sure." Gretchen tilts her head, a coy smile on her lips. "But never dismayed."

Tee taps her spoon against the rim of a pot. Loudly. "You have question for the customer?"

"Oh, yeah. Right. She wants to know if the lemon barley soup has any dairy in it. You know, milk, cream, butter."

"I know dairy," Tee snaps. "I milk the cows with these hands before you are born in the earth. I beat butter up and down. There is no sticks in box to buy in store, to make easiest for you. None. *Nixto.*" She says all this while making charade-like motions with her hands, squeezing and yanking invisible teats, churning invisible cream, chopping the air with each negative word.

Gretchen remains unfazed. "So, is there dairy or not?"

"Nei," Tee says, turning away.

"That's no," I say.

"I got that." Gretchen gives a wiggly-finger wave to Jonathan and, with exaggerated hip movement, leaves the kitchen.

"I'm afraid I didn't get to meet your . . . uh . . . charming cook the last time I was here," Jonathan says, and Tee shuffles pot lids with much clanging and growling.

I take a deep breath. "Jonathan, really. I *am* surprised to see you. But I'm assuming you must be here for a reason. So, can I help you with something?"

"Actually, I was hoping you had a little time to talk." He looks around at the others. "Privately."

Seamus's hands tighten.

"Okay, sure. We're closing soon anyway. How long do you think it will take?"

"Awhile."

I turn to Seamus, touch the back of his wrist; the sleeves of his work shirt are rolled and his hair is against my fingers. I have brushed his arm before, I must have, but in the heat of the crowded room and dying wood fire and Jonathan's presence, it feels bristly and untamed. "I guess, then, I'll see you two tomorrow, after school?"

He nods, and then leans in and kisses my cheek. "Call me later."

I stand there, stunned, my hand pressed to my face, the scraggy texture of his beard lingering on my skin. He's never kissed me. He's never told me to call him; I hear it as a command, somewhat casual but edged with possession. He's marking his territory.

He and Cecelia go, and I offer Jonathan a stool at the kitchen's proofing table. Jonathan says, "I was hoping for more privacy than that."

I glance at the clock on the wall. "We close in ten minutes. Then we can sit in the café area."

"Are all your employees gone at that point?"

"No."

"Maybe I should come back when they are."

"Well, Gretchen's the last to leave at five." I slip the elastic band from my hair, pluck out the barrettes keeping my unruly bangs in place. "We could go upstairs, I suppose."

"I'd appreciate that. I need to be back in the city for tomorrow, and the earlier I can leave, the better."

I open the kitchen door a crack. No customers in the bakehouse. Gretchen closes out the register and Ellie sweeps the floor. Jonathan follows me outside and up the stairs to the apartment. "Have a seat," I say, motioning to the kitchen table. "Can I get you something to drink? I can make coffee or tea. And there's water or orange juice."

"No, thank you, though."

Sitting across from him, I rub the backs of my hands over my thighs, crumbs of dried pumpernickel dough powdering my dark jeans. "I have to admit, you're making me nervous. I can't imagine why you'd be here, except maybe to tell me I don't get to keep the prize money. Though I suppose you'd have a lawyer call me for that."

"Liesl, relax." He laughs. "And there's nothing to be nervous about. I do have news, but it's the kind of news I thought best delivered in person. The network was very impressed with your episode." He squints at me. "You did watch it, didn't you?"

"Yeah."

"Oh, good. I wouldn't put it past you to skip it. What did you think?"

"Patrice was right about the editing. I didn't look like a complete imbecile."

"You looked fantastic. The camera loves you. I'm serious. You're a natural."

I snicker. "I don't need flattery. I would just like you to tell me what this is all about."

"It's not flattery and that is what it's all about. When I saw the show, I was really, really blown away. As were the powers that be. So I pitched an idea to them, and they loved it. Now it's up to you."

"What idea?"

Jonathan holds up his open palm and drags it through the air, as if highlighting his next words. "*Bread Without Boundaries*. You. Me. Traveling the world, finding the best bread, and teaching viewers how to make it."

"I don't get it."

"Your own show, Liesl. On the Good Food Channel. With me."

"You've lost your mind."

"Dead serious here. The network wants you. All you need to do is say yes."

"Jonathan, come on. Even if what you say is true, I have my bake-house. I can't leave it."

"No one is asking you to. The filming schedule would only be three months out of the year, with travel and some work back in the New York studios. There may be some other appearance obligations, but not many. You'd have eight months, at least, here at the bakery."

I shake my head. "I can't even consider this right now. I hardly believe you're telling the truth."

"I am," he says. "In a few days you'll get a package with all the details—contract, itinerary, information on the format of the show, salary, expectations—you name it. Take your time. Read through it all. Have someone look at everything with you. Talk to people. Whatever you need to do. My number will be in there too. You can call at any time."

"You really are serious."

"I am."

Settling back in my chair, I brush the rye dust from my legs. My pumpernickel dough waits for me, uncovered and half-kneaded downstairs. I wish my hands were in it now, my umbilicus to the familiar. "I don't know what to say."

"I know. Trust me."

"How long do I have to decide?"

"About eight weeks. We'll begin production in January in order for a September premiere." He stands. "So, unless you'll agree to grab a bite with me before I make the long trek back to the big, bad city, I'm on my way."

"I can't eat. I'm sorry."

"Understand." He offers me his hand, manicured, slim-fingered, much smaller than Seamus's, scalier than I remember. I shake it. "Hope to hear from you soon."

I don't move to show him out, and he doesn't expect it, leaving on his own. My stomach pitches; I wrap my arms low across my belly, taking hold of my hip bones and folding forward until my insides are too compressed to move on their own and the nausea passes. I straighten and the blood pours from my face back into the rest of me. This is what an hourglass feels like, all its sand dripping away and powerless to stop it. I can't stay here, though. There is bread to be made. Once in the kitchen again, they all look at me—Tee, Gretchen, Rebekah—but do not ask. I knead my dark rye dough and, counting each stroke, each turn, try to forget everything else.

Pumpernickel Onion Sourdough Bread

Makes one large or two smaller loaves

LIESL'S NOTES:

Baker's ratios can be confusing at times. In general, it is the ratio of liquid ingredients to flour. This recipe calls for a 100% hydration starter, which means there are equal parts water and flour. The starter on page 45 is a 100% hydration starter. If baking this recipe with a starter of an unknown ratio, the proper hydration can easily be obtained by taking 112 grams (approximately 1/2 cup by volume) of the "old" starter and mixing it with 225 grams of water (approximately 1 cup) and 225 grams of flour (approximately 2 cups). Using a mixture of wheat and rye flour will enhance the pumpernickel flavor. Continue feeding the starter every 12 hours until it doubles in size; with a healthy, active starter, this may only take one or two feedings.

INGREDIENTS:

220 grams (1 cup) hot black coffee (water can be used, if
   necessary)

18 grams (2 tablespoons) caraway seeds

240 grams (2 cups) pumpernickel flour (pumpernickel flour is
   coarse-ground rye meal containing the germ and bran; rye
   flour, organic if possible, may be substituted)

280 grams (1 1/3 cups) wild yeast starter, 100% hydration

60 grams (1/2 cup) chopped onions

18 grams (2 tablespoons) vegetable oil

12 grams (2 teaspoons) salt

85 grams (1/4 cup) dark, unsulphured molasses (buckwheat
   honey may be substituted, or any honey if necessary)

120 grams (1 cup) whole wheat flour, organic if possible

360 to 480 grams (3 to 4 cups) divided, bread flour or all-
purpose flour, organic if possible

60 grams (1/4 cup) water

EQUIPMENT:

kitchen scale (optional but recommended)

2 large glass or ceramic mixing bowls

wooden spoon

plastic wrap or clean kitchen towel

stand mixer with paddle attachment and dough hook (optional)

olive oil

parchment paper

proofing basket (also known as a banneton or brotform,
optional)

baking or pizza stone

broiler pan

serrated knife or baker's lame

baking thermometer (optional)

DO AHEAD

To prepare the sponge, pour the hot coffee over the caraway seeds.
Allow the seeds to soak while the coffee cools. Once the coffee is
room temperature, add the pumpernickel flour, wild yeast starter,
and onions. Stir until well combined. Cover the bowl with plastic
wrap and allow the sponge to ferment for at least 5 hours, or overnight. The longer it stands, the more "sour" the bread will taste.

ON BAKING DAY

To make the dough, stir the oil, salt, and molasses into the
sponge. Stir in the flour 1/2 cup at a time until the dough is a
consistency that can be kneaded (about 360 to 420 grams, or
3 to 31/2 cups), then allow the dough to stand for 20 minutes.

Turn it out onto a lightly floured surface and knead for 5 minutes, adding only enough more flour or water to keep it from being too sticky. A dough with rye flour will never lose its tacky feel; knead it until pieces of dough no longer adhere to your hands once you remove them. If using a stand mixer, combine all the ingredients using a paddle attachment, adding the flour 1/2 cup at a time, until a shaggy ball has formed. Switch to a dough hook and mix for 4 to 5 minutes on low speed, adding more flour if the dough seems too wet, or a little water if all the flour is not incorporated.

Lightly grease a ceramic or glass bowl with oil. Place the dough in the bowl and cover with plastic wrap. Allow the dough to rise until it is 1 1/2 times its origanal size, approximately 2 to 4 hours.

Gently shape the dough into one large or two smaller freeform boules, and place them on a sheet of parchment paper sprinkled with pumpernickel flour. Or shape the dough into loaves and place in a large 10 x 5-inch bread pan or two 8 1/2 x 4 1/2-inch pans. A brotform may also be used. Cover the loaves with a damp kitchen towel or lightly oiled plastic wrap. Let rise again until 1 1/2 times its original size, approximately 1 1/2 to 2 hours.

Preheat the oven to 375 degrees Fahrenheit with the baking stone on the middle shelf and broiler pan on the bottom shelf (if the bread is being baked in loaf pans, there is no need for a baking stone). Transfer the loaves to the oven. The free-form boules can be kept on the parchment paper and set on the baking stone. If using a proofing basket, turn the dough out of the basket directly onto the stone. Score the dough with a serrated knife or baker's lame. Add 1 cup of water to the broiler pan and close the oven door. Bake for approximately 35 to 45 minutes, or until the bread reaches an internal temperature of 195 degrees Fahrenheit. If using loaf pans, remove the bread from them. Allow all loaves to cool for at least an hour before slicing.

❦

The next afternoon Cecelia doesn't get off the bus. I hear the familiar rumble, wait for the trailing song of the breaks and a flash of yellow-orange through the window. But the bus doesn't slow; it's already turning the corner by the time I'm standing on the sidewalk, calling, "Wait," and waving both arms above my head.

Back inside, I shuffle through phone numbers and find Seamus's, calling his cellular phone first. Four rings and then voice mail. "Could you call me as soon as you get this message? It's about Cecelia. And important." I try the home number, but there's no answer there either. I don't leave a message when the machine clicks on.

"What's wrong?" Gretchen asks. "You look like you've seen a ghost."

"Cecelia wasn't on the bus."

"Did you call Seamus?"

I nod. "He didn't pick up."

"Call the school."

I find that number in the phone book. The receptionist tells me Seamus picked up Cecelia at dismissal.

"Thank God," I say, the adrenaline diffusing from the center of my body, spreading to my limbs, pooling in my fingers and toes. I curl my feet inside my shoes, repeatedly open and close my hands. I've never panicked like this before. It's the terror of mothers in department stores and amusement parks, when they turn and find their child gone, every kind of nightmare scenario in their heads before they discover the girl hidden between the dresses on a clothing rack, or the boy staring at a game in the arcade he's already been told he can't play. *Maternal* is not a word I've ever used to describe myself—nor anyone else—but Cecelia has managed to become more than a kid I watch after school. I know this already, but admitting things . . . not something I do well.

The phone rings. It's Seamus. "I have her."

"I know. I talked to the school." The fear shifts to anger. "Why didn't you tell me she wasn't coming today?"

"I texted Jude this morning and asked him to let you know."

"He's seventeen. Of course he's not going to remember."

A pause. "I'm sorry," Seamus says.

"Yeah. Okay. I was just worried." I take a deep breath too. "So, I'll see her tomorrow."

Another silence, this one long enough to have me shifting the receiver from one ear to another, something to do to fill the awkwardness between us. Finally, he says, "I think we might have intruded on you long enough." He's pulling away and taking Cecelia with him.

I haven't the energy to argue, all rinsed out of me from the bus incident. And the anger creeps back in. He's doing this because of yesterday, because Jonathan Scott showed up here.

He's sulking.

"Fine, then," I say. "Maybe I'll see you Sunday at church."

It's not fine, though. I hang up and emptiness mingles with the anger. I want Cecelia here. She's come to belong to this odd, growing Wild Rise family of immigrants, high school dropouts, nerdy engineers, flighty artists, fundamentalist farm girls, and everyone else. Seamus too, if I'm honest. I miss both of them.

I clang and clatter about the kitchen nearly as loud as Tee, and the staff avoids me as I sidestep the looks they shoot one another from various corners of the room. It's another layer of tension added to the day; no one has come out and directly asked about Jonathan's visit, but it's been whispered about enough, and both Xavier and Jude knew about it when I came in this morning. "You had a visitor yesterday," Xavier said, and when I didn't respond, he asked, "Care to talk about it?"

I shook my head. "Not yet."

And I couldn't. Can't. Because I haven't the slightest idea where I stand in the midst of it all.

It's not the show that has ensnared me. I don't want to be on television. I want the things the show allows—the travel, the interaction with other lovers of bread, a chance to help people appreciate something simultaneously a simple staple of life for so many in the world and yet so intricate in its history, its science, its art. I think of Xavier's words, of ego, passion—and if the difference between the two is as distinct as he seems to believe. No. They are parent and child, one birthed from the other, a chicken-and-egg scenario and it doesn't matter which comes first. I already have Paris and Germany, my *Bake-Off* winnings tucked away for my trip, the one I plan to take in the unhurried weeks of February next year. Now it's not enough with the world dangling before me.

Finally, I'm alone in the kitchen, Tee and Rebekah and Gretchen gone home for the night. I feed my starters and mix three batches of dough I'd rather Kelvin not touch, and think about how much more *full* I feel when Seamus comes to help. I wash my hands and, picking up the phone, scroll through the previously dialed numbers until I find his. I don't call yet, wanting to wait until Cecelia is in bed. Instead, I take the phone upstairs with me and try to keep busy. A shower. A load of laundry. Some time paging through old cookbooks I've collected over the years, mostly at rummage sales or used-book stores. A few minutes of some banal movie. As soon as the microwave reads nine, I take the phone into the bedroom and close the door. "It's me," I say when he answers. "Do you have a minute?"

"Okay." He sounds tired and cautious. Water runs in the background; he washes the dishes after Cecelia falls asleep.

"Jonathan Scott came yesterday to offer me a cooking show."

"Like, a real one on that food channel?"

"Yes."

I hear him turn off the faucet. "What did you say?"

"Nothing yet. I'm still in shock."

"What's Xavier think about it?"

"He doesn't know. No one does." I hesitate. "Except you, now."

"Oh," he says, and the single syllable echoes with every uncertainty both he and I have in regard to each other. Seamus is braver than I am, though. He recognizes I've reached out to him, and while he doesn't understand why—I'm not certain I do either—he's willing to be the one to expose his heart first. "I'm here, whatever you decide."

"I know," I say.

The line, the miles, between us bloat with silence. We're both so unsure of it all, clumsy with our emotions. He's been torn apart by a divorce and has a child to protect. I'm still nursing the wounds of a twelve-year-old who found her mother dead in the garage. "Then I guess I'll let you go," Seamus says. "You have to get up way before I do."

"Wait. Will I see Cecelia after school again?"

"I don't know, Liesl. I don't want you to feel obligated to have her there."

"I don't. Really. I'll miss her if she doesn't come." I swallow. "I'll miss you, if I don't see you when you pick her up."

"Well, when you put it like that," he says, each of his words dressed in a grin, "I guess we'll both see you tomorrow."

That wasn't so hard, I think as I turn off the phone. Not hard at all.

Sixteen

We're two magnets of the same pole, my father and I, an invisible force keeping us apart. That force is his God, an ever-increasing intrusion in our lives. He goes to the church two, sometimes three or four days a week. He hums. He reads thick, gilded-edged books in the living room, under the floor lamp, multicolored highlighters on the arm of the sofa. He tries to love me better, probing all those places I used to let him into, asking about schoolwork, friends, activities.

I want none of it. He's allowing his God to replace my mother. *It hurts less*, he says over the phone; now I don't listen at the closed door of the library but hold down the mute button and pick up the receiver in my bedroom. *It's getting better.*

Not for me. I forget how to function without pain. When any moment of confusion comes, of anxiety or stress, I find the hairbrush. The leg beatings increase from once every week or two, to almost every day, sometimes twice a day. I buy a brush with a larger, flatter head and carry it with me in a purse I buy for it. I bring it to school and wait until all the girls leave the bathroom before slapping my thighs. The bruises puddle there, purple, blue, brown, green, speckled red—the colors of grapes and dried berries and wine—a large stain on each leg spreading from groin to five inches above my knee. I draw a line there, in black Sharpie, retracing every several days. My barbed wire fence, keeping the damage contained, the bruising from dripping low enough for someone else to see.

In gym class I wear bicycle shorts beneath my Umbros, the Spandex a second skin, tight and long enough to keep my self-inflicted injuries concealed even as I run the field. I'm not the only girl to make such a fashion statement, and no one pays attention to me. Most of my friends have drifted away months ago. I understand. I have the tinge of death all over me while the adolescents charging through the halls of the high school have yet to experience more trouble than forgetting their lunch money, or getting detention two afternoons in a row, or painful menstrual cramps. Their mothers never told them of grief, and they step over the pieces tumbling from my body; I can't collect them quickly enough to keep me whole.

The gym teacher wants me to collect the cones and flags. I do, carrying them inside with a cardboard box of mesh blue and gold pinnies. She'll give me a pass if I'm late, and I will be, lingering in the equipment room until I know the locker area is clear. The pass isn't necessary, though—I've become one of the forgotten things, an unmatched sock crammed in the back of the drawer, a candy wrapper on the sidewalk. Something no one notices until it's the only pair of socks that matches a suit worn once a year, or until the wrapper sticks to the bottom of someone's shoe and he's forced to peel it away and throw it in the trash. The teachers pay me no mind until grades are due, or the guidance counselor asks how I'm doing in their classes. And I do well enough to keep from drawing attention, camouflaged in the safety of the mean.

Or so I think.

As I change from my gym clothes, I hear the locker room door open and she's watching me, Sara Kempf, cheerleader, honor student, and the most popular girl in school. We've not exchanged more than a mouthful of words since the beginning of the year. I'm wearing my blouse but haven't removed the bike shorts yet. I don't know what else to do but stare back.

It's smart, to use your legs, she says.

I don't know what you're talking about, I tell her, but my entire body ignites beneath her scrutiny.

She wears her cheer uniform, complete with a Spandex undergarment beneath the skirt, not nearly as long as the shorts I wear. Carefully, she stretches the elastic hem of the shorts and lifts, exposing a slender, irritated line. A healing cut, shimmering with ointment. *I got caught because I did it on my arms at first.*

I don't cut.

You do something.

I hesitate, and then remove my own shorts.

Sara doesn't react, other than to press her perfect lips together. *I talk to someone now.*

A shrink.

It helps.

I see that, I say, jerking my head toward the scratch on her own thigh.

I hardly need to do it anymore.

Thanks for the PSA.

Nodding, she readjusts her uniform. *You can find me around,* she says, *if you want to,* and spins to leave, her body with the control of a gymnast, the control of someone who can slide a razor blade across her own flesh and draw blood.

In three long steps I'm peering around the end of the locker wall, the bottom half of my body hidden again from her. *Wait. How did you know?*

She turns toward me, a Mona Lisa of a smile appearing and

disappearing as quickly as the shrug of her shoulders, and, pulling the handle of the door, she leaves.

∽

We have dinner together at Wild Rise, the three of us, and I cook. Seamus offers, but I admit I fear what he'll serve. Cecelia tells me it's often boxed Kraft macaroni and cheese or hot dogs. Seamus insists he can whip up food to rival Jonathan Scott, and when I look at him with something well beyond disbelief, he reminds me of the fiber tour and his spinning. "I am a man of many hidden talents. They're just wasted on a six-year-old."

"Daddy, I'm seven now."

I don't cook well either, but don't tell him that. The bakehouse always has homemade tomato sauce around for its pizza days, a thick, roasted flavor instilled by the more than twelve hours of slow simmering upon which Tee insists. Cecelia's new favorite food is *farfalle*, which she tells us tastes much better than plain ol' spaghetti because "it just does." And it's cuter than spaghetti too. So I boil two boxes of semolina bows, planning to send her home with plenty of leftovers.

Cecelia sets out plates and glasses; we're eating in the kitchen, on stools, around the proofing table. I drain the pasta and add sauce. Seamus pesters me to let him help; I give him a knife and direct him to the cooling garlic bread. He slices it with precision, each piece appearing, to the naked eye, exactly the same size. He layers them in a linen-lined basket.

"Show-off," I say.

"I told you."

My mother was skilled in hospitality, reveling in the details of pretty printed napkins and slices of lemon in a glass of water, and those finishing touches of ribbon and cocoa powder few think of but all see and recognize as special. I can't be bothered to get caught up in those things. Throw the still-warm pot of food on the table—I will remember a trivet so the wood isn't scorched—and let everyone serve themselves. But I won't be outdone by Seamus. I spoon the farfalle into a ceramic bowl, grate on fresh parmesan, and tuck a sprig of Tee's parsley on top.

"Ooh, pretty," Cecelia says.

Seamus rolls his eyes.

"Let's eat," I tell them both.

Cecelia asks the blessing and Seamus serves her food. She asks for more, but he tells her to finish the mountain of pasta he's given her first and have some salad.

"I only like the cucumbers and tomatoes, and there aren't any," she complains. "Lettuce makes me choke."

"I can slice some cucumber for you," I say. "Skin or no skin?"

"No skin."

"Let Liesl eat," Seamus says, but I'm up already, digging a cucumber from the crisper and then looking through Tee's drawers for a peeler. I try not to disturb anything, but will hear it on Monday, I know. "Ta-da," I say, presenting a dish of pale green rounds.

"Thank you," Cecelia says.

"You are more than welcome."

We listen to Cecelia chatter about first grade, how she likes it so much better than kindergarten because they don't have to take naps anymore, and she hates to take naps at school—the floor is always cold, even through her mat, and if she's the one on the end next to the bookcase, she wakes up with gray balls of fuzz in her hair because the bottom of her ponytail likes to sneak under the shelf while she's sleeping.

"Your hair," I say.

She nods, looking at me with round, serious eyes. "Sometimes it has a mind of its own."

I shift on the stool, keeping my legs crossed, awkward in the new skirt I wear, one of three I bought last week when Seamus mentioned having dinner. All women eventually care about how they look, don't they? I tell myself I'm a late bloomer.

"So," Seamus says. He swallows almost his entire glass of iced tea. "Anything . . . new?"

He wants to know if I've decided about Jonathan Scott's offer. I shake my head, because I haven't. The only other person I've told is Xavier. When the large FedEx envelope came, I simply handed it to him and asked him to look through it. The next morning he motioned me out to the back delivery area with his eyes and, once I was with him, asked me if I was seriously considering doing the show.

"Considering? I guess I am. I don't know how seriously, though." I didn't tell him that his own words taunt me, the ones he spoke on regret and ego and wanting more. A television show is the most *more* I could imagine. "Would you do it?"

"In an instant," he said.

"That doesn't help me."

"Are you looking for a reason to say no?"

"I'm looking for someone else to give me one."

Xavier clucked his tongue. "You won't find it here."

I don't want to want the show; that's my problem. I want to believe I'm above such things, that Wild Rise is enough for me. Seamus tells me to pray about it, and I try, but either I fall asleep while doing so or I stare at the darkened ceiling in my bedroom, hearing all manner of answers in my head, unsure if any are from God.

I poke at my noodles. Seamus stabs his; they fall from his fork and he uses his fingers to push them on again. Cecelia waves her spoon at him. "It's easier like this," she says.

"Real men don't use spoons. Except for cereal. And ice cream," he tells her.

The phone rings. After hours I will let the machine deal with it, but I'm thankful for the distraction. I reach over and snatch it from the cradle. "Hello, Wild Rise."

"Hi, yes. I'm looking for Liesl McNamara." A woman's voice.

"This is she."

There's silence.

"Hello?" I ask.

"I'm sorry. I just can't believe I'm talking to you. We saw you on television and we—oh, you don't need to hear any of—"

"Who is this?"

"My name is Dana. Dana Preston. My mom thought it would be easier if I, well . . . if I did the calling. Oh, I don't know now. She's here. I'm going to get her to come to the phone—"

"I'm sorry, Dana. I'm in the middle of dinner now. Would it be okay if—"

"You're my sister," the woman blurts.

I blink. "Excuse me?"

"Well, half sister. We share a mother."

I laugh, a part-nervous, part-annoyed titter. "That's not possible." Seamus looks at me, brows low. Shakes his head slightly and mouths, *What's going on?* I wave him off. "My mother didn't have any other children."

"Not Claudia McNamara." She says it the American way—*claw, claw, Clawdia*—and images of my mother's funeral assault me. The broken trough on the floor. My broken father on the floor. Something, though, worms even deeper. "Mary Preston. My mother. Your biological mother. She was Mary Lombardi then."

"Look, I don't know what kind of—" I am saying words, but the woman on the other end of the line is talking over me, things about dates and towns and being too young, and will I wait a minute because some other person wants to say something but can't because she's crying, there's too much crying, and finally I can't take the roar anymore. My head is filled with sand crabs and burial urns and the crashing of the waves against my skinny seven-year-old legs.

I hang up.

"Liesl?" Seamus is on his feet, at my elbow. I blink, waver. He steadies me. "What's going on?"

Laugh it off. Say it was a wrong number. A prank. Sit down. Finish dinner. Ignore. Bury. Let the waves come in and sweep it all away. I can't follow any of my brain's commands, however. For the first time in years I want a hairbrush and a locked bathroom, and five minutes to beat my thighs until my skin splits.

"Liesl?" he asks again.

"Just go."

Cecelia hunches beneath her sweatshirt. She's pulled the hood up and sucks the ends of the drawstring. Her hair, French braided today, won't reach her mouth. She whimpers a little.

"No, I'll go," I say, shaking Seamus from my arm and finding my way upstairs to the apartment, my entire body a pulsing mass of heat and thundering blood. *You look like your father's Aunt Elinor,* they told me. They showed me photos. They wiped globs of green mucus from my toddler nose, stayed up all night with me during my second-grade bout with chicken pox, fed me, clothed me. Loved me. My father taught me to drive. My mother taught me bread.

I'm in the bathroom, the hairbrush on the counter. The three-day stubble on my legs stands upright with anticipation. I look in the mirror, face pale except for two rouge-red circles on each cheek—no, deeper than red. Purple, in that bloody, recently butchered meat way. *If your right eye offends you.* Taking the brush in both hands, I position it over the edge of the vanity, bristles scratching the Formica as I press down with one hand on that side, with the other hand on the handle until it snaps off.

I fling both parts into the shower.

There's a story in the Grimm Brothers' *German Tales* about a poor widow whose only child dies, and it grieves the woman more than anything that this child has no shoes. Her beloved cannot be buried barefooted, so she bakes shoes of bread and puts them on the child's feet, and the coffin is lowered into the ground. But the child will not rest, appearing again and again to its mother in anguish, and this continues until the townspeople dig the coffin from the earth and replace the shoes of bread with shoes of leather.

This is *bread sin*. Giving loaves to the dead is an honor. Placing it on their feet is a horror, for now they must walk upon the sacred food for eternity.

And more stories are told. A woman is turned to stone for rubbing bread on her son's clothes. Cities sink into the sea because the people who live there use bread to block rats from leaving their holes. Even Shakespeare, in his *Hamlet*, writes of a baker's daughter who, after refusing bread to the Savior, is transformed into an owl. These fables infiltrate the world over, told and retold, heightening the importance of bread to levels reserved for God himself. In Germany, the bakers won't turn their backs to an oven, as it's disrespectful. Loaves are not to be laid on a table without cloth or cover, so the "friend of man will not have a hard bed." Even today, in some cultures, bread dropped on the floor is quickly retrieved and kissed, a holy apology.

I get in the car and drive home.

Do people ever stop thinking of their childhood houses, cities, towns as home? I've lived away from Sutter's Point nearly as long as I lived in it, and still it's where I'm going now to seek out answers and comfort. I can phone my father, but my interrogation is a face-to-face one. My mother is still in that house too. I want both of them there.

Tomorrow's Sunday. I don't have to worry about preparing dough or opening the bakery. I put the mess in the kitchen out of my mind. Seamus probably will take care of it anyway. He'll be worried, looking for me tonight, in the morning. I tell myself I owe him nothing, no explanations, no courtesy calls, no excuses, really. The coolness of my internal protests unsettles me. I thought I'd been making progress in the relationship arena.

The sun sinks behind the mountains as I drive, a cling peach stewed in its own juices, the horizon saturated with cool orange light. I scan through the FM stations. The radio doesn't block my thoughts. I make conversation in my head, practice posing difficult questions to my father. My mother too. I think over the inches of my life, feeling through the pockets and zippers and lint-caked corners, trying to recall some hint of—*anything*—indicating I am not their biological child.

Nothing.

In first grade, Deena Howard told everyone she'd been adopted. She'd known for, well, as long as she had the ability to know things. Her parents didn't keep it a secret from her; as a small child, the story of her origins was a favorite bedtime tale. Her mother drew pictures and wrote a poem about it and stapled the pages together, and they would read it together before the good-night kiss and lights-out song. Deena brought the handmade storybook in for show-and-tell, and when I came home from school, I slurped down my mother's chicken noodle soup and told her, "Deena Howard got adopted. That means her mommy and daddy bought her as a baby." I have no memory of the conversation beyond that, if my mother corrected my inaccurate definition or if she said anything at all. I only remember the soup, not too hot, the chicken shredded into toothpick-sized strips, the potatoes nice and mushy, and little, slick oil bubbles bobbing over the surface. I didn't look at her when I told her; I was trying to keep the carrots off my spoon.

Another friend, in high school, confided in me about her adoption. Her parents revealed it to her only days before, when she turned sixteen. Of all the emotions she felt and was still feeling, surprise wasn't one of them. "I never fit," she said. "I never truly felt a part of them."

I have no feelings like that. I always seemed the perfect-sized puzzle piece, like the baby Jesus hand-carved and balanced in Mary's arms in my grandmother's antique German crèche. She would wiggle him out *just so* in order for me to hold him, and then when I finished turning his tiny, crazed body over in my hands, she gently maneuvered him back into place, so firmly in the virgin's grasp that not even my knocking the figures off the side table shook him loose.

Still, I have no doubt the words of the woman on the phone are true. As I drive, it's this certainty with which I wrestle. Why do I believe it? Why don't I discount the woman as a hoaxer or a loon and simply put the conversation away, into a place I'll never visit again? I pull into the driveway of my childhood home, the answer settled. I know because Truth recognizes truth.

I haven't been here to visit in three years, not since Wild Rise opened, despite living only two hours away. The front door is unlocked; I go inside and am struck by how little has changed over the years. The couch. The mat in the entryway. A soap dispenser on the kitchen sink. A telephone. The television. Otherwise, it's the same as the day my mother died.

"Dad?"

He doesn't answer. I open the basement door, the light on down there, and descend to my father's workshop, to a room that's really not more than a cellar, with an uneven stone floor and damp walls, and beams sticky with cobwebs above. He's standing at his bench—always stands when he tinkers—unscrewing some small part from some bigger one, bug-eyed safety glasses across his face. "Dad," I say again.

Looking up, Alistair wipes his thumbs across the goggles and then simply snaps them off his head, knocking his prescription lenses from his nose. He fumbles to reclaim those before they fall to the floor, and he does, catching them against his shirt before tucking them back onto his face. "Liesl. Did I forget you were coming?"

"No."

"Then why are you here? Not that you're not welcome any—"

"Who is Mary Lombardo?"

"Lombardi." He sets down his screwdriver. "It's Lombardi."

He takes off his glasses again, huffs on them. Wipes them on the hem of his shirt. Sighs. "Mary Lombardi."

"Yeah."

"We should go upstairs." And then, as if he's decided he has no right to ask anything of me, he adds, "Please?"

I nod, wait to follow him. In the kitchen, he motions to a chair and I sit. "Your mother would make that tea of hers. In the milk."

"With honey," I say.

"And bread. Always, always bread."

"Sometimes she made muffins."

"I suppose you're right." He takes two white teacups from the cabinet beside the refrigerator, each ringed with brown stains. "You'll have to settle for scorched coffee. I did brew it this morning, though. Not yesterday."

"It's fine, Dad."

He pours the black liquid into the cups; they rattle in the saucers as he carries them and slides them both in front of me. I move one across the table as he brings a carton of milk and the sugar bowl. "I'm out of half-and-half." He sits, opens the carton, and sniffs. Wrinkles his nose. Turns the container and checks the date. "I'm not sure this is good still."

"Just sugar is fine." I add a teaspoon. He adds three and then splashes the suspect milk into his cup anyway. He stirs the coffee, spoon chattering against the porcelain. Sips.

"We never meant to keep it from you."

I wait. His glasses come off again and he rubs his eyes until they redden. "How did you . . . I mean, what—"

"I got a call today from . . . a woman who said she was my half sister. I didn't get everything she was saying. It was kind of a . . . shock and I, well, I hung up on her."

"She saw you on television?"

"Yes. I think so. How did you—"

"You look so much like her. Mary, I mean."

"You know her, then."

He grabs the skin of his cheek and pulls at it absently, releases and repeats, making a wet, sucking sound. "Where to start."

"The beginning?"

He sighs again. "Your mother loved you more than anything, you know? She loved you so much, even before she knew you, that she wouldn't do anything to harm you. And that meant, to her, giving birth to you. She wouldn't allow even the possibility her . . . illness would be passed on to her child.

"We were married, oh, eighteen months or so when it started. The sadness. The odd behavior. I didn't know who I was living with, this stranger who sometimes went days without leaving the bedroom closet, or days without coming home. I was ready to give up on her, and then she . . . well, she bought bottles of pills from the pharmacy and took them all. Someone found her in a movie theater, unconscious, and called for an ambulance. It was in the hospital they gave it a name. Manic depression.

"It took another couple of years to truly get her back to being my Claudia. By then she wanted a child, and so did I, but we waited. We wanted to be certain she was truly stable. So nearly ten years after we were married we adopted you."

My father—yes, still my father; I won't let my world tilt so far as to shake him from this position yet—swallows some more coffee. I take a sip too, and it's like drinking sweetened smoke, the taste in my mouth that comes when I smell a wood burning stove on a frigid day.

"Things were different when you were born. Now, people get married all the time and don't have kids. Then it was assumed we were trying and couldn't get pregnant, and we let everyone believe that. Your mother's doctor had no problem deeming us infertile after ten years of marriage and no babies. We used that on the adoption application. We also, for wrong or right, didn't disclose Claudia's condition. We were afraid no woman would give her baby to a couple with such a family secret.

"It didn't take long for the call to come. A young woman picked us to adopt her baby. Mary Lombardi. We met her once, before you were born, at the agency office. She was seventeen and scared but also determined. She left the meeting and we were there, oh, I don't know, several more hours filling out paperwork and making arrangements, and all that time she waited for us in the parking lot, and when we got back to our car she gave Claudia a little square of paper and said she had no right to ask, but would we consider letting her know how you were doing from time to time? Your mother hugged her and said she would. And she did. Every year around your birthday she sent a photo and letter. After she died, I didn't think about it until I found Mary's address in some of Claudia's papers. It was a PO box. You were about twenty, I think. I scribbled a quick note about Claudia's passing and let her know you were well and in college, and that I wouldn't be sending any more correspondence now that you were an adult. I don't know if Mary received it or not."

Finishing his coffee, Alistair pushes back from the table and pours a refill. He opens the small cabinet above the stove hood, reaches back, and removes a bottle of Baileys Irish Cream. "I knew I was saving this for something," he says, shuffling back to me. He spills some liqueur into his cup, drinks deeply.

"You said you were going to tell me."

"We were, your mother and I. We discussed it until we turned blue and croaky. We went back and forth on when the right time was. Eventually we settled on you being twelve or thirteen, somewhere in there. Claudia wanted you to be able to understand the reason for it, all of it. She didn't want to scare you with details of her illness too soon. She thought you'd be able to handle it then."

"But she died."

Alistair nodded. "She died. And I chose not to say anything because I didn't want you to lose her twice."

We're silent. My father fiddles with the Baileys cap; if he had coffee left in his cup, I'm certain he'd add more alcohol. I feel like I've had a few too many drinks, all woozy-headed and working too hard to put all I've heard in tidy order. It's nearly eleven. "I think I'll crash here tonight," I say.

"I'll get some sheets."

"No," I tell him, sharp little teeth in my voice. I take a deep breath. "No. It's okay. I'll get them."

He closes his eyes. "Don't hate us."

I nod, knowing I should hug him, a quick squeeze around his shoulders, but I have no comfort to offer.

I'll find that bottle empty in the morning.

Upstairs, I open the linen closet, a narrow door between the bathroom and my bedroom, painted white and raised-paneled. It was my favorite door as a child because the knob is violet glass, faceted until it sparkles. The others in the house are white or brown, ceramic-like, cool, smooth eggs in my hand. I would pretend the special knob was put there by a fairy, and if I opened the door at the right time, I'd find passage to her magical land. I decided the time would be the stroke of midnight, and I would stare at the ceiling, chanting, "Stay awake, stay awake," eventually hearing my parents turn off the television, brush their teeth, flush the toilet, and close their bedroom door. "Stay awake, stay awake." But I couldn't. And by the time I was old enough to make it to midnight, I didn't believe in fairy stories anymore.

The sheets aren't folded, but balled and shoved onto the shelves. I find a fitted and flat one for the twin bed in my old room; they don't match but it doesn't matter. In my room, I move the plastic totes of Christmas tree lights and Alistair's old sweaters from the bed to the floor and make up the bare mattress. Switching on the ceiling fan, removing my skirt and sandals, I climb under the thin sheet. I shiver, but don't get up to lower the fan speed, and fall asleep listening to the rattle of the pull chain against the light globe.

Seventeen

I want you to come to church with me, my father says.

    I'm sixteen, angry, ignoring his words and Christmas Eve, the fourth since she's been gone. The first since his new best friend is Jesus. I watch a Lifetime movie about finding the perfect man for the holidays, even if he happens to be a former convict in a Santa hat. My father stands in front of the television, wearing galoshes with his only suit, his parka, and a woolen hat with ear flaps. He holds my own peacoat out, an offering.

    Liesl.

    I heard you.

    Get your coat on.

    I'm not going.

    He drapes the coat over the arm of the sofa and leaves the room. The kitchen door hinges squeak. I hear the garage open, the car start—a Taurus, purchased the month after my mother died, her Buick traded to a dealership without its history disclosed; does the new owner sense what took place where she sits?—and the garage door once more, closing now.

I've defeated him. Again.

The battles give me purpose. How many ways am I able to pierce him? How many times will he struggle to his feet after I strike? This is my crusade, declared against him because he dares move on with his life. And he must turn the other cheek. His God commands it of him.

The front door opens and my father is back. He gropes the length of the television set, touching buttons until the screen goes black, the picture sucked into the center before it disappears. *I don't ask much. I don't know that I ask anything. This once, please, come to church with me.*

I snuggle into the leather sofa, my head on the wide, puffed arm, and, tugging my coat over my body, close my eyes.

If you don't come, you won't get your driver's license.

His words electrocute me, and in a surge of defiance I'm standing before him, almost as tall as he is, my pupils dilating with venom. *You can't do that.*

It's done.

In one strike he has amputated my limbs. All of them. I can remain here, at home, and bleed to death. Or for the sake of my teen-aged social life, I can allow the stretcher to carry me from the field of battle, have my own gushing wounds dressed, grow stronger, and devise a new strategy with which to crush him.

This is not for you, I say.

I turn, walk into my own rubber boots waiting near the door, cross the snow-covered lawn, and slip into the car. It's frigid outside; my nostrils freeze and my throat tastes of metal in the few moments I'm exposed to the air. I wear thin Tweety Bird pajama pants and a sweatshirt. My father brings my coat but I won't use it. When he covers my lap with it, I ball it up and heave it into the backseat.

I remain silent. My father introduces me to people before the service. I ignore them and their *I've heard so much about you's*, crossing my arms over my chest—I'm also braless—and staring at some invisible point above their heads and to the left. I see Sara Kempf standing not far from us. She nods to me. I turn my head. During the worship time, I slump in the chair. I don't stand. I don't sing. I don't open any hymnal to page two hundred and whatever-whatever. I don't light a candle and hold it toward the ceiling as far as my arm will stretch, at the end of "Silent Night" in representation of the Light of the World.

I seethe.

Two old women serve birthday cake for Jesus in the lobby. The children clamor around first, frosting on their fingers and in their hair. We don't stay, and this time the car is freezing when we get into it.

Only a fifteen-minute drive home.

My father turns the radio on and scans, choosing a station playing instrumental renditions of holiday songs. "Joy to the World" ends, and then another arrangement I recognize but can't name until the announcer identifies it as "Waltz of the Sugar Plum Fairy."

And then—

No, I breathe.

"Es ist ein Ros entsprungen." My mother's most beloved Christmas carol.

I clench my teeth so I won't sob, but my tears flow without sound. My father sniffs, and I roll my eyes toward him as far as possible, until they throb, and in the headlights of the oncoming vehicles, see him crying as well.

I haven't stopped missing her, he says. *I never will.*

He feels around for my hand—I sit on them for warmth—and I bite my lip as his fingers dig it out from beneath my bruised thigh. But I let him. And when he squeezes it, I squeeze back.

I wake in a tight ball beneath the sheet, head tucked between my knees, toes as cold as timid souls. Out of bed, I throw on my skirt and dig a sweater from the castoffs, an ecru cotton button-up without its buttons. Another clear tote holds boxer shorts and sport socks. I snag a pair for my feet and carry my shoes downstairs. I hear my father's snores, loud and full of gravel, from the bedroom down the hall.

In the kitchen, I check the refrigerator for something to drink before I go. A plastic bottle of Tropicana, expired two months ago. The milk from last night, stuck back on the top shelf rather than dumped down the sink. A couple of apple juice boxes, and why he has these I can't imagine. I take one anyway, tapping the straw on my leg to remove the wrapper and then popping it through the foil hole. I'm so dry my saliva is sticky, bitter, and I suck down the entire box, squeezing the cardboard to get the final mouthful. I drink the second one too and toss both empties in the garbage can. The Baileys bottle is at the bottom, half-covered with a paper towel.

I want to leave before my father wakes. There's no way I can stand with him in the kitchen and make small talk while the coffee percolates. Or, even worse, discuss the things revealed last night. But he'll sleep until noon, at least, and I think I should make him bread so he will know I still love him. I can't bring myself to stay any longer, though. I leave a note—*Be in touch soon. Love you. Liesl*—and tape it to the can of Maxwell House on the counter.

I drive back to Vermont and the trip is hard because I don't want to think about anything. I try counting barns and admiring the old farmhouses. I stop for gasoline and another apple juice. Finally, I force the picture behind my eyes to become a sheet of clean white paper. Whenever a word drifts onto it, I erase it. This works, for a while, but the words come faster and faster, and like playing Missile Command on my father's Atari, eventually I can't keep up. I know this; as a child I would imagine all sorts of scenarios, from decorating elaborate cakes to simply pulling up a zipper, and the more I tried to control the daydreams, the more independent they became, spinning in a reality all their own. Now all the words begin piling in the center—*adoption, illness, suicide, secret, Mary Lombardi*—each one larger and darker than the previous. I imagine the corners folding in, covering all the accumulated words, but the other side of the page is gridded and filled already too, in handwriting I recognize as my mother's, a single, neat, accusing letter in every box.

"Stop," I shout, and then a moan. "Please, please stop."

They do. My mind clears. Perhaps God takes mercy on me.

Early Sunday morning streets in downtown Billingston are blank canvases, waiting to be colored by people still in bed, or in church, or driving from a few hours away for a lovely day trip of leaf peaking and antique markets. I park the car behind Wild Rise and enter the back way, directly into the kitchen, and it has been cleaned by Seamus, no trace of last night's dinner seen. He's left a note too—it's a day of notes—*Call Me. S.* Underneath, a young girl's still-developing penmanship, *and Cecelia.*

It's almost ten. I can find him at Green Mountain Community, but no. I'm too bruised to sit through a service, too bruised for anything but handling soft flour and cool water. I'll plant my hands in dough, root them there, to keep from being pulled from this firm, kitchen world back into my head. I touch my mother's trough, trace the repair line where my father glued it together, and when my finger reaches the end, it balances precariously on the lip of the wood, nowhere to go but back the way it came.

I can't go back, though.

I've been orphaned by my bread.

Not only have I lost a mother and a father, but my heritage disappeared with the word *adopted*. I am no longer a *Tochter von Brot*, a caretaker of the *Anfrishsauer*. There is no blood binding me to Oma and her mother, and to all the others, one ancestor passing the craft of baking to her daughter a generation at a time, a loaf at a time. This love of bread I think I have been born into, I believe I must follow because I can do no other—it is simply something I have been taught, not something I *am*.

Who does that make me?

Taking off my father's sweater, I scoop a measure of flour from the bin, hold the cup high over my head, and let it fall into the trough. I do it again, again, dust particles whitening my arms, tickling my face. I sneeze into my shoulder. And then water, adding it the same way, from the sky; it splashes down, sloshing out of the bowl, cutting the mountain of flour. Erosion. Everything washes away, eventually.

I knead not only with my hands but my arms as well, coating myself with dough. It's weak and pasty, not enough flour to bind it; I open the bin with my elbow and manage to get more, dripping white water on the floor while doing so. Now the dough is tough, but I continue to work it, pressing, rolling, squeezing until my breath comes like razor blades and I bury my face in my sweet-smelling hands and finally cry.

Barley-Wheat Sourdough

Makes 2 loaves

LIESL'S NOTES:

Experimenting with flours other than wheat is another adventure in bread making. Barley always reminds me of Jesus' miracle of the loaves and fishes—the feeding of five thousand. Barley bread was the bread of the poor for much of its history, but many now respect the health benefits of this low-gluten, high-protein grain. Bread made with barley will have a different flavor than one made entirely of whole wheat, earthier and slightly sweet. This recipe combines both types of flour for a chewy crust and crumb.

INGREDIENTS:

100 grams (1/2 cup) 100% hydration sourdough starter (see page 45)
150 grams (2/3 cup) water
120 grams (1 cup) all-purpose flour, organic if possible
160 grams (1 1/3 cups) whole barley flour, organic if possible

520 grams (4¹/3 cups) whole wheat flour, organic if possible
360 grams (1¹/2 cups) water
113 grams (¹/3 cup) honey, raw if possible
12 grams (2 teaspoons) salt

EQUIPMENT:

kitchen scale (optional but recommended)
2 ceramic or glass mixing bowls
wooden spoon
plastic wrap or clean kitchen towel
stand mixer with dough hook (optional)
olive oil
2 proofing baskets (also known as a brotform or banneton),
    optional
parchment paper
baking stone
broiler pan
serrated knife or razor

Do Ahead

Combine the first three ingredients (sourdough starter, water, and all-purpose flour) in a bowl and mix well. Cover with plastic wrap and allow to rest for 12 hours or overnight.

On Baking Day

In a large bowl, combine the starter with the remaining ingredients, mix until everything is incorporated, and allow to rest for 30 minutes. Turn the dough out onto a lightly floured surface and knead, by hand, for 5 to 8 minutes. If using a stand mixer, combine all ingredients and stir with a wooden spoon until a dough forms. Allow to rest for 30 minutes, and then mix for 5 minutes on medium-low speed with a dough hook.

Lightly oil a bowl and place the dough in it, covering with plastic wrap or a clean, damp kitchen towel. Allow to rise for 1 hour, then gently turn the dough out onto a lightly floured surface and "stretch and fold" three times. Return the dough to the bowl, cover, and let ferment another 1¹/2 to 2 hours.

Again, remove the dough from the bowl and divide in half. Shape the dough into loaves (boules or bâtards work well), place on parchment paper, and cover with a damp towel or lightly oiled plastic wrap. (If using proofing baskets, allow the dough to rest for 15 minutes before transferring it into them.) Allow to proof for 2 to 3 hours, until the dough, when gently pressed with two fingers, returns slowly to its original shape.

Preheat the oven to 475 degrees Fahrenheit with the baking stone on the middle shelf and empty broiler pan on the bottom shelf. Score the loaves (either once down the center for a bâtard, or three times across the top for a boule) and move them, on the parchment paper, onto the baking stone. (If using proofing baskets, either turn the dough out onto parchment paper, score, and place on the baking stone, or turn the dough out directly onto the baking stone and score there.) Add 1 cup of water to the broiler pan and close the oven. Bake for 15 minutes with steam, then remove the broiler pan and bake for another 20 to 25 minutes. Check the loaves during baking to make sure they do not overbrown; if the crust browns too quickly, cover loosely with aluminum foil to prevent continued darkening.

Remove from oven and allow to cool on a wire rack. Wait 2 hours before slicing.

I shower and stand naked, hair wrapped in a towel, before my open closet door. I don't know what to wear. Nothing feels right—old clothes, new clothes, clothes for the person I thought I was, for who I am now, for who I wish I can be. I've made it too complicated. Finally, when I'm shivering, I grab something for all those parts. One of my new skirts, a long-sleeved T-shirt with screen-printed dandelions that doesn't quite match, and because I hear thunder, a pair of brightly patterned rain boots, gifted to me by a customer because I complimented hers. I tie back my hair in a stumpy ponytail and don't bother with makeup. As I'm leaving through the kitchen, I grab the sweater I borrowed and shrug into it. I'm stitched together by these clothes, not quite a whole person despite having enough toes and fingers to make me seem so.

The rain comes as I drive to Seamus's home. I've not been there before, but I know the road and figure the mailbox will be marked. I switch the wipers from delay to high and peer at each house I pass. There are no names on any of the mailboxes. I turn around in someone's driveway and try again, finally peering through the trees into the yard of a small house with two bicycles leaning against the shed— a small pink two-wheeler with faded plastic streamers in one handle and a larger men's mountain bike. I pull toward the house and see the glider swing Cecelia told me about, the one she likes to rock on while she colors. A Hello Kitty pillow sits on the canvas seat cushion, leaning against one arm of the rusted frame.

They're still at church. I wait in the car, windows steaming, shifting so my back leans against the door and my legs drape across the passenger's seat. I'm cold, though; tucking my legs to my chest and wrapping them with the sweater only works so long until my feet begin to tingle. I won't run the car while it sits idle, ever.

I decide Seamus isn't a person who locks his doors, and this isn't the type of house that needs locking, so I run up the cracked cement stoop and twist the knob. The door opens. I slip inside the house, into a kitchen–living room combination, generic brown carpet denoting one side, plain beige tile marking the other. Miniature dog and cat figurines swim over the rug with their hairbrushes and beds and tiny sneakers. Books and papers and clean laundry cover the one kitchen counter. This morning's breakfast keeps watch from the table: a yellow box of Cheerios, a milky bowl and spoon, the crusts of some supermarket bread toast, a glass with a pulpy puddle of orange juice at the bottom, and an empty coffee mug.

I'm freezing. I check the thermostat only to find the heat off, but I'm not so brazen to turn it up. Instead, I leave my wet boots at the door and tiptoe through all the plastic puppy shrapnel to the couch. I shake open the fuzzy brown blanket crumpled on one end and fold it around me. Then I lie down, crooking my elbow beneath my head.

I'm awakened by puffs of warm breath in my face and open my eyes to find Cecelia's nose inches from my own. "Daddy wanted me to see if you were up yet."

"I'm up," I say, and sit, aware the blanket has come apart and one side of my skirt is twisted over my hip. I cover again, but Cecelia doesn't notice. She plops next to me, offering me one of her kittens.

"This is Zoë," she says. The cat is yellowish with purple-tipped ears and a disproportionately large bobbling head. "She's my favorite. But I only tell her that, not the others."

"Oh," I say. I'm still waking, having slept hard enough to drool all over my arm and congest my nose. My hair flops around my face. I search the cushions, find my elastic, and redo my ponytail. When I smooth my hands over my head, though, I feel all the lumps and puckers of unruly hair. So I shake the rubber band loose and tuck it behind my ears.

"I didn't make you get up, right?" The little girl closes her fist around her kitten and tucks it beneath her chin. "Daddy said not to, just to check. I didn't make noise or touch you or anything. I was just looking."

"No, you didn't make me get up. Don't worry."

"Tell Daddy, okay?"

"Tell Daddy what?" Seamus asks, looking even more a giant in this cramped house.

"Cecelia didn't wake me."

"I didn't, promise." She traces an X over her chest and then kisses the tip of her finger. "She got up all by herself."

"Okay, now. Why don't you go into my bedroom and turn on the movie?"

"We're supposed to watch it together."

"I'll be in soon. Now go."

"Can Liesl come?"

Seamus narrows his eyes and silently mouths, *Go.* Cecelia scrunches her lips to one side and swats her nose, but does make her way down the hallway, albeit with slow steps and neglected sighs.

I twist the blanket tighter around me.

"So," Seamus says. "Breaking and entering. Not all that smart, for a celebrity."

"There was no breaking," I say.

"Cold?"

"I'm fine."

He shakes his head and adjusts the thermostat. "I try not to turn it back on until November first."

"It was warmer before the rain."

"Want some coffee or something?"

I shake my head now. "What time is it?"

"A bit past two. You were out."

"Yeah," I say, voice airy with sarcasm. "I didn't sleep so great last night."

"We waited for you, at the bakery, I mean. After church. We went to see if you were there." He sits on the sofa, on the opposite end. As far from me as possible, really.

"How was church?"

"Good. How are you?" I open my mouth and he looks into me and says, "Don't say good."

"I don't know what to say, then."

"Anything but that."

"I'm adopted."

Seamus blinks. "Okay."

"No, I'm—I just found out last night."

"Oh," he says, the word sounding the same way I feel, dull and ill at ease. "How did you . . . I mean, was it that phone call?"

"Yeah."

He waits, expecting more of the story to be forthcoming, but telling it seems such work, as if there are dozens of marbles in my mouth I need to speak around, or my jaw is dislocated, and I need to manipulate each word with my hand too, opening and closing my mouth, marionette-style. Exhausting. But I did come into his home and sleep in his bed, the Goldilocks of family dysfunction, so I owe him at least a nibble more.

"I told you my mother was mentally ill. She and my father wanted a child but she didn't want to chance passing on her . . . problems. So they adopted. Me."

"They never told you."

"My father said they planned to. Then my mother died and everything pretty much fell apart. But the TV show. They saw me. My biological family." I wipe my palms over my face, from my oily nose to my ears. I almost pinch a chunk of cheek and stretch it, like my father did last night. Stop myself. It's too much to be like him right now. My hands still smell of flour; it's there, dried in my cuticles. I pick at them.

Biological. The word means nothing to me outside the freshman science lab I'd been required to take, at least before yesterday. Now it's five syllables capable of altering a life. More than one.

Seamus extends his long arm—he reaches me without leaning—and touches an unseen part of me at the bottom of the blanket. My ankle. "What can I do?"

"Take me back in time. Keep me from going on that stupid show."

"You'd rather not know the truth?"

"What has it done?"

"It's given you the truth. That should be enough."

"I don't want it."

"Too late."

I'm annoyed. Who is Seamus in my life that he thinks he can speak to me this way? "Do me a favor and don't comment, please. You're not helping."

He takes his hand away. "I'm sorry," he says. "I just . . . well, I guess I just think it's a good thing. If it were me, I'd want to know. Like about where I came from, and those things."

But Seamus is a wanderer, never staying too long in one place. To him, this is romantic and exciting, a chance for me to explore the newly discovered topography of Liesl. I don't want it, though. I am the child who felt safe nestled between my parents, watching *The Cosby Show* and eating popcorn made on the stove in my mother's blue enamelware pot. My father ate his popcorn with cinnamon and sugar. So did I. My mother wore two pairs of socks because her feet were cold. So did I. I liked being part of them, believing God plucked this piece from him and that one from her, and stirred them together to make me. I liked coming from somewhere utterly recognizable.

I like blending.

"I don't know," I say.

"You've gained, Liesl. More knowledge. More family. I guess, though . . . I mean, how much you take of it is up to you."

"I've lost—"

—the bread.

I stop. Seamus doesn't need me to finish. He touches me again, a little higher up my leg, but still far enough away from my heart to be safe. "It's not gone."

"But it's not me anymore."

"It's more you than anything else. Your mother, she nurtured that bread down deep into you, deeper even than if it had been planted there by blood."

The bedroom door opens. Cecelia shouts down the hallway, "Can I at least come out to get a Capri Sun?"

"You can come all the way out," Seamus says.

She skips into the kitchen and yanks open the refrigerator. Bottles jingle in the door. "I'm sorta hungry too."

Seamus meets her at the fridge and peers inside. "Want a sandwich?"

"Nah."

"Apple?"

She shakes her head.

"Cheese stick?"

"Don't we have anything good?"

"Hey, Miss Gratitude. Shopping day's tomorrow."

She crinkles her nose. "Is there any popcorn?"

He spins the revolving corner cabinet, holds up two cellophane-wrapped rectangles. "Ta-da."

"Can you come watch the movie with me now? And Liesl too?"

"Tell you what. You grab the disc and bring it down to the living room. I'll make the popcorn. And we'll ask Liesl if she wants to join us. How about that?"

"Liesl, will you? We can start the movie over, I don't mind watching the beginning part again."

"Okay," I tell her. I'm cold and tired and it's still raining, and I don't want to be alone right now.

She squeals and runs for the movie. Seamus opens the popcorn bags and starts the microwave. I try to readjust my skirt beneath the blanket. Cecelia returns, lugging her princess sleeping bag and pillow-shaped plush unicorn. "Pick up those Pet Shops too," her father says. She dumps her armful on the recliner and crouches, using her arms to bulldoze the figurines into one pile. Then she scoops them into the sparkly pink pail beside the television.

Seamus glances over. "Where do they go?"

"I'm going." She huffs a little, dragging the bucket to her bedroom and racing back. Seamus empties the steaming popcorn into three bowls. Cecelia digs the movie disc from inside her sleeping bag and drops it into the player. Turns on the television. "I can't find the remote."

"Check the cushions."

It's there, in the crack beside me. She begins the movie and pauses it, tosses the remote back onto the couch before shimmying into her sleeping bag and hopping, like in a sack race, to settle next to me. "Do you like dolphins?"

"Uh, sure."

"Good, 'cause this movie's about one."

Seamus comes with popcorn and sits on Cecelia's other side. "Press play."

She pats around. "The remote's gone again."

"Under you," I tell her, and she struggles around in her polyester cocoon until she finds it. Then she nestles between us, yellow crumbs escaping from her mouth as she smiles at the movie and chews, legs thrown over her father's, head on my shoulder.

"Do you want her to move?" Seamus asks.

I shake my head and realize, oh, how easy blending comes.

Eighteen

We survive, my father and I, rebuilding the bonds I tore down. He has his church and I go with him when asked, which is only three or four times each year. I stop beating my legs, mostly, and when the more intense urges come I phone Sara Kempf, and we talk about nothing until they pass. She would be more of a friend, I think, if I wanted her to be, but I avoid her in school because I don't deserve her, and anyway, the world turning around her—the other cheerleaders, the youth group, her quarterback boyfriend—want nothing to do with me. My grades improve, and by my senior year, with excellent standardized test scores and letters from the guidance counselor explaining the extenuating circumstances of my first two years of high school, I manage to be accepted into one of the best computer science programs in the state. My father wants to know what I'm studying, exactly.

Coding languages. Graphics. Computational theory.
But why?

Because it's the furthest thing from bread I can imagine. I don't say that, but tell him instead, *It sounds interesting*.

We pack my car. He asks again if he can drive out with me. I say no, and he lets it be.

I worry about leaving him.

He tells me, *Go, go*, placing his hand atop my head and gently pulling me toward him. He kisses me between my temple and ear. *Only two hours away. I'll be home to do laundry.*

I drive, relying on my door mirrors because the backseat is stacked high with boxes and totes and blankets, and I can't see out the windshield rearview. I merge onto the highway northbound. Two exits later I swing over to the right lane, take the off-ramp, and swing back around to go south again.

I decide I can't leave without it.

Parking at the curb, I leave the car running so I have an excuse not to stay. I love the Rausenberg house, so much like my own, built not long before the turn of the century and charming in its details, from slate roof to eight-inch baseboard moldings, to the quirky under-the-stairs passageway leading into the bathroom. I ring the doorbell and Jennie answers; we've long been estranged, our talents and circumstances leading us in different directions. Not hostile toward one another. Simply untied.

Hey, she says.

Hey back. Is your mom here?

She holds the screen door open. It's green, like the wide plank floorboards of the front porch, extra glossy, paint flaking beneath the handle. *In the kitchen.*

Mrs. Rausenberg hugs me when I enter, knowing better than to say she's not seen me around for a while or that she's missed me around here, and asks instead for me to sit with her and have a glass of lemonade. *Fresh squeezed, the way you like it.*

I can't stay. My car is running out there. I'm leaving for Clarkson.

She presses her lips together in a bittersweet smile. *I read that. In the paper.* And then, sweeping my untrimmed bangs from my eyes, says, *You made it.*

Yeah. I guess I did. I tug the hem of my shirt; it's shorter than I normally wear and I'm self-conscious about it. *Do you think . . . I mean, do you still have—*

Yes.

The kitchen is remarkably modern compared to the rest of the house, with stainless steel appliances and bright aqua and lemon pans hanging from the rack in the center of the ceiling. She opens the refrigerator, so much larger than the one we have, cleaner, without clots of dried sweet-and-sour sauce on the shelves or shriveled carrots in the crisper. She reaches deep inside, nearly disappearing, and emerges holding a Mason jar and Oma's stoneware crock. With her knee she shuts the door. *They were fed three days ago. They're always hungry, still.*

Thank you. For keeping them all this time, I mean.

Thank you for asking me.

I don't need them both. There's no difference between them, especially now as they've been given the same flour for years. I take only the crock from her and say, *You keep that one.*

She embraces me again, more firmly, the cold crock between us, against the bare skin of my belly where my T-shirt rides up because I've thrown my arm around her neck. She whispers, *Be good, you hear?*

I nod my head against hers.

Back in the car, I belt my crock of starter into the passenger seat and tuck a pillow around it to keep it safe.

Two days after the movie with Seamus and Cecelia, my father calls. I consider ignoring his message but don't want to make him more concerned than he already is. I, however, am not ready to talk. There's nothing new to add to the adoption conversation, and I have other things on my mind as well.

One other thing.

The cooking show.

I'd been leaning toward accepting, especially after Xavier gave his approval. I read through every word of the information the Good Food Network sent, logistics and contract and legalese. The first season of *Bread Without Boundaries* would feature twenty-four episodes, and I'd be paid five thousand dollars each—four times the salary I take at the bakehouse. Add to that airfare (first class), hotels (only the best I imagine, if Jonathan Scott accompanies me, or at least very good ones), food (whatever I want to eat), and the experience of the best breads from around the world (to quote the credit card commercial, priceless). Only a fool would refuse.

But something happened the other day, when I went to Seamus and shared with him about the adoption. When Cecelia snuggled between us. I caught a glimpse of another possible future, one I never expected I might want. No. In those deep recesses where I tuck the memory of family, the way life was before my mother's death, I always have wanted it. I have been afraid to lose it again.

I'm caught off balance, though I shouldn't be. Seamus and I have been flirting around the edges of this for weeks, him subtly pursuing but interested in more, me undulating in bewildered attempts to understand my rather erratic—and unpracticed—emotions. He's been more patient than I deserve. I've been, well, a bit of a handful. As improbable as it seems, when I stack Seamus—a divorced, blue-collar single father packaged with a precocious little girl—beside all the Good Food Network offers me, I'd rather have him.

What do I do?

Ask me.

I haven't prayed over the decision. Will seeking the Spirit ever be my first inclination? After three years, I think I'd be better at this

Christian thing. Others come to faith and within hours have boarded a ship to deepest Africa with only two dollars and a granola bar in their satchel, trusting the Lord to care for their every need. I don't remember to thank him before a meal.

No condemnation. Ask me.

I close my eyes and see Cecelia sucking her pigtail to a wet point, and then she grins, her father coming from behind to cocoon her in his stout arms.

Jonathan Scott's card is in the mess of pages on the kitchen table. I sift through and, before I change my mind, dial his number. He answers, and I tell him who's calling.

"Liesl, I was wondering about you."

"I'm not going to do the show. I appreciate your generous offer, but—"

"—it's not for you."

"In some ways it's too much for me, I think."

"You know I understand." He says this in his other voice, not the showman one he uses while the cameras roll, but the tired, generous one with which he told me about the old boulanger who let Jonathan wash his floors to earn admittance into his world of bread and war.

"Yeah, I do."

"Any chance you'll change your mind?"

"Slim to none."

"How slim?"

"Okay, none to less than that."

He laughs. "I hear you. But listen. Keep my card. If you ever need anything you think I can help with, please call. Seriously. I mean it."

"I will."

I gather the show documents into their envelope and, before dumping them into the trash can, hesitate. Do I want to save them so one day, perhaps five years from now, when I realize my life is exactly the same as this instant, I can look back and think, *I was offered more and I chose this?* I shake my head despite being alone in the kitchen. To choose means owning the decision. I cram the envelope down the side of the bag and shut the lid. I do keep Jonathan Scott's card, taping it into the cover of my mother's *Beard on Bread* so I won't lose it.

Wild White Sandwich Bread

Makes two loaves

LIESL'S NOTES:

This wild yeast loaf is soft and airy without the use of commercial yeast. The taste is mild with only a hint of sourness. Translation: even the kids will love it. Because butter and milk powder are added, this bread would be considered enriched, which is why the crumb is so tender.

The windowpane test is used by bakers to gauge gluten development. Take some dough from the larger mass, approximately golf-ball sized or a little smaller. Stretch the dough. If it doesn't tear but the windowpane (thin dough membrane) is mostly opaque, there is only a low level of gluten development. If the dough stretches to a thin, translucent windowpane, the gluten is highly developed. This recipe calls for the gluten to be developed somewhere between these two extremes; the membrane will be opaque in places and translucent in others, but the recipe works best when there are more translucent areas than not.

Please remember, the "standard kitchen measurements" are close approximations. For best results, use a kitchen scale.

INGREDIENTS:

700 grams (5 3/4 cups) unbleached white flour, organic if
　　possible
355 grams (1 1/2 cups) water

18 grams (1 tablespoon) finely ground sea salt

65 grams (4^1/$_2$ tablespoons) unsalted butter, softened to room temperature

42 grams (2 tablespoons) honey

23 grams (^{1}/$_3$ cup) instant non-fat dry milk

400 grams (2 cups) 100% hydration sourdough starter (see page 45)

EQUIPMENT:

kitchen scale (optional but recommended)

stand mixer with dough hook

wooden spoon

olive oil

plastic wrap

butter (for greasing pans)

two 8^1/$_2$ x 4^1/$_2$-inch bread pans

baking stone

broiler pan

DO AHEAD

Make sure the starter has been fed and is ready to use for baking.

ON BAKING DAY

Combine all the ingredients in the bowl of the stand mixer. Using the dough hook, mix on low speed until the dough forms a ball of medium dough consistency—a little more water or flour may be needed. Increase speed to medium and mix for approximately 8 minutes, until the gluten has developed sufficiently, as described in the notes above.

Lightly coat a large glass or ceramic mixing bowl with olive oil and move the dough into this bowl. Cover with plastic wrap or a clean kitchen towel. After 1 hour, turn the dough out onto a lightly floured surface and "stretch and fold" four times. Return it to the bowl and cover for another hour, and then "stretch and fold" a second time. Again, return to the bowl and allow to rest for 1 more hour (this is a total of 3 hours of fermentation time). Gently divide the dough in half and shape each into a log. Allow the dough to rest on a floured surface, covered, for 30 minutes.

Generously grease the loaf pans and, after reshaping the dough to fit, place it into the pans seam side down. Cover and let the dough proof for approximately 3 hours, or until the dough has risen at least 1/2 inch above the pan.

Preheat the oven to 450 degrees Fahrenheit with an empty broiler pan on the bottom rack. Place the loaves in the oven and add 1 cup of water to the broiler pan. Close the oven door quickly and reduce heat to 400 degrees Fahrenheit. Bake for 45 minutes, checking at 20 minutes to see if the loaves are browning too quickly; if so, cover loosely with aluminum foil. (If you don't tent the tops with foil at 20 minutes, you'll want to continue to check every five minutes to make sure the loaves aren't getting too brown. To simplify this process, you can cover the loaves with foil at 20 minutes even if they're not dark enough for your liking, and then remove the foil the last 5 minutes of baking to brown them more.)

Remove the loaves from the oven and carefully take them out of their pans. Cool for at least 1 hour before slicing; allowing to cool to room temperature works best if the bread will be sliced thin for sandwiches.

I leave the bakehouse around noon, telling Gretchen I have errands, and go see Seamus. I can wait for the next morning, at church, but don't want to try to find a way to get him alone and have a serious conversation. The words rattle around my head, each imaginary conversation I have with him longer and more heartfelt than the previous, and I'm afraid, given too much passing time, these words will decompose and be reabsorbed into myself, and I'll have nothing left to say at all.

I bring bread, white loaf bread, because I know he likes it best, a new formula I've decided has been perfected, made with sourdough but also ideal for sandwiches. When I knock on the door of his house and he answers, I hold the two paper sacks out to him and say, "I've come bearing gifts."

"It's Saturday," he says. I think he's been napping, his hair matted flat on one side of his head, the top slightly greasy and standing on end.

"Playing hooky," I say. "Someone I know told me it would be good for me."

He briskly buffs his face in his hands, fights a yawn. "Oh."

"Can I come in?"

"Yeah, sure. Sorry." He moves out of the way.

"Thanks." I set the bread on the table. "Is Cecelia here?"

"At a friend's. Which is why I was catching up on a little rest."

"I didn't mean to wake you. I can go—"

"No," he says. "I'm up. Really."

This is not how I pictured things going, him half-asleep in baggy sweatpants, his stomach speaking in short, audible growls, me foolishly waiting on his porch, grinning with all the enthusiasm of a Crest Whitestrips commercial. Seamus turns on the tap and drinks a glass of water. "Are you hungry? I can make us lunch."

I dangle one of the bread bags in front of him. "Sandwiches?"

"I'm always up for one."

He unloads his icebox, all the cold cuts, spreads, condiments, and anything he deems sandwich worthy—a chunk of London broil, egg salad, cold French fries—lined up on the kitchen table. "Thick or thin?" he asks, a steak knife positioned over the bread.

"Thin," I say, and he cuts two slices for me. I dress mine with turkey breast and provolone, lettuce, tomato, and Dijon mustard, while he hacks off a two-inch-thick piece of his own, smears it with cream cheese, and then tops it with coleslaw.

My poor bread.

We make small talk. Our interactions feel clunky today, strained even, as if we're both trying too hard to be casual. I can't read him, and I see none of what I'm looking for—that is, interest from him, in me—to give me that last push into saying what I came to tell him. I'll do it anyway.

I'm terrified.

"So, I have news," I begin, and Seamus pauses, mid-bite, and returns his sandwich to his plate. "About the show. I'm not going to do it."

His entire face wrinkles. "What?"

"I've turned it down."

"Why?"

It's not the response I expect. Crowing, quacking, shouting, "Yaba daba do" as loud as possible—those are Seamus reactions. Defensiveness prickles in my armpits, at my hairline. "I have reasons. I don't want to abandon the bakehouse, for one. I know the network says I'd only be away twelve weeks maximum for filming, but there's some clauses about special appearances and other obligations, and I don't want to be roped into something I don't want to do."

"Oh."

I turn my head, unable to look at him as the next words leave my mouth. "And there's you and Cecelia to consider." Seamus doesn't answer. I wait, every skin follicle responding to the embarrassed silence, tightening with anxiety and perspiration. "Well then. I guess I'll be going now—"

"Liesl."

"What?"

"You can't say something like that with your back toward me."

I don't move. He stands and rotates my chair. My feet tangle in the legs, ankles kinking, one heel twisting out of my shoe. Sitting again, he leans in close enough for me to see his eyes aren't completely gray but centrally heterochromic; a ring of amber glows around his iris. And he grins so brightly, so contagiously, that I smile as well. "Tell me again."

"I don't want to leave you. Or Cecelia."

He catches my face between his hands and, rising slightly, kisses me at the intersection of my nose and forehead, where I pluck my eyebrows to keep them from meeting. "I love you," he says.

"I think I might love you too."

Nineteen

We eat at Pane Pappa, a bakery chain close to campus and open until eleven. My roommates rave over the desserts, which are dry enough to be Sheetrock, and the bread. I don't give my opinion of the gummy, flavorless loaves, instead ordering tea and lentil soup—without the roll.

It's a celebration tonight. We graduate in two weeks. Mia's boyfriend proposed the other night; she wears a pavé ring of grayish diamonds all clustered in a pear shape and tells us Bradley promises to give her something more significant as soon as he's working. Cassandra has been accepted into the competitive master's program she wanted. And I already have a job with a technology consulting firm in New York City, as an entry-level software developer. We reminisce over the past four years—three foolish freshmen thrown together by random computer generation, kept together by the bonds of individuality. That's why we're still friends. There's never been competition between us. Different majors, different goals. I don't think we've shared a class since first semester. We pledge to keep in touch, but I'm not certain we will. Maybe the other two, but I'm Teflon when it comes to relationships.

We're the only people remaining in the restaurant. A blackhead-speckled teenager mops the tile floor, and an older woman gathers all the leftover loaves of bread and drops them in large, clear plastic garbage bags. She fills three of them.

What waste, Mia says, shaking her head.

The teenager, hearing her, says, *They're not going to the dumpster. Some church picks them up and does something with them. Gives it to poor people, I guess.*

What church? I ask.

He snorts. *How should I know?*

On the way out, the woman at the counter tells me the church's location and food distribution times. I thank her and, after we leave, watch through the glass door as she berates the boy for being rude to customers.

The next morning I skip my information systems security class and walk four blocks to an asbestos-shingled house that's been annexed for a church building. Inside, I follow a paneled hallway to a back room. Several long folding tables stacked with clear garbage bags greet me. An elderly lady asks if I've been here before. I shake my head and she hands me two balled plastic sacks. *You can take as much as you can fit in these.*

I move between the tables, glancing into the bags. Some are filled with a variety of unwrapped loaves, the ones from places like Pane Pappa. Others contain bread in cellophane or paper bags from the bakery of the local grocery store or the Walmart. There's a bag with wilted vegetables and fruits, one with muffins and stale bagels, and another of donuts, all squished and disfigured, the jelly fillings bleeding over the fudge icing, the custard smeared around the inside of the plastic.

A half dozen people, all women, paw through the bags with their bare hands, and a preschooler sits beneath one of the tables, devouring the donuts he's plucked from the heap above him.

Are you doing okay? a cheerful, obese woman asks. Her wooly, pale hair frizzes in two springy clips on either side of her head. She looks more poodle than human. *You seem a little lost.*

I think I'd like to help. The words spill out even while my mind protests. I'll be gone in a month and what will it matter then?

The woman's face swells with a jack-o-lantern grin. *Wonderful. Praise God. Let me get your name. We need people to be here on Tuesday and Friday mornings, and always to pick up the food. Do you have a car? We're always—*

I'd like to organize the bread.

Her smile collapses, slowly, like unrelaxed dough pulling back in on itself when someone tries stretching it. *I don't understand.*

It's all thrown together. I'd like to separate it into its different kinds and tell the people who come what they're eating. Perhaps even package it into—

Darling, no one getting stuff here cares about any of that. Bread is bread is bread. As long as it doesn't break their teeth when they chew it, they're happy.

Sometimes if you know better, you care better. That sentence belongs to my mother, and it's odd for my tongue to wear her words; it's like speaking with a mouthful of pebbles, and perhaps the woman hears it that way. By the way she looks at me, she thinks I'm some wealthy, out-of-touch college student whose parents give me carte blanche on the credit card and who doesn't understand poverty in the slightest. My mother, though, knew poverty. She came with Oma and they had nothing but a steamer trunk and two baskets of belongings. Oma scrubbed floors and took in laundry. My mother plucked chicken feathers for the butcher in their apartment building and earned a nickel a bird. But still they ate good bread, and gave it to others so they, too, might taste the stars. So when I came home from school at nine years old, complaining that all my friends ate white bread with fluff and chocolate puddings in plastic containers, my mother explained to me that good things, things prepared with delight by someone who knows they are good things, can bring hope to those who otherwise may never experience it.

Well, I thank you again for your offer, but I think we have all the help we need right now. The woman turns away, and I am left to wonder if I'm the only person outside a boulangerie or *Bäckerei* who thinks bread has a beauty beyond eating.

I unlock Wild Rise at six in the morning and know, the moment I walk into the building, something isn't right. I stand in front of the door, the cold from the glass chilling my back, waiting for my front side to absorb the warmer temperatures of the café area, heated by the brick oven despite it being in the other room. I'm greeted, however, with more cool air and the haze of sunrise. And I wait for the vibrations of human energy to come over me; I've always been able to feel the presence—or absence—of life.

There's no one else here.

To be certain, I slip my messenger bag off my shoulder as I cross the room; it tumbles somewhere behind me, and in my rush to get to the kitchen I hear its contents spill onto the floor, my Sigg water bottle, a collection of pens and Tic Tacs and lip gloss, a hairbrush. It doesn't matter, and I'm through the swinging door into the shadowy kitchen. No fire in the oven. The proofing baskets and shaped loaves Kelvin prepared last night untouched on the center table and counters.

Xavier hasn't missed a day of work in three years.

Fear blisters within me. I check the answering machine. No messages. I fumble beneath the counter for my Rolodex and reconsider having a cell phone in which to keep my contacts programmed, or some other kind of electronic directory. I spin through the cards until I find Xavier's, dialing first his mobile and then his home. No answer. Beneath those is Jude's cell; I punch in all eleven digits for the out-of-state number and wait as it rings. "'Lo," he grunts.

"It's Liesl. Where's Zave?"

A yawn. "I don't know. Call him."

"Jude, wake up. It's past six."

He mutters something unintelligible. Bedsprings shift.

"Jude," I shout.

"What?"

"You were supposed to be here three hours ago."

More fumbling. Something crashes to the floor. He groans again but sounds more alert. "Pops didn't wake me."

"That's what I'm trying to tell you. Something's wrong. He's not here either."

"What do you mean?"

"Do I have to spell it? Xavier didn't come in to the bakehouse this morning." I'm screeching at him. "Go check on him."

"Oh no, no," he says, and I hear him stampeding through the house shouting, "Pops? Pops!"

My breath prays on its own, *Please, God, please, God, please, God.* And then Jude wails, and I recognize the sound.

It's grief.

"Liesl, he's not waking up."

"Is he breathing?"

"I think so."

"Call 911. Now. I'm coming."

"Liesl, I can't—"

"Now, Jude."

"Okay, okay. Okay."

The line goes dead.

I crouch and scoop all my scattered things into my bag; the floor against my kneecaps impels me to prayer, and I press my forehead to the ground, searching for the words. I have none. I weep instead, and when I finally stand, the knees of my jeans are stained with tears.

Somehow I manage to make it to Xavier's home without being

pulled over by the police for erratic driving. The ambulance is already there when I arrive, Xavier strapped to a stretcher, one EMT pumping air into him with a mask and rubber balloon, the others lifting him into the vehicle. Jude slouches on the front porch in boxer shorts and nothing else, face swollen, eyes dim. I go to him.

"Liesl? You're here."

"I told you I was coming."

His skin is veined with purple. "Yeah."

"Where are they taking him?"

No response.

"Jude?"

"They told me . . ." He shakes his head. "They told me."

I run to the driver's side of the ambulance and the EMT rolls down the window. "Which hospital?" I ask.

"St. Mary's," he says. "You got the kid?"

I nod. "Can you tell me anything?"

He flips on the flashing lights. "It doesn't look good."

Jude hasn't moved. I shepherd him into the house. "We should get to the hospital." He shivers, and I look around for something with which to cover him. "Jude. Clothes?"

"I don't know."

Searching for a dresser, a closet, I find a laundry basket of socks and towels at the top of the stairs. Everything in it seems clean. I grab two socks of similar length—though the ribbing doesn't match—and move into the first bedroom I see. It's Xavier's, the bedcovers thrown back, the photo frame on the nightstand overturned. I set it upright. A picture of his Annie.

The next room is empty, and the one after that is where Jude sleeps, his clothes flung around the space, on the floor, hanging on the footboard, the open dresser drawers. I grab the first shirt and pair of jeans I can reach from the doorway and rush back to the living room, slipping on the narrow farmhouse stairs. I scrape my spine along the treads until

261

I hit the floor at the bottom, crashing hard on my tailbone. Shaken, I bite my hand to keep from crying out, roll onto my side and curl up until the pain subsides, and then I stand. Again, Jude hasn't moved. His feet and lips are zombie white. "Can you get dressed?" I ask, tucking the clothes in his arms. With jerky, automated motions, he manages to slip into his pants and shirt. He fumbles with his socks, losing his balance because he doesn't sit. I take his elbow and lower him into a chair, and I bunch up each sock and roll the fabric over his bird-thin feet. "Shoes?"

He licks his lips. "The mat."

His sneakers are there, and I kick them over to him. He worms into them without untying the laces.

"Do you have your phone?"

"I left it in his bedroom."

"Okay, I'll get it. Go to the car and wait for me."

Back upstairs, I shake the blankets and look under pillows before finding the cell phone under the bed. When I finally collapse behind the steering wheel of my Civic and turn the key in the ignition, I see only a bit more than an hour has passed. I hold out Jude's phone. "Can you manage a call to Seamus?"

"No," he whispers. Sleek, silent tears cut a trail down each cheek, each one dangling at his jaw until the next one slides down and bumps it off.

I dial and Cecelia answers. "Hey, Jude," she says, and giggles.

"It's Liesl, sweetie."

"Oh. Daddy's phone said Jude."

"I know. Can you put your dad on?"

"Daddy," she yells.

I cringe as her sharp little girl's voice pierces my eardrums. I hold the phone away from my ear until Seamus's voice comes on the line. "Liesl? What's going on?"

"Xavier has been taken to the emergency room. St. Mary's. Can you meet us there?"

"Oh, sure. Yeah. We'll come now." A pause. "Is it serious?"

"Yes."

We drive. The hospital isn't far. Jude sits rigid beside me, hands clamped between his legs, staring ahead. He doesn't wear a seat belt, which makes me much more conservative as I stop and look and turn. I park the car, but as I open the door I realize Jude isn't moving. "We should go in," I say.

He begins to shake. "He can't die. I have no one else."

"Let's just get in there and see what's happening."

"I know he's gone. I saw how those ambulance guys looked at him." I try to leave the car again and he grabs my arm, his fingernails pricking my skin through my sleeve. "Pray, Liesl. Please."

I slam the door. I want to tell him I'm a sorry excuse for a follower of Jesus, a fraud, really. I give bread to the hungry because it's what I do—bake bread. It doesn't require effort or sacrifice, only twenty cents per loaf for a custom-printed paper bag, which in turn I deduct from my yearly taxes. I go to church now, but that's to spend time with Seamus and Cecelia. Otherwise, I can't be bothered to crack open my Bible for five minutes a day. I shouldn't be allowed to pray for anyone.

Jude waits, though. I reach for him and place my hands on the back of his neck. The weight of all my awkwardness and shame drags him toward me until his forehead rests on mine. His eyes are closed. I shut mine as well and offer my own silent petition first, that I'll have the words to comfort this boy.

I start there, asking the Lord's peace and comfort on Jude, his guidance and protection. I implore him to spare Xavier, to heal him, to give wisdom to the doctors and strength to us. I ask for mercy. And finally, I ask for him to give us the grace to accept his will, whatever that may be. Jude echoes my "Amen," and we go into the hospital where a doctor waits for us with the news Xavier is dead.

"Can I see him?" Jude asks.

"Of course," the man says.

"I'll wait here," I tell Jude. He bobs his head at me, and it continues to seesaw as he walks down the sterile hallway.

I drop into a molded plastic chair, orange, too cheerful a color for this place of death, and hard as a seashell beneath my bruised tailbone. I shut my eyes and lean my head back against the wall. The world throbs around me, each ping of a monitor, burst of oxygen, staticky message over the intercom magnified in my sightlessness. Heavy footsteps, and a mountain of body and denim stops above me, blocking the bright lights still able to penetrate my eyelids. I know it's Seamus.

"He's gone," I say, eyes still closed.

He sits beside me and folds me against his neck.

And then the bread bleeds.

The priests find them, the guarded wafers, surfaces crusted with red. It looks like dried blood. What else can it be? Yes, they are certain. The bread is being crucified again, and who else but the very people who killed him the first time would want to inflict this pain on the Christ?

They blame the Jews.

Of course, the Jews have no part in it. They don't believe God can be incarnated in such a vulgar thing as bread. So why would they bother stabbing at bits of baked wheat when they think it no consequence whatsoever?

Logic does not prevail. It's the Middle Ages, a time of darkness and fear. Already anti-Semitism flows through the church as freely as the wine it calls his blood. It is far too easy to allow hatred to rule the mind. Jews are tortured publically, stretched in half on the rack, and in their agony they confess, *Yes, we pierced the bread*. Others are then rounded up en masse and beheaded, burned, or forced from their homes before they, too, can perpetrate such evil.

Five hundred years later, in an age when reason overcomes

superstition, and when bleeding food is not something to be feared but explored, a scientist discovers *Monas prodigiosa* in the lens of his microscope—a bacteria that, in the proper humidity, secretes a harmless red substance on bread.

I close the bakehouse for the week, the sign on the front door announcing a death in the family and apologizing for the inconvenience. During that time, I do little but sleep and wander through the apartment trying to fill the hours. I don't bake. I don't step foot into the bakery kitchen. Kelvin feeds the starters and manages to fit most of the daily sourdough buckets into the cooler; the rest end up in my refrigerator. They'll be fine until we reopen.

I desert Jude, wallowing in my own sadness. He has Seamus, I tell myself, but I know I'm a coward. I don't want to deal with Jude's grief, or sweep up the pieces.

Seamus calls to check on me. He tells me the funeral plans. Xavier's son Ray oversees the details. The oldest one, not Jude's father. He asks if I'm okay. He asks if he can come visit me. I decline, feeling inadequate and lost and undeserving of his attentions. He shows up anyway, Chinese takeout and new movie release in hand, Cecelia home with a sitter. I let him in, my hair unwashed, still wearing the flannel pants and thermal Henley I put on two days ago, and he loves me with my underarm odor and plaque-stained teeth. We sit on the couch twirling lo mein noodles around forks and eating our rice with spoons, and throwing greasy wads of napkin at the horrible movie. "So much for direct to video," he says. We still watch the entirety of it.

As I wrangle the disc from the drive of my computer and snap it back in the case, Seamus lingers around my bookshelf, a self-constructed grid of plastic milk crates and pine boards. College chic. Tonight is the first time he's been in the apartment for any length of time, the first since that day with the photographs. "You have a lot of books on bread."

"Observant," I say.

He laughs softly, touching the spines of each one, pausing at the khaki-covered *Beard on Bread*. I think, *Don't open it;* I don't want him to see Jonathan Scott's card taped to the cover. He doesn't take it from its spot, but raises his copper brows, wooly bear caterpillars without the black stripes. "Tell me this is someone's name."

"It is. James Beard. He was a celebrity chef back in the day. Someone gave that book to my mother. She hated it."

"Why?"

"Because Beard was down on sourdough. He didn't think it was worth the effort and called it unpredictable. He includes one recipe for those who might want to haggle with it, but his starter has commercial yeast in it."

"The philistine."

"I certainly think so."

His fingers continue their travels, and he pulls out another book, *German Bread*. Seamus flips through the pages and reads, "'Germany prides itself on having the largest variety of breads worldwide. More than three hundred basic kinds of bread are produced with more than one thousand types of small bread-rolls and pastries.' Well, that's impressive. No wonder you bake. How could you not?"

I'm not German, remember? I want to tell him, but as he closes the book he notices a handwritten date and short note in the cover. Reads it to himself. "Paul?" he asks.

I jerk my shoulders. "No one. Some guy."

He returns the book to its place. "I have one of those."

"It's less than yours. Not really serious at all." I stack the dishes on the coffee table into a pile, close cartons of rice and seal the plastic lids on foil trays of beef and broccoli.

"Should I take this as a hint?" Seamus asks.

I stop. Sigh. "No. I'm sorry. I'm not trying to kick you out of here."

"Good," he says, coming up behind me and looping his arms across my breastbone, each of his hands cupping my shoulders. I sigh again and melt back into him, his collarbone rigid against my skull. I still hold a container of fried rice.

"How's Jude?" I ask, because I'm too comfortable here, with him. I don't deserve to be soothed while the boy suffers.

"He's holding up."

"Is he still at the farmhouse?"

"No. His uncle wanted him out, like, yesterday. They're getting the place on the market as soon as the ink dries on whatever papers need to be signed."

"Then where is he? With you?"

"I offered, but he said no. He's staying with Tee."

"Tee? Really?"

"That's what he told me."

"How's that going to work? She rents a room in someone else's house."

"No. Jude said she's in an apartment now."

"She must need her bathrooms scrubbed or something."

"I think she just has a heart for the wounded."

I shrug free of Seamus's arms and carry the food to the kitchen, packing it into the Bacardi box from which it came. "Why is it Chinese places are always near liquor stores? One of the universe's great mysteries, I suppose. Anyway, you take this with you. It will just go bad here, and I bet Cecelia would like it."

I'm embarrassed. Seamus is so much more generous with people than I am, more perceptive. I don't know Tee in full, only scraps of her story culled from things she's said over the years, but well enough to hear truth in Seamus's assessment. Her father was an alcoholic, or is one—he may still be living, I'm not sure. Her mother I've never heard her mention, except to say she sometimes made brown bread, and perhaps I should consider making some for Wild Rise. She immigrated from the Ukraine with her older sister in the eighties, arriving here unable to speak English. She worked hard as a child. She works hard now. She wears a gold Russian Orthodox cross every day, the kind with three crossbars, a short and long one near the top, a crooked one toward the bottom. Tee is a rescuer of stray dogs and nestlings with broken wings, fallen from their nests. She nurses them with her cooking, Jude and Cecelia and Seamus. And, I suppose, me. She doesn't prepare special desserts for me like the others, or hot cocoa or sandwiches of cream cheese and coleslaw, but the bakehouse wouldn't be what it is without her food. Some of my customers come for her, for what she provides; to them my bread is something to dip in her delicious soup.

She has cancer.

Seamus picks up the box. "See you tomorrow at the funeral, then?"

I nod. "Yeah."

"I love you, you know."

"I don't know why."

"One of the universe's great mysteries, I guess."

I can't help but chuckle and shake my head. "Go on. The babysitter is wondering where you are, I'm sure."

He closes the front door and I hear him lumbering down the stairs, and his truck's ignition turning over with a pig-to-slaughter squeal. He's so big, he leaves a pit in the room when he goes, a giant-sized vacuum. It takes time to refill with my previous, pre-Seamus existence, each time slower, each time less, and I realize sometime soon, the hole will be one only he can occupy. What will I do then?

Twenty

Five years in a cubicle, and my hands itch. The money is good and the work challenging, but there's too much plastic beneath my fingers. I wake in the mornings, stare at my reflection while brushing my teeth, and want something else.

I don't allow myself to consider what that something else may be. *Hello, earth to Liesl*, Paul says. *Is everything okay?*

I like him. He's nice, steady, the kind of college-educated man who can buy Star Wars memorabilia without seeming socially inept, or creepy, for that matter. We have lunch together every day at work. He brings the same thing: ham and yellow American on white bread, Miracle Whip on the side so the sandwich doesn't become soggy, rippled potato chips. A kosher dill. *And a little something sweet*, he says, opening his hand to offer me one of his two Hershey Kisses or similar foil-wrapped treat. Sometimes miniature eggs at Easter, or the bite-sized candy bars he snagged for 70 percent off after Halloween. He tells me his mother packed his lunch for school the same way, with some tiny treat. *She counted out the M&M's. I always got twelve.* I don't tell him my mother, father, and I would eat an entire bag of chocolate in one sitting.

I'm good, I tell him.

Sometimes we talk on the phone, but mostly we don't. He kisses me on the cheek after work, outside the office building when we separate to go home, each in our opposite directions. Occasionally we pucker our lips to dry prunes and touch them together, a show of affection more for the great-aunt occasionally visited at the nursing home, the one with the beard who smells like urine. Now, after eighteen months of this, we add an *I love you* in there. I don't mean it, and I doubt he does. We're free variables for one another, *notation*s in the code of our existence specifying a place where *substitution* may occur. I'm twenty-seven, he's twenty-nine. It's easier to have someone to tote around if needed for a wedding or party, to be able to say to that nosy mother or friend, *Yes, of course I'm seeing someone.* We're the not-so-favorite-but-affordable shoes, knockoffs of the real deal. The pair of trendy designer jeans found at the thrift store, hot this season but a size too small, and we squeeze into them anyway, no matter how uncomfortable, for the sake of fashion. We're biding time together for the right person to come along, instead of waiting alone.

It's Saturday. Paul asks me to brunch with him and a married couple he knows from college, visiting from south of here. *They're activists,* he says, and we meet at Housing Works in Soho, a café and used-book store staffed by volunteers, and all profits fund the charity of the same name, battling homelessness and AIDS. After eating, the other couple disappears into the depths of the store while Paul and I poke through the discount bins. We're not readers, neither of us.

How long do we need to stay with them? I ask.

I know. They're not nearly as fun as they were when we were drunk together at frat parties.

I see it then, a book nearly as large as my torso, foggy cellophane cover taped around it, library call number sticker on the spine. *Breads of Germany.* The photos are full color and glorious, the recipe pages stained with crusty dough or oily fingerprints. I turn through it, mouth open and juiceless as I breathe my saliva away.

The bread found me.

Do you bake? Paul asks.

I shake my head. Swallow. *My mother did. She was German.*

Of course she was, with you having a name like Liesl. Either that, or she really liked The Sound of Music.

It's Austrian.

What is? Liesl?

No. The Sound of Music *takes place in Austria.* I have this exact conversation often, as most people have never heard my name outside the movie.

But it's under German rule at the time.

That makes all the difference, then.

Paul looks at me. *I offended you.*

No.

I did. I'm sorry. He reaches for the book. *Let me buy this for you.*

I hug it beneath my arm. *Really, that's not necessary—*

Please. I want to.

I check the inside cover, where the price is written in pencil. Five dollars. *Okay.*

He pays for it as I wait by the bin, shaking his head when offered the receipt. Then he takes it from the flat paper bag and, borrowing a pen from the clerk, writes something in the front cover. Returning the book to the bag, he gives it to me as the other couple appears, each with armfuls of paperbacks. I plead fatigue and thank the couple for lunch, wishing them well and lying about looking forward to meeting again the next time they're in the city. I squeeze Paul's hand, a surge of genuine warmth in the gesture, land a peck on his baby-smooth cheek, and hail a taxi.

My mother's starter, in Oma's crock, sleeps in the refrigerator at my apartment. I've been a neglectful caretaker, going weeks or months between feeds. But now I spoon the contents into a bowl. I wash the crock, refill it with half the starter, a cup of water, and two cups of flour, stirring to a batter-like consistency. I'll leave this on the counter, lidded, and feed twice a day in hopes a few resilient microorganisms still exist. To the rest of the starter in the bowl, I add the same, cover it with a damp towel, and stick it in the oven; the extra warmth from the oven light will incubate the yeast colonies more quickly, if there's anything left to grow.

By midnight, the mixture bubbles with life.

I quit my job, and Paul, on Monday.

Xavier's memorial is at Frederick & Sons, and I wonder about all the funeral homes I've seen with *& Sons* tagged on the end. What keeps these men glued to a business of bereavement and finality, following in the ways of their fathers? What child wakes and thinks, *I want to be a mortician when I grow up?* Perhaps for them it's an inherited fascination, the grim reaper gene. Or maybe the father simply gives his kid a nice cut of the profits.

The room is plush and gold, the rug squishing beneath my feet, all the mirrors and candelabras brass-toned, the long burgundy drapes tasseled in yellow. The chairs are brocade, the air sodden not only with the scent of dozens of floral arrangements around Xavier's closed casket but with some kind of perfumed aerosol I saw one of the attendants spritzing in the corners.

I wear my one black dress with black flats and a gray sweater, the cardigan kind with no buttons, and feel underdressed, even though the majority of people I know here—my employees and customers— are not attired much differently. The strangers, like Xavier's extended family, all wear suits, ties, and shiny shoes. I mingle and accept condolences, and it seems so strange to have others apologize to me for my loss. It is a greater loss to me than they realize. Xavier, the man who peered through me like glass. I'm still mostly opaque to Seamus, though I've become translucent around the edges.

In the tsunami of events recently—Jonathan Scott's offer, Xavier's death, everything defined and undefined with Seamus—I've been able to sidestep most of the emotional turmoil of the adoption revelation. *Most.* It's been difficult not having the long hours at the bakehouse to keep focused elsewhere. Years of avoidance, however, have given me an arsenal of techniques to stuff feelings, so if one fails me, I try another.

This week I tried reading the Bible.

Sleeping kept the memories from snapping at my heels, so I didn't get out of bed until close to noon. However, those hours after dinner, when tiredness won't come because I've dozed the better part of the day, those are the difficult hours to fill. I moved to another of my most trusted approaches: organizing something. This time it was my closet. I stripped the hangers of my clothes and sorted them into items I would keep and items I'd donate. I swept storm clouds of dust from the floor, piles thick enough to be spun to yarn, like the roving on the fiber tour my first time out with Seamus and Cecelia. I restacked the items on my topmost shelves. And, in doing all this, I found the Bible I stuffed up there because I couldn't stand it accusing me of unfaithfulness when it was somewhere I saw it every day.

I remember my father, when he first began attending church with a coworker, spending so much time with the Word flopped open on his lap, scrutinizing and underlining, the message a salve for the gaping chasm left by my mother's suicide. One flesh torn asunder, like a man who's lost half of himself in battle. I was jealous of his spiritual attentions. I wanted him to continue hurting as I hurt, for us to be fused in our grief. I never expected him to begin healing, and despite knowing even today that my father isn't whole again, he's much closer to it than I am.

So I opened the book, hardly larger than my hand with an olive faux-leather cover embossed with a swirly cross. The ribbon marker rested somewhere in Romans. I scanned the first passage my eyes fell on.

For all who are led by the Spirit of God are sons of God. For you did not receive the spirit of slavery to fall back into fear, but you have received the Spirit of adoption as sons, by whom we cry, "Abba! Father!" The Spirit himself bears witness with our spirit that we are children of God, and if children, then heirs—heirs of God and fellow heirs with Christ, provided we suffer with him in order that we may also be glorified with him.

I've heard this passage before, used to spur those in the pews to adopt children. If God adopts us, the argument goes, should we not emulate him and do the same? Not to mention all the other times we're told to care for orphans. It doesn't help me think more positively of my own circumstances. I'm confused, disoriented, and in some ways, I question my entire existence.

There is anger too, and it's directed, unexpectedly, at my mother.

It's been there since the hours after I found her, simmering, a pot of linguini on the back burner, heat turned up too high. The water foams and threatens to overflow, but I always snatch the pot away in time, moving it to a cool place until the torrents subside. *She was ill. She didn't know what she was doing.* I can't allow myself to be mad at her, though. It means—

No. I won't consider this today.

Jude sits hunched in the corner, Tee standing over him, a diminutive sentinel in black slacks and turtleneck and turban of silk around her bald head. He wears his everyday jeans but his newly dyed hair shimmers black like crow feathers. He stares at his scuffed boots. She presses an embroidered handkerchief to her nose, moving it left or right to absorb her tears before they travel all the way down her face.

"You're crying," I say.

She must hear disbelief in my voice. "It is my sadness. I am able to have it."

"I know, but—" I stop myself from the rest of it, the *you never liked him anyway*, because it's a repulsive thing to say. Death is here, she weeps for it. It doesn't matter if Xavier was her least favorite person in the world.

Tee is no fool. She reaches for my hand, holds it open, palm up, and bunches her handkerchief into it. Then she curls my fingers around it. "You take. The compassion I have, maybe you wipe it on you. Maybe you see something not your bread," she says, and she walks briskly toward the ladies' restroom.

"Tee is Tee," I mumble, as if her behavior excuses my own, and cram the hankie in my sweater pocket. To Jude, I say, "You're really staying with her?"

"Pops would want me to. She acts all tough and whatever, but when she's home you can see how sick and tired all those cancer drugs make her." He sticks his finger through a shredded patch of denim, close to his knee. "Nan was like that."

Nan. His grandmother. Xavier's Annie.

I start to ask how he is managing, but a man approaches, one of the dark suit brigade, his silver shirt and tie the same color. His stomach hangs over his belt and the skin of his face seeps downward, toward his neck, pooling in a fleshy wattle beneath his chin. He reaches us and holds out one fat hand. "Bill Potter."

"Liesl McNamara," I say, shaking it. Now it's my turn to guard Jude, and I push in closer to him, resting my arm across his shoulders. "I'm sorry for your loss."

"Yes, of course. But my father led a full life. That's the way to go, in your sleep, isn't it?"

"I imagine so."

"We should all be so fortunate." He adjusts his pants, tugging them up at the waist. "Well, we're starting soon. But I wanted to intro-duce myself."

"It's good to meet you."

"That it is. And I do understand how you might be somewhat . . . shorthanded now. In the bakery. If that changes how you feel about possible business decisions, please feel free to get in touch with me. I'm still very interested in potentially working with you."

"I appreciate your concern," I say. "But I'm sure Jude will be able to step in and handle things just fine."

The man nods. "Jude."

"Dad."

And he limps off to the front, where a similar-looking man, slightly thinner, slightly taller, his shirt and tie navy blue, talks with the rent-a-chaplain. Jude half-whispers something I think I hear, a string of words found in rated-R movies. I drag the closest unoccu-pied chair next to him and sit. "Are you okay?"

"How can Pops and I be related to that?"

"I hear chronic imbecility usually skips a generation."

Jude allows himself the tiniest grin. "What does that say for my kids?"

"Two generations, then."

I hold Jude's hand between both of mine as the memorial begins. I wish Seamus had been able to come; Cecelia took ill with a stomach virus this afternoon. He called after picking her up from the school nurse's office to say he would be home serving ginger ale and saltines to his little girl, and most likely cleaning vomit from the bathroom floor. Had he been here, he could be a citadel for Jude and me. I need something between us and the rest of this place.

Xavier's sons and daughter speak. Some of the grandchildren too—both of Jude's brothers and two younger girls. Then the chaplain blabs his regular script about the frailty of life, appreciating everyday bless-ings, and how Xavier has moved on to that elusive-sounding *better place*.

His words crush me, their weight heavier than the wood on the back of Simon the Cyrene.

Never once did I speak of faith with Xavier.

I begin to cry.

"Liesl?" Jude asks.

I wave him off and leave for the restroom, jiggle the handle. Locked. A woman waiting beside the door says, "There's a line." I push outside instead, sucking lungfuls of late October air, steam pouring from my nose and mouth. I shiver, legs bare, soul fractured, and the door opens again. It's Jude. He stands frozen for a second, and then shakes out of his hooded sweatshirt and wraps it around me.

"I didn't tell him. About God," I say, voice rough with mucus.

"I did."

I wait for more, but instead he removes a crumpled pack of cigarettes from his front jeans pocket and shakes one into his hand, closes the end between his lips as he lights it with a Bic he fishes from another pocket. Inhales until the tobacco burns brimstone red.

His smoke joins my breath, whorling into the evening sky.

As much as the bakers of the Middle Ages are mistrusted, the bakers of ancient Rome are revered. But they must have something with which to make bread. When the empire begins, Italy does have grain, more than it needs to feed its people. As the years turn to decades and the decades to centuries, the wealthy landholders find it more lucrative to raise sheep and cattle. The poor farmers—formerly soldiers given small parcels in payment for battles well fought—can no longer afford to grow wheat and move to the cities for their families' survival. The grain must come from somewhere because the people demand their bread. So Rome takes it from the *bread lands* it conquers: Egypt, Spain, North Africa, Sardinia, England.

As cities grow in Italy, so do populations. Many of these people are unemployed and receive free grain by order of the emperor. The provisions stave off revolts and civil unrest. Eventually bread is given instead of wheat, each person receiving two loaves each day, and at times more than three hundred thousand people flood the streets of Rome for their share. When the right to receive the dole is declared hereditary, the urban poor begin having more and more children.

While Italy feasts, other countries throughout the empire are stripped of their wheat and forced to send it far away for those who did not toil for it to fill their bellies. The people of the bread lands go to sleep at night without bread. And it's into this hungry world Jesus is born.

It's my father's turn to show up unexpectedly, sitting on the top step leading to the apartment when I arrive home from the funeral. His arms are across his knees, head kinked in the crook of his elbow, wheezing in that light, uncomfortable sleep way. As soon as I climb the first stair he opens his eyes and finds his glasses between his feet, slips them on.

"You said you weren't coming for the service," I say. I don't want him here—he's intruding in my mourning. "And anyway, you missed it."

"I'm here for you," Alistair says.

I unlock the door. "You could have just called me."

He peers over the top of his lenses, his face contorting into some expression more at home on the face of a teenaged girl, one who can't believe her best friend forever is dating the class clown. And we both chuckle in that family way because neither of our telephone habits lend themselves to communication. I unlock the door and he follows me inside, removing his coat but not his scarf, a camel-and-red wool plaid he's had for as long as I can remember. My mother bought it for him, I'm certain. Another trait we share, being unable to rid ourselves of anything related to her. He keeps her clothes in the attic. Her teas, now more than twenty years old, still stacked in a kitchen cabinet. Her cosmetics in the bottom vanity drawer. I have her bread, of course. I'd say it's a family thing, a genetic propensity, but I know better now. Nature. Nurture. None of it makes sense to me any longer.

I offer him coffee. He declines. I sit on the loveseat and he takes the wing chair across from me, crosses his legs, slips his finger inside his loafer, and itches the underside of his foot. I wait; my silence tortures him. Finally, he says, "I did call and leave a message."

"I know."

"How was the funeral?"

Shrugging, I say, "Like any other, I guess."

"You were close to him. I'm sorry."

"These things happen."

I don't want this harshness between us. It oozes from one of those lesions I try to keep undisturbed, but in my despair over Xavier and the confusion of my adoption I'm unable to control it. My father shuts his eyes and lets the barbed words slice over him. "I deserve your anger."

"I'm not angry—"

"You are. It's allowed. We keep too many things shut up inside, Liesl." He shakes his head. "Not this too."

"All right. I am mad. I understand why you and Mom didn't tell me about . . . things. All of it. But I can't stop feeling like, I don't know. Not that my life has been a lie, exactly. You both weren't a lie. Your love for me. I suppose I feel displaced. I thought I fit somewhere. Now I don't. It really, really hurts."

"I can't imagine. If I could go back and make different choices, you know I would." Alistair holds his hands out toward me, palms up, a gesture I imagine Jesus made when he presented his wounds to Thomas. Christ's actions comforted. My father's are empty. He and I both know that, and he says, "I can only say I'm sorry, and pray it means something to you. And hope you'll forgive me."

The tears drip from my eyes. I say, "I'm going to get in touch with her. Mary Lombardi."

I haven't actively been working to decipher the labyrinth of issues surrounding my adoption, but subconsciously—and in the Spirit, perhaps?—there's been a churning of possibilities. Yes, Xavier's death plays a prominent role in my decision; no one knows the day or the hour, and I feel I owe this woman for allowing me to be born. If something unexpectedly occurs to make our meeting impossible, I'll carry the guilt over it. My father sitting here only deepens my resolve. Do I tell him of my plan now to hurt him? Maybe I do, a little, so he, too, can feel the sting of losing a piece of himself. He simply nods, though. "I think that's right."

He's offering me up to her, my birth mother, returning me, in a sense. And I realize then I don't want to be returned. As hurt and upset as I am, I still belong to him. To both of them, Claudia and Alistair McNamara. Those ties—our pasts, our shared experiences, our devotion—none of it can be severed.

"I forgive you, Dad."

He weeps too, quietly, and comes to me on the couch. I lean against him and we sniffle together, wiping our runny noses on our wrists until he snatches the roll of paper towels from the kitchen and returns to my side. Conversation eludes us, and we're both fine with that, having had years of practice with silence. Eventually the room darkens and I plead fatigue and offer my father my bed for the night. "You can't go home now," I tell him. He doesn't drive well at night.

"Where will you sleep?"

"Here."

"I won't take your bed and make you be crushed up on this little excuse for a couch. I'm fine on the floor."

"Dad."

The word is nothing but a casual address to me, but it stops my father and he touches my face, his recently upturned, empty palm warm on my cheek. "That's right."

I nod and gather blankets and pillows to build his nest on the carpet.

⁓

When Wild Rise reopens, I'm back on three a.m. duty. I set the most irritating alarm possible thirty minutes before then on my new cell phone—yes, I break down and buy one; it's a tax write-off, I rationalize—my body creaking and moaning from bed to the bathroom. I manage to brush my teeth, splash cold water on my face because I don't wait the necessary thirty seconds for it to heat, and wrangle my hair into an elastic. It's unruly now, my hair, the layers at odd, in-between lengths, my bangs shaggy and over my eyes. I position my lower lip over my upper one and blow, the strands parting in the center of my forehead, and then I twist them into an unattractive bunch, clipping them atop my head, away from my face.

So much for all León's artistry.

I dress and leave my bed unmade, since I'll be coming back to it in a few hours, and go downstairs. Jude either waits for me or he's bouncing down the street with that tiptoed gait of his, hands deep in the pockets of his hooded sweatshirt, stocking cap stretched over his head; Tee's apartment is close enough he can walk to work.

He's learned to use his alarm too.

"Where's your coat, for goodness' sake?" I ask.

"Don't have one."

The first couple of days we light the fire together, but then I allow Jude to do it alone, and it's clear Xavier taught him well. He stacks the wood expertly and we wait for the oven to heat to the proper temperature. Because Kelvin does much of the shaping the night before, there are only a few types of dough left to proof and form into loaves. Jude and I tarry. I make coffee and sort through notes left by Gretchen. Jude slips a Bible from his pocket and reads aloud, asking questions I usually can't answer. "Try Seamus," I tell him.

"I will. I'll see him tomorrow. He's helping me study for my license. And he found out for me that I can have help on the written part of the test. Someone at the DMV will read me the questions."

We talk about things, about how he's concerned for Tee. "She cries sometimes. She turns on the shower and radio and thinks I can't hear her, but I do." Most often he tells stories of Xavier, remembrances, like about the time he was three and his grandfather said if he planted a twig in the yard, it would grow. "Pops was trimming the hedges and gave me a trowel and told me to find the perfect baby tree. I scoured the yard until I found one with a single leaf still stuck on it. I dug a hole and stuck it in, and tromped down the dirt with my feet. Pops told me not to forget to water it. I sprayed it with the hose until it fell over." He laughs. "The next week I came back and there was a tree in the ground where my stick had been. Pops went to the nursery as soon as I'd left and bought a sapling, this tiny thing, about as tall as me. I think I was ten before he told me the truth."

"Is it still there?"

"The tree? Heck yeah. Know that big maple in the front? That's it. I can't believe my dad's selling the place. I mean, I can, but . . ." He swats his eyes and makes a disgusted little snort. "I better check the oven."

"You know, I could have Kelvin start it before he leaves. That would give us an extra hour or so to sleep in."

"I don't mind doing it," and he means, *No, I need to do this, please don't take it from me.* It's his connection with Xavier, what he learned first. He can't lose it.

I understand. I have the sourdough knitting me to my mother.

No, not my mother. I've not yet found my peace with her, even though I offered forgiveness to my father.

Jude takes a handful of flour and tosses it around the oven. I watch as the fine white powder darkens, first to gold, then to brown. "We're good," he says.

"There's a thermometer for that."

He shrugs. "Pops told me not to trust it. What if it breaks or something? He said I need to know how to know if it's time without it."

We begin baking, and he's as dexterous as Xavier with a lame and peel. I take joy in watching him move, the sleek muscles in his arms, his shoulder blades, his hands. As the room crackles with cooling loaves, I disappear into the euphony of the bread, and for a time nothing exists but the radiant heat of the bricks, the in-out waltz of baking, the sweat of our brow. By seven, Ellie has unlocked the front door and Tee is here; she comes earlier now because of the expanded breakfast menu, stays through lunch, and leaves detailed instructions for Rebekah to prepare for the next day.

We're all learning how to relinquish control a little.

While Jude helps with the front counter and Ellie waits tables, I tell Tee, "Jude doesn't have a winter coat."

She removes a wild yeast breakfast cake from the oven. "I not his mother."

"No, but he needs one."

She doesn't ask which I mean, a mother or the parka, but shuts the oven door with enough force to rattle the entire kitchen, signaling the end of the discussion.

I'm falling asleep on my feet by the time Rebekah starts her shift at nine, so I sneak back upstairs for a couple hours' worth of nap. How I used to run this place all on my own, I can no longer fathom. The community that Pastor Ryan is constantly imploring us to develop in our own lives—it's happened here in the bakehouse, a wild yeast colony, expanding and adapting, nourished in the care of one another. I climb beneath the blankets but can't find my way into sleep.

I decide to call my birth mother.

I took the number from the caller ID weeks ago, wrote it on an order receipt from the café, and stashed it in my freezer beneath the ice cube trays I don't use. I remove it now, unfold the brittle paper, and dial my new cell phone. "Hello?" a woman says.

"Is Mary Preston home?"

"Speaking."

"This is Liesl . . . McNamara."

Deep, overwhelming silence. And then the smallest of sobs. A hiccup, a sniffle. A trembling voice. "You called. I didn't think—I didn't know if I'd hear . . . How are you?"

I can't make small talk now. "I thought you might like to meet."

"Yes, oh my, yes. Of course. When? Where? I'm only six hours away. I can be there tonight, or tomorrow. Or—"

"Friday evening. Would that work for you?"

"Yes, that's perfect. I'll bring your sister with me. Dana. The one you spoke with before, if you don't mind, that is."

"That's fine." Lack of sleep, the emotional toll of this conversation, of the past several weeks, builds in my head. "Call me when you get into town and we'll decide a place."

"I will. Okay. That sounds perfect."

"Good. I'll talk to you Friday."

"Liesl?"

Oh, my head. *Please, stop talking already.* "Yes?"

"Just . . . thank you."

Hands shaking, I grope through the medicine cabinet, knocking toothpaste and deodorant into the sink, along with a bottle of ibuprofen and my tweezers, which slip down the unplugged drain. I'll fish them out later, or better yet, have Seamus do it for me. For the moment, I take three Advil and then swallow two acetaminophen tablets for good measure. I burrow into the mattress, covering my face with a pillow, and don't wake until Gretchen comes to find me, tapping my forehead with an infuriating woodpecker of a fingernail, letting me know it's closing time. "It must be nice to sleep on the job."

❧

The next day Jude walks through the doors with the shiniest marsh-mallow of a down jacket I've ever seen. I raise an eyebrow.

"Tee," he says.

"Well, it looks warm."

"Warm enough I'm willing to wear it." Hanging it on the kitchen coatrack, he adds, "I think it's a girl's coat. When I zipped it this morning, the zipper was on the other side. I couldn't figure out what I was doing wrong."

I chuckle. Tee will always be Tee. "At least it's black," I say.

Twenty-One

I want to open a bakery, and I want to travel to Paris.

For the time being, I do neither of these things. I simply bake bread. My hands must reacquaint themselves with dough. My eyes must learn the respiration of yeast, the rise and fall of proofing, how each formula reacts to oven spring and steam. I line the wire racks with baking tiles and do the rest of my cooking and reheating on the stovetop.

I've lived frugally the past six years. My home is a basement studio outside Manhattan, in a house owned by senile Mrs. Brownell and her daughter; they charge four hundred and fifty dollars a month and make me take care of my own garbage and snow shoveling. I keep the water temperature low and the thermostat lower so they won't think to raise my rent. I use public transportation. I don't purchase clothes or shoes unless an absolute necessity, like when the soles separate from the leather and flap as I walk. I eat canned tuna with Italian dressing over lettuce almost every day for lunch, something else from a can—beef ravioli is a favorite, but I don't mind noodle soup or baked beans on occasion—for dinner, and skip breakfast altogether, except if there is free food in the office break room, which there usually is, some client thanking us with a fruit basket, some administrative assistant bringing in cake for a coworker's birthday. My student loans are almost paid off. I have a nice double-digit nest egg to draw from until I figure out what comes next.

Until then, bread.

I read the books—Peter Reinhart, Jeffrey Hamelman, Maggie Glezer, Joe Ortiz, Daniel Leader. I employ the techniques—cold fermentation, long fermentations, high hydration dough, whole grains, sprouted grains, hand-milled grains. I produce a dozen loaves a day, giving them to the mailman, Mrs. Brownell and her daughter, the woman at the organic store where I buy my flour. My flavors are complex and developed, the crust what I consider the perfect shade of honey-brown. I control the sour tang of the bread, more or less depending on the taste I'm seeking. But one thing eludes me.

Those beautiful, large rooms in the crumb.

Oh, I covet them.

I see photos in books and on artisan baking websites. I follow formulas to the gram, the minute, the degree. I remove the loaves from the oven, forcing myself to wait the required cooling time, and then I slice into them, each movement of the knife heightening the expectation. It's receiving the most elegantly wrapped gift, all tight corners and spiral ribbon, knowing the surprise inside can be anything from boring items of clothing to matchbox cars to the Easy Bake Oven at the top of the Christmas list for the past three years but still undelivered. I spread the halves of the loaf and look.

I sigh. A tight crumb with a dime-sized hole here and there. Underwear again.

When I tell Seamus my birth mother is coming, he asks if I need him to go with me. I shake my head, touched by his offer but feeling the need to do this on my own.

Mary Preston calls, and I direct her to Green Mountain Community Church. A diner seems too public, unrestricted, and I'm not certain how any of us will react. But I don't want this woman—this stranger—at Wild Rise. Not yet. That's mine. And having her there, to me, is nothing short of allowing her to trample my mother's— Claudia's—grave. The church is quiet enough to allow conversation but with enough people coming and going to the Friday night ministries that it won't seem we're all alone.

They wait for me in the lobby. My father is right; I look like her, Mary, or a version of her pinned up on the clothesline and left too long, stretched by gravity and wind and time. Taller and thinner, but our features are nearly identical. It's startling, to both of us, I think. She blinks away tears when she sees me, clings to her daughter's hand. I stop about three feet from them, a safe distance.

"Oh, my sweet Lord, I can't believe you're here," Mary says.

I don't know if her exclamation is reverent or blasphemous. I motion to the far corner of the room, near the gas fireplace, where a quartet of tub chairs face one another around a squat coffee table. "Is this good?"

Mary nods. Her daughter leads her by the elbow and they sit. I choose the chair facing Dana because sitting across from this woman who gave birth to me is like something out of a gothic story and I'm staring into a haunted looking glass that shows what I'll be twenty years from now. It almost frightens me.

"So, I'm Dana, by the way," my half sister says. "Obviously. I'm sorry my phone call last month was so . . . unsettling. We didn't mean to do that to you."

"I don't know what way it could have been done to not be unsettling."

"We just don't want you to feel—"

"It's fine."

Dana breathes deeply. "Oh, that's good. I was worried I really screwed things up."

A clumsy silence follows. My legs tingle, my scalp. I scratch my calf through my jeans, only intensifying the creeping sensation. I'd like to gouge my skin. Instead, I cross my legs in an attempt to dampen the itchiness. Mary has her own nervous ticks; she slides the gold pinky ring on her right hand up and down, from nail to knuckle. She jiggles her knees. "You talked to Alistair, then."

I nod. "Yeah."

More silence.

"I don't know how to do this," she says.

I crack my thumbs. "I suppose you could ask me some questions, if you have any."

"Okay," she says. "How long have you had your bakery?"

"Going on four years now."

"And you like it."

"I wouldn't do anything else."

"Did you go to school for it?"

"My mother taught me." She flinches, the heart-shaped ring tumbling from her pinky. Dana quickly drops to the carpet and finds it beneath Mary's chair. Gives it back to her. Mary squeezes it in both hands. "I'm sorry," I say.

"No," she says. "Don't be. I understand. She is your mother."

She asks a few more questions. *You're not married?* No. *Someone special?* Yes, someone. *Is Alistair well?* Hanging in there. How probing this all feels, coming from some person I don't know. It becomes clear the interrogation isn't moving things forward in a way either of us thought it might, and the conversation lulls again. A few women I know walk by us. "Hey, Liesl," they call, and I wave back. Finally, Mary tries again. "Do you have anything you want to ask me?"

I have to know. "Do you bake?"

"Not really."

Dana laughs, a combination of nerves and humor. "Mom can't even make those Pillsbury cinnamon rolls, you know the ones that pop out of the can? She always messes them up somehow—" She stops, clearly afraid she's said the wrong thing.

For me, however, it's the only thing I want to hear. If they had said, "Oh yes, Mary is a fantastic home baker. She makes bread from scratch every day, and pies and cakes and muffins, and wins blue ribbons at the county fair in every baking category every single year," it would have devastated me. I would have, as my father feared, lost my mother all over again, never knowing if the bread had been loved into me, or was simply a genetic by-product of an accidental teenage pregnancy. But there is no doubt now. I am Claudia McNamara's daughter, wild yeast harvester and keeper of the bread. It's mine and hers and Oma's—our bond, passed down through the generations. I'm still Liesl, and no matter what blood I have in my vessels, the brot is what sustains.

Mary slides a folded rectangle of blue paper onto the table. "This is your fa—birth father's phone number. He'd like to hear from you. When you're ready."

"He knows you're here?"

"Yes." She spins her engagement ring around her finger, the solitaire not large but bright. "We . . . I mean, we were in love, as much as two naïve teenagers can be. We were just so young, and things were different then. We both thought adoption was best. But after . . . well, we couldn't even look at each other, it all hurt too much. We kept in touch, though. A Christmas card most years, a phone call now and again, to catch up. He's happily married with two sons, and a grandbaby too. He's really looking forward to you getting in touch, but he knows it's . . . a lot to, well, digest."

Another stretch with no words. One of the meetings ends, and people stream through the sitting area. Mary says, "I think we've probably taken up enough of your time."

I ache for her. We both want the impossible. Her the daughter she never had as if she hadn't given her away. Me the mother I did have, and only her, whole and alive. Opposite desires. I close my eyes, compelled by the tickling of the Spirit, and ask, *What now?*

Trust me, and tumble into the midst of it. There's a place you will meet her, eventually, in the middle.

"I'm sorry. This probably wasn't what you were envisioning when you called me," I say.

"It was more than I could have hoped for," Mary says. She touches the tiny gold heart again, now back in place on her finger. "This ring. I bought it on your first birthday. I've looked at it every day and thought of you. I've had thirty-three years to prepare for this day and I'm at a loss. You've had three weeks. I know it's overwhelming. I'd like to stay in touch, but would understand if, for some reason, you didn't want that."

What did Seamus say? I haven't lost—I've gained. "I'd like to try to get to know you better." I look at Dana. "All of you."

My birth mother finds a travel package of Kleenex in her coat pocket, wads three or four tissues together, and lowers her face into them. Her body trembles, and Dana rests a hand on her curved back. She sniffs, mops her eyes, and tries to smile at me. "I can be patient."

We stand, our bodies contorted in odd configurations because we don't know what to do with them. Dana tells me they have hotel reservations about two hours from here. Mary offers both her hands to me. I take them, and she tightens her fingers around mine. "Thank you," she says.

I move my head, nearly imperceptibly, more a tremble than a nod. She wants to embrace me, but I'm not ready for that yet. She gives my hands one more squeeze and they go out as they came in, her daughter leading her by the elbow. I wonder what they'll say about me during the drive home.

Sourdough Breakfast Cake

Makes one cake

LIESL'S NOTES:

Sourdough isn't only for bread. Any grain-based baked good— from crackers to waffles, from muffins to pasta, can be made with a wild yeast starter. Why would the home baker want to incorporate sourdough into their regular baking? First, it's an excellent way to use the starter you remove during feedings. Instead of throwing the excess in the trash, add it to your pancake batter or chocolate chip cookies. Second, a sourdough starter is an ecosystem of wild yeasts and beneficial bacteria that work together to add B-vitamins to grains, to break down gluten for better digestion, and to neutralize phytic acid and enzyme inhibitors. In other words, it's good for you. And finally, because sourdough eventually becomes a way of life. Experimenting with different ways of using it is one of the most satisfying aspects of using wild yeast in your kitchen.

This recipe requires 24 hours of fermentation time. Begin the sponge on the morning of the day before you plan to serve the cake for breakfast. Also, please note this is not a sweet cake and really is more suited for a healthy breakfast than for a dessert.

INGREDIENTS
FOR THE SPONGE:

100 grams (1/2 cup) active sourdough starter

120 grams (1 cup) white whole wheat flour (unbleached all-purpose flour, or a mix of all-purpose and whole wheat, can be substituted)

120 grams (1/2 cup) water

FOR THE BATTER:

180 grams (1¹/2 cups) white whole wheat flour (unbleached
    all-purpose flour, or a mix of all-purpose and whole wheat,
    can be substituted)

245 grams (1 cup) buttermilk or soured milk

55 grams (¹/4 cup) oil or 57 grams (¹/4 cup) melted butter

2 eggs

200 grams (¹/2 cup) sugar

3 grams (¹/2 teaspoon) salt

5 grams (¹/2 teaspoon) vanilla extract

Zest of one lemon

9 grams (2 teaspoons) baking soda

2–3 cups of berries of your choice (fresh or frozen), because
    the weight of different fruits vary, no gram measurement is
    given

EQUIPMENT:

large glass or ceramic mixing bowl
plastic wrap or clean kitchen towel
9 x 13-inch baking dish
electric mixer or stand mixer with paddle attachment

DO AHEAD

Twenty-four hours prior to baking the cake, combine the sponge
ingredients—sourdough starter, flour, and water—in a glass
or ceramic bowl. Cover with a damp cloth or plastic wrap and
allow to rest for approximately 12 hours in a warm place (an
oven with the light on works well).

The night before baking, add the rest of the flour, buttermilk, and oil. Mix well. Re-cover and allow to rest for another
12 hours.

ON BAKING DAY

Preheat the oven to 400 degrees Fahrenheit. Grease a 9 x 13 inch baking dish. To the sourdough batter, add the eggs, sugar, salt, extract, and lemon zest. Mix well with an electric mixer. Sprinkle the baking soda on top of the batter and mix again. Pour the batter into the baking dish. Gently scatter the berries across the top of the cake. Bake for 30 minutes or until a knife inserted in the center of the cake comes out clean.

Let cool for 5 to 10 minutes. Serve topped with freshly whipped cream.

Seamus's truck rattles up to the loading area, and he bursts through the screen door, into the kitchen, leaving the engine to idle. I'm about to make a joke about it, a half joke, since he knows how I feel about the exhaust billowing into the bakehouse, but I see his face, lips white and eyes frightened, and ask, "What's wrong? Is it Cecelia?"

He shakes his head. "My mother. She's had a stroke."

"Oh no. What can I do?"

"Pray," he says. "And I need someone to watch Ceese for a few days. Do you think you could—"

"Done. She can stay with me as long as you need."

He fills his barrel-sized chest with air, and while exhaling, envelops me in his arms. "Thank you, thank you," he says, rocking me a little, more for his comfort than mine. And then releases me. "I have to go. My flight's at five. I'm already cutting it close."

"Just go. We'll be fine here."

Again he hugs me. "Okay. I'll call you both later."

Cecelia knows, when she gets off the bus, she's staying with me. "Daddy told the school. And the teacher told me. She said Grandma is sick and it's a 'mergency."

"She's right."

We drive to their house to pack a bag for her. Seamus forgot to leave a key for me, and he did lock the door for the trip out of town. Cecelia, however, knows which rock in the flower bed is the fake one with the trapdoor in the bottom. She crawls under a shaggy evergreen bush and returns only seconds later. "Ta-da," she says, holding the rather unrealistic resin stone in her hand. I unlock the door and we scramble through the house, collecting clothes for school and clothes for play, pajamas, toothbrush and hairbrush, and all her Littlest Pet Shop figures.

"Don't you want to pick out a few and leave the rest here? That way they don't get lost," I ask.

She scrunches her nose. "I guess you're right," she says, and dumps the container's contents into the middle of the living room rug. While she's choosing, I wash the dishes left on the table and in the sink. No one should come home to a dirty kitchen.

We pack the car with Cecelia's suitcase and Pillow Pet unicorn, and I assure her I have plenty of blankets so she doesn't need to bring the three fleecy ones from her closet or her sleeping bag. "But where will I sleep? Do you have two beds?"

"No. But I do have an awfully comfortable couch the perfect size for you."

What I don't have is food, at least food that isn't claimed by Tee to be used in the café. I'm tempted to swing through some fast food drive-through window, but that won't solve the dinner issue for tomorrow, or however long Cecelia stays with me. We go to the grocery store instead, the little girl tossing hot dogs and buns and cherry Pop Tarts into our basket. "This is for tonight. And we need school lunch stuff too," she says. I exchange our basket for a shopping cart and mentally berate myself for not thinking to take things from Seamus's fridge. In the end, I have eighty dollars' worth of kid food and no idea how I spent so much.

I boil the hot dogs because Cecelia tells me that's how her father makes them, and she eats three with so much ketchup the rolls fall

CHRISTA PARRISH

apart. Then I help her adjust the water for her shower, and while she's washing—and singing the *na-na-nas* of "Hey Jude"—I make up the couch, tucking sheets firmly into the crevices of the cushions. She skips from the bathroom not quite dry, her pajamas sticking to her here and there, her hair dripping down her back. I soak the moisture from her ends and she asks, "Can you brush it for me?"

"Sure." I have her sit cross-legged on the floor in front of me, like my mother did for me, and work her brush through the tangles. "I'm trying to be gentle."

"We forgot my spray. It makes the knots disappear."

"Well, we can get it tomorrow, if we have to. There, you're done. Teeth now."

She scampers back to the bathroom and I pack a lunch for her, peanut butter and jelly with baby carrots, pretzels, and two packages of fruit snacks. I remember how my mother used to write notes on the napkins in my lunch box, so I find an ink pen and draw a heart, printing beneath it, *Have a happy day! Love, Liesl*, and tuck it under her sandwich.

"Can we call Daddy?"

"We can try," I say, but the call goes straight to Seamus's voice mail. Cecelia leaves a rambling message about hot dogs and Pet Shops and the rock with the key in it. "And we put it back right where it's s'posed to go. Cross my heart." Then I cover her with blankets and tell her if she needs anything at all, I'll be right down the hall. "I'll leave the bathroom light on, so you can see."

"Wait. You hafta pray with me."

"Oh, right." *Oh boy.* I close my eyes and begin, "Dear God—"

"No, not like that. The prayer Daddy says."

"I don't think I know that one, sweetie."

"I do. I got it memorized. In peace, O God, we shut our eyes. In peace, again, we hope to rise. While we take our nightly rest, be with those we love the best. Guide us in your holy way. Make us better every day. Amen."

"Amen," I repeat.

"'Night, Liesl. If Daddy calls when I'm sleeping, tell him I love him."

"I will."

Seamus does call later, while I'm in my bedroom dozing with the light on, waiting for him. "I woke you," he says.

"Just tell me what's going on."

He says his mother has had a moderate stroke. She's conscious and recognizes him, but her speech is uneven and she's lost maneuverability on the right side of her body. The prognosis is good for an almost full recovery, but how long that will take is a guessing game. "She won't be able to be alone at home, once she's out of the hospital."

"Well, there are nurses and home aides, right?"

"Yes," he says, the word drawn out, my drowsy mind aware of the change in his voice but unable to process what it may mean. "Are you sure you're okay there with Cecelia? I think I'll be home on Tuesday."

Five days. "We're fine. Did you get her message, by the way?"

"I did."

"She wants me to tell you she loves you."

"Tell her I love her back. I'll call earlier tomorrow."

I smother a yawn against my shoulder. "Good. Three in the morning comes soon, you know."

"Liesl?"

"Hmm?"

"I love *you* too."

I nod, even though he can't see me. "Same here." I don't tell him his words make me tingle. A girl has to keep some secrets.

Twenty-Two

I pack my suitcase for Paris. My flight is in less than a month, and I plan my travels around the bread—boulangeries I must visit, regions known for certain techniques or varieties, rural one-baker villages that may or may not still exist, mentioned in obscure and possibly obsolete guides. I do the same for Germany with thoughts of taking the Eurail, or perhaps purchasing a small automobile—which may double as my sleeping quarters—and moving freely between the two countries. Or more. I have enough savings, if I'm wise with my money, to stay for five months and still buy an airplane ticket back home. Perhaps longer if I subsist predominantly on bread. *Der Mensch lebt nicht vom Brot allein*, my Oma would say. Man does not live by bread alone. I intend to prove her wrong.

I don't give up my studio yet, but do have fantasies of not returning at all.

And then I see the advertisement. A small space in Billingston, Vermont, population fifteen thousand, former pizzeria already outfitted with a wood-fire oven in a building with a one-bedroom apartment above the restaurant space. I blink at the rent. Surely it must be a typo—or perhaps I don't know the cost of things outside Manhattan—and if it isn't, the place will be leased by now. I pace several days and finally call the phone number. Yes, the price is correct and yes, it's still available. Would I like to see it?

I drive four hours and as soon as I cross from New York into Vermont, I feel a shift in my soul, something I've not experienced since my mother was alive and I came home from school to bread cooling on the counter and her, simply *being* and being there, offering me a snack and milk, her hair curling over my face when she bent close, the scent of honey and lemon verbena. The restaurant space seats thirty comfortably, crudely painted murals of grapes and wine and meatballs on the walls. The kitchen is dominated by the brick oven, but large enough for three people to work without tangling together. The realtor apologizes for the size of the apartment; I don't tell her it's more than triple my studio space.

I am supposed to have Paris, like my mother was unable to. I am supposed to visit her homeland and immerse myself in all things bread. Starting a business will empty me, my time, my bank account, and I know enough about life to realize if I don't go on my trip now, there may not be another chance. Still, this opportunity begs me to consider it.

Why don't you stroll around? the realtor suggests. So I do. Following the sidewalk, I leave the small downtown area—perhaps thirty independently owned shops, galleries, and eateries. No chain stores, one local bank, and several professional offices. I pass into a residential area. The houses hunch together, mostly turn-of-the-century homes, longer than they are wide, with picket fences and wicker chairs on front porches, not unlike the one in which I grew up. I slow as I approach a white chapel, stop at the bottom cement stair, and touch the metal railing, tracing the twist in the wrought iron with my finger. I feel as though a rope has been tied around my waist and someone—something?—pulls me toward the door. It has to be locked, I think, but when I press the latch and yank, it opens. I glance left, right, and duck inside. I can use a place to sit and think for a few minutes.

The carpet is worn and red, the padded chairs gray, the walls some sort of paneling painted white. Water has damaged one corner of the ceiling, a *café au lait* spot I half expect to look like the face of the Virgin Mary, since that's what happens in places like this. I stare at it for a while but can't even manage to see a pair of eyes, let alone some recognizable person. I sigh and close my eyes.

What am I going to do about the bakery space?

Take it.

I jump, the words so vibrant and clear, and look around for the person who spoke to me. There's no one. I'm alone. I tell myself it's all in my head but, remarkably, unexpectedly, don't believe it.

Who do people say I am?

My father's God has come to me.

I watched him for years, how easily he slipped into his faith, the one I mocked and railed against, the one I wanted no part of, the one that replaced my mother. I swore I was above such primitive mythologies. My father needed a crutch. I was the brave, strong one who could overcome in my own sufficiency. Now I hear voices. No, one voice. It's a light switch, an open circuit now connected, a burning bush. A miracle.

His God is now my God.

I walk back downtown, to the realtor's office, and sign a lease for the bakery.

The days pass uneventfully and that makes them special, Cecelia stitched into the shirring of my routine. She joins Jude and me downstairs in the morning once she wakes, around seven, and sits on a tall stool at the proofing table, asking sleepy questions about the bread. I answer them all, reminding her not to poke at the dough, but invariably she does, and when she goes upstairs to dress I find one mound or another degassed, flat as a punctured inner tube, with a handprint patted into the center, or a tunnel of a little finger, or a pinch and pull. I explain to her again how delicate dough is, and like a balloon it needs all the air inside it. "What fun is a balloon if it doesn't float?" I ask, but I can't be upset with her. Dough is magnetic—everyone wants to touch it.

Tee comes a bit earlier to cook Cecelia breakfast, whatever she wants, and it's been bacon and more bacon. And cinnamon buns. On the days she has school I drive her. She returns on the bus and contin-ues her regular afternoon routine, bouncing between doing homework, helping Gretchen, and chattering to whoever will listen. By Sunday, Seamus's absence is magnified because he's not at church with us, not around to go to lunch, and, as Cecelia puts it, we miss him like crazy.

He does make it back Tuesday evening, trying to surprise us by coming quietly up the stairs to my apartment, but nothing about Seamus is quiet and we hear his exaggerated tiptoe, the treads shift-ing beneath his weight. We pretend he's successful, though. "Shh," I whisper to Cecelia as she giggles. "We don't know it's him."

The door flings open and Seamus says, "Who forgot about me?"

"Daddy," Cecelia shouts, lunging into his waiting arms.

"Ooof. You're heavier."

"That's because Tee spoils her rotten," I say, feeling a bit Donna Reed-ish, drying my hands on a dish towel as my man comes home. Perhaps I need heels and pearls.

Seamus pulls me into him too, and it's family. We've adopted one another.

"Is Grandma okay?" Cecelia asks.

He sets her on the floor. "She's getting better. Now, go grab your stuff. I'm beat, and you have school in the morning."

"I'll help you," I say, and together we make sure she has kittens and puppies—Zoë and Daisy and Justin B. and Firefly; I can name them all now—and her autumn leaves poem she wrote for homework, as well as her clothes. I zip her coat for her, tug on her hat, and kiss her forehead. "I'll see you tomorrow."

She hugs me around the waist. I look at Seamus and know he's troubled. He tickles her ribs so she releases me and then picks her up again. "We'll talk later."

I nod and mouth, *I love you.*

When I emerge from the kitchen at eight thirty the next morning, Seamus is waiting at a table with coffee and a croissant, one of the items I added to the menu once Kelvin arrived. I gesture to Ellie to come back into the kitchen with me. "How long has he been out there?"

"I don't know. Half hour, maybe?"

"Why didn't you tell me?"

"He never asked me to."

I go to him, touch his arm. He looks more ragged than yesterday, dusky pits beneath his eyes, his face thinner than a week ago. "What's going on?"

"Do you have a minute?"

"Yes, of course. Let's go upstairs," and once we're in my living room he consumes me in his embrace, inhaling the scent of my hair and trembling. I twist my head so I can see him, and he's crying.

"What's wrong? Seamus, is it your mother? Did something else happen?"

He wipes his sleeve across his eyes. "No, nothing's changed with her."

"Oh good. You had me worried."

"Liesl, I need to go to Tennessee."

"Again? Yeah, sure. Not a problem. Cecelia is fine staying with me. Really. I love having her—"

"I need to move there."

I blink. "What do you mean?"

"I told you, my mother can't be alone anymore. Someone needs to stay with her."

"But a nurse—"

"—is fine for part of the day, but I don't want her with strangers all the time. I'm her son. I have a responsibility—"

"I understand that. But can't you move her here?"

"No," he says, shaking his head. "The doctors say she needs to be in her own familiar environment for the best chance of recovery. Plus, it's too cold here. Her arthritis." He throws up his hands. "It just won't work."

"It won't work, or you don't want it to work?"

"That's unfair, and you know it."

I sink onto the loveseat. The upholstery has been flawless up until this past week, Cecelia not only splashing milk and squishing cherry filling onto the cushions, but also wiping her hands on the matching throw pillows. She did it absentmindedly while engrossed in a movie, tossing Cheese Puffs in her mouth and either licking the fluorescent orange powder from her fingers or sweeping them over the nubby fabric. I gave her a stack of napkins and washed the spots as best as I could when she wasn't here.

I'll miss her. I'll miss them both.

"Well, people do the long-distance thing all the time. I guess we just try it and see what happens," I say, forcing a good attitude. But I already know the outcome. He won't be able to leave his mother, and I can't leave the bakehouse, and in two months it'll be over. We'll hang on a few more weeks because we don't want our hearts broken. Eventually the phone calls will lessen and our feelings will cool, and we'll part as so-called friends but in reality never speak to one another again.

Seamus sits next to me, our inside knees touching, and takes my hands. "Or you can marry me."

"I'm sorry. What?"

"Marry me. Come with us. I don't want to wait and see what happens. I want you."

"Seamus, I'm flattered, really. But it won't work."

"Why not?"

"Well, Wild Rise, for one."

"It's not like you can't open a bakery down there. All you'd have to do is advertise your *Bake-Off* win and people will flock to buy your bread."

"But I'm established here. This is my home, Seamus. I've been working for this my entire life, even before I knew it. It's all I have."

"You have Cecelia and me."

"Now you're not being fair. You're asking me to drop everything for you, but you're not willing to consider the same."

"My mother's a person. You're talking about a business. And one that can be replaced, at that. They're not even remotely the same."

You cannot serve two masters.

I am hiding behind the bakehouse, huddled in the shadow of it, using the bread as an excuse to avoid opening up that area of my adolescent self that atrophied after my mother's death. The part capable of loving and receiving love. I've been hiding since the very moment I saw her lifeless body in the front seat of the Buick, using whatever means possible to keep from facing the agony she caused. *No*, I tell myself. *It wasn't her. It was the illness. She didn't have control.* My mantra, the one I've repeated all these years to keep the anger in its place. Only now it doesn't work as well. Instead, I swallow my feelings; it burns like vomit on an empty stomach, all digestive juice and gall.

I will not blame her.

I disengage my hands from his, take a deep breath. "People have long-distance relationships all the time. Let's just see what happens."

Seamus presses his lips together, cups his mouth with his hand, pulling downward at his beard. Bobs his head. "Fine. You're right.

They do." And then he leaves me there, sitting on the loveseat, picking at the stains left by his daughter.

∞

The first thing Christ is tempted with is bread. After fasting forty days and forty nights, the adversary comes to him and says, *If you are the Son of God, tell these stones to become bread.*

And why should it not be this way? God in flesh wears humanity in full; he hungers as his people hunger so they may never claim he doesn't understand the gnawing in their bellies. But he also knows something their eyes have not yet been opened to, that man shall not live on bread alone.

Five thousand people believe otherwise.

They follow him because he heals the sick, but the day is long and they are tired. And hungry. Jesus has compassion on them, and breaking five loaves of barley bread—the bread of poverty—he feeds them until they have their fill. He desires to be their provision, teaching them to implore God for their daily bread, allowing the apostles to glean on the Sabbath, reminding the multitudes of the Father's care for birds and grasses. How much more will they be satisfied?

The next day the people search for him because they want more. That is the crux of hunger—it always returns. For the wealthy, this is a minor inconvenience, nothing more. For this crowd, however, it is a way of life. They want the bread of heaven to rain down on them, like their ancestors received in the desert, so they will never again worry where their next meal comes from.

I am the bread, Jesus says.

Hearing this, most of his followers turn their backs to him; they want the food that perishes. He will not feed them so they have no reason to stay.

Do you want to go away as well? he asks the twelve.

Lord, to whom shall we go?

In less than a week Seamus and Cecelia are packed and on their way, a For Sale sign hastily pounded into the ground at the end of their driveway, all their ends in Billingston knotted up and the bakehouse in mourning. The two of them park Seamus's truck in front of the building and come through the front door—a gesture, separating themselves from this place; they are no longer heirs, but guests, no different than any other paying customer—and they come to say good-bye before beginning their twenty-hour trek to Nashville.

Seamus keeps the truck running. He knows that trick too.

Tee, especially, takes their departure hard. She gives them boxes of food for the trip. She pinches Seamus's cheek, tugging it, slapping it twice in what I imagine she means as a gesture of endearment, but she does it with enough force that we all hear the dull skin-against-skin blows. She kneels before Cecelia, shrinking to half the girl's size. Tee rocks her and whispers against her hair. Cecelia nods, crying. Tee gives her a handkerchief, this one cross-stitched with teeny blue blossoms, and I remind myself to dig out the one from the funeral, still in the pocket of the sweater I wore, and return it to the cook.

Cecelia comes to me next. "I don't want to go."

I smooth her hair away from her face, unsticking the strands from her tears. "I don't want you to go. But sometimes things happen that get in the way of what we want."

"Daddy says God has a plan."

"You need to listen to your daddy."

She nods. "I love you, Liesl."

"Love you too, baby girl."

While the other employees hug her and talk to her, Seamus approaches. We've spoken since his proposal of marriage—Cecelia still came after school and he picked her up when he was done making deliveries—but the conversations were limited to perfunctory inquiries about the move, his mother, and the logistics of it all. We didn't talk of us, if there is such a thing anymore.

He will go, it will fade, and everything will be back to the way it was before I got the foolish notion that I am capable of having an intimate relationship with someone.

"So," he says, and opens his arms to me. I have promised myself I won't cry, but I do, and I step into his offered comfort but find none. "We'll call when we get there."

I nod. "Be safe."

And they go. Gretchen and Rebekah and Ellie return to their duties. And Tee stares like only she can, face tight, eyes small, an aura of resentment hovering around her. I can almost see it, like mist low to the ground.

"I'm going upstairs," I say.

I don't know what I hope to accomplish in the apartment. I throw a small load of whites into the washing machine, and as I'm shutting the lid I think of the handkerchief. I retrieve it from my sweater and it opens. There are no stitched flowers on it, but initials.

X.R.P.

I return to the kitchen and give the cloth to Tee. "Xavier Robert Potter."

Her fingers, so skeletal, tighten on her spatula. She swings it around toward Gretchen and Rebekah. "You. Go out."

"I'm busy," Gretchen says.

"Robota ne vovk, v lis ne vtiče."

"You know I can't understand a word you're saying."

Tee uses the metal utensil as a prod, moving Gretchen toward the door. "Work is not wolf, it does not run to the woods."

Gretchen holds the door frame. "What the heck?"

"I think she means you can get back to what you're doing later," I say, and I nod at her.

"Alrighty then," Gretchen says, and she disappears into the café area, but not before yanking the spatula from Tee's hand and throwing it across the room, into the sink.

Tee turns to Rebekah. "You too, tall helper girl."

The teenager glances in my direction. "We still have orders to fill."

"Tell them cook is sick. Tell them no more food until tomorrow."

"Go ahead, Rebekah," I say. "It's okay."

Xavier's absence is still palpable, like sepsis, flowing through every vein of Wild Rise, but all the more here, in this kitchen, where I still think I see him sometimes, clutching the warm miche to his chest, his lips against it, eyes closed, soul nourished. I motion to the handkerchief, still safe in Tee's grasp. "It's Zave's."

"Ah. I see it. You come out from under your hill of *hleeb* and open eyes."

"You can't blame me for not figuring it out. I mean, I saw how you acted around him."

"What is it you know now? Nothing. You let the girl go, and the father. You give them up for—what is this? You think you are some—what?—a hero to the bread? You are only frightened child. The man and I," she says, shaking the cloth in her fist, "we have the companionship. What it is to you?"

"But Annie . . ."

"You can love a someone who is gone and a someone who is here, both together in time," Tee says. "That I know." She turns her back to me, kissing the handkerchief and rolling it beneath the scarf trussing her bare head.

It's grief, I hear my mother say. I've been walking all over Tee's and have done nothing to sweep it away.

Twenty-Three

I'm seven and at Oma's house, visiting for the weekend, alone.

I love when we are all together, when my mother and grandmother speak their own special-secret language and I listen, not understanding but still enraptured at the way the words flutter in my ears. I like when we all eat around Oma's table in the sunroom off the kitchen too small for the four of us, but we squeeze in anyway, me in the back because I can crawl beneath the table and through all the legs and make it out the other side if I need to use the bathroom. In the cold weather, my back presses against the glass and makes me all shivery, like Christmas. When it's summer, my grandmother pulls the blinds so we don't bake like bread during dinner. She doesn't make picnic foods, the kind of things we eat at home when my mother says it's too hot to cook—hot dogs on the outside grill, sliced tomato and cheese, grapes, potato chips, or mayonnaise-covered salads from the deli. Oma always prepares a good German meal of meats or stews or cabbage, always served from the stove at mouth-burning temperatures.

I love when we're together, but sometimes I want her all for myself.

This is my second sleepover, and even though she's old and gets tired and needs to nap every day, we still have fun. She lets me play with her delicate tea set and the china dolls she collects, and I have tea parties with real tea and cakes. We watch cartoons of Tom and Jerry or Sylvester and Tweety, Grandmother laughing even harder than I do. She teaches me card games two people can play without anyone else. And she takes me to the German market, where other old ladies speak to me in *Deutsch* and Oma tells them my mother hasn't taught me any of her mother language, and they cluck their tongues and talk even faster. It hurts her that my mother hasn't raised me bilingual. She replies to the women, and even though I don't know the language, I realize she's making apologies for her daughter. Or perhaps blaming my father; I hear her say *Katholik*.

Her kitchen is brighter than ours, cabinets made of thin wood with no doors and painted yellow, walls covered in paper printed with cherries who have eyes and noses and smiles. *Are we baking?* I ask when she ties a half apron around my waist and sits me on a chair she's dragged close to the counter. *Nein*, she says. *It is time to learn.*

About talking German?

She slides a stoneware crock in front of me. *Über Sauerteig.*

About sourdough.

Opening the crock, she holds it beneath my nose. It smells strong and bitter, with a hint of something I recognize from my mother's party punch. I sniffle and turn my head, but she follows. *Breathe deep. You must know how it is.*

I don't like it.

It makes the bread you eat.

That?

It is Anfrishsauer. It is very old.

Is that why it smells?

It smells because it is good.

I pinch my nostrils and peer into the jar. Inside, a sticky beige foam clings to the walls. *It doesn't look good.*

It is very good. A long time ago my own Oma took dough and put it in this pot with flour and water to make Anfrishsauer. The dough is Anstellgut; *it is saved from the baking early in the day. Oma mixes the Anfrishsauer and keeps it warm and gives it more flour to eat so it becomes* Grundsauer. *More flour, more water, more warmth and time, and it changes again. Now it is* Vollsauer *and can be made into brot. A little bit of Vollsauer becomes the Anstellgut, fed to the pot with water and flour to make more Anfrishsauer. Again and again, every day so the children have brot. Always something is in this pot, waiting to eat.*

I poke my finger into the crock; the gooey mass surrounds my nail and tries to suck in the rest of my pointer. I yank my hand away. *I didn't know bread was so hungry all the time.*

We are all hungry all the time. Every living thing. Oma caps the pottery jar and holds it close. *You will try to know this always, Liesl. Please try.*

I nod, the strange and lovely words already fading from my mind. *I will try.*

Sunday. The day of rest. I stay in bed and ignore the cell phone rattling on my nightstand, Jude's number flashing on the screen. I had told him I'd drive him to church, but I have no desire to go now. I should answer and let him know; instead, I wrap the flattened pillow around my ears and block out the buzz and shimmy. He'll figure it out.

Eventually my phone goes still.

Tee's right. I don't care about people.

With the body idle, the brain moves faster. I try to shut it down, first with vain attempts to empty it of all thought, and then by actively directing the images in my mind. This also fails, each seemingly innocuous mental snapshot conjuring another that only aggravates my gloom. Fat, fuzzy cartoon sheep jumping fences become memories of the fiber tour, my first outing with Seamus and Cecelia. Images of hands kneading dough start me thinking of Xavier, or Jude, or my mother. I try tapping my knees together and counting each beat, but the motion focuses me on my joggling thighs and I begin craving a hairbrush, despite not having hit myself in years. I'm a dry alcoholic of self-harm.

Every sensation begins irritating me—the sheets against my toes, my hair on my neck, the elastic waistband of my flannel pants. I grunt, throw off the covers, and take a shower, scrubbing all over with a bath puff until my skin settles. I dry and use a little olive oil to soothe the inflammation; my only lotion is scented and will burn the places I've washed raw.

I rake my hair into an elastic without brushing the snarls from it, fashion myself a skirt from my bath towel, and search my drawers for my softest T-shirt. My Bible stares at me from atop the dresser. I've been better about reading it, just a few verses here and there, but I felt the inklings of accomplishment the past week or two.

I hurl the book across the bedroom. It thumps off the wall, falling like a bird that has bashed into a clean, closed window, stunned. Or perhaps dead. I don't know. I don't care.

I'm angry.

Finally, all the flotsam I've spent twenty years siphoning down, down, down foams to the surface. It's triggered by loss, all of it. Xavier, gone. Seamus, left. My father, around in body only, and then escaping into the church. My grandmother, taken too soon.

My mother.

It's not her fault. Not her fault. Not her fault.

"Yes, it is," I say aloud.

And I hate her for it.

Or which one of you, if his son asks him for bread, will give him a stone?

My mother gave me stones instead of bread.

If you then, who are evil, know how to give good gifts to your children, how much more will your Father who is in heaven give good things to those who ask him.

"I don't want you," I whisper, crying. "I want her."

She loved me so much, my father told me, she chose adoption so there was no chance I would inherit her illness. But she didn't love me enough to stay. To her, ending her pain through death was better than all those milestones I had and will have without her—my first period, my first kiss, my wedding, grandchildren, Wild Rise, birthdays. And bread.

It isn't like I can believe she had one microscopic moment where she thought, *I wish it was over,* and in that moment pressed a gun against her temple and fired. No. She had to choose to sit in that car until the carbon monoxide overtook her. How long was that? An hour? Two? Was there no part of her, in all those minutes, that said, *Liesl. You have Liesl,* and if there was, why didn't it compel her to turn off the engine?

I know all the psychological explanations, that she was unable to reason such things in the throes of her depression. But what does reason mean to a twelve-year-old with a broken heart? Which is why I hide in the bread and have refused, until now, to open myself up and be vulnerable with another person. Which is why I am afraid to marry Seamus because, what if he, too, decides I'm not enough? What if, in all my brokenness, I can't be enough?

My grace is sufficient for you, for my power is made perfect in weakness.

Then why can't I feel it?

"Oh, Jesus. I want to believe. Help my unbelief."

There is no sudden crash of peace over me, no tongues of fire, no physical sensation of the Spirit coming over me. Not even a still, small voice. I sit on the bed, rocking gently back and forth, humming "Es ist ein Ros entsprungen," and, cautiously, I allow my mother's face to come into my mind. *I forgive you,* I think, and I exhale until my lungs are so empty they hurt. Then I stand and finish dressing. I have dough to prepare for tomorrow and a plane ticket to buy.

My God has provided a new home for me.

I will go to Seamus.

The twelve stay.

They eat a final meal with Jesus, and with his hands he tears the unleavened bread and holds it up to them. *This is my body*, he says. *Remember me.* And he tells Simon that the adversary has asked to sift them all like wheat, but their faith will be restored. The next day the Christ is lifted up at Golgotha, nailed to a tree, dead before sunset. And when his Spirit leaves him, the temple curtain rends, a veil between God and man. Left exposed in the holiest place is the ark of the covenant, and in that, the manna given to the Hebrews in the desert, life-giving for those who ate of it, but only for a short while here on this earth. And the people remember his words on the shore of Capernaum: *Your fathers ate the manna in the wilderness, and they died. This is the bread that comes down from heaven, so that one may eat of it and not die. I am the living bread that came down from heaven. If anyone eats of this bread, he will live forever. And the bread that I will give for the life of the world is my flesh.*

His body, crucified, given for them so they may taste eternity.

Three days later, resurrected, so those who believe can come to his banquet table and be filled.

His followers obey. They devote themselves to the breaking of the bread. They remember him each time they eat of it, and offer thanks. They are sustained in the world and rescued from the world because God became man, and man became bread.

There are phone calls to make.

Not Seamus. I will surprise him, certain he will still have me. But telling him gives me too much accountability. I don't want his antici-pation driving me, his knowledge of my arrival ensuring I'll still go. I do have to tell my father, praying briefly before I dial he'll pick up, and he does.

"I have news," I say, and I explain the situation.

"I thought there might be something between you two," Alistair says, "that day they taped the show. But, Liesl, are you certain? You're giving up . . . well, everything."

I hesitate. Leaving Wild Rise doesn't seem so frightening anymore. Seamus was right—I can bake anywhere. I have the prize money, if I want to use it to begin another business. I no longer feel as if the opportunity to travel to Europe will never come again. If the Lord wants me to have the trip, I will.

Leaving my father, it's more difficult, but he isn't alone; he has community too, those who have worshipped alongside him these two decades, who accept his quirks and who were so faithful to love him out of the shadows of his grief. Those in his church, they were Christ to him. He will be fine.

No, what scares me now is this faith to which I've been called. It's larger than me, outside of me, against my control. My first real act of submission to him. To God. "I'm not sure," I say. "But it's obedience."

"That I understand," Alistair replies, and in his voice I hear the joy of a father who is watching the seeds of the sower sprouting in the good soil.

After we say good-bye, I take a deep breath and call Mary Preston. She's not home. I leave a message with my cell phone number and let her know, honestly, I hope to hear from her soon.

When I tell Jude the bakehouse is his, he blinks at me from behind his glasses and bites his bottom lip into his mouth, stretching the skin around his lip rings.

"I don't know what you mean."

It's early morning, our time together before coworkers or customers arrive. I covet this time, and though our relationship is nothing like the one I had with his grandfather, having Jude here keeps Xavier a part of things and Wild Rise needs that.

"I'm leaving for Tennessee today," I say.

"I talked to Seamus last night. He didn't tell me."

"He doesn't know. No one does."

Jude grins. "You sly dog."

"I assume that's a compliment."

"He loves you, you know."

I nod. "That's why I'm going. And that's why I want you to be head baker here. If you want it."

"I'm a high school dropout who can't hardly read."

"But you have the hands. That's what Zave told me when you first came. You've proven yourself, and there's no one I trust more with my bread."

I hold my arms open to him and he steps in, bony against me, Xavier in miniature. He squeezes me so tightly my ribs pop. I ruffle his hair, now algae green, and straighten his apron. "This is our secret, got it? I'll e-mail Gretchen tonight and we'll figure things out, but I don't want any fanfare. Besides, it's not like I'm gone for good. I'll be back every month to check up on all of you."

"Y'all," he said. "If you're living down there, you better learn to talk like them."

"I'll work on it."

I spend the rest of the morning wandering around the bakehouse, committing the smells to memory, running my hands over the wainscot, enjoying the cadence of Tee's chopping and Ellie's laughter. At lunchtime a class of kindergarteners comes for their field trip, thirteen this time. I write their names on the paper chef hats. I tell them about dough, giving them some to work into crusts for their pizzas. And as they flatten and knead and pinch, I watch their hands. No Poilâne. No Jude. Simply a table full of six-year-olds who may one day remember their time with the bread and come to love it in ways unexpected.

Everyone's busyness makes me invisible. I take the stoneware jar of starter from the cooler. When the children's class is finished, I take one last look around Wild Rise and slip out the front door with them, up the stairs to my apartment. I spin layers of cotton towels around Oma's crock, thinking this must be how she wrapped it before leaving her home behind, traveling thousands of miles with her daughter to an unknown land. I asked my mother once why they came here, and she gave a generic immigrant answer: "For a better life." But my grandmother loved her country, and they were no more poor or burdened there than in the United States, perhaps less so. I won't ever know what Oma would say was the true reason that stirred her away from all she knew. But I see now through a glass less dimly, with eyes of faith, tracing the thumbprint of God from one event to another until here I am, bubble wrap and masking tape wadded thickly over the towels, trusting the Anfrishsauer will safely make another journey to a new home.

Twenty-Four

I'm young, eight, home from third grade because of snow. My mother and I spend the morning playing Pick Up Sticks and Old Maid because the television doesn't work. *But the lights turn on*, I say.

The cable is out. She offers to put a video in the VCR, but we don't have many to choose from, only Christmas movies, aerobics tapes, and a flat, brown box with a picture of a man and a woman on the cover; her neck is long and gold, and he hovers above her as if he'll bite it. *Gone with the Wind*, I read. *What's this?*

A very long movie.

Is it good?

If you're a grown-up.

I want to play outside, but it's an icy storm, each flake a tiny, sharp dagger, the front patio shiny as a skating rink. Instead, I build a fort with the couch cushions and a bedsheet; it's cool and crackly and smells like only a fresh bedsheet can. My favorite scent in the world, even better than bread in the oven. I don't tell my mother, but I think she knows. She sees me press my face into the smooth fabric and finds me some mornings hugging a wadded sheet I've taken from the linen closet because I wake in the night from a bad dream and can't bear to slip back into sleep without the smell in my nose. My own twin-sized sheets don't offer the same comfort, the flannel too fuzzy and hot, saturated in my own skin oils and dust mites.

My mother lets me eat an early lunch in the fort. SpaghettiOs, a special treat. She keeps a can hidden behind the green beans for days when she has her pains and Daddy needs to feed me dinner. She doesn't get them often, but when they come she can be in bed for days, the bedroom shades pulled all the way to the sills. I hear her cry, and my father tells me the pains make her sad. I don't know where they settle, but I have had enough earaches and sore throats to understand what it means to hurt.

I bring my empty bowl to the kitchen sink. My mother captures me in her apron, tying me in it, and says, *It's time.*

Are we baking?

You are. The canister of flour is on the counter, the measuring cups, the ring of spoons. *Show me you have learned.*

I don't understand.

I want to see you make the bread. All by yourself.

I need the cookbook.

No, she says, crouching, placing her palm over my heart. Her touch magnifies the beating somehow. *The recipe is here. Tell me, what four things do you need?*

Flour, water, salt, yeast, I say, the words an incantation, spurring my arms to motion. Closing my eyes, I conjure images of my mother the last time I watched her bake, and I do as she does. Three cups flour. Two cups water. One tablespoon each of yeast and salt. I stir until the mass of dough thickens and traps the spoon. Then I sprinkle flour on the counter and begin kneading. My hands stick. I reach into the canister for more, hold it high and let it rain down like fairy dust. No, my mother doesn't do this, but I am the sorceress today.

I work the dough and she tells me of the past, how older women taught young girls the art of bread, how the children were included in these things from an early age and they take them in as the right way to do it. Perhaps the only way. The new bride buys butter or oleo for her home, a choice depending on what her mother has always done. She folds socks or rolls them into balls. She adds washing soda to the laundry or chlorine bleach. She does what she knows; it's imitation at first, but somewhere the lines blur and it becomes her way, no less a part of her than the hue of her eyes or the crookedness of her teeth.

I cover my dough with a damp towel and place the bowl in the oven with the pilot light on, and we wait together, watching Scarlett O'Hara lose more than she gains, and when intermission comes I shape my loaf into a fat braid—again because it's mine and I want to—and let it puff again under the towel, on the counter this time, and play the remainder of the movie. I don't care for it, but happily sit through the characters' pouting and drinking and shouting at one another if it means I spend the afternoon tucked beneath my mother's arm, my cheek on her soft breast, her fingers twining my hair.

The bread goes into the oven. I keep the light on and watch it bake as my mother prepares our beef stew supper. My father stumbles into the house, weary from his daylong battle to keep the delivery truck from skidding off the weather-beaten roads, kisses my mother more tenderly than Rhett ever did Scarlett, and changes into dry socks. I set the table and she spoons hot meat and root vegetables into bowls, and I take the bread from the oven, burning my wrist on the rack. The loaf is too flat and dark, and it should cool but we don't let it, instead slicing it with Oma's long, toothy knife, the still-humid crumb tearing unevenly.

It's beautiful, Liesl, my mother says.

For real?

Yes. Her cool fingers touch the blister on my wrist. *You are now a keeper of bread.*

Recipe Index

Reading Group Guide

1. Liesl's grandmother quotes a German proverb to her: *Whose bread I eat, his song I sing.* What does she mean by this? How does this relate to your daily life? Your faith journey?

2. When Liesl's grandmother dies, Claudia says to her, *"It will come again, Liesl. Grief always does. And in the face of it, you'll need to decide if you'll step over the pieces and leave them to be trampled, or if you'll gather them up for salvage."* How have you reacted to grief when you've seen it in the lives of others? In your own life?

3. Seamus isn't the typical romantic interest often found in novels. How do his authenticity and idiosyncrasies give him the ability to draw Liesl from within herself? What about him helps Liesl come to view him as a safe person?

4. In an age when so many people are searching for—and in ways, creating—their own fifteen minutes of fame, do you think it's realistic for Liesl to turn down her own television show? How would you choose if you were in her position?

5. Seamus has told Cecelia her mother left them because she "never learned how to love." Cecelia, however, states she didn't realize

loving someone was something needed to be taught. What do you think? Do you agree with Seamus or Cecelia?

6. Intergenerational ties are strongly represented in *Stones for Bread*, particularly between Liesl, Claudia, and Oma. Do you think we, as a society, have lost some of those bonds today?

7. Liesl, Xavier, and Jude all share an intense love of bread and baking, and it knits them together in a way that gives them a deeper understanding of one another. Have you had a relationship based on the sharing of a skill or passion? How has that influenced your life at present?

8. Did you learn anything new about the history of bread and how one simple food has shaped the human experience? What fact did you find most interesting?

Acknowledgments

I always come to the acknowledgments scratching my head, knowing there are more people to thank than I can ever fit onto these pages. Here is my non-exhaustive list, with apologies to all those I've neglected to include, compounded by the fact I wrote this while thirty-nine weeks pregnant, which any woman who's been pregnant understands is a rather forgetful time.

Thank you:

Thomas Nelson Publishers, for taking a chance on this novel.

Amanda Bostic, editorial director at HarperCollins Christian Publishing, and my personal editor, for being my champion and advocate. Your enthusiasm for *Stones for Bread* means more to me than I can express.

Line editor extraordinaire, Rachelle Gardner.

Bill Jensen, my agent and friend and fellow home artisan baker, who offered this idea to me.

Those who helped with the languages represented in this novel: Claudia Bell (whose name I borrowed for Liesl's mother and who

I hope ins't too disappointed by her fictional namesake), Melinda Bokelman, and Jen DeBusk.

All my recipe tasters and testers.

Everyone who has prayed for me, my writing, and my family, especially the people of Clifton Park Center Baptist Church, Redeemer Reformed Presbyterian Church, and Gentle Christian Mothers.

My parents, Ann and Joseph Parrish, for their continued and seemingly endless support.

My sister, Laura Parrish Combs, for loving me even though I hate to answer my phone, and for all the hand-me-downs.

My children—Gray, Jacob, Claire, and Noah—who continue to challenge and grow me.

And Chris, who tells me every day he loves me. No regrets.

Invaluable in writing the history portions of *Stones for Bread* was H. E. Jacob's brilliant *6,000 Years of Bread: Its Holy and Unholy History*, published by Skyhorse Publishing (2007), forward by Peter Reinhart.

About the Author

Author photo by Allen Clark

Christa Parrish is the award-winning author of four novels, including the 2009 ECPA Fiction Book of the Year *Watch Over Me*. Married to author and pastor Chris Coppernoll, Christa co-labors with him in co-leading their church's youth ministry program, and weekly Bible study. When not writing, she is chauffeuring her Grand Champion purple belt to and from Taekwondo classes, teaching a preschooler the alphabet, and changing newborn diapers. She is now also slightly obsessed with the art of baking bread.